Praise for author Mindy Tarquini

For *The Infinite Now*

2017 USA Best Book Awards Winner in Fiction: LGBT,
and Finalist in Fiction: Fantasy

2017 Foreword Indies Gold Winner in Adult Fiction: Fantasy,
and Finalist in Adult Fiction: LGBT

2017 *Today Show* winter book selection

"Replete with poignant details, Mindy Tarquini's *The Infinite Now* is an engrossing tightrope walk over the relational lines that connect human beings to each other and to time itself…*The Infinite Now*'s potent sorcery doesn't lie primarily in its forays into fantasy and myth, but rather in the humanity of its characters and the energy of its storytelling."

—*Foreword Reviews*, 5 out of 5 stars

"This book offers a well-researched and engagingly drawn portrait of a displaced Italian community in one of America's most turbulent years. Fiora is a forceful, determined protagonist among an intriguing cast of supporting characters. The first-person descriptions of her life are both vivid and tender…A well-woven tapestry of history, character, and charming mystery."

—*Kirkus Reviews*

"Historical fiction is portrayed in a new way . . . Told in first-person prose, this novel blends history with science fiction. Those who enjoy a story that appeals to the mind (and STEM topics) will gravitate to this work. Twists and turns in the plot are unpredictable but still believable and will leav⸱   ⸱hanges course.
VERDICT: T   *Library Journal*

"Tarquini uses words like a composer. Her word choices crescendo into sentences that read like majestic musical scores and artfully explore the angst, fears, and emotional struggles of a confused teenage girl... Overall, though, this is a beautifully written book with heart, humor, and just enough magic to make things a bit dangerous. Unexpected and poignant: I recommend it."

—*Historical Novel Society*

"An easy read with likable characters and a story about love and acceptance, Tarquini's latest...will captivate readers until the very end."

—*Booklist*

"As an original and deftly written novel that is a consistently and absorbing read from beginning to end, *The Infinite Now* reveals author Mindy Tarquini's genuine gift as a narrative driven storyteller....Unreservedly and enthusiastically recommended, especially for community library collections."

—*Midwest Book Review*

"Mindy Tarquini beautifully weaves a tapestry of superstition, time, and hope in her most recent novel, *The Infinite Now*...Those who enjoy magical realism mixed with a bit of mystery will find themselves highly entertained, and the story reminds readers that hope and love are always good guides when we feel we've lost our way."

—*Manhattan Book Review* (4 out of 5 stars)

"Mindy Tarquini does a phenomenal job at capturing not only the feel of the time but the feel of people who would have lived there...If you want to lose yourself in a fantasy that feels all too real, look no further than *The Infinite Now*."

—*San Francisco Book Review* (5 out of 5 stars)

"Take a break from reality with this whimsical plot set in flu-ravaged 1918 Philadelphia for some spellbinding magic at your fingertips."

—*Working Mother*

For *Hindsight*:

Redbook **Best Books of 2016**

2017 Benjamin Franklin IBPA Award: Gold

USA Best Book Awards: General Fiction - Finalist

"Tarquini's innovative concept is paired with realistic characters and sparkling wit, making this enjoyable novel a keeper."
—*Publishers Weekly*, Starred Review

"A unique and innovative reminder to enjoy life like it's the only one you'll have."
—Bookstr

"*Hindsight* is an evocative and inventive reincarnation tale. Drawing on snippets of wisdom from long-gone literary giants, including Chaucer, Dante, Goethe, and Kipling, Tarquini illustrates the eternal universality of human behavior . . . the narrative emphasizes the importance of acting in the here and now: saying what should be said, forgiving what needs to be forgiven, embracing opportunities to deepen connections with others, and seizing moments of happiness when they're presented. Consequently, Hindsight is a sustaining and deeply personal reading experience."
—*Foreword Reviews*, FIVE STARS, Book of the Day Selection

"This contemporary jewel is a literary parade that reminds us to live life fully in the now."
—*Working Mother*, "21 New Books to Fall for This Autumn"

"Witty and thought-provoking, Mindy Tarquini's debut is a must-read for lovers of Chaucer, magical realism and literary ingenuity."
—Buzzfeed

"Funny and irreverent, this modern fable is a good reminder to love the life you have."

—*Real Simple*

"This quirky and often funny novel is a satisfying debut and will pique readers' interests right off the bat."

—RT Book Reviews

"This charming contemporary fable marks a fabulous debut for author Mindy Tarquini."

—SheKnows, "The best books written by women you need to read this fall"

"*The Infinite Now*'s combination of suspense, tragedy, and coming of age is sure to be the next book on your TBR pile."

—PopSugar

"Author Mindy Tarquini glues readers to the page with her insight into character and her signature irreverent humor. Hindsight is a debut you don't want to miss."

—Stephen Parrish, editor of the *The Lascaux Review*

"In Eugenia Panisporchi, Mindy Tarquini gives us a heroine for the ages and for right now, combining the concept of past lives with a witty and entertaining take on the timeless task of being true to ourselves."

—Kamy Wicoff, author of *Wishful Thinking*

Deepest
Blue

A Novel

Mindy Tarquini

Published by SparkPress, a BookSparks imprint,
A division of SparkPoint Studio, LLC
Tempe, Arizona, USA, 85281
www.gosparkpress.com

Published 2018
Printed in the United States of America
ISBN: 978-1-943006-69-4 (pbk)
ISBN: 978-1-943006-70-0 (e-bk)

Library of Congress Control Number: 2018942981

Formatting by Kiran Spees

For Avi, for Rosie, for Ian, for me.

For all who love like us, all who grieve like us.

With respect. . . .

One

In dreams of light, I search for thee. . . .

Outside, empires rise. They fall. The moon waxes. It wanes. Days break, nights pass, clocks tick. Calendar pages turn. A cascade marking every event, large or small, notable or not, with dependable and tyrannical regularity.

Inside, our hearts keep what time we must, allowing what is necessary for ideas to be born, dreams to blossom, and hope to flower. We note deeds, not dates, joys, not sorrows, strengths, not shortfalls, our milestones marked at Midsummer's Eve, when we each plot our progress, our points in our constellation, and dance.

The Midsummer's Eve I ran away, my brother Antonio brought me back.

He made the long climb to join me at the cliff edge, fiddle in hand. "Matteo! Where do you think you're going?"

I pointed over the valley to the silhouette of a new horizon—light-filled towers and pinnacles soaring to the heavens—visible only at twilight on those rare evenings when the fog lifted and most strongly

1

on Midsummer's Eve. "I'm going Outside. To be with Dante and Ilario."

The bit of iron hanging at my neck whispered words of sadness, of despair, of yearning for my little brothers. The words tugged on the iron's chain, fighting our world's magical pull. "I won't go for long, I won't go for always."

"You won't go at all. Insiders don't go Outside. Outsiders don't come Inside. Not anymore." Antonio took hold of my iron, wrapped his fingers tight. "Say it, you have to say it."

Because words have power. "I won't. Dante and Ilario left a trail. The maestro told us—we always leave a trail."

The maestro told us everything. How the bird decides where to place its nest, why the butterflies return every spring, and the exact count of honeybees.

I thought Antonio would fight me. Thought he'd argue and flail, the way he had when Dante and Ilario left. I pointed to his scar, jagged across his cheek, then to Antonio's iron, trilling a tune of longing, of remorse. "You're sorry. I know you're sorry. Come with me."

Antonio let go of my amulet and shoved his under his collar, but the iron fluttered beneath the deep blue fabric, whistling like a caged *rigogolo*. He smacked the flutter to his chest, then swiped at a swath of hair the color of new-tilled earth, shoving it up and off his forehead. "We can't go back. Not once, not ever. The maestro told you that, too. Outside is not like Inside."

Music swelled in the distance, floating in from the festival fields. My urgency drained away, replaced with a different need, pulsing, primal, one I didn't have the years to understand, but which already had hold of Antonio. His mood grew dreamy and he raised his fiddle. "Let's go. Mamma expects me to play."

"But—" Dante. Ilario.

"But nothing. The maestro told us—remember what helps, forget what hurts, give what stars remain permission to rise. We'll work together. I promise."

—

Permission to rise. In Antonio's lexicon, *rise* meant *grow*, and that meant a garden. A place to which Dante and Ilario could return. A place we could always find them.

Then Antonio handed me a seed and assigned me to grow the tree. "Use your words," he urged. "It's only bark and branches."

Easy enough for Antonio. One scherzo from his fiddle and poppies leapt from the soil, cosmos orbited the boxwood, laurels leafed the crown flowers, and silverbells tinkled a carillon—a compendium of miracles for which my magic had no definitions.

I asked the maestro for guidance. "Tell me about trees. Not of their grace, nor their nobility, not how their souls creak in the wind, tell me . . . how do trees become?"

He explained about cambium and heartwood, xylem and pith and, most wondrous of all, food made from light, a process he called *photosynthesis*. I planted and pruned, watered and shaped, every leaf, every limb. I spoke the roots deep into the ground, bid the canopy reach to the sky. I declared its leaves ever green, no matter the season, and ordained them widespread enough to provide shelter from any storm.

I described the fruit last. Delectable. Intriguing. Small and succulent and bursting with possibilities. The work of years, grown on a promise. Antonio's promise.

Then that son of a hog root cut it down. The whole damned tree. He chopped the limbs into firewood, left the stump, and made a run for our illusory horizon. Who knows what he did with the fruit. My first job as Protector of Panduri, our *ducato*, was to retrieve him.

"The Heir must return before nightfall," was all my father, Panduri's Duca, would say. The craggy ridges which passed for his eyebrows twitched in temper.

My iron again whispered on its chain—hard-tipped defiance, spiteful and brazen and blatantly unrestrained. "Antonio knows his duty," I added.

Father drew himself up, his spine stiffening until his height exceeded my hubris, his hair blowing wild, an oak in a squall.

Hedgerows rattled. Thickets shuddered. Roses climbing past the windows fell.

I planted my feet, became the rock upon which Father's displeasure broke. "No."

Father sent Salvatore and a contingent in my place.

They returned twenty minutes into twilight, shaking and sweating, a disgruntled Antonio in tow. Salvatore shoved him forward, bestowed the deepest of bows on my father, the barest of nods on my brother, and departed.

Antonio charged out of the room.

I charged after. "That's it? No explanations?"

"You told Father I left. You let Salvatore go to find me."

Because I didn't want to let you leave, didn't want to make you return, didn't want to fix your messes, didn't want you to fix mine.

And I didn't want to obey our father.

Antonio nabbed my amulet—the piece of iron which connected me to my source, connected Antonio and me to each other, the bit of metal without which my life in Panduri could not persist. He yanked the iron from its chain. "Why?"

The world went wavy. So did my knees. The floor fell away and I lost my footing. "You cut down the tree."

Antonio threw the amulet back at me. "Put it on. Then cease to call me *brother*."

And so I did, for the rest of Midsummer's long, enchanted interval, referring to Antonio only when the *duca* required and then only as The Heir, as in, "The Heir will be late, his hangover requires his full attention." Or, "The Heir will be along as soon as he finds his pants." And also, "The Heir will be happy to join you the moment he sobers up."

Until Antonio stumbled into the kitchen, stupid and stinking and full of apologies, a brace of quivers crisscrossing his chest, our bows clutched in his fists. "Let's practice targets."

I tilted my head toward the window, where dawn had not yet appeared. "The field will be pitch. You'll skewer yourself."

"If I do, you have to be Heir." He headed for the door and into the night.

I followed, moving in a quick-step to match Antonio's stride. "Did you run because Father locked away Dante's and Ilario's star charts?" All those lost hours, tracing the possibilities. Father said we needed to look forward.

A melody rippled from Antonio's iron, whimsical and winsome. Then the music grew harsh. "I ran because of Uncle Giacomo."

He'd just left us, in his spectacular and legendary fashion, making mountains from molehills and howling at the moon. Antonio was first on the scene.

I got a few steps ahead, turned and walked backward, forced Antonio to look me in the eye, "And the tree?"

"It was ugly."

Whatever his argument, whatever his complaint, Antonio didn't give a damn about our uncle or how much work I'd put into that tree. Antonio cared about Antonio. And left everything else to me.

I again fell into step. "You missed the Promise."

"Whose Promise?"

"The maestro's daughter. She married one of our air spinners. A better match than I'd have expected for an Outside-born. Mamma arranged it. I conveyed your good wishes."

That information troweled like tar across Antonio's path. His tempo slowed to an *adagio*. "What good wish was that?"

"Long life and happiness."

The tar must have gotten deeper because his *adagio* lengthened to a *largo*. "Long life and happiness is a powerful wish."

He was Heir. Of course his wishes would be powerful. "Should I have gone with something less onerous?"

"No. That's fine. Very generous. The daughter has every right to find her place. The maestro has been very . . . well, he's been a great help to Panduri."

We traversed the garden. The remains of Antonio's bonfire still smoldered near the stump, hot enough to roast marshmallows.

Antonio bypassed it, his gaze overtly averted, then ducked under an arch and into our practice field, illuminated by the glow of a thousand tiny lights. Trumpet vines announced his entrance with a flourish. "Antonio, first son of Bartomeo. Panduri's Heir, most blessed, most beloved."

"Most in need of a bath." I ducked around him, making a show of holding my nose, then pointed to the little dancing glimmers and did some quick calculations. I tilted my chin toward Claudio, our younger brother, waiting by his targeting stake. "These shouldn't be here. The star count will be short tomorrow night."

"Beautiful, aren't they?" Claudio upturned his face, his song lilting. The glimmers danced along his grace notes. "They're Mamma's doing."

Antonio clapped Claudio on the back, then wrapped him in an inebriated bear hug snug enough to make a prostitute cringe. "Because we're celebrating."

Claudio's song went somber. He twisted clear and rubbed at his neck, where his collar, stiff and new as his divinity, was already leaving its mark. "We are not celebrating."

"Relax." Antonio patted him twice on the cheek. "You've only just taken the cloak. Your account's still clean."

He pulled the strap of my quiver over his head and settled it around mine. He handed off my bow. "Tell him, Matteo. One sin won't matter."

"And dozens are hardly worthy of mention. Not on Midsummer." I nocked an arrow, sighted on the dark cloth tacked to the middle of a hay-stuffed canvas sack at the opposite end of the field, and yet again read the poem Father had graciously ordered engraved along the weapon's belly:

Forsake not thy spirit;
Nor honor lost condone;
Maintain well thy merit;
By these things, thou art known.

6

Antonio's bow was engraved with musical notes, Claudio's with songbirds. The bows were gifts from Father, commissioned to commemorate our elevations to our charted offices. Mine alone carried a permanent admonishment.

I adjusted my aim. "Which sin are we not celebrating?"

Antonio answered. "No sin. A very sad occurrence. Ursicio's wife has died."

My arrow went wild, embedding in the trunk of a poplar well behind the target. Death on Midsummer's Eve, even at its terminus, was a bad omen.

"The baby's fine." Claudio tapped one of Mamma's happy little pinpoints. "Bright-eyed and bawling. Blessed to have been born before Midsummer's end."

I lowered my bow. "Why are you both so giddy? Ursicio is our cousin."

"Our distant cousin." Antonio drew and sighted. "Our very distraught and distant and resourceful cousin. Overwhelmed with responsibility. Three children. All girls. No heir. And a dead wife."

He let fly. "Perfect for Luciana."

His arrow landed in the same tree to split mine down the middle. I paused to admire the shot. "You want our sister to marry Ursicio."

"Luciana has to marry eventually. Ursicio is a fine choice. He's loyal. He's resourceful."

He has a nose like a rutabaga and an imagination to match. "Luciana won't like that. She's promised to Ruggiero."

"Luciana's fine with it. Ruggiero beats whores." Antonio waggled his bow at Claudio. "Your turn. Go for one of the closer targets. Success emboldens the reach."

Claudio drew and sighted, wavering worse than a young man presented the choice of two virgins. He let his arrow fly, then checked where it landed, shoulders tensed like he worried he'd accidentally spitted the cat. "Has anybody seen Topo?"

"In the kitchen," I assured him. "Lapping the last of the cream." And hissing every time I got near.

I chose another arrow from my quiver. "This will bring trouble. Ignazio will see Father's refusal to let Luciana marry his son as an insult."

The air pulsed, the tiny lights faltered. Antonio snatched the words from my mouth. "Ignazio is fine with it, too. Father's exchanging enough to cover any insult."

He dropped his bow and grasped my shoulder, fingers tense. "Say it. Ignazio will be fine."

I couldn't, not without my iron betraying me. Ignazio could whip a gentle breeze into a tempest or calm a gale into the doldrums, go unnoticed as a rock, or command the attention of a kettledrum. Ignazio could be clever or dull, his words sparse, or flowing off his tongue like a marimba. Always charming, never forthright, Ignazio followed only those rules he found convenient. Because he was inimical, born under a contrary star and was rarely, barely, almost never ever *fine.*

And neither was Ruggiero.

I crossed my fingers behind my back, a trick that sometimes worked. "Ignazio will be fine."

The air settled. Mamma's glimmers resumed their gentle glow.

Antonio released me. "Ursicio will cast off his wife tomorrow. He's asked Claudio to perform the elegy, so you'll need to write one for him to sing. The Promise will be the following afternoon. Mamma says there's no use giving grief time to seed."

Or Ignazio time to smooth talk Father back to the original arrangement.

I nocked another arrow. None of this had anything to do with me. Marriage negotiations were Antonio's province. Luciana was fine with them. I was to depart with the dawn, take up my position and chart my course in Panduri's constellation. Her Protector. Legendary, storied, larger than life.

Like Uncle Giacomo.

I sighted on Antonio's arrow, meaning to split it as he had mine. I again drew.

"Here's the rest," Antonio piped up. "With so much upheaval in the current casts, Father agrees. Best you stay to chart the happiest course for our sister's new life. I'm going to the border in your stead."

I swung around. My shot again went wild, arcing over Antonio's head. "But you're Heir. It's official. They gave you the ceremony, the parade."

Mamma had my uniform fitted, my buttons polished. Even my pen nibs were new. "The women threw flowers at you."

"They can throw them again next year."

Anger raced up my gullet. I nocked yet another arrow and drew, leveling it at Antonio's chest. "They won't have to."

Claudio's bow creaked. "If you think I'll let you shoot him because you're annoyed, you're wrong."

Antonio drew. "And if you think I'll let you shoot Claudio for not letting you shoot me, you're more wrong."

My face went hot. "Fine. Shoot me. Then we will all have something to celebrate. Especially Father."

Antonio lowered his bow. "Shut up, Matteo. Nobody's shooting anybody. I have to get out of here. One more day plotting star charts and I will shave my head and take Claudio's place at the monastery."

The next morning, Claudio sang the elegy I wrote for Ursicio's poor, dead wife. Both she and the elegy were forgotten by nightfall. Antonio composed a fanfare for Luciana's Promise so luminous, people still remember it in song.

Antonio found me in my study before he departed. He carried both our bows. "Words and music, Matteo. No use breaking up a set."

"Get out of here, and take your damned bow with you. You've stolen my destiny. I'm never practicing targets with you again."

"I haven't stolen your destiny. I'm borrowing it for a while. I'll return it as soon as I can face mine. Then we'll find better ways to pass our time, happier times to remember." He hung his bow by the door. "Until then, keep this safe for me."

Antonio did return, but we never found better ways to pass our time, nor happier times to remember. And we never again practiced targets. One day, Antonio's destiny faced *him*. He followed it back to the horizon, and he crossed to Outside for good, leaving me no trail to follow, no trace to hold onto.

But I still have his bow, forever, for always, my hope ever strong Antonio will find a way to cross back.

Two

The reminders of my brother are before me every day. . . .

*F*or what reasons did we war? A boundary here, a birthright there, the roles we were each expected to play. Excuses meant to explain the Great Upheaval, our vendetta against our cousins on the other side of the valley, the Ducato of Careri.

Fingers pointed. Egos bruised. Tempers flared. As only families can. Raising blame deeper than any magic. Strong enough to shake us from our foundations.

What did we expect? All those slings and arrows and young hotbloods. What else did we expect?

Claudio tired of my questions. "Enough, Matteo. It was only a tree."

Dante and Ilario's tree. It had been shocked, been broken. Ill-used and misrepresented. I'd pressed my ear to the bark, listened for its heart. Of life, of love, of a yearning to heal. "All that tree needed was time."

"Stop. You're making the willows weep. Here. Write it down." He handed me a journal. No. A tome. Three inches thick. "I commissioned it from Salvatore's father."

I flipped through the leather-bound volume, admiring the smoothness of the parchment. "So many pages. You must think I have a lot to confess."

"Scream your anguish from the parapets, howl it to the moon. But have a care." Claudio took back the journal, turned the spine toward me, and shook it inches from my nose. "Your words contain power. They have substance. Don't waste them wallowing in your misery."

"You think I wallow."

"Like a pig after a rainstorm."

Claudio has it wrong. I do not wallow, I rage. At Antonio.

Not for being first. Nor for being foremost. I rage because Antonio refused to let me be second.

The First is Heir, renowned and irreproachable. Like Father. He stays home, attends ceremonies, gets married, makes new Heirs. And plots the fucking star charts.

Second is Protector. Legendary and celebrated like Giacomo. Panduri's defense in our vendetta against the Careri, Protectors are supposed to be first on the scene, last to leave in a scuffle. And living at the goddamned border.

Third sons are Panduri's priests, her Gentle Guardians. There's no third son in Father's generation, but if there were, he'd have been like Claudio who lives at the monastery and. . .

. . . actually, I've never been clear what Claudio does.

No matter. We were pieces of the puzzle, my brothers and I, dominoes aligned by the Deep Lore with well-planned precision. Like dominoes, one knock was enough to send us tumbling.

Dante and Ilario were explorers, set sail in a joyous and well-attended ceremony. Every Midsummer's Eve, we stood in their garden and awaited news of their arrival.

A year after Antonio chopped down their tree, and several Midsummers before he left us, I found him in the garden with Claudio, hop-stepping off the stump and making a cheerful noise. I hop-stepped past them and searched out a contribution for Dante's Wall, a masterpiece of intertwined twigs and bric-a-brac arranged with careless exactitude, and the only one of Dante's many constructs Ilario had never tried to take down.

I chose a sharp-edged flint from the bank of the stream which ran along the garden's edge, then slipped the rock into a likely slot. I considered the construct's persistence a sign all was well with my little brothers, so I watched, breath stopped.

The structure held.

Antonio tucked his fiddle under his chin. He played the happiest of ditties, one eye to the sky, purple-washed pink in the day's last display. He tossed me his score, the notes lighting on the paper as his bow moved across the strings. "You're late, word master. Claudio's awaiting his lyrics—where are Dante and Ilario now?"

I climbed onto the wall, wanting to look taller, grander, more authoritative than Antonio. I marked the score. "Messina. Or possibly all the way to Gibraltar."

Claudio's voice rose from his diaphragm, singing the line in a sustained crescendo, a call to adventure. Antonio tapped his bow to Claudio's shoulder, a conductor leading a chorus. "What should Dante and Ilario send back when they get there?"

"Oranges and figs." Claudio sang full and sweet. So sweet I tasted the figs plump and rich on my tongue, inhaled orange fragrance rising from an imaginary peel. Still...

I pointed my pen at him. "You sang oranges and figs last year."

The starch went out of Claudio's collar. His shoulders slumped. "I like oranges and figs."

"We already have plenty of both."

"Fine, Matteo." Antonio climbed onto the wall, also, and towered his typical over me. What do *you* want them to send?"

I gazed at Dante and Ilario's constellation twinkling in the twilight, imagined fair seas with a following wind, their ship landing on far-off shores. "I want them to send us stories. Hours and hours of them. Enough to fill a dozen Midsummer's Eves."

Antonio made an approving grunt. "We will perform them together." He pulled Claudio onto the wall with us, then drew us close in one-armed embraces. "The three of us. One for all and, well . . . you know."

All for one.

The procession that Midsummer was grand. Antonio was grander, resplendent in deep blue vest and shirt, his boot tops overflowing with treats, his fiddle buffed to a blinding polish.

The Deep Lore claimed seventy sirens had worked seventy Midsummers to create that fiddle. Antonio's music, spirited and strong and strongly suggestive, had the *signorinas* hanging on his every string pluck, sighing with his every *spiccato*. He strode the streets, the hope upon which Panduri's star rises, playing his role with the artistry of a harpist performing an arpeggio. Benevolent, beloved, tossing trinkets to his admirers and candies to the children.

I strode with him. Panduri's Protector. Trying not to sputter. "What do you mean you're not staying home? Look at this parade. And the ceremony was lovely."

I dodged a flower meant for Antonio, then pointed to the double row of moon-washed buttons gleaming across the bright red of my Protector's doublet. "How do I explain to Mamma about the uniform? She ordered it special. It's new."

We passed the reviewing stand where Mamma and Father waited with the rest of the *signori nobili*. Each of the *signori* stood and nodded to Antonio, the nod meant for the Heir, bestowed upon him every time he passed. Antonio raised his fiddle and I my pen, the customary salute and the official end of the procession.

Antonio stopped tossing candies and popped one into his mouth. "Store the uniform in moths' balls; it will be just as new next year."

Moths' balls. I'd never get out the smell. "Okay. Fine. Go back to the border. But take me with you. Father has secretaries. He doesn't need me."

"*I* need you. Here. Doing what you're doing, keeping Father off my back and out of my business." He stepped out of line and headed off.

I chased after. "What about my business?"

"What business is that?"

"The same as yours. Private."

Antonio smacked my shoulder. "Listen to me. Life is miserable out there. The vegetables are always mushy, the cream always sour. You go days without a bath, sometimes weeks, and who would you fuck?"

"The same as you."

"Milkmaids. Camp followers. Trust me, sheep smell better."

"You fuck sheep."

"Not if I can help it." Antonio looked over his left shoulder, then his right, then leaned in like he was going to let me in on a secret. "You don't want to live your life like Salvatore. As Father's thug."

"Salvatore's no thug."

"Sure he is. First on the scene, last in the scuffle. What do you think being a protector means?"

I thought it meant I'd live far from Father. "We talked about this. And I've been patient. Haven't sent you so much as a protest—"

Something rustled in the leaves overhead. A sprite flitted before us, young and eager, her wings lacey and translucent. "Did you say you needed to send something?"

We looked to each other. A sprite, once summoned, even without intention, could not be ignored. Antonio emptied his boot tops, scooped out the candies and trinkets. He handed them to her.

She held the trinkets to her ear. "These do not say where they are bound."

Antonio smiled a smile only second to a string pluck for eliciting a lady's sigh. "They have no destination. They are yours, compliments of Midsummer."

"A gift?" The sprite dropped the trinkets into her messenger pouch, then did a backflip, tracing an exuberant, silver-tinged arc. She nodded, deep and respectful. "Someday, Panduri's most generous, most gentle, most generally liked, will need me and I will know exactly where to go."

I watched as she spiraled with her treasures into the treetops. "Why would you ever need to send anything from this part of town?"

"The maestro lives here. Salvatore, also. You've never been?"

The only things there were crafter stalls and donkey carts. "What for?"

"How can you be Protector if you don't even know whom you protect?"

"Let me be Protector. We'll find out. Stay home. Plot a few charts to keep Father happy and go back to doing what you do best—as you please."

Antonio indicated a tiny clearing crammed between the bracken. "If I could do as I pleased, I'd pitch a tent, right there, right now. Make my way as a street performer. I have the fiddle for playing and the cap for collecting the coin."

Antonio took off the referenced headgear. Ridiculously pleated, bearing a braid of silver laurels and shaped like an overturned urn, the hat was meant only for the Heir and was large enough to cook soup.

He shoved it at me. "Here. Tell Father I tried, but I can't do it. I can't walk around with people bobbing and nodding and announcing me with superlatives. Not yet."

I admit I was tempted. Not forever, nor always, just for the experience, the memory. Of being first, of being foremost, of basking in the adoration of all.

I shoved the hat back. "Sure you can. It's charted in your stars."

"No." He loosened his collar. "It's like I can't breathe. Like I can't—"

"Can't what? We're sons of the *duca*. We lead processions or fuck sheep."

"Only because you accept the underlying premise. There's a whole world out there." Antonio threw out his arms, sweeping to one side then the next like he were leading a dance. "Keep your eye open, your heart alive. Maybe you'll find your bliss in the last place you imagine."

I snapped my fingers in front of his face, the way Luciana does when she raises the dawn. "If you're talking about going Outside, you can't. Your music would drive the Papists to madness. They'd burn you at the stake."

"Outside has no magic, deep or otherwise. My music would have no effect." Antonio rubbed his neck. "I don't think they burn people at the stake anymore."

"How would you know? Did you ask the maestro?" I grabbed him by the arm. "Have you already been?"

I told him he was foolhardy. Hollered and railed. Then I tried to get him to tell me what the Outside was like. "Are the buildings tall as I saw? The lights bright as I remember? Is it true what the maestro tells us about how they close off their houses? When they crawl into their beds, do they truly sleep cut off from the stars?"

Antonio never let on whether I'd guessed right or not, and the Heir cannot be ordered, he can only be swayed. "Grant me one more year, Matteo. One year more to settle my fancies and I'll come home. Stay here. I beseech you. And keep Father quiet."

Keep Father quiet. Ha. If only I could, but after Antonio left, Father grew uncommonly chatty. He deemed my didactics deplorable, my arguments amateurish, my rhetoric sophomoric, my penmanship illegible, and my star casts inept. I wrote to Antonio of Father's complaints, long epistles meant to persuade, but no amount of cajolery or conceit, conspiracy or contempt could convince my brother to do his duty so I could do mine.

Sheep-fucking could not be worse than the misery Father and I subjected each other to, so three months after Midsummer's end, I tossed a week's worth of weather mapping on the fire and gave the moths back their balls. I donned my uniform and headed for the border.

At a gallop.

I found Antonio under an olive tree fiddling to a field of maiden ferns, grey-green leaves in his hair and ten days' growth on his chin. "*Buongiorno!*" I called.

Antonio's bow screeched to a stop. He shushed the maiden ferns, then lowered his fiddle and lifted an eyebrow, his expression teeter-tottering between dismay and disbelief. "Is it a year already?"

"No, but you have to go home."

"Has something happened?"

Not really. "Plenty has happened."

I dropped my saddlebags and clutched my chest in what I hoped looked like horror to cover my iron, then I spoke twice as loud and half as fast as necessary to give any truths a chance to outrun all the lies. "Panduri is in a panic. Grain won't ripen, bears refuse to hibernate, the days won't shorten, and the crocuses have sent notice that without at least one snowfall they will not bloom in the spring. Mamma and Father's timing is in a spiral. They need reliable stars to chart Panduri's course. They need Panduri's Heir to cast them. Panduri's true Heir, not this pretender to the position."

I dropped my hands in mock despair at Panduri's manufactured plight and left my iron uncovered. Big mistake.

My iron whispered and Antonio's gave off a faint harmonic. He flicked my nose. "Your speech is bullshit."

I fell to my knees. "Please, Antonio, go home."

"Impossible. The *folletti* are in a froth. We tossed them treats; all that did was spoil their suppers."

Folletti are sugar imps, worse than sprites, placed by the *signori* to keep the Careri out. "Talk to Ignazio. A cloudburst might clear the air."

"No." A deep rumble pulsed from Antonio's iron. "Ignazio claims consideration at every turn in this conflict, sends squalls when sunshine might serve, lifts fog when cover might be desired, all the while making his mistakes look like strategy, then sends invoices to the *signori* to correct them. I won't give him reason to confuse the situation into the next cycle."

"Forget Ignazio. I'll sweet talk the *folletti* myself. Later. Or sooner. It doesn't matter. Go home, I implore you. Give Panduri its due. Do as I beg and in exchange, I'll write you a panegyric worthy of a god extolling your efforts. A panegyric Claudio can sing for your worshipers next Midsummer's Eve." I got off my knees and stood tall. "I'm invoking my rights. I'm Panduri's Protector. This is my place, not yours. So pack yourself up. I'm taking your tent."

Antonio let me take his tent, but he didn't pack up. He attached to me like a bad habit. When I rose early, he rose with me. If I slept late, he brought me breakfast. Did I need to stretch my legs? So did Antonio. Inspect the woodwinds? So did he. We drew up word lists together. Composed cricket song together. One day he followed when I went to piss. I bent backward, arced my stream over his. "Stop it."

He buttoned his fly. "Stop what?"

"Stop following me. Every time I eat beans, you fart. It's unnatural."

He rosined his bow and made a big show of tucking his fiddle under his chin. "This vendetta moves to its own beat. You have to watch your tempo."

Since I'd arrived, not so much as a harsh word had whispered across the valley buffering us from the Careri. I began to believe Giacomo had made the whole fight up. An excuse to get away from Father.

Until the day I woke to a thrumming in my temple, a tremolo like tree frogs in my ear, and the staccato sprints of stretched horsehair on sheep gut.

Antonio's fiddle, playing a sprightly tune. "It's only cuts and bruises," he told me. "They'll heal. I told you to watch your tempo."

"There were trolls." Great bumpy beasts with feet the size of planks. I grabbed my jaw, tonguing along a newly emptied space. "And maybe the tooth fairy. She got a molar."

"No trolls. No tooth fairies. *Folletti*." Antonio pinched forefinger and thumb together to show me how small. "Armed with sticks and stones. You have to stop all the name calling."

They were rude.

"Salvatore says you followed their bells."

So delicate. Fanciful. The call . . . irresistible. "Yes, they distracted me from the trolls."

A swath of hair escaped the thong binding it behind Antonio's head and fell across his face. He hooked it behind an ear and pressed a vial into my palm. "Use this for the confusion. Shake it when you feel uncertain. The music is soothing. It will take your mind off things."

Liquid tinkled in the glass container. I tilted the vial this way and that, fascinated with the way the tones shifted. "Off the trolls?"

"Off going home. You're too much for the border, Matteo. You're just too much. Your ego's too large, your equanimity's too small. Take a measure, take two. Give yourself time to mature, time to ponder, time to examine all your possibilities before forcing yourself along this path."

"But—"

"I'm sending you with enough chart templates to plot stars into the next generation. Give Mamma a hug for me, tell Father hello and please, see if you can find a few of Dante's and Ilario's stories hiding in your heart to comfort Claudio. We'll switch places next Midsummer's Eve. As promised."

Stories. Hugs. And star charts. "You're supposed to stay home. I'm supposed to stay here. You're supposed to be Renowned. I get to be Legendary."

I babbled for a while, whimpered, then wailed, then touched his scar, jagged across his cheek, desperate to make him understand— even cuts and bruises can kill if left to fester.

Three

From Despair's abyss, my words retrieve. . . .

Beware the pull of a false promise.

The following Midsummer's Eve, Antonio did not come. He sent a sprite instead: *Perhaps next year. Or the year after.*

Beneath he had the sprite play an end note: *Until then, you wear the hat.*

I fought my way past Father's sparring ficus and into his office, then flung Antonio's foolscap onto his desk. "I've already sent Salvatore. He cannot find him."

So much for being first on the scene.

Father pointed to the gossamer-wrapped collection I carried on my back, a mighty bundle that weighed more than my woe. "Are those star charts regarding Ignazio?"

And a dozen other matters Antonio hadn't bothered to attend. The charts took me forever to find, longer to cast. Antonio had tossed half the stars into a bucket. Chaotic, disordered, worthless to our next generation. "Our Heir is missing. You're not going to do anything?"

"He'll show up. Midsummer is stronger than any stubbornness." Father put out a hand. "The charts, please."

I shrugged the sack to the creeping nettle carpeting the floor, then plucked Ignazio's from its bundle and unrolled it so Father could see, pointing to the outermost pathway. "Ignazio has reached the limit of his appeals. You've ceded him twice Luciana's promised dowry and Ruggiero's married a suitable substitute, one who promises many heirs. Ruggiero's path continues on course. You owe neither him nor his father further legal obligation for Ruggiero's failure to marry my sister."

Whatever stick Father carried traveled a little further up his backside. "Re-plot the particulars. Not all obligations fall within legal definitions."

"You want me to change the chart." Charts were supposed to be fixed at origination. Only Panduri's Heir could propose a change.

Father eyed my shirt, defiantly red and rebellious and again out of the moths' balls. He wrinkled his nose.

No. Father didn't want me to change the chart. He wanted me to figure out the problem so Antonio could change it. "I understand Ignazio is your friend," I said, "but why pander to him?"

"Ignazio is not my friend."

Father's soft-spoken announcement arrived with the force of a mudslide, shifting the ground beneath my boots.

"But . . . that is, I thought. . . ." I struggled to keep the I-have-no-idea-what-I'm-talking-about out of my voice. Ignazio spent more time with Father than Mamma ever had. "You've always kept him so close."

Father reached across his desk and rerolled the scroll. He looked to the window, to a sun that appeared glued to the horizon. "Antonio's tarried long enough. Find your brother. Return him to me."

I threw my arm across my midsection and bowed, my slant more exaggerated than my attitude and my best foot so far forward that I near toppled into the tumbleweed. "I will depart at once. I will check every hollow, peruse every path, consult every oracle."

"Don't be ridiculous." Father plucked a tiny marshmallow from the sprite collection he kept on his desk. He popped it into his mouth. "Don't look for Antonio, look for the lady with whom he is . . . engaged."

Sometimes Father can be so old-fashioned. "You mean fucking." Antonio wasn't missing, he was getting an early start.

"I mean making love. With somebody he cares about. This close to Midsummer, it's the only way to avoid the lure."

Conversations with Father flashed their own lightning. This one came with a steady supply of thunderbolts. "Then rejoice. If Antonio has found a lady, a Promise will not be far behind. In a year, maybe two, we will be knee-deep in potential Heirs. Antonio will return to home and hearth and you may cease to torment me."

"Torment you how, Matteo?" Mamma stood in the doorway, her hair draped in bluebells, her dress deep as twilight.

I went to her and kissed her cheek. She smelled of lilacs and lavender, sweet peas and baby's breath. "By keeping me from my appointed role. I'm Panduri's Protector. It's Antonio's problem to fixate planets and arrange cloud sculptings. I'm supposed to be at the border. Protecting."

Mamma smiled and twirled a finger through my hair, straight and lank and nothing like Father's. "The stars you plot direct our paths. Without them, we are petals gusting in a chaotic wind. What could be more protective than that?"

She grew serious. "Enough stormy words. The maestro's son-in-law has died. Such tragic tidings and an ill-portent so close to Midsummer's Eve. So sad for the maestro's daughter. Her baby is still an infant."

The air spinner. I'd wished the maestro's daughter long life and happiness in Antonio's stead. It never occurred to me those conditions might not include her husband. "I didn't know about a child. I didn't plot his star."

Father made a harrumphing sound. "Antonio is the child's benefactor. He plotted the chart."

As Pretender Heir, it was my duty to mark these milestones, note these relationships, find their influence in the intricate gravity which held our *ducato* together. Midsummer hadn't even begun, and I'd already had enough of it. "Fine. Tell Antonio to stay home and plot the rest. I don't want to play Heir anymore."

A flicker shot across the room, inches from my nose. It streaked toward the ceiling branches.

A star. Unplanned, unplotted.

My iron tugged on its chain, my heart halfway to following without taking a step. I looked to Mamma, to Father, then bowed to them both, my mind in loop-de-loops. "My star finally rises. I am off to follow it. I shall let you know where it leads."

"No. You cannot leave." Mamma glided to Father's chair and put a hand on the ivy twining along its back, closing the invisible divide between them. "The Deep Lore requires your presence."

"I'm Protector, not Heir. All the Deep Lore requires of me is to do my best by Panduri." I pointed to the flare strengthening above our heads. If the Papists' legends could be believed, a less obvious star had sent three wise men across a desert. "I must go."

"Tell him." Mamma nudged Father. She worked the vines between her fingers, her voice taut and trembly and tinged with fear. "You are Duca. Tell Matteo he cannot—"

Father cut her off with a curt *zzzzt*. He planted fist to palm, his determination dense enough to cast shadows. "You will not leave."

I was beyond listening. I headed for the door, my star's guidance bright and clear and blinding me to all else.

Stranglevine sprang to block my path, thick, strong, faster than quickweed. It twined my wrist, then my arms, then twisted me around to face my parents.

Tears streamed down Mamma's cheeks. "Please, Matteo. You must not forsake Midsummer's Eve."

Memories flooded in with her tears. Of Dante. Of Ilario. Of being restrained and Mamma crying crying crying. *You must not go.*

I pulled against the bonds. "Why not?"

Father closed a hand over the amulet hanging about his neck, covering its gentle green glow. The creeping nettle browned, the wolfsbane whimpered, cut off from their source. Their words reached me, minute murmurings of despair. I stopped struggling. "I yield. I *yield*."

Father released his iron. The nettle plumped, the wolfsbane

calmed. The stranglevine released me. It shriveled, retreating back into the earth between the floor stones. My star darted out Father's window, the tallest, the most impressive, the window from which Father surveyed the entire *ducato*. It disappeared into the twilight.

Midsummer's first twinkles peeked over the treetops, Midsummer's first music rose in the festival fields. Father sighed, the sound long and lush and rooted in the Earth. "Maybe you did not choose the field you are plowing, but you can determine the quality of your planting."

Was he talking about sex? Farming? I had no idea. "My star has gone rogue, sir, rising over a sun which finally dips below the horizon. A sun beholden to an Heir who must have finally arrived, yet feels no obligation to his place in Panduri's constellation."

"That is why you must stay, to hold safe Panduri's soul. To perform as her Heir until Panduri's charted Heir sees fit to return to his responsibilities."

Fury rose. Reckless, rebellious, full of reproach. "Tell me something, Father. Did you hand your brother his noose? Or did he tie it all on his own?"

Mamma gasped, her hand flying to her mouth.

I stalked off.

Because it is Claudio's responsibility to hold safe our souls.

I found a bottle and headed for Dante and Ilario's garden, there to see if my star had returned and to muse on what route Giacomo might have taken. "Egypt, perhaps. Or possibly Morocco."

Claudio, downcast, dour, disagreeable as donkey-breath, wasn't drinking that night. "Uncle Giacomo didn't go exploring. He hung himself from Dante and Ilario's tree. Then we cast him off."

I flopped by the two purple-capped pixies we'd positioned at the garden's center. One for Dante, the other for Ilario. I pulled candies from my boot top and placed one in each of their marble palms, as I did every Midsummer. "Did I ever tell you Uncle Giacomo showed me his maps? Here, I'll show you."

I found a stick and scratched in the dirt. A circle to represent Panduri. "This is us."

I drew a second circle around it. "This is Outside."

I drew a smaller circle on our border, nudging Panduri as one star conjuncts another, placing the circle mostly Outside, but still a little Inside. "And this is Careri."

I drew an orbit for Careri, spiraling it in the ether between Outside and Inside until it came to rest within Panduri's influence, making a binary star, orbiting one about the other. "Careri went exploring. Just like Dante and Ilario. Someday all will return with plenty of stories to share. They will enthrall the *folletti*, convince them to leave. Then maybe this vendetta will end."

Claudio pushed his cowl off his head. "Careri's orbit is Outside because they've lost hope. Lost purpose. They find no joy in what they have and seek it among what they don't."

"How do you know?"

"The maestro told me."

"My explanation is better."

"Your explanation is a lie."

"My explanation is an agreeable fiction. There's a difference." I ran a hand along one of the patterns in Dante's Wall. "Did the maestro tell you why Ilario never tried to take this one down?"

"Because they built it together."

I tossed the stick to the ground. "Then if I want to believe Uncle Giacomo went exploring, why do you have to tear that down?"

"Because you hide behind your stories and ignore the underlying premise."

"Did the maestro tell you that, too?"

Claudio sank back into his cowl.

He wasn't always like that. Before the cloak, before the shaved head, before the thorny righteousness which lately crowned his conversations, Claudio was more like Antonio. And like Antonio, he'd have listened to my imaginings and joined right in. "Okay, fine. Which underlying premise am I ignoring?"

26

"The premise that the hero is not allowed to take the castle until the villain stops fighting him."

"Ah. And Antonio is the villain."

"No. Antonio is your brother. Your villain lives here." Claudio tapped his temple. "He tells you all the things you cannot do, all the paths you cannot follow."

Claudio clapped his hands over his ears. "Don't listen to him. Listen to what matters. To what makes your spirit pulse, what makes your soul sing. Then dance. Dance for purpose. Dance for your heart's desire."

"The way Careri did."

"The way Careri didn't. That's why they lost hope."

Twilight deepened. Midsummer's music grew louder, its rhythm steadier. I stepped onto the stump. "Did the maestro tell you that, too?"

Claudio stepped up with me. "No, the Deep Lore."

We gazed at the horizon and watched Dante and Ilario's constellation climb to its zenith. I could dance for them, for all the places they'd been, all the places they'd yet to see. Experience the one adventure Antonio couldn't usurp. "I want a life of my own."

The air vibrated. My amulet quivered. My intention set. I tugged on Claudio's robe. "Do you ever listen to your own advice?"

"Never."

Twilight deepened and we were off.

The gathering seemed subdued, the dancing not quite started. Antonio stumbled onto the festival field, looking sullen and sleepy. The ravens seemed uncertain what to squawk in announcing his entrance. "Hail, Antonio, first son of Bartomeo, the . . . quiet, the . . . reflective . . . the. . . ."

The ravens trailed off and I feared Antonio's dancing would also, his timing chaotic, his heart obviously elsewhere.

HEEL.

to toe.

andbackagain This last all in a rush and stuttery.

The dancers faltered.

Salvatore plucked me from my square and dragged me to Antonio's. "Take over for him."

I nodded to Antonio, paying him more obeisance than had Salvatore, mindful of the audience, and concentrated on correcting Antonio's cadence, on regaining his pulse,

Antonio matched my swagger. The music picked up our rhythm, others fell in behind, our Heir the lodestone upon which Midsummer depended.

I fell into my own beat, moving partner to partner until one took my hand, her touch soft, her eye clear, her gown the color of pomegranate. My star returned and circled above her. The iron hanging about my neck shuddered. It let out a roar.

The girl broke from the group. I followed, scampering into the woods and down a moss-covered trail lined with glowstones. Our path terminated at a stream. I lifted my heart to her. "Please. What is your name?"

She giggled, dulcet and delicate, skirts rustling like leaves in autumn. "Go away, boy. I will not tell you. Protectors do not marry."

I looked at my shirt, at the red I'd worn in rebellion, disheveled from the stranglevine, the buttons still unpolished. "Protectors may not marry, that does not mean we do not love."

"Why should I love you? Have you consideration? Position? Do any call you by title?"

"None." I shook my head, trying to look mournful, happy, for once, Antonio's recalcitrance had denied me a position and given my amulet no reason to announce a lie. "The most beautiful consideration I shall ever earn stands before me, the noblest title I shall ever hold is if you'd call me *Lover*."

The air between us twinkled, sparkling with truth. I pointed to my star, subdued in the twilight. "The heavens agree."

She examined the star for what felt like forever, then took my hand. "My name is Ceres."

The blood-rush in my ears went silent, lost in a cascade of hair the color of acorns, my reason in a mingle of maiden grass and musk. My resentment over Antonio, my anger toward my father, my frustration with my circumstances drained away. I would stay in town, go to the border, surrender myself to whatever course the stars cast me, so long as I came home to her.

Somebody invoked my name, the tone crass and crude and pointier than porcupine quills.

The invocation pulled me away from her, a fish on the hook, forced me to retrace my route, along woodland lanes, across well-tended fields, through rose-lined streets. Back to the ducal mansion, up stone steps, through the colonnade twined with wandering thyme and summerberry, near tripping over Topo, trembling under the tempest. "Matteo has found a lady. His stars have aligned. Let him have the succession. I'll return to the border."

Antonio.

Claudio stopped me. He pulled me under a bower of Sheltering Monks Ease. "Leave. Now. Let Antonio handle this."

"Handle what?"

He glanced at his cloak. "I can't tell you."

Of course not. But I could guess. I wasn't deaf. I straightened my clothes, buttoned my shirt, searched for any evidence of my Midsummer's success, then pushed past Claudio, and into Father's office with a curse strong enough to send the sparring ficus into full retreat.

Antonio and Father stood nose to nose across Father's desk.

Father turned to me, his face red, the vines twining his chair blanched. "Whatever promise you've made your lady must be forsaken. Whatever plan you and your brother have devised forsworn. Panduri must not follow Careri's path. Our place in the celestial dance must be maintained, with no cracks at our center, no chips on our surface, no imperfection from which our enemies might hang a complaint. We will not return to the days of the Great Upheaval. Our Heir must be clear in his duty. Our Protector's passions must not be divided."

Protector. Did he mean me? "There's no promise. No plans."

"And the lady?"

"None, sir." The declaration slipped through without thought, following on my tendency to answer any of Father's inquiries in the negative.

I dove to retrieve the words, to unmake them before any had time to settle, but Father was on a plow, his furrows deep and definite, cutting through my intention and sending my declaration out the window. "Antonio has one more year, one year only, to indulge his fancies, avoid his obligations, pretend his stars do not exist. Then he must return, accept his title as Heir, make his choice, and marry, or Panduri falls, our flame forgotten, and all we love turned to ash."

Father slammed his fist to his desk. "Panduri needs its Heir, the one we have charted, not the one you two decide. If either of you utters a word to the contrary, composes a refrain in protest, he will spend the rest of his life at the monastery, picking stink beetles off the cow patties and in silent contemplation of his failings."

Outside Father's window—the tallest, the most impressive, the window from which Father could survey the entire *ducato*—my declaration overtook my star, still shining in the twilight.

And sent it hurtling.

Four

Forgive me all I failed to do, forgive me all I did;
Recall the words I failed to say, forget the sins I hid.

ntonio returned to the border. I spent a long and unsatisfying year writing plenty of dodgy but heartfelt poetry and pondering what had happened.

I sent Antonio a sprite: *What in hell did you tell Father?*

He sent one back: *I told him you could be Heir. Don't be angry, it was just an idea.*

I sent another: *It's a terrible idea. I don't want to be Heir. I want to be Protector. I want to live at the border and far away from you.*

He made me an offer: *If you're Heir, you live in town, still far away from me, plus you get your lady, get to lead the procession, get all the flowers thrown at you, and get to wear the hat.*

It *was* a mighty fine hat: *Forget it. I'd have to be Duca. I'd have to use Father's office. It's a mess.*

He doubled down: *You don't have to use anything until Father dies. And he'll never die. You declared it yourself.*

I had. But I was drunk. So it probably didn't count: *No. It's too risky. Fire. Flame. Destruction. Ash.*

He didn't care: *Don't worry about all that. I'll figure some way around it.*

I didn't answer.

A last sprite fluttered outside my window: "He says, 'I promise.'"

Words have power. Power to unmake my denial of Ceres. Words organized by meaning, by emotion. Words subdivided by color, by size, by tone, by inflection. Words arranged in the proper order, to be spoken at the proper time, to arrive at their purpose like stars coursing across the heavens: "This is my lady, and never again will I say otherwise."

Antonio's promises have none.

Midsummer approached slower than any I'd ever known. The *ducato* gathered, eyes shaded, and gazed at a sun which refused to set, delayed, yet again, by Antonio's obstinate absence.

Father sent out those in whom he had the most confidence.

They returned disappointed.

Father sent them again, Salvatore at their head, his warning clear. "Do not return empty-handed."

I searched for Antonio in Dante and Ilario's garden, my uniform pressed, my buttons polished, my expectation I'd be heading for the border while Antonio planned his Promise. I found Claudio perusing the primroses, Topo purring on his shoulder. "Give him over," I said.

"The cat?"

Claudio had recently been made head of his order. He'd been given the best room at the monastery, the simplest, the most meditative, the room with the clerestory windows. He'd also received a new collar, higher and pointier than his old one, no doubt to match the new stick he seemed to have shoved up his ass.

"No, idiot. The cat hates me." I rattled the raspberries, rustled the bergamot, I climbed onto the stump, and peeked over Dante's wall. "Knock it off, Antonio. It's Midsummer. You have no choice but to dance."

Antonio stepped from behind a stand of climbing bellflowers. He laid a hand on the blooms to stop their pleasant *ring-tinga-tingle*. "I have a choice."

The sun commenced its downward dip. I pointed toward where the music swelled, my heart skipping a hopeful beat. "You have dozens of choices, hundreds. They're waiting on the festival field. Pick one."

Anyone. I didn't care who because the moment Antonio did, I intended to find Ceres, unmake my declaration and set her up in a suitable situation. No more milkmaids. No more camp followers.

Thank what gods there be, I'd never gotten to the sheep-fucking.

Antonio's eyes closed, he swayed to the music, his arms rounded before him like he danced with a partner. "The Papists have a story about an apple, have you ever heard it?"

"When would I have met a Papist who could tell me a story?"

"If you did, the Papist would tell you this apple grew from a very special tree in a very special garden." Antonio kept on swaying. The breezes came alive with his rhythm.

"Did this Papist have a brother?"

"He did, a brother who was drawn to the apple, wanted it more than any other fruit of the garden, yet it was the one fruit the Papist forbade him."

I glanced pointedly at the stump. "So the Papist chopped down the tree."

Claudio flung his cowl up over his head.

Ha. I'd walked into a conversation ongoing between them, a conversation unlike any Antonio and I had ever had, unlike any Antonio and I ever would. A conversation Antonio was at liberty to divulge, but Claudio never could. I'd walked into Antonio's Underlying Premise. "What's going on?"

Antonio stepped heel to toe, then toe to heel, then he stopped. "I don't want a marriage like Mamma and Father's. Convenient. Proper. Void. I don't want to spend the rest of my life standing on ceremony when I could be standing on the shoulders of giants. There is more. So much more. I hear it when I play my fiddle. In the trees, from the flowers. It's like the whole earth sings to me. Can you understand?"

That's because sirens made the instrument. "I understand until you live your life, I won't get to live mine."

Antonio threw his arm about my shoulder. "You are only unhappy because you believe you can't do what you want. But you can and you should. With all your heart. And you will, no worries." He clapped me on the back. "I have a plan."

A plan. Oh no. Oh holy hell, no. "What's your plan?"

But Antonio was off, and I was after him because when Midsummer descends, it refuses to let go.

Antonio burst onto the field with a mighty yell and a great, spiraling leap. Willow wisps announced his entrance. "Antonio, first son of Bartomeo, the exalted, the excellent. . . ."

Etc. Etc.

The unmarried women of suitable lineage formed a circle around him. He extended a hand and walked along its inner edge, gaze intent.

I nudged Claudio. "What's his plan? Did he tell you?"

Claudio looked at his cloak, the shroud by which all secrets are covered, and his mouth was closed.

Damn. Damn damn damn.

Midsummer's Lore claimed the first would be final. Heads turned this way and that, eager to see who the *duca's* Heir would choose. The willow wisps followed Antonio, to and fro, crisscrossing in a complex tizzy. They coalesced, their tiny lights arrayed like a crown behind the circle's edge.

Antonio's iron sounded a jubilant rhapsody, all but leaping from his chest.

My heart leapt with it. Antonio would be happy. I'd be happy. I just had to find Ceres. Unmake my denial. Make a new declaration.

The circle reformed, moving back and around, making a place for the Heir's choice. A murmur went up, then a cry. Affectionate, amused. The lady was shy. The lady was nervous. The lady was. . . .

Ceres.

Breathless, beautiful, her acorn-colored hair twined with berries and her gown dizzy with daisies.

Panic flashed from eyes grey-green as moss. Her gaze swept the clustered faces.

And met mine.

The music took over.

Antonio took her hand and led her in the first lengthy circuit. Others fell in—behind, beside—and moved with him, heel to toe, toe to heel, backward and forward, crisscrossing as had the willow wisps, around and turnabout, in a rhythm as old as memory.

I moved with them, helpless against the tide, keeping one eye to my brother, the other to Ceres. I maneuvered my way toward them, determined to make my claim, determined to separate her from Antonio.

The music stopped.

I faced a girl, wearing a dress, flimsy and feathery, of a hue which makes every person in Panduri well with emotion.

Deepest blue.

The girl twirled into the following measure, her skirt fluffing in the rising breeze. My heat fluffed with it, and when the twirling stopped, we again faced each other, her color too high, my breaths too deep. She pulled me through the next chain of steps, her hair moving with the turns in flashes of silver and gold.

The music again changed and Ceres again whirled into view, cheeks round as apples and skin aglow. I reached for her, the move instinctive, certain there'd been some error, some miscalculation of the magic, intending to draw her away, unmake my denial and correct our courses. My mouth moved, my words low and insistent, filled with every last longing of my unmasked heart.

Ceres listened, expression serious. Then the damned music moved Antonio between us. Her iron pulled toward his.

Taking my hope with it.

My intention cracked.

All the longing, the planning. All the poetry I'd written . . .

The dance moved on, presenting me with the next woman in line, the girl with the deep blue plumage. The music swept us away, turning me in time to see Antonio take Ceres's elbow. When next I turned, Ceres was gone.

So was Antonio.

The rhythm picked up. Couples began to splinter. I searched the crowd. The girl cuddled close. "Come with me."

Her voice was soft, its timbre resonant against my throat. Her amulet shivered against my chest. I took her hand, desperate for the connection. She drew me away from the field, skipping down one leaf-covered path after another, a series of twists my Midsummer-addled brain gave up trying to follow. She sank into a sprawl of purple sedum and pulled me on top of her.

It was wrong. I knew it, but the sounds of others likewise succumbing rose with the song of the cicadas. Her skin, so smooth and welcoming warmed to my touch. Her fingers feathered tiny whispers along mine.

That was the time to draw back, the time to satisfy her in other ways. This woman promised release, but no succor. Pleasure, but no purpose. I did not love her, I only wanted her, and only because the tyranny of Midsummer's Eve denied me the one I loved.

I did not withdraw. She made the invitation, I accepted, moving deeper when she pleaded and harder when she begged, frantic to chase away the image of Ceres wrapped around Antonio as this woman wrapped around me, creating a child which should have been mine.

A cry in the night threw ice water on my release. I stopped my movement, as did she.

The cry came again, the wail of the wounded, pitiful and meek. I rolled off the girl, secured my britches and headed for the sound, my blood again rising, this time with apprehension. I turned and turned again, uncertain of direction, then the *thwap* of fist on skin pulled me into a clearing.

Ruggiero was there. With his new wife.

Her hands covering her face, his fist raised to strike another blow. I pulled him off her and pushed him against a tree. She scrambled up, adjusting her skirt. I averted my gaze, appalled at her obvious state and shook Ruggiero. "She's with child. Do you wish to kill your heir before he's even drawn breath?"

"I'm not hurting her. She enjoys it."

Impossible. "No woman enjoys that."

"Leave us be." He shrugged me off. "You're not Heir, you're not Protector. And you're sure as hell not Gentle Guardian. You're Pretender. This is none of your concern."

I looked to his wife, to the bruise swelling on her cheek. She raised frightened eyes to me, her expression pleading.

For what?

Aid? Forbearance? Understanding?

She could have been Luciana.

I threw Ruggiero to the ground and fell atop him, rammed my fists into his face, one after the other.

Bone broke. Blood sprayed.

I grabbed his iron and yanked it from its chain, fingers clenched about it. Its heat seared into my palm. Ruggiero's life source faded under me.

I squeezed, feeling what Ruggiero felt in those moments before I tackled him, the rage mixed with sexual tension, the arrogance, the . . . hubris, rising like victory, like glory, like freedom. I wanted to do as he had done to her, to hit him until he crumbled, until he groveled at my feet, until he begged for comfort, for mercy.

I again drew back, this time meaning to finish him.

Antonio caught my arm. He encircled me with his other, clasping a fist about my amulet, then pulled me off Ruggiero. "Matteo. Hold your temper in check."

His compassion sliced through my spasm, deep and whole and boundless. I dropped Ruggiero's iron. Claudio scooped it up, fixed the amulet to its chain. He held it against Ruggiero's chest, singing benedictions.

Ruggiero's eyes cleared. Color returned to his face. Claudio helped him to his feet. A gaggle of ladies swept in. They swept Ruggiero's wife away in a cloud of soothing words and tongue clicks. A crowd gathered. Watchful.

Antonio handed me to Claudio and drew Ruggiero aside. Separated from the warmth Antonio imparted, my rage again rose.

Claudio tried. He wrapped his arms as had Antonio, but my body would not quiet, my spirit would not settle, my fury would not abate.

I looked to Antonio as I always had. He spoke to Ruggiero in a low and authoritative rhythm, and I fought jealousy because he did not speak to me. He laid a hand on Ruggiero's shoulder, and I fought Claudio's grasp, resentful Antonio did not take hold of mine.

Ruggiero caught my gaze, his belligerent and baneful, the bruises I'd bestowed already blossoming in shades of purple and black, a blood-soaked handkerchief pressed under his nose. "For this, you will be sorry."

He flung the handkerchief at my feet and walked off. The crowd dispersed.

Salvatore scooped the handkerchief from the ground. He handed it to Antonio, then tilted his head in the direction Ruggiero had gone. "Monastery?"

Antonio looked toward Claudio. "Can you keep him there?"

"Yes." Claudio's affirmation exited with a heaping spoonful of *no*. "I can try. We all will. But the monastery holds no man against his will."

"Well, we can't let him go home." Antonio shoved the handkerchief into his vest pocket. "Ignazio collects plenty of consideration in the vendetta, it's time his son makes a contribution. Find Ruggiero, Salvatore. Take him to the border. He's had enough of Midsummer. So have I. I'll go with him."

Leaving Ceres alone.

I imagined her here. In town. And Antonio away. At the breakfast table. And dinner. Making polite conversation with my parents while my brother's child grew within her. "I'm Protector of Panduri. I'll go. You can't make a Promise and leave."

"Promise?" Antonio spat out those syllables like they were slathered in horseshit. "Who said I'm making a Promise?"

"Mamma. Father." Deepest blue faded before me, replaced by hope, soaring and sweet. "Ceres. . . ."

"The only promise Ceres and I made is to stay as far away from each other as we can manage." He threw his arms wide. "Were I a betting man, I'd wager she's home safe in her own bed upholding her end of the bargain."

At home. All this time. Not . . . where I'd imagined. "But Midsummer Lore says . . . I mean the amulets. . . ."

Antonio waggled his. "This? This is a hunk of iron. What happened tonight was a show for the *ducato*, a way around Father's fire and brimstone, the death and destruction, my intention set to choose the one woman among all those suitables who had no interest in me."

He smiled. "I told you I had a plan."

A stain bloomed from the blood-soaked handkerchief Antonio had secured in his vest pocket. Ruggiero's blood, seeping close to Antonio's heart. My own lurched. My now shattered intention to unmake my declaration. The crossed purposes.

The ground trembled, a great and ominous roar.

And the woman. The other. The dress of deepest blue.

Five

My wife's gone to see her mother;
Let the revelries begin;
How nice to be alone at last
For Debauchery and gin.

It's a drinking song, no more. One men sing in public houses. I drew another pitcher from the well, my confusion foaming like piss on snow. "How in hell did you think choosing someone you don't want and who doesn't want you would somehow get Father to stop bothering you about being Heir?"

Yes, Antonio was supposed to be long gone, supposed to be happily sleeping off Midsummer from his tent at the border, but . . . parents. Parents with plenty of questions and exclamations of delight over Antonio's choice of consort. Parents less than pleased to be told Antonio had meant it all as a joke.

I fixed Antonio with my favorite of Father's glares, condescending and contemptuous and harsh enough to bleach bed linen. "'Her iron pulled toward yours, my son. She is meant for the Heir. You have a duty. To your *ducato*. And your *duca*.'"

I upended my drink. "Your plans stink."

Antonio blubbered into his bass clef. A series of notes, low and portentous, bubbled a counterpoint from the well's depths. "Any explanation I give won't seem enough. The solution will seem simple. But—"

"Shut up." He was beer-soaked and bleary-eyed. As Panduri's Protector, it was my duty to cut him off. Heads were turning. People were muttering. And I wasn't so drunk I couldn't figure out the inevitable end of his blathering. "There's somebody else, somebody unsuitable."

Antonio's iron let out a honk like a swan dying in winter. "Define *unsuitable*."

I slumped into my chair, too drunk to define anything. Stupid love. Stupid impossible love. The tragedies of the Outsider poet, Shakespeare, had better outcomes than me. "That's it. Until I'm done drinking, I'm done with love. Done with all love's stupid stupidness."

I raised the pitcher. "To Salvatore. May he swiftly get Ruggiero to the border. At least somebody will get out from under this Midsummer's Eve."

A dram for my tankard,
I plan not to be bored;
Does life get any happier?
Absent wife and here—my whore.

I nudged Claudio, all but buried in his cowl. "Let's salvage the twilight. What about Pieta? She was my first."

"Mine, too."

Why did that surprise me? Claudio's a cleric, not a saint.

"Yes. Pieta is very talented." Antonio snapped his fingers in front of my face. "All you had to say was, 'I have a lady. Her name is Ceres.' And we wouldn't be having this problem."

"We have a problem? How could we? You chose the woman I love. I fucked another. I'd say the situation is about as good as it can get."

"It can get better. Have you any idea who the other was?"

Antonio went for the pitcher, but I held it away and drank directly from it. "No idea."

Antonio leaned across the table to tell me. "She is Careri."

I stopped drinking. Beer dribbled down my chin. "How do you know?"

"The maestro told me."

When had Antonio found time to talk to the maestro? "No doubt he also told you how she got here, this supposed woman of Careri. The valley is teeming with *folletti*. No doubt she took wing and flew." I took another drink. "You're lying."

"Am I?" He held out his iron so I could check. It was silent. He pulled the pitcher from my fingers. "You better hope the maestro doesn't tell Father."

Go gently now, dear woman,
Be careful of my back,
For it has been some time
Since I played roughly in the sack.

The temperature rose, along with a sex-sweet stink. It emanated from the bushes, from behind hedges, from private rooms swaying gently in the treetops.

The press on my uniform had wrinkled, the buttons had tarnished, even its red color felt sticky and hot. I loosened my collar, wondering why I'd bothered. "Nobility is stupid, too. All this talk of suitable matches, whose iron pulls towards whom, doom, gloom, and stars falling from the sky. How we're all connected, part of the celestial dance. Inside is not like Outside, my ass."

I pulled back Claudio's cowl and indicated the singers. "Look around. Look at all these noble sons. Half of them are married. Tell me, you who claims to understand the Underlying Premise—Why don't protectors marry? How come clerics can't?"

Claudio peeked around his whiskey. "So nobody feels bad about the milkmaids and camp followers."

Or the sheep-fucking. "No, my happy little holy one. It's so there's not a lot of extraneous offspring clogging the lines of succession. Oh, to be an everyday person, work my craft, live my life, love whom I please."

Antonio corralled Claudio's whiskey and sucked it dry. "Do without question whatever the nobility chart for them."

What else were they supposed to do? "Do you think they care?"

"Have you ever asked one?"

I hadn't. "What for?"

"They're not puzzle pieces we can arrange at will. Neither are we."

"Are you sure? Mamma's already making the arrangements for your Promise. Flowers and fancies and comet trails and starbursts. Look." I pointed to the sprites, darting tree to tree. "She's already sending out invitations."

"Then she can rescind those invitations. I'm not getting married on Mamma's say-so, nor steering my life by the whims of an arbitrary star." Antonio placed his palms on his temples and rubbed with enough friction to spark a fire. "Listen to me, Matteo. See Ceres. Talk to her. Then give me a little time. I will find some way to fix this mess, some way we can all be happy."

He shoved that stupid swath of hair out of his eye. "I promise."

Kiss all the tender places,
I dare not ask my wife.
She's for bearing babies,
Not for sharpening my knife.

I stood. "I have plans. Don't wait up."

"Nothing to do with the Careri woman, I trust."

"Don't be ridiculous." I slapped a hand over my iron, then stepped back to give my lie a little legroom. "I'm off to find a lonely wife. Judging from this crowd, there are plenty available. If I'm unsuccessful, I'll look for someplace more discreet. I don't like fucking in public. Claudio, where did Salvatore find Father the last time we lost him?"

Antonio clapped a hand over Claudio's mouth. "You don't want to find a lonely wife. Or a brothel. You don't want to do anything stupid."

No, I planned to be like Antonio and do something deliberate. "How will you avoid what the Deep Lore says must be? Change the star charts?"

Guilt glinted in Antonio's eye. A tone rose from his iron—furtive, deceptive, and like everything having to do with my brother, hidden.

I picked up the pitcher and poured the contents out on the floor. "If bullshit were beer, we'd all be drowning. Go home, Antonio. Plot stars until you bang your head against the wall so hard you see them before your eyes. Then admit the truth. It's not that you don't want to be Heir. You don't want to be part of Panduri."

The words wedged into the space between us, bowing the floorboards. An awful, awesome, awkward truth.

I'd had enough. "I'm leaving."

Antonio grabbed my arm. "Don't. Rebellion changes a man, in ways you can't imagine."

"I can imagine plenty." I headed for the door.

It took me hours to find her because I didn't have any notion where to find a stray Careri and neither did my amulet. I traveled the wrong road, strolled the wrong street, turned the wrong corner, hoping to pick up her trail. I mounted the wrong stairs, knocked on the wrong door, conveyed my apologies when the wrong occupant answered, traversed the wrong room, and escaped out the wrong window. Back on the street, my iron finally, finally, *finally* climbed me up the right trellis and through the right window.

So I could mount her.

Happy dagger, please release me.
From this wanton's lips shall fall
Pleasant words and pleasant actions
Upon my noble balls.

Ah. The heat escaping her skin in frantic waves, the feel of her, thighs clutching, fingers grasping, our amulets quivering at all the right moments. The branches of her bower were bursting with greenery, the canopy thick. The breezes carried a hint of perfume. Nightingales sang, fireflies glowed. And this woman, this . . . vision, was open and eager and enjoying it all very much.

So was I, until I felt the familiar peak. Then I slid away,

She crossed her ankles. "What are you doing?"

"You are Careri." And the Maestro had told me of how babies came to be on the Outside. "Docs it . . . I mean . . . just, Careri may be different."

She arched under me, ran a finger along my cheek. "Do I feel different?"

"You feel wonderful. What I mean is. . . ."

She giggled, then drew me close. "You're talking about babies!" Her tone was happy and husky and a little on edge. "You and I are Inside. That means the Deep Lore holds. And that means we do not make babies we do not want."

Her iron did not betray her. "So you agree you don't want to . . . start anything."

She tightened her thighs on my hips, got hold of my backside and rolled on top of me, her frenzy rising, her moans coming short and deep. "Start anything? My goodness, yes! The moment we are finished. And then again after."

Ha, so did I. Not babies. Sex. Lots of it.

I obliged her. Then we slept. And fucked some more. Then slept. And fucked. Sometimes we ate. Sometimes we peed. On occasion, we bathed. I looked for my uniform, thinking it was past time to leave, but I couldn't find it.

"It will turn up." She ran fingers through her hair, her breasts lifting with the movement, then poured us both wine, rich and red, of a vintage both familiar and foreign.

And oh so warming, sparkling in goblets of polished crystal, my desire to drink of it, overwhelming. A drop caught at the corner of her lip. I licked it off.

Then we fucked again.

The stars outside her window continued to shine. Midsummer music continued to play. We continued to fuck, trying new and varied positions, using new and unbridled words to describe them. We reveled in unabashed pleasure without purpose, her willingness and wine driving me to new limits, wishing her more than I had to give, wanting to please her, to satisfy her deepest desires until a spark, the tiniest illumination, the sensation unique, untried, and impossible to define.

Claudio burst through the door and pulled me off her.

"Let's go." He tossed me a pair of pants. And a clean shirt. Both Antonio's. "You've had enough of Midsummer's Eve." He turned to the Careri, who gathered the sheets about her. "So have you."

But we hadn't. There was the spark. The tiny glimmer. I needed to return, to discover the meaning.

Claudio gave me a shake. "I've been looking for you forever. Antonio's camped at the horizon, worried the Careri would convince you to cross. All Father does is pace. He held the stars as long as he could, hoping Salvatore would pick up your trail."

"Good. Let Father pace. And let Antonio do his duty. There are a thousand women in Panduri. Tell him to stop mooning over the one he can't have." I shrugged him off. "I'm going back to bed. Collect me when Midsummer is over."

Claudio snapped his fingers in front of my face. "You're bewitched. Do not trust what she shows you, trust less what she says. You need to leave. Midsummer has been over for days."

I pointed to the window, where underdown, delicate as her dress, filtered a twilight that seemed never-ending. "Are you mad? The stars still twinkle."

Claudio tore at the feathers. He flung the window wide and pointed to the sky beyond. "Matteo. Open your eyes."

Day appeared, bright and blinding. I blinked, unable to reconcile what I saw, then leaned over the sill to see Panduri bustling in its midday concerns. Shopkeepers presided over stands, craftspeople busied themselves in their stalls. Children played. Dogs barked, donkeys brayed. Sprites darted hither and yon, making deliveries for spun sugar treats.

In sunlight, the Careri's bower felt more like a nest, its branches twiggy like kindling, their leaves dry and dead. The goblets, over-turned amid a flotsam of threads and bits of twine, were not crystal, but rough pottery. The dregs of the wine jug stank of sour milk. The Careri seemed different also, her face more angular, her nose beaky, her hair without highlight, and her manner shrewd.

My ardor faded. "Why?"

She reached across the bed and pulled her dress from the chair, no longer fluffy and no longer blue, but of a brown plumage suitable to one who hoped to escape notice. She stepped into it, and, I swear, her arms changed to wings. "I found you . . . useful."

I pulled on Antonio's pants and shirt. I tightened the buckle to the last notch, rolled up cuffs and tucked in all the extra fabric, my attention fixed on the task and away from her increasingly birdlike appearance. Was this how she got here? Had she actually taken wing and flown, or was I imagining all of it? I turned to Claudio. "Why didn't you bring my clothes?"

"Because the house brownies think you're at the border. If your street clothes suddenly went missing, it would seem strange." Claudio dropped a pair of boots at my feet. He waited while I stomped into them, then turned to the Careri. "Were you wise, you'd be gone by nightfall."

Then he pulled his robe up and over his head, tossed it over mine, and pushed me out the door.

No greater love could I have
For my wife so fair.
Yet it's nice when she is absent,
For then I screw without a care.

Six

On hopeless paths, I waste my wrath. . . .

o urs later I stood in Father's study, Claudio's cowl catching at my neck, horror catching at my craw. What had I slept with? What had I drunk? "She was a woman, then a bird. How is that possible?"

Father transplanted a clump of *sotto voce* to his window sill, their large blooms a shield against the world beyond. The sounds of the *ducato* went silent, absorbed by the *sotto's* spongelike leaves. "She shifted her shape, a powerful magic she combined with illusion, to be what she needed to get what she wanted."

Father's words echoed around me, despite the plant, like I stood in a hollow. He leaned toward Claudio. "You took precautions?"

"We traveled back streets. Matteo kept the hood up at all times." Claudio's expression went sheepish. "I couldn't find his uniform. She must have used it as a talisman to hold him."

"She will sleep in it to strengthen her hold."

Hold. "What hold? We had some fun. I don't even know her name."

Father tilted his chin toward me. "Good, then your ignorance will be real should anybody ever ask about her."

"Why should anybody ask?"

"Nobody will if we handle this correctly and that means you have to leave. The *signori nobili* think you're already at the border, awaiting your brother's arrival to settle this new threat."

Threat.

Father leaned back in his chair. "A woman of Careri has crossed our border and is exposed for a spy. The *signori* are very concerned. All saw her at Midsummer's Eve, and it is said she found herself a partner."

He turned to Antonio, standing by the sparring ficus. Like a waxwork. "Have you any idea who that partner might be?"

"Tendi." Antonio danced without hesitation and so lifelike, I never saw the strings. "He is young and foolish and has never been to the border."

"The Careri made a poor choice. Tendi couldn't have told her much. I will order him to monk's robes. The *signori* will be relieved."

Border. Monk's robes. I'd slept with a bird. Didn't anybody care? "Father, you can't. She's no spy."

"If the *signori* decide she's a spy, she's a spy. Why else would she be here, trawling for a partner? Have no worry. Tendi's consideration will go to his younger brother at the proper time. Except for the monk's tithe, of course."

"Tendi is Ignazio's kinsman. He won't stand by while you discredit his cousin's son."

"Ignazio will not protest. Nobody will protest."

"You are wrong, sir. I'm protesting." I struggled with Claudio's robe, near drowning in the volume. I finally got it over my head and stood straighter, feeling giddy. "Whatever the madness behind this fiction, leave Tendi out of it."

"You, they would have to exile."

"They won't have to." New life flooded me. I headed for the door. "I'll exile myself."

"Matteo, no." Antonio's voice followed me, desolate and dejected. "Outside is a crude, indelicate place full of rules without reason, where every unpleasant thing is remembered. Their music is muddied, their colors dull, their words coarse. They do not value poets."

No. There were light-filled towers, pinnacles soaring to the heavens. "Dante and Ilario are out there, you puffed up bag of privilege. They left a trail. The maestro told us. We always leave a trail."

Antonio shook his head.

I crossed the distance broadening between us, yanked the iron from Antonio's neck, then plastered it against Antonio's scar, jagged along his cheek. "Say it. You have to say it. Dante and Ilario will always have a place in Panduri."

Antonio did not waver, did not faint. His knees remained steady and his music true. "As Panduri will always have a place with them."

His melody exited on butterfly wings, wrapped my declaration, and carried it skyward.

I dropped the iron into Antonio's palm and closed his fingers over it. He was Heir. Strong beyond measure. Separating him from his source would not change that.

And I'd slept with a bird. I turned to Claudio. "Did she look like a bird to you?"

"She looked like an ordinary woman. Older than you and bent on a purpose." Claudio pulled a chart from a pile on Father's desk. He unrolled it and laid it out. A genealogy. He traced one path, then another, stars catching fire under his fingers. They came to rest near the bottom of the page. He pointed. "This is her, we believe. She is the wife of a powerful *signore*, a man in line for the Careri *ducato*."

My spirit shrank, along with my anger. I'd found what I'd voiced, a lonely wife. "I see no purpose here except she wanted a little adventure and didn't want to be discovered. Good. Neither do I."

Especially if it turned out she were actually a bird. "Why is everybody in a panic?"

Something, perhaps compassion, perhaps not, flickered across Father's face. "She wasn't looking for adventure. She was looking for you. Probably because you look like her husband. You really had no idea?"

I'd had warmth. I'd had pleasure. I'd had freedom. More than seemed possible for one man. Without promises, without constraint, but not, as I was coming to understand, without regrets. "Looking for me for what?"

Claudio showed me the paths leading from the woman, from her husband. All were dark. "They have no children. She wanted a baby."

The gravity of Claudio's words weighed on me, their meaning heavy to hold. I needed to be out from under the awful burden, needed a place to fling it all.

Antonio. "You let me go."

He drew me close as he had the day he pulled me off Ruggiero. "Get hold of your emotion, or you will not survive the coming storm."

A baby.

Impossible.

I'd have known. I'd have sensed it. Even drunk and near unconscious. Not without my consent, not without my willing participation.

Not without her wine, so sweet on my lips, the desire it engendered. To give her more than she begged while between her legs. To give myself over completely, just for the moment.

And the spark, the glimmer, the tiny illumination.

Claudio rolled up the chart. The one that showed the Careri and her husband had no children. "She found you useful."

Uncle Giacomo once told me casting stars is like casting dice. When the parchment first goes down, all odds are even, all possibilities on the table. For intelligence, potential, career, and talents. For good, for better, for contentment and satisfaction.

"The twists come from the parents," he used to say. "Look to them, and you will see the gravity with which each cast must contend."

Odd observations from a Protector, yes, but free of the Heir's constraint, who must plot not just for the baby, or its parents, but also for Panduri.

Or so I once heard Antonio complain. He cast stars about as well as drunks walk tightropes. That's why he left his charts to me. Still, it did not keep him from opining about them. Even in camp. Even when I escaped my tent to do my casting at the border's edge.

He leaned over my shoulder. "Enough with all the nudging. She's only an infant. Grant her a little room to explore." He took a breath and blew. Stars and planets skittered across the parchment.

I caught one before it went over an edge. "Knock it off. Her parents hope for delivery this week. The mother's very uncomfortable."

Antonio snatched the star from my palm and tossed it back onto the parchment. "Call for a stork. Deliver the chart to Claudio now."

"I can't. It's not done."

He tucked his fiddle under his chin and played a measure, happy and hopeful. The stars fixed into place. "It's done now."

Antonio pointed his bow to a meteoroid which had landed in the chart's far corner, what we call a fireball. "Imagine when that one finally comes to earth. Who knows how her planets will develop?"

Or collide. Antonio kept on playing. Bells responded from the valley, high-pitched and sweet, tolling a star I wanted to experience in private, one rising over Careri and fixed to my path.

I shoved the remaining charts off my lap and smacked Antonio's fiddle to the ground. "Shut up."

Antonio scooped up the instrument, then tested its tune, plucking each string and twisting the pins, his expression thoughtful. "Where's Salvatore?"

"Digging mushrooms for my supper." I tapped the side of my palm to my stomach. "Even a prisoner must eat."

Antonio peered into the surrounding trees. Maybe he thought he could summon Salvatore with the force of his splendor. "He's assigned for your protection."

The border settled in for the evening. Squirrels scampered up the gracious oaks. Birds returned to their nests, lambs to their pens. "This is the quietest vendetta in the history of vendettas." Peaceful enough for a lullaby. "From what am I being protected?"

"From yourself." Antonio stopped perusing the trees and returned to tuning the fiddle. "You'll always feel it, always be aware. You'll always want to know more."

"He. My child is a boy." And the connection so strong. "How could she hope to fool her husband? How could he not know?"

"Perhaps her husband does know." Antonio ran his bow over one string, then the next. The notes danced on the breeze. "Perhaps she was here at his bidding."

Despair washed over me. A moment of passion might be forgiven, a desperate ploy understood. But to plan this, plot this, carry it out in such a cold and cruel manner . . . for what? A *ducato*? The chance to be announced every time you walked past? "I have to save him. I can't let my child live in a house filled with lies."

"What if the house is filled with love?"

What if it wasn't? I pulled at the silver buttons on my shirt, stripping them from the fabric. Took off my vest. Turned it plain side out. "I'll put on everyday clothing. Borrow something from Salvatore. Walk among them, maybe catch a glimpse. I won't go for long, not for always. I just need to see him, make sure his situation is sound."

Antonio threw himself in my path. "No. You must not cross."

"Are you worried about the *folletti*?" I pulled at Antonio's buttons. "You can come too, play your music to calm them. Then play your music for the Careri. You wanted to go, I've always presumed you would. Panduri doesn't need you for Heir, doesn't need me for Protector. Panduri has Claudio. Leave him to do our jobs."

Antonio dropped his fiddle and got hold of my shoulders. "Claudio can't be Duca, can't be Protector."

"Because he's dedicated to the Deep Lore?"

"Because he'd piss his pants. Then who'd get to be Duca?"

Ignazio. Most consideration, most allies among the *signori*, most able to convince anybody to do anything.

"Fine." I shrugged off Antonio and gazed at my son's star, strengthening as he grew, seeing a path I could follow, a dream I might realize. "I'll cross alone. But I'll clear the *folletti* first."

The bells went tinny. Antonio clapped a hand over my mouth. "*Shhh.* They heard. Then somebody might get hurt. Like you did."

I struggled, but Antonio held fast. He turned me toward my son's star. "Say you get past the *folletti*. Say you manage to see your son. If the Careri *duca* found out who you are, found out why you were there—you, true father of the child of the woman married to the man in line for their *ducato*. They would not let you take him. They might not keep him there. Maybe they'd send him beyond your reach, beyond Careri's reach, into the true Outside."

I dropped the buttons, letting each slip from my fingers.

Antonio released me, then played a simple song, somnolent and unhurried. The song spoke of happiness and ease, of looking forward and forgetting the past.

I covered my ears. "Stop. He's my son. What memories I keep are mine to choose, for help or hurt. You have no right to choose them for me."

"Then you must find some way to make those choices, some way to hold him near. Your words, my music. We'll work together."

I turned my back on Antonio. I gathered the charts and the stars. And I left.

Some days later, on a hot, humid, fly-ridden afternoon, Antonio found me. "Claudio sent a sprite. She is dead."

I looked up from my star plotting. "The sprite?"

"Ruggiero's wife. In childbirth. The baby also."

The pleading eyes, the swell beneath her waist. . . .

"Impossible, I just cast the baby's stars." I groped for the bundle at my feet, the stork's next delivery. The baby's chart was a masterpiece, labored over for days, to set this child on a better path than his father's. So loving, so fortunate. "His aspirations always on an upward spiral, his destiny always for Panduri's best."

I unrolled the scroll so Antonio could see, then traced the

Matteo

paths, but they were dark and cold and no longer lighting with the possibilities.

Ruggiero must have gotten to her before Salvatore found him. Must have taken the shame of my beating and visited it on her. I gripped the parchment, edges crinkling. "I should have killed him. You should have let me."

"Stop." Antonio took the star cast from me. He turned it this way, then that, eyes desperate. He laid it out on my desk, fingers tapping a pattern along its origin. "I should have ordered Ruggiero to monk's robes, never allowed him to marry. Then I should have followed the path I'd been charted, let you follow yours."

He dropped into the chair, dropped his head into his hands. "I've sent us all spiraling."

I gazed at Antonio's scar, jagged along his cheek. My reminder of every unabsolved remorse. Every unspoken rebuke. Every unvoiced regret. Every semblance of normalcy we'd pretended into our lives. Every day. Every hour. Every minute. Since Dante and Ilario left us.

We were already spiraling.

In the distance, lightning flashed. "I'll find Ruggiero."

Antonio sprang to his feet. "No. Let me."

"I'm Protector of Panduri. First on the scene, last from the scuffle. It's what we do. It's what you told me. Our laws are clear."

"And our way of enforcing them just as clear. The *signori* will gather. There will be a tribunal. A decision."

"Like the one they gave Tendi." The ground pulsated, pushing against the pressure in my chest. "Don't you understand? Ruggiero's wife could have been Luciana."

I found Ruggiero in the swampiest part of the border, his buttons rusting, his face caked in mud to keep the mosquitoes away. Overhead, storm clouds gathered.

Because Ruggiero knew. A husband always knows. The Promise is like that, even shoddy Promises like the one Ruggiero had made.

Ruggiero removed his iron. He flung it at my feet. I picked it up. The heat again seared into my palm and I experienced his anguish, his woe.

That was the time I should have sent him on to Claudio, should have shown him mercy, should have remembered my part in it. That was the time I should have given Ruggiero his chance to make amends, to ask forgiveness, to seek a better way.

I did none of those things.

And I did not hold my temper in check.

Seven

In dreamlike guise, our longings lie. . . .

On the day we cast off Ruggiero, I headed home under a sky thunderous as my mood. Salvatore came with me, charged with my constant and consistent protection.

I needed to see Ceres. Needed to unmake my declaration in front of whoever happened to be there when I arrived. "Find her for me, Salvatore, and I will grant you enough consideration to restore your father to his place among the *nobili*. Enough for him to declare you his heir."

"No consideration outweighs Duca's orders." Salvatore laid a hand over his breastbone, where his iron hid beneath his shirt. "And Duca orders me to deliver you directly to Ruggiero's castoff."

"The way you delivered Antonio." I pointed to where Panduri's treetops swayed in the gathering storm, then to the cliff edge beyond, fog-shrouded and secret, so Salvatore would know I meant the time Antonio ran before the ceremony which officially made him Heir. "I'll bet you were first on that scene. Did Antonio scuffle?"

My curiosity overwhelmed my anger. "What did you see?"

Salvatore wouldn't even look to where I pointed. "Lost loves, crushed dreams, hopes abandoned like the forget-me-nots we braid for May Day. And people, so many people, pale and hurried, focused on nothing, gusting past me without notice, as if I were some figment of their imagination, a trick of the light."

I pulled out my pen and a scroll. "What were their buildings like? Their streets?"

"Lifeless, stale. Stone and brick plastered with more stone and brick. People there keep their purpose in their pockets and their greenery in clay pots, and when it rains, they run for cover."

Cover. From rain. Ridiculous. I tried to imagine Panduri the same, gone Outside like Careri, her grass-laid thoroughfares covered over in marble, her roofs made solid, her windows paned. "Why would Antonio go there?"

Salvatore didn't tell me to ask Antonio, didn't think it odd I asked him and not my brother. "The hopeful man creates a path if he believes his retreats are blocked."

"Then let me create such a path for you." I leaned toward him. "Let me go. Find Ceres for me and what I have is yours. You won't have to be a protector anymore. You can marry, have a home."

"I already have a home, filled treetop to root with siblings I have to help my parents support. I'm not giving up a private tent at the border to add to the chaos." Salvatore moved his mount a hoofsbreadth closer to mine. "So stay with me, or I will bring you back in chains."

Claudio drew me aside the moment I dismounted. "Ignazio will be here any minute. We do not have a moment to spare." He put out a hand. "Give it to me."

I dug Ruggiero's iron out from where I'd kept it warm, next to my own, happy to be shed of it.

Claudio clasped the amulet against his chest, closed his eyes, and did his tinkering. "I'm leaving Ruggiero's iron with only grief for his child and solitude for his wife. I'm filtering the rage, the betrayal he felt toward his father."

"His father."

Claudio's song wavered with dejection, with disappointment and despair. "Ruggiero did not start as he ended. There was a time before."

We're not supposed to speak ill of the dead. In Panduri, we rarely speak of the dead at all. But I was heartsick and horse sore, my struggles outweighing my mercies. I'd known Ruggiero all my life. "There was never a time before."

A hand landed on my shoulder. "Then we must work together to improve the times after."

Claudio and I both answered, "Niccoli." Ignazio's second son.

He opened his palm. "You have my brother's iron?"

Claudio handed off the amulet. Niccoli wrapped it in his fist. The sky rumbled, but a warm wind blew between us. "Thank you. I know this was difficult to carry. All of this has been . . . difficult."

Niccoli's tone was kind and thoughtful and filled with concern, like Claudio's when his collar's freshly starched. He left us humbly and I watched him go, all but expecting bluebirds in his wake. "So understanding, so forgiving. Yet he did nothing to pull his brother out of his depths."

I turned to Claudio. "He should have been a cleric."

Claudio's prosaic bearing is the result of his professional training, but his outrage is always real. I expected a full-blown response to my insult, but all my brother did was sigh, the tone somber enough to flatten bubbles. "Niccoli would have been a cleric. He's third son. There was a baby before Ruggiero. A boy. He died."

The Deep Lore claims we cast off as we lived. Ruggiero's wife and child caught the first wisp, their spirits fragrant like honeysuckle and gone in a breath. Ruggiero's hung heavy, a sore in need of lancing. Claudio sang for minutes, then hours, the day held steady by Luciana, but Ruggiero's sorrows continued to hover.

Finally, Niccoli wove a wreath of soul's ease. He lifted the wreath to the sky and whistled, the note sustained and sad. The wind responded, swift and strong and smelling of autumn. The season changed in a blink, and Ruggiero took flight, his burden lifted. All that turmoil, and then . . .peace.

It didn't seem fair.

Antonio presented the star charts. Ignazio lingered over Ruggiero's. Perhaps it was grief. Perhaps he perceived Antonio's rearrangements to remove my star from what happened.

Claudio approached Ignazio, hands outstretched. "Let me take their charts. I will burn their stars with the proper laments."

Ignazio stepped away. He tucked the charts under an arm. The sky darkened, dropping hail with the rain. The breezes turned violent. Mourners scattered.

I scattered with them.

Antonio caught me up. "Ignazio wants to send Niccoli to the border to negotiate with the *folletti* in Ruggiero's place. He seeks consideration to declare Niccoli his heir before his time. Father's in a furrow. What should I tell him?"

"Whatever you like. I am not Protector. I am not Heir. It is not my decision."

"You said Ignazio would be fine."

"He is."

"His son is dead."

"I never said anything about Ruggiero."

I backed away, my intent to find Ceres, but Claudio swept in. He flicked his head at Antonio—"Father needs you"—then turned to me. "Where are you going?"

"To practice targets." Almost true, my Midsummer's arrow was still embedded in the poplar tree at the far end of the archery field, still split cleanly by Antonio's. I meant to fix that. Meant to fix a lot of things Antonio might have split.

My amulet didn't give me up, perhaps confused by my circuitous thinking. I walked off, expecting to finally be free to pursue my own business.

But— "I'll come with you."

Fifteen broken arrows later, Claudio got to his point. "Trouble is coming. Ignazio would not let me take the star charts; he plans to study them at length."

I drew again, again sighted on Antonio's arrow, taking a perverse satisfaction in how the rain obscured Father's poem. "Ignazio can study the charts all he wants. I didn't kill Ruggiero. He'd made his decisions before I got there."

Claudio caught my arm. "But you didn't stop him. Didn't try."

"Stop him? It was all I could do not to join him. That's what you're all afraid of. The reason everybody's sticking to me like fresh dog turds."

"We want to make sure you're all right."

"You want to make sure I do what I'm told. Well, I'm done begging permission to live my life, done asking Father to explain his actions, done expecting Antonio to explain his. Tell them from now on they offer or I live in ignorance." I reclaimed my arm. "And tell both there is no way I'll let either come between me and Ceres."

The air pulsed, a breath, a warning.

Claudio must have felt it because he flicked at his ear. "Stay away from Ceres. Give Antonio time to find a solution, to settle the deep magic, settle Ignazio. Give Father the same."

"You're nuts. I'm not waiting my happiness on the hope one of Antonio's half-cast plans pans out."

"This has nothing to do with Antonio's plans, half-cast or not. It's about working together." Claudio scooped up a rock and inserted it between one of the crevices in Dante's Wall. "Look how well this stands. We add to it, it becomes stronger, but if I take it apart. . . ." He pulled at a twig, a pebble, a branch. Mud poured through. The far edge started to crumble.

I pushed him away, then pulled the branch from his fist. "What do you want from me?"

"Your patience. Please, I'm begging you. You will find your happiness. A man cannot outrun his stars, and yours are beautiful."

"You've seen my chart." Charts are private, personal, plotted at birth, passed on at death, and perused in between for only the most dire of reasons.

I unstrung my bow. "You are all so far up the Deep Lore's ass you can't see the obvious. This isn't about walls and constructs. It's not about birthrights or boundaries."

I pointed to the horizon, to where my son's star was fixed behind Ignazio's clouds, my urge to be with him strong and steady and swamping all other concerns. "I'll never hold him. He'll never know my name."

I found Ceres with the setting sun. She stood by the stream where we'd first joined our spirits. I took hold of her amulet and felt the longing, the yearning, how comfortably it fit in my hand. "Is this what you want? To be removed from me forever?"

She laid a finger on my amulet and her answer filled me, speaking only of the change of season, the bountiful time before our world's long rest, of woolens wrapped against a rising wind, and children sleeping peacefully in our arms.

Then her emotion changed. "I'm told I'm meant for Antonio, because he's Heir. I'm told the Deep Lore must be honored. I thought I was meant for you. I also thought you were nobody, a protector, like anybody." She released my iron, pried my fingers from hers. "You lied to me."

The ground grew unsteady as it had the twilight Antonio promised to stay as far from Ceres as he could manage, the twilight I betrayed her trust while she held mine. "I did not lie to you. I just lost my way."

I wanted to retrieve the days, rewrite the lines, recover all the squandered emotion. Make the claim I should have made then, create the child which would always be ours. I dropped to one knee and removed my iron. I held it out to her, palms up, my intent to reset our paths with a new declaration, one which would hold until the end of time.

"With opened hands, I lay bare my soul, and Promise myself to you. Sun to sun. Moon to moon. Midsummer to Midsummer. For now and forever. In this life and beyond. Refuse me, I will still belong to no other. Send me away, my heart will only beat for you. Hear my troth and let my star bear witness—my words are true and will never be unmade."

Ceres removed her iron and laid it over mine, clasping her hand around both. Every leaf on every tree changed with the season, bursting forth in yellow and red, orange and purple. The wind picked up, sending the branches creaking.

I wrapped my arms around her and we lost ourselves in each other, awaiting the glimmer, the spark, the tiny illumination.

The earth cracked, a single great, soul-shaking heave.

Rocks tumbled. Trees toppled.

My spirit settled. Clouds cleared, revealing my witnesses, stretched from one corner of the sky to the other.

Not one star, a thousand. Heaven's hosts.

Twinkling in a mantle of deepest blue.

The day after the earthquake, Antonio married Ceres.

The day after their Promise, Claudio finally pulled the blanket from over my head. "Be reasonable and I'll untie you."

I stopped struggling, cold stone under my back, my clothes still in unembarrassed disarray and my defiance shining in what light filtered through the clerestory windows of the monastery's upper branches. I blinked, half-blinded.

He loosened my binds. "It wasn't Antonio's decision. Neither was it Father's."

I rubbed my wrists, at the raw places left by the ropes, then tore at my gag, spitting out the fabric with a mouthful of bile. I headed for the door.

Claudio's voice vaulted over my vexation. "Father's ordered you to stay and Salvatore's in no mood. Half his quarter came down."

I whipped around, memory of the Midsummer Antonio and

I walked there fresh. The twilight we accidentally summoned the sprite. The twilight he challenged my ability to be Protector, accused me of not knowing the people I was supposed to protect.

He was right.

"Who was hurt?" My question, husky with thirst, echoed into the vastness.

"The maestro and his daughter. He broke a leg, she an arm. Her child is unharmed. Antonio went to see them, to survey the damage. He was in the quarter for hours, moving branches, digging through collapsed earth, crawling into the deep places. The people swarmed him. They are frightened. They blame the quake on Antonio's recalcitrance regarding the deep magic."

Claudio dipped a cup into a pitcher plant near the great alderwood doors and handed it to me. "The *signori nobili* went to Antonio and demanded his compliance. He had no choice but to marry."

I raised the cup to my lips and drank deep, wishing I could drown in it, then dragged a sleeve across my mouth. Her scent, still strong on my hands, filled me, fragrant like apples and allspice. "He had a choice."

"He has the choices the *signori* give him. They are convinced the quake is part of some scheme by the Careri. Ignazio is even suggesting a connection to the death of young Ruggiero. The *signori* want to talk to Tendi."

Every nerve in my body fired. I dropped the cup and again headed for the door. Claudio threw himself past me and blocked my path. He held up the gag. I licked the corners of my mouth, raw as my wrists. "You told me the monastery holds no man against his will."

"The weight of your words holds you here, not the monastery." He dropped the gag to the floor. "Use them wisely. Free yourself."

"Tendi—"

"We told the *signori* he is in seclusion, suggested they make their request again in a month, maybe two. All is calm now. Panduri's Heir has returned to his duties and her Protector to the border. You must accept, the Promise is done."

"It will not hold. I already made a Promise to Ceres. She is already pregnant."

The lilting hum which always accompanied Claudio stilled, replaced by a cold, inflexible silence. His every angle and line, from forehead to feet, took on the serenity of a statue, carved in marble and as immutable. "The *signori* will interpret that information as favorable—that the deep magic holds, and the rightness of the marriage is confirmed. This child is meant for the Heir. To tell the *signori* anything else will get the child labeled outcast and you lorebreaker."

"I can take Ceres. We'll go Outside. Antonio can choose another."

"They will send Salvatore to retrieve her. You would fight. One of you would die. Maybe both. Maybe her, your child."

"Claudio." My voice broke, along with my heart. "The child is meant for me."

He put a hand over my mouth. "Don't."

Too late. The air between us shimmered, reflecting my words like star shine on water. I raised my arms to them, to a freedom I'd always believed unattainable, a freedom lifted on a swell of certainty and propelled by love for a heart that did not yet beat, but which held the promise of a future I'd thought lost. A promise strong enough to muffle the call of the other, the son I'd never know.

Claudio reached for the declaration, a starling startled from his perch. He flocked this way, then that, his song deep and true, but the words rose past the treetops and fixed themselves in the heavens.

He let out a wail, laden with lament, then fell to his knees, doubled over, and pounded a fist to the floor. "I begged you to stay away from her. Begged you to give things time to settle. The heavens have not placed you at its axis and that knowledge makes you so bitter, you've sent us all spinning out of control."

Eight

By what brilliance brief does memory live. . . .

Two months later, on a windswept, wintry morning Antonio joined me at the border. He arrived amid wailings rising from the valley.

A couple of snow bunnies I'd been plying with carrots announced his entrance. "Antonio, first son of Bartomeo, the unwelcome, the uninvited, the unilaterally unimpressive."

Antonio walked right past them, grunted something he may have meant as a greeting, then went to stand before a cast of the area tacked between the polls of my tent. "How's Niccoli?"

"Only cuts and bruises. He'll heal. He followed the bells. Here." I pointed Antonio to a wandering star, skirting the upper edges of the cast. "He was looking for a way through."

"Pull out your pen. We don't have much time." Antonio unhitched his fiddle from the strap he used to holster it to his back and plucked the strings, testing their tune. "Ignazio's in a tumult. He's sending a storm, a tempest. With thunder enough to make the *folletti* fear, lightning enough to drive the *folletti* mad. And. . . ." He yanked a paper from his pocket. "Oh yes, 'enough snow to bury the *folletti* for a dozen Midsummers.'"

He threw the paper to the ground. "Father wants us to compose a tune strong enough to turn the storm aside."

"Don't be ridiculous." I pulled a wad of dandelion fluff from the bowl on my desk and stuffed it into my ears. "Listen to that pandemonium, the gnashing of teeth."

"You don't understand." Antonio tucked his fiddle under his chin. "Strife begets strife. Those *folletti* leave peacefully or not at all. Now please, help me compose something."

Compose something. Antonio usurps my position, marries my wife, pretends to have fathered my child, then waltzes in and expects me to write poetry. "No. I'm Protector. What transpires at the border is my province, unbeholden to yours." I stood straighter. "Just like Claudio's."

"Except when Ignazio sends his son to observe."

I made a big deal of smacking my forehead. "Niccoli's here to spy for his father. Thank you for the insight. I'm too stupid to figure that out on my own."

"Ignazio told the *signori* you sent Niccoli in on purpose."

"Ignazio is correct."

Antonio stopped tuning his fiddle. "Excuse me?"

"I needed incentive, something that would make Ignazio willing to give up all the consideration he earns doing nothing and do what he should have long ago—clear the *folletti* so we can make a path to the Careri and settle the vendetta. I think Giacomo would be proud."

"You know less about Giacomo than you think."

"You're just angry you didn't come up with the idea yourself, didn't send in Ruggiero while you had the chance. The *folletti* might have finished him before he had a chance to finish himself. But Father sent me here to torture me, and you were so worried I'd cross Outside. Well, you and Father have other worries now, don't you?"

I threw down the scroll and stuffed my pen into Antonio's breast pocket. "How's Ceres?"

I suppose I expected Antonio to rage and rant. All he did was lower the fiddle. "I'm not sure. Fine, I presume. She doesn't talk to me much. We have separate bedrooms."

I don't know why I felt so victorious. Ceres wasn't talking to me, either. I'd tried sending her a sprite. She broke the poor thing's wing and returned her on the back of another.

I grabbed Antonio by the collar and pulled him close enough to count his nose hairs. "You have it all. Position. Power. And Father's love. Fate hands you the most bountiful woman in the *ducato* and you don't even want her. Fine. You don't deserve her. Don't deserve Panduri. But you are going to do your best to serve both, because my child will not live his life like me, without love, without caring, without respect. Go back. Build a home for which he is worthy. Make it bright and cheery. Fill it with music and song. Or I will take Ceres, take my son, and build that home myself. I do not care if the result sends every rock in Panduri toppling."

I meant to let go of him, meant to drop him on his ass. Hard. But Antonio wrapped arms around my shoulders. He spoke to me, his breath warm on my ear. "Matteo. You have Father's love."

Longing, deep and achy and sharp as shards, shot down my spine. I wanted to believe him. Wanted to let that belief enfold my hurt as Antonio enfolded me, but my brother lived in a house walled by half-truths and roofed in delusion.

He was Heir. He refused to accept it. That meant there was nothing left for me.

I threw him off, wrapped another scarf around my neck and made my way to the stables, cold slicing across my cheeks. I picked a horse and headed to the ridge, storm clouds close behind me.

Salvatore close behind me, too. "Where are you going?"

"I have no idea." All I was, all I'd ever be were not mine to define. I belonged to Antonio. He did not belong to me. The knowledge smacked me in the chest with the power of a runaway ox-cart.

I paced my mount. This way, then that. The *folletti's* wails rose to a wince-worthy pitch I felt deep in my soul as yearning for my children, the one I'd know, the one I wouldn't. I bent, checked billets and buckles, desperate for distraction.

Ignazio's storm rolled in, with a clash like cymbals and a roar like a waterfall after winter melt. The rush windmilled me from the saddle. My horse bolted, my heel caught in the stirrup, bumping me through a world of white and shadow.

Ice shoved under my shirt. Snow packed into my mouth. Time pulled taut.

Every word spoken, each to come. Every line drawn, each erased. Every thread woven, those long-frayed. Who I was. Who I had been. And who I was meant to be. Every connection to every person, every place, every event.

Snapped.

The world screeched to a stop. My insides sloshed from hip to hip, sternum to skull. Then Antonio was over me, groping at my neck, pawing at my scarf, his music damped, his voice panicked, his words echoing from a far-off place. "Salvatore, help me. Matteo's iron. I can't feel it."

I couldn't feel it, either.

Clouds darkened under a twilight exposed to a world indelicate and crude like Dante and Ilario's. And like them, I'd go exploring. As I should have at first. Set sail with them on an Outsider's tide. To see what we did not know, send back stories of what we learned. Always with the knowledge we had a place in each other's hearts and a place in Panduri.

I stepped nearer, the horizon clear before me. And stopped.

Warmth flooded my chest. Faith filled my heart. I reached for my iron and found Antonio's instead. All he was. All he had ever been. Wrapped around my soul. As I'd always wanted.

The happiest of ditties returned me to my tent. Antonio played by the window, fiddle poised, swath of hair falling across his forehead. He laid into the refrain, his notes rising with their own light.

Tuck of the chin. Set of the shoulder. Tremor of each finger for the *vibrato*.

Every detail carried an importance I'd never understood, an exquisiteness I'd never noticed. Each a beginning, each an end, and each whispered.

Pay attention. Have a care.

Remember.

The music cut off. Antonio shoved the hair out of his eye and looped it behind an ear. "You're going home. It's only cuts and bruises. They will heal."

Home. A woman with hair the color of acorns, a child meant for the Heir, another lost forever across an unfriendly border. "I have no home."

I felt myself shrinking, the horizon growing. The spiraling towers, the light-filled pinnacles. Dante and Ilario stood on the far shore, full-grown and fearless, finally arrived. How I wanted to hear their stories.

Antonio leaned over me and laid a hand over my heart. "Matteo." My name fell in fragments at his feet. "Don't leave me."

"Don't send me away."

"I have to. This vendetta must end. Either I find a creative way to end it, or it will end us all. Here, we found your amulet." He fastened it about my neck. "Keep mine, too. Words and music. No use breaking up a set. I'll ask Claudio to make me another."

I didn't know how he'd managed so long without his iron, how he'd manage until Claudio sent him a new one. I was jealous, so damned jealous, that he could, that I couldn't, that despite my best efforts, his efforts always overshadowed them.

I clasped the irons, pulled his from my chain and flung it to the floor. "Don't bother. We're already broken."

Cuts and bruises. And a snapped shinbone corkscrewed in my somersault from the saddle. I returned to research and star charts, my crutch my constant companion.

Ceres rounded with the days, our child strong within her, our contacts brief, our conversation careful. Somewhere in Careri, the other was born, the birth tossing me from a troubled sleep. I plotted his star in private, my joy crowded by tears. His chart was the only way I could think to keep him connected to me, to connect him to Panduri, the only way to pave a path along which we might someday meet.

And the *folletti*? Back, stronger and louder and more furious than ever. So loud, we sometimes heard them in town.

I took to spending time in Dante and Ilario's garden, pouring out my heart to the pixies and lodging candies between their little marble fingers.

Claudio arrived from the monastery, Topo hissing and spitting at me from the depths of his cowl. He brought musical scores, addressed to me in Antonio's no-nonsense script. "Antonio asks that you take the time to listen. He says you will understand when you do."

I folded the scores in plain paper, addressed them to Antonio with every flourish I could muster, and summoned a sprite to return them.

Claudio's face turned the most unattractive shade of purple. "Why?"

Because Dante's Wall, so stalwart and strong, was warm in the sunshine, its gentle curve pleasant on my back. Perhaps not quite a trail, but a message I did not until that moment fathom—when the one did not tear down what the other built, what they made together was invincible.

I tried to explain. "Without words, Antonio's music means nothing. He begged me to stay, then sent me away. I'll speak to my brother in person, or not at all. Tell him that, then tell him to find me."

Midsummer's Eve approached. I planted myself in Dante and Ilario's garden to await news of Antonio's arrival, the words I wanted to share strong on my tongue. The *folletti* were subdued, their complaints a subtle contrast to the buzzing of the honeybees. Then their complaints went silent. A sprite flew past. "The child is coming."

I tucked the words away and hobbled back to the mansion, the dutiful uncle.

The heat grew heavy with humidity. Afternoon lengthened. Tempers got short.

Luciana emerged from the lying-in, eyes shaded, and stared at a sun which refused to set. She turned to Father. "Any news of Antonio?"

Ceres cried out and Luciana hurried back, affording me a glimpse of my love through the opened door, face pinched, perspiration-darkened tresses plastered to her brow in sodden rivulets. She caught my eye, her expression accusatory. The door swung shut.

I decided to wait in my study.

I'm not sure why Salvatore sent the sprite to me and not to Father. Perhaps because my title, if not my occupation, was still Protector. The truth was in the sprite's face before she opened her mouth to deliver her message, but I refused to see, because the moment I paid attention to her, the ground shook and a cry went up. My son had arrived.

Music swelled, wafting in from the festival fields.

And with my son's arrival, the Heir.

I stood and breezed past the sprite, my pulse already picking up that of my son's, down the passage, across the great hall, and up the stairs, my crutch clumping on every step.

I found a scene of confusion, not celebration.

Claudio pulled me aside, face contorted. "What have you done?" His voice was low, frightened. "Antonio is not here."

I looked out the window. The sun, blood-orange, sank below the horizon.

Mamma swept out of the room, a bundle in her arms. "Behold. The Heir's child."

Ruddy and roaring and full of life.

A child I could coddle if not claim, protect if not parent, a child not plotted in my stars, but by whose star I would set my course.

I retreated to a corner, heart full, worried my joy would escape my lips. And finally let the sprite deliver her message.

She made no sense, a jumble of syllables and diphthongs. I fought to force her consonants and vowels into words, her words into sentences, to comprehend the meaning taking shape in fits and starts.

My tongue froze. My eyes clouded. My ears buzzed.

I turned away from the sprite, wondering why Salvatore would send her at all. If he meant her as some kind of joke. The sun had set, the music played. Midsummer had arrived and with it the Heir.

That's how it was. How it had always been. How it would always be.

Mamma placed the child in my arms. "Say hello to your nephew."

Ceres let out a wail. Not of pain, but sorrow.

She knew. A wife always knows. The Promise is like that.

Mamma and Father groped, one for the other. For the connection I now knew well. Sun to sun, moon to moon, Midsummer to Midsummer. Until the day I departed or did one of my children.

The room quieted. The sprite repeated her message, my silence insufficient response for her to call her commission completed.

With a heavy heart. . . .

Regret to inform. . . .

The most sorrowful of incidents, unexpected of events. . . .

Jumbled, twisted, disjointed with disbelief.

Ending with a phrase that would follow me into the future, haunt my every footstep, wake me from every peaceful sleep.

"Antonio, Most Beloved and Blessed Heir of Panduri, is dead."

I gazed into my son's eyes. A long, quiet moment during which I let him know: I was his. He was mine. And as long as he needed me, I would never go exploring.

Those gathered arrayed around me. Father came forward, eyes bright with tears.

He nodded.

Followed by Mamma and Claudio. Luciana and Ursicio. *Signori* and servants.

The nods deepened, growing more respectful as they moved down the ranks.

The nod meant for the Heir, bestowed upon him every time he passed, and every nod directed . . .

. . . to me.

—

Words have power. Power to heal. Or hurt. To clarify. Or confuse. The power to laud. To lambast. To defend.

Or damn. Their substance judged by the quality of the speaker and shaped by his most closely-held belief.

I meant to tell Antonio, with words spoken in truth, in fairness, words meant to be said at the proper time, in the proper order. Words meant to chart a new course, plot a new path, build something together that our circumstances would never tear down. Words still tucked under my tongue. Because I squandered them.

Claudio handed me a journal bound in leather and filled with the finest parchment. He told me, "Make an accounting."

Write the story. Draw the lines. Trace the steps. It does not matter. The truth is still the truth.

This is my confession. And to it I hold.

Antonio is gone.

Because I squandered him, too.

Claudio

Nine

The Midsummer's I first shaved my head, Antonio handed me the razor. In those days, before I'd reached my full height, Antonio towered tall as a tree, arms outstretched like limbs and hair waving in all directions. As did mine. For another few moments. "I'm supposed to pick up the razor myself."

"To show you take the burden freely. I understand." Antonio closed my fingers around the mother of pearl handle. "But should you decide to lay your burden down, I will be here to help you find it a soft landing."

I couldn't imagine laying down the burden. Being third meant I didn't have to chart stars, nor hit a target with accuracy, nor scratch my balls at the border wondering when I'd get my next bath. Being third meant a room at the monastery, far from Father, from responsibility, from expectations. Being third meant freedom.

I embraced the burden a few hours later when I heard my first confession, from a lonely wife in search of release. Fully clothed and upright against an alder tree, her knees high on my hips, my hand over her mouth, aware, Midsummer or no, our act was forbidden.

I embraced the burden again a few hours after when my second lonely wife confessed. Also upright, also fully-clothed, this time against a huckleberry hedge. She bit my lip.

The third confessed to me from behind, her exaltations muffled in a stand of wisteria.

By the time number four tracked me through the dance steps, freedom's burden weighed a little heavier and my balls were sore from the constant chafing.

"Please, *signora*." I indicated a moss-filled copse, soft as cygnet feathers. "Let us lie down."

"Are you mad? What if somebody should wander this way? We must be ready to flee."

I'd ignored the first of the monastery's many lessons meant to guide me along the path of enlightenment: Pace thyself.

Antonio's body arrived with Midsummer's end, cold and still in the rising sun, the manner of death not apparent, the explanations few.

"*Folletti*. He went out alone." Salvatore looked shaken and stiff. He handed me Antonio's iron, then stepped before Matteo, shielding me from his view. "He left his fiddle in camp, did not bring it with him, so he could not calm them with his music."

Matteo put down his bottle and tore through the bloodstains on Antonio's shirt, traced scratches and bruises, deeper cuts, and abrasions. "None of these wounds look mortal. You were first on the scene. Tell me more."

Salvatore couldn't tell him much. "His horse was not harmed."

Folletti like horses. They like most creatures, except rude Protectors, people who betray their purpose, and children who try to escape. But Salvatore couldn't tell Matteo that, either.

Matteo shoved Salvatore aside, ripped Antonio's iron from my hands, wrapped his fingers around it and closed his eyes. He shook the iron at me. "There's nothing. How can there be nothing?"

I'd had no time to tinker, to tease out those truths Matteo would find agreeable. I'd had to let Matteo take a blank iron, an iron Antonio had asked me to make for him but never used. "Sometimes a shock is enough to send the memories into stasis. Give the amulet back to me. Tomorrow, the day after, we will try again."

My brother-in-law Ursicio joined us, bearing a basin and towel. "We need to get Antonio ready. The women want to see him." He pointed down the hallway, toward Antonio's room. "Is there nothing you and Matteo would cast off with your brother?"

I touched Antonio's scar, jagged along his cheek, then followed after Matteo, counting every thump of his crutch, every sway in the stone, his turmoil threatening to send the Deep Lore topsy-turvy. Antonio's room was austere, unembellished, wiped clean of telltales, scoured of tip-offs. Concertina vines twined from his bedposts. Campana moss chimed from the sills.

Matteo poked through a cabinet, flinging boots and breeches behind him. "Help me, Claudio. What am I to choose?"

The first time Matteo was injured, he returned to us unsteady and raving about trolls. A sprite returned with him. She handed me a score. "From Antonio."

I broke the seal and the sprite wailed Antonio's worry: "Help me, Claudio. What am I to do? Matteo is impulsive and will not bridle his words, shouting insults over the valley and debating when there is no need. Do not sing to me of Father or bury me in lore. Protector is not Matteo's path. Charting stars is not mine. Tie our brother to the bedposts if you have to, but keep him home."

I obliged Antonio and tied Matteo to his post. In a sense. I sent him requests for star charts, sometimes dozens at a time, making sure he had to dig them out from the deepest archives. I dug in there ahead of him, to confuse their locations, tossing unfixed stars into the disarray. Poets thrive on order, on meter, on every word placed exactly.

The mess made Matteo crazy. "Obviously, filing systems are of no concern to our Heir."

Watching Matteo rummage among our brother's few possessions

—Antonio's notes lined up least to greatest, thirty-seconds to wholes, his chords arranged in perfect fourths and fifths, everything in its place and easy to score—it seemed impossible Matteo had fallen for my deception.

Matteo held up Antonio's fiddle, returned to us along with his body. "There is only this. And my regrets."

I am not spiritual, despite my vocation, but this I heard, clear as if Antonio had walked into the middle of our search, and so repeated, "The Deep Lore says seventy sirens worked seventy Midsummers to produce that fiddle, and now you want to cast it to the winds."

The fiddle responded, tripping a series of notes across the strings.

Matteo whipped around, eyes bulging with fright. The floor stones upheaved in response. "Did you hear him? Was that you?"

It may have been a breeze. Or an accidental nudge by the fiddle's bow, which Matteo held in the same hand. Perhaps a stray thread hanging from his jacket, an accidental swipe by his shirt cuff, an unnoticed fly bouncing off the instrument's frets.

It may have been any number of possibilities, but Matteo chose a message from the Great Beyond, a remonstrance from his conscience and so demonstrated the monastery's second lesson: Contentment is fragile; self-reproach will withstand the most stalwart of assaults.

I took the fiddle from him. "Let Antonio wear his uniform. We will blanket the stains with our love."

"He is Heir. It is not appropriate for him to wear his uniform."

"You are Heir."

The subtle shivering under my feet, present since we'd received the news, stilled. So did Matteo, my statement seemingly having the power to freeze flesh. His face went thoughtful and his eye sober. "What we cast off with our brother should have meaning."

He dug under his waistcoat and pulled something from an inner pocket. A bundle of paper, wrapped in deepest blue. "Antonio's scores. The ones he sent to me. I found them on my pillow, Topo sleeping beside."

My spine chilled. I hadn't left the scores there and Topo never went in Matteo's room. "You should listen to them first."

Matteo pressed the bundle into my hand. "I no longer have the right."

The service went as expected.

Mamma and Ceres cried together under clear skies and bird chatter. Father rooted at the head of the assemblage. Matteo, a monument to his foolhardiness, took on the mantle of Heir along with the blame, our brother's stars scrolled under an arm. He kept his gaze to the treetops. "Is there a way to be certain Antonio's spirit takes flight?"

I mouthed platitudes meant to placate our mourning, intoned prayers made meaningless by repetition, performed rituals I'd long ago relegated to rote, my well gone dry.

Luciana slipped her hand into mine, her belly ripe with new life. "Sing a deeper song. For me. For Mamma."

I kissed her cheek and tried again, grateful for my sister's light, hoping it shone bright enough to convince Matteo and conceal my worries. Whether Antonio had gone, whether he lingered, whether he'd left a trail.

With trembling hands, Father hung Antonio's fiddle from a willow weeping near the stream. He returned Antonio's star chart to me, its seal intact, his stars unperused. "Leave the women to their sorrow, shake off yours, sober up your brother."

"Sir?"

"The *signori* are gathering. They want to speak with Matteo."

To discuss the vendetta. Discuss the loss of their Heir. Discuss the setting of Panduri's star in hushed and awkward tones.

Father stopped them. "Our star is not setting, our Heir is not lost. Matteo is now the oldest son of the *duca*. He stands before you, ready to do his duty."

Ignazio, always an ill-wind, had something to say. He was short and often unsubtle, with eyes sharp as flint, skin pruny as an old pepper, and ears as red and disc-shaped as a couple of cippolini onions. The better to eavesdrop, I supposed. "A Protector is not an Heir. Do we pretend what has happened has not happened? Claudio is now Duca's second son. Does that make him Protector?"

The *signori* looked to Father.

I held my breath. Memory is malleable as clay, the bad ones best left by the wayside so better remembrances can take their place. The Deep Lore, however, is granite, and Father its champion. "The Heir is the Heir. Ursicio will take on the role of Protector until Matteo produces a son."

Another of the *signori* stood. "Matteo cannot produce a son without a consort. He should marry the woman meant for the Heir."

A half-hour later Matteo and his crutch *thump-thump-thumped* back, then forth, across Dante and Ilario's garden. "I'm a fool, Claudio. I should have followed my star that Midsummer I complained to Father about having to do Antonio's work. The star was right there, plotting a new path with my words. I should have gotten on my horse and gone."

He should have gotten drunk, passed out, and woken the next morning, unencumbered. "When I advised you to dance for your heart's desire, I thought you wanted to get out of town. I didn't know you wanted to get married. Protectors never do. You told me yourself. Milkmaids and camp followers."

Matteo pulled a bottle from behind the stump. He popped the cork. "Sheep-fucking."

That, too. "Maybe this is where your star was leading the whole time. Maybe you are here because you are meant to be Heir."

"You're saying my star might have led Antonio to his death."

That hadn't been my intention, but my good ones often go awry. I'd cast that star into Matteo's conversation with Father on a whim, hoping Matteo would follow, hoping Father would have the courage to let him and see where it led.

82

The monastery's third lesson came home to roost: Fuck with the Deep Lore, the Deep Lore fucks back. "I'm saying Ceres is the mother of your child. The woman you were willing to defy our laws and our lore to obtain."

"And she's just lost her husband, she's just given birth, and she's still figuring out how to breastfeed. You'd think the *signori* could give her a few hours." He took a long, long pull off his liquor. "Ceres and I would only be going through the motions. I've already made her a Promise, she's already sorry."

Uncertainty took hold, cancerous and dangerous. The ground again trembled. "Stop. Do not use your words to make the untrue true."

"If my words had that kind of power, Antonio would again be alive."

I scooped Topo off my shoulder and settled him into my cowl, like a baby in need of tending. Antonio once told me of Outsider stories about people who came back from the dead. They were called vampires and zombies and had names like Dracula and Frankenstein. Antonio had the impression none of those stories ended well.

Topo growled. I guess he agreed with Antonio. "No power is greater than Death. Death is. We continue our course."

"But which course is right?" Matteo ran a hand through his hair. "Help me, Claudio. What am I to do?"

Four hours after I cast off Antonio, I stood in Dante and Ilario's garden and married my brother to his widow. "Do you take each other in a lawful and spiritual manner? Sun to sun, moon to moon, Midsummer to Midsummer?"

Matteo seemed nervous, Ceres exhausted and resigned. I studied the chart Matteo had hastily cast before the ceremony, hanging my hopes on a rose-colored star, a twining of their spirits that might yield a happy harvest. I pointed them both to the possibility.

Matteo's hand groped for Ceres's. She took it.

Panduri's autumn arrived in a lush and bountiful rush, its grain ripening, and its fruit grown plump. The witnesses dispersed, a fresh wind at their backs.

The Deep Lore had one last sting to visit on Matteo, a sting I'd been given the honor to bestow. "The *signori* insist the Promise is not complete unless you formally acknowledge your son as Heir after you."

Never have I seen my brother at a loss for words. He swept his gaze from one end of the garden to the other, like he'd misplaced them under a scatterberry bush. "Of course my son is Heir after me."

"You don't understand." I stepped in close, lest prying ears lingered. "They insist you acknowledge him as Antonio's son, son of the true Heir, and your every other child subordinate to him. It is the only arrangement they believe will settle the Deep Lore and allow Panduri's constellation to again rise."

Matteo let go of Ceres's hand. "He's an infant, not an arrangement. Why should such details matter?"

Like Salvatore, I couldn't explain much more than I had. "The *signori* are cautious. In time, memory of this urgency will fade, along with memory of Antonio. Then it will be up to us, you and I and Ceres to ensure he always has a place in Panduri. All of us together, because . . . you know."

All for one.

Antonio's music woke me in the night. Clashing and commanding and repeating the same refrain he'd had the sprite play when Matteo arrived home after his fall from the horse, his complexion pale, his heart sore, his shin snapped.

"Help him." Antonio's melody had despaired. "He is sucked dry. I would keep him here, but his soul is freezing. In my shadow is no place for a poet. Remind Matteo who he is, before he is lost to us forever."

The memory rolled me out of bed. Had Antonio given me permission or just guidance?

I pulled on pants, Antonio's irons heavy against my heart, and ran outside, my failures leading me to the practice field.

Matteo was already there, dressed in Antonio's shirt and britches, loosing one arrow, then the next in feverish ferocity, moonlight bright overhead. He used Antonio's bow.

I followed his sightline to pick out his target—the tree where Matteo had lodged an arrow all those Midsummers ago. "What are you doing?"

"I cast off my brother at dawn, married his widow at midday, and denied my own child at twilight. Antonio's dead and I'm Heir. No ceremony, no procession, not one damned flower." He nocked another arrow, sighted, and let fly. "Who knows where Antonio stashed the hat."

He shook the bow at the night sky. "Is he happy, Claudio? Does he think our account squared? Today has been shit, and were there even one true star shining on Panduri, I'd at least be able to split Antonio's arrow."

He threw the bow to the ground, then balanced on his crutch and lifted a boot, also Antonio's and obviously too large. "I'll never be able to fill them."

Antonio's irons grew weightier around my neck, burdened by the dense core of truth. Antonio was gone, taking his secrets with him.

I unclasped the new iron and handed it to Matteo, bearing the one small memory I'd managed to transfer in all the day's chaos. No harm could come from the giving, and no amount of tinkering would provide the soft landing Matteo so desperately sought. "Take this. There isn't much more than there was, but perhaps it will give you comfort."

Matteo hung onto the iron like a drunk in a windstorm. He closed his eyes. "I see Antonio looking into the distance to a new horizon. How does that help?'

It doesn't. A lesson I'd taken far too long to learn: Freedom is an illusion. Expectations cannot be outrun. And no desire can be set without consequences.

I left Matteo, returned to my room, and finally laid down my razor.

I hid the mother-of-pearl handle beneath my tears and retrieved the compositions Matteo believed he no longer had the right to hear.

Because I'd accepted Antonio's star chart from Father, but not his passing, and I could not burn Antonio's stars while my burden remained. Antonio decided his path the Midsummer he usurped Matteo's. I stood with him, and so decided mine. I may have cast off Antonio's body with all the laments and petitions, muses and meditations my vocation requires, but until I make things right, I will never be able to cast off Antonio.

Ten

For what reasons did we war?

For what we wanted to do, what we didn't. The roles we were born to, those we were not. But mostly for all the things we couldn't do much about.

I found Matteo sorting through star charts in Antonio's study, tossing his compositions into chaos and the house brownies into an uproar.

"These charts shouldn't be here." Matteo showed me a few, crackly with age. "They should be in the archives."

Where Panduri's memories go to die.

And her archivists. The place is dark and dusty, its original order laid out by deranged gnomes.

I shouldn't have left all these charts and compositions. I'd meant to clear them away. Meant to organize them as Antonio had asked, arrange them as he'd planned, find some way to present them that wouldn't have me crossing the Deep Lore, but . . . grief. "Three months after your Promise is not the time to be concerned about these matters."

In those three months, Matteo had exchanged his crutch for a cane. He used it to poke at another pile of scrolls. "Since Antonio left, being concerned about these matters is all that keeps this happy husband sane."

That's how Matteo referred to our brother. Like he'd gone for a walk. I half-expected to hear Antonio's boot in the hall. *"Claudio! Leave your petitions and prayer beads. The stars can find their own paths for a few hours. The moon shines on the meadow, but not for long. Father's asked Ignazio to provide rain before sunrise. Where's Matteo? Without words, we are lost."*

Antonio had liked nothing better than making music under moonlight.

"Leave the charts," I told Matteo. "Their location doesn't change one thing you or I do today."

He rattled the jumble. "The Heir may cast charts where he pleases, but they may only be stored in the archives or the *duca's* office. You're the one always babbling about the importance of keeping the Deep Lore. This doesn't bother you?"

I took Matteo's bottle and corked it. "These charts look ancient, like dead stars. Their owners must have been cast off long ago. I doubt the Deep Lore remembers them."

"These casts do not belong to people. They're agreements, consideration exchanges, long out of date. At least, I think so. They're near-unintelligible." Matteo tossed the charts into the air. "It's like Father cast them in code."

I gathered them and dumped them back among Antonio's scores and notations. "Do not blame Father. Giacomo cast these charts."

"Giacomo?" Matteo unrolled one and laid it on the table, gaze flitting from corner to corner. "How did you know? More importantly, why? Was Father's arm broken?"

I ignored his questions and asked another, hoping Matteo would be too drunk to notice. "What are you looking for?"

"The family charts. They're in the deep archives and I can't get to them. Father's magic has them locked up tight." He leaned on his cane and tapped his good foot. "Believe me, I've tried."

"I'll bet you haven't tried asking Father."

Matteo gave my statement far more consideration than it deserved. He hobbled around it, examined it from all angles, then ran the cane over the word *Father* and knocked it away. "You know I can't."

Ah, yes. Matteo's declaration after Ruggiero's castoff. The one about never again asking Father for that which might explain his actions. "Maybe Father thinks it better you chart your new course unencumbered by the past."

"Then Father should have put me up for adoption on the day I was born. If I can't learn from the past, I can't avoid repeating it." Matteo took back his bottle and uncorked it. "Yes, I know. Radical thoughts. No doubt the Deep Lore will kick them in the ass when it's least convenient."

I dug deep into my supply of banalities. "Be a little more generous with yourself. It takes time to adjust."

"Ah, so I'm adjusting. I'm relieved. I thought I was falling apart. No doubt the *signori* likewise adjust. No doubt so does Panduri. That's probably the reason the ground still shakes. All this trouble. Death, marriage, denial, acceptance. No doubt we're lucky the earth doesn't open and swallow us whole."

"I'm sure you're exaggerating."

"Am I? Ignazio has the *signori* who support me convinced the instability is some ploy of the Careri, and he has the *signori* who don't support me convinced my refusal to settle things is some ploy to gain consideration. They talk of revenge, but I'm not sure against whom. Father? Me? The Careri? Maybe they mean the *folletti*. How do you take revenge against a bunch of imps? Cut off their sugar supply?"

He pulled a roll of gossamer from his pocket and began gathering the charts into bundles. "Revenge. Ridiculous. We don't even know what happened to Antonio. Why he left us, why he left his fiddle."

The endpoint of our every conversation in those days, the funnel into which all possibility of happiness disappeared. "We'll talk more about this when I return."

Matteo drew the gossamer threads tight. "Return from where?"

"The monastery. The farmers are filling their storehouses, the alewives fermenting their ciders. Autumn is upon us and so I must depart. I came to fare you well."

"Fare what well? Father sent Ursicio to the border. How am I supposed to navigate the *signori*? And the charts. You should see my study. They're piling past my ears."

"I'm a cleric, not a negotiator. I don't cast charts, I meditate on them."

"Meditate on them here. Eat lunch on them for all I care. You cannot leave. I forbid it."

"You cannot forbid me. I have obligations."

Matteo smacked the bundles to the desk. "I have obligations, too. And my obligations affect all of Panduri."

"So do mine." I headed for the door.

Matteo chased after, his cane *rat-tat-tatting* beside. He brought his bottle with him. "Know what your problem is? No imagination. The Papists' Jesus walked on water, and then he turned it into wine. He healed the sick, fed thousands with a loaf of bread and two fish."

"Then they hung him from a cross."

"Right. But he rose from the dead. And only three days later." Matteo shifted from one foot to the other, steady on his cane, waving his arm the way he used to when we were boys and he wanted me to stop. "I'm not asking for anything near so complex. Just that you meet your obligations from here. Set up an adjunct office. Someplace private. So you can . . . you know . . . pray."

Truly, to this day, I do not think Matteo has any clue what my duties entail. "I am not the Papists' Jesus."

"And I am not Heir. I'm a poet trying to keep up. Either I concentrate on the politics and ignore the charts, or I cast the charts, and forget about Ceres." His sentences slurred, his stance listed leeward. "I haven't written a word since Antonio left. Not a line, not a stanza, not a single rhyming couplet comes off my pen. My star is sinking and I've no way to express it."

I didn't give a fuck. I wanted to get out of there. I had my own bottles to hide behind. "Your star isn't sinking. It eddies while you try to circumvent Father's magic, lies buried while you dig through Antonio's things. You've mired your star where your heart is, not where your heart should be. Change your desires, your star will follow."

I headed down the pathway, my destination Dante and Ilario's garden, always my last stop before I took my final leave. Matteo got ahead of me.

"Claudio, please. I need you." He hung his head. "I cannot talk to Father."

"You've been talking to Father since Antonio died, talked to him for years before. Talked until Father twisted in frustration."

"And it's gotten me nowhere."

I opened my mouth, meant to answer. Matteo clapped a hand over it. "Quiet. Father's in the garden."

Sitting on the stump of Dante and Ilario's tree, the sun shining on his hair and Matteo's son in his arms.

I pulled Matteo's hand off my mouth and stepped forward, thinking I'd say hello.

Matteo got me by the cowl and yanked me back. "Don't. He has my son."

"His grandson. Why are we whispering?"

Matteo dropped into an awkward crouch. He shimmied the hook of his cane over my collar and pulled me down with him, then sidled us to a stand of undercover berries and peeked through the thorns. "*Shhh.* I can't hear."

Father was humming, a little strain Antonio composed as a child, a tune of greening, of life. Better suited to spring than autumn. "First to come are the crocuses, then tulips and daffodils. After, there are poppies, followed by morning glories, and jasmine." He pointed to blooms swaying deep blue and defiant in the waning sun. "Cosmos are mighty, expansive and enduring and steadfast into frost. When all other flowers shrivel, cosmos remains, Panduri's last bulwark against winter. As are you."

Matteo stirred. I put a finger to my lips, put my faith in Father's next actions.

Father pointed to the treetops. "Up there, the bird builds its nest." He showed the baby the delphiniums. "These blossoms are why the butterflies return every spring and beyond the path, you'll find the best place to count honeybees."

He showed the baby the snowdrops and moonflowers, the winterblooms and blushing brideberries. "This garden is springtime, it is summer, it is autumn, and winter. This garden is Panduri, all Panduri has been, all Panduri is, all Panduri will be, planted so you'll always have a place you can find it, tended so you'll always have a place to return."

Matteo gasped. Not out loud, inside, like a constriction in his throat, his veins drawing taut and his jaw tight. I wanted to gasp also, wanted to scream and cry and pound my fist in frustration.

We were eavesdropping. We were hiding. We were behaving as intruders in our own place. A place we'd built to remember our brothers, a place we alone planted, we alone pruned, we alone protected.

Father stood. He held the infant more securely, stepped onto the stump, and pointed to the horizon. "Where are Dante and Ilario now?"

A place where we alone performed our private little ritual.

In that moment, I hated Father. Hated his presence now, his lack of power then. We were sick on that long ago Midsummer. We were burning and babbling and brimming with so much more. More questions, more quandaries, more reasons to care. Mysteries to puzzle out, answers that needed telling. We needed Father to stand with Giacomo, to stand up to them all.

And we needed our brothers. Needed them with us. Needed them to stay.

Not a garden.

I think Antonio had agreed.

Matteo grabbed my arm, his fingernails digging into my sleeve. "The sun is setting, If Father stands there much longer, he'll see."

Dante and Ilario's constellation. It could only be seen from the garden. Cast by Antonio, held aloft by our love. A balm to arguments and annoyances, petty hurts and prolonged animus, Dante and Ilario's constellation would never set, so long as one of us were there to sing their song.

I meant to stop Matteo, meant to hold him, counsel him as I had the day he went for Ruggiero. Meant to do as I was trained. Bring consolation, not contention. Order, not disarray. "Matteo . . ."

He catapulted onto the scene, cane waving, finger pointing.

". . . hold your temper in check."

He dropped the cane and took the infant, near ripping the boy from Father's arms. "You were not there for Dante and Ilario then, you will not speak of Dante and Ilario now."

His words exited in a huff and a puff. Had there been a house nearby, Matteo's statement would have blown it down.

Father came down off the stump and stood tall. "For all my lacks, I was their father. As I am yours."

Matteo clutched his child to his chest and took Father's place on the stump, though how he managed it with that leg and carrying a baby I still cannot fathom. He blocked Dante and Ilario's constellation from Father's view. "I'm not your son. I'm your vassal."

Never has truth been spoken with so much heartbreak. Panduri's star was setting and Father was using an infant to prop up his failures. I'd encouraged the chicanery, convinced Matteo to go along, helped secure Panduri's succession along a path of shame, and I was tired of carrying that burden. If Father could claim Matteo, then Matteo could claim his own.

I stepped forward. "Father."

Something in my timbre must have alerted Matteo my intention to set the charts straight, ensure Father knew whose son Matteo held. "Do not come to his defense, Claudio. This garden is meant for poetry and song, music and joy, rising stars and dawning hopes. Grief has no place here."

He turned his attention to Father. "And neither, sir, do you."

I expected Father to fight, expected him to assert his authority, his rights as a grandfather, as Duca.

Father didn't. He nodded to Matteo, respectful and deep.

And left.

I watched him go, uncertain if I witnessed a tragedy or a miracle. Or merely the power of Matteo's words.

But Matteo was bitter. "Father loves this child because he believes he's Antonio's."

"Father loves this child because he's his grandson. If this child were Antonio's would you not love him?"

"If this child were Antonio's, Antonio would still be alive."

Words have power. So do regrets. "You can't know that."

Matteo crumpled, stumbling from the stump, hard, yet soft, still holding the baby and despite his leg. As only a drunk can manage.

Then he cried, in the silent way of men, hand clasped around Antonio's iron, always close to his heart. "He only had cuts and bruises."

The lamb's ears started bleating, their soft, silvery leaves twitchy with dismay. Tiger lilies growled. Bullberries snorted. Vines shriveled. Blooms browned. Frost set in, and the flowering cosmos, Panduri's last bulwark against winter, succumbed.

Dante and Ilario's constellation descended, sinking under the onslaught, their light fading.

I've trained my whole life for these moments, pledged an oath to minister to the miserable, pity the pitiful, comfort the comfortless. To see my brother there, sloppy and slobbery, his son in his arms, his tears soaking his shirt, the creeping knowledge to which I'd paid passing homage since assuming my vocation faced me front and center and hit me on the head.

I'm a cleric, yes, but I'm not a very good one.

I again woke in the night, my heart sore, my bottle empty, Antonio's music reverberating off the walls.

In our world we'd thought ourselves blessed, separated from the Outside in our connection to each other, our orbits in perfect alignment, our charts in perfect balance, our courses decided, our fortunes set to rise.

Antonio left us. That meant I had to stay.

Because I love my brothers. Because I love Panduri. Because even cloaked in lies, the truth is the truth—in a constellation as complex as Matteo's, we are all sinking stars.

Eleven

*n*o good intention escapes unscathed.

By the following Midsummer, Matteo's star appeared on the rise. He cast off his cane and settled into his role, the ground beneath us steadying along with his stance. He plotted charts, cleaned up the filing system, counseled with the *signori* regarding the vendetta. And hid his bottles.

No matter. I found them.

I didn't mean to. I meant to be present, be supportive, be interested in all Matteo did, ready with an encouraging word, a gentle admonishment, a pithy observation, my purpose clear—preserve the deep magic, protect Panduri's path. And prevent Matteo and Father from killing each other.

But life at the mansion was chaotic, and forever under scrutiny, and well . . . not private.

I'd forgotten.

And there was the matter of Tendi, one of the ever-present passengers on Matteo's cartload of guilt. "Father, you must give him back his birthright."

"I've raised the matter with the *signori*. They side with Ignazio." Clearly, Father was tired of hearing about it. He returned to the pile of plottings Matteo had placed before him to approve.

"Then we shall raise the matter again." Clearly, Matteo was only getting started. He shoved the plottings to the side. "The reasons for Tendi's confinement are long past and would be forgotten but for Ignazio's constant reminders."

I raised my flask to my lips, grateful for the cover provided by my cowl, and mentally searched my portfolio of Aphorisms for Every Occasion. "Perhaps we should leave well enough alone."

Matteo dove under my cowl, grabbed the flask, and emptied the contents onto the sparring ficus. "Next time you come in here bring a clear head. Your counsel's become clichéd."

He picked a scroll from the plottings and unrolled it. "This is a cast of the current situation at the border and our possibilities for settling matters in a peaceful way."

Matteo pointed to a star along the edge, floating gentle and unassuming in a sea of contention. "Tendi's talents are wasted at the monastery. His capacity to calm chaos is without compare. We should send him to the border to help Ursicio."

"You can't do that." My outburst surprised me. I'd long ago given up on meaningful input in matters of import. "What would Ignazio do?"

"What he's been doing. Nothing."

"What I mean is, we put the man in the monastery thinking only to solve our problem, and now we remove him without consideration. Tendi is happy there."

Matteo took the time to weigh my words. "Tendi's supposed to be his family's heir."

"Maybe Tendi doesn't want to be."

Father reached across his desk and rerolled the chart. "Enough. Tendi stays at the monastery."

Matteo whipped around. "But—"

"Matteo. Please. In this one small thing, trust me." Father reached for the next scroll on the pile. "Midsummer approaches. Let us move on to other business."

Matteo plucked the scroll from father's fingers and tossed it aside. "Old business before other business, Father."

He pulled two more casts from the collection on Father's desk. Two I thought I recognized, crinkled, worn about the edges, as happened when parchment is rolled and unrolled, time and again, their starpaths traced, all the possibilities. Like Dante's and Ilario's.

The ground beneath us, steady for so money months, trembled. I groped for my flask. Not the one Matteo had emptied, for my other one.

Father's face turned purple, like poison ivy in autumn, his miff mottling the leaves always draped about his collar. He reached for the charts. "How did you get these?"

Matteo held them away. "I am Heir. And I may have learned a few skills during my brief sojourn as Protector to get around your chains."

Father fell into his chair. "Panduri looks for direction. You look to the past."

"I looked for the truth."

"And you couldn't ask because of your declaration. Fine. Let that be a lesson to you about speaking without thought."

Matteo shifted left, then right, turning Dante's and Ilario's scrolls over and over in his hands. "Well, sir, there's the other half of my declaration. You could have offered the information."

"I tell you what you need to know despite your ridiculous declaration. Everything else is a distraction. From your purpose, Panduri's purpose. Our status is fragile, this transition still in question. Or would you rather Ignazio took my place as Duca?"

"I'd rather you'd tell me what happened to my brothers. Why they had to leave."

Mamma interrupted from the doorway. "Because it was best."

We all turned. Ceres stood with Mamma. She looked hopeful, her hair twined in bounty, but Mamma's song was wrapped in darkness, her high notes dampened, her expression sad.

She rubbed her forehead. "Our lives are overwhelmed with whys without answers, our charts crowded with truths without adequate interpretation. We must choose which we carry, or we'd never continue."

"The truth is the truth, Mamma. It requires no interpretation, only that it be stated." Matteo tapped Dante's and Ilario's charts to his palm, his face pensive, his iron whispering words of sorrow, of confusion.

Mostly confusion. That confused me. I scooped a handful of marshmallows from the bowl on Father's desk. I popped one into my mouth, threw a second at Matteo. "Enough. It is Midsummer. Only happy songs. Matteo, come with me. Bring Ceres. We will go to the garden first, then onward to the festival fields."

Outside the window, the sun hovered over the horizon. Matteo put the marshmallow in his pocket. "I can't."

Mamma went to stand by Father. "You must. There have been so few babies since last year. Because Antonio . . . because Midsummer was so short."

She worked a finger into the vines twining Father's chair. "You are Duca. Tell him."

"You must go, you both must." Father's voice was parched, dry like crinkled leaves. He took Mamma's hand, on his own and without the purpose of public consumption, for the first time in my memory. "So must we. We cannot forsake Midsummer's Eve."

In the skies, sparrows moved, this way, then that, their path uncertain, knowing it was time to roost but without sunset's guidance. The nightingale began her song, then stopped, with no emerging star to sing along.

Ceres joined Matteo, hand outstretched. Still, Matteo stood, stone-faced and solemn, his song fading.

He was Heir. He could not be forced. He could, however, be questioned. I wrapped an arm around his shoulder, drew him close. "What is it?"

"I do not have the right."

Matteo's words have power, even those whispered in his brother's ear.

Because the last time Matteo uttered them, he was in despair, regretful he had not heeded Antonio's last message. Because the last time he stood at a window awaiting Midsummer's Eve, the onset brought disaster. Matteo's recalcitrance now, his mood before, his reasons for holding me here, keeping me close, had been birthed from the same star.

Midsummer was coming, as it would every year. And Matteo was terrified. "You have the right," I said, "by every measure that matters. We will go together. As always."

Matteo's words sharpened, slashing through my good intention. "Don't make promises you won't keep."

He whisked out of the room.

We all stared at the place Matteo had been, like some appropriate amount of time should pass to let his image fade from the location, to acknowledge Matteo, in fact, was no longer there.

Then I went after him, my place beside his. As wonderful counselor, promoter of peace, chasing out of Father's office, then out of the mansion, past Dante and Ilario's garden and on up the hill all the way to the cliff edge, to the silhouette of a new horizon—the Outsiders' city, its light-filled towers reaching to the heavens. I wondered if Dante and Ilario ever got to see it, if Antonio ever regretted he'd gone, transfixed as I'd been as a boy, and wishing I had the courage to know.

Fog rolled in, reminding me of Matteo and why I stood there. "You can't do that. It's Midsummer."

"I'm Heir. I can do as I please."

"As can your wife. And she's one lyrical punk like we once were from being seduced into becoming a lonely wife. Do you want her to end up in some stranger's bed? Is that what you've decided your marriage means?"

"Don't worry about Ceres. I'll satisfy both her and Midsummer later." He walked off.

I followed him again, all the way to his study. Truly, I cannot imagine the Papists' Jesus could have kept up any better. "When did you grow so callous?"

"The day Antonio left me with this mess." He pointed to charts piled past his ears.

I'd presumed he was exaggerating. No wonder he kept his study locked. "Have you been doing nothing?"

"I've been doing my best, but my best is inadequate without information." He clasped Antonio's iron, then took it off his neck and pressed it into my palm. "You've trained your whole life to know these things. Tell me what Antonio did not want me to know, tell me why you felt the need to tinker with Antonio's iron until it yields nothing."

His tone was pleading, his yearning clear, but my vows were to the deep magic, to Antonio, to the others involved. And to a pile of charts and compositions, scores and secrets I still hadn't found the fortitude to arrange. A complex tangle I struggle even now to phrase in a way which will not brand me lorebreaker. At that moment, however, I thought the chains imposed by my vocation might have broken. "You have Dante's and Ilario's charts. They can help you plot your path."

Then I gave in to my deepest desire since perceiving what Matteo held in his hand. "May I see them?"

"These?" Matteo held the charts aloft. "These are not our brothers' charts. I cast these this morning, on ancient parchment stock I found in a closet. They plot the fortunes of a couple of kittens my son's taken a liking to. I hoped to trick Father into divulging what might be lurking in Dante's and Ilario's stars, why Father is so determined to keep them hidden."

"You're charting stars for kittens." Relief fought with disappointment to realize my burden had not lifted. Then disappointment fought with rage that Matteo would play so loosely with my feelings. Then rage gave way to sentiment at the efforts my brother took to father his son.

Matteo is often an ass, but sometimes he's an adorable ass.

He grabbed me by the collar. "I need you to get me into the deep archives. I've tried every way I can think of: voiced invocations, charted directives, cast spare stars plucked from other plots against the framework. I've tried every word, every query, every pleasantry, in every tone from pleading to commanding. The doors hold firm."

And most of the time Matteo is just a stupid ass. "I can't get into the deep archives. Not without compelling reason. The deep magic won't let me."

"My sanity is not compelling enough?"

In those days Matteo had no idea about sanity, no idea his was improved by not knowing, no idea the burden enlightenment brings, no idea how my world was so filled with truth I sometimes buried myself in my cowl and screamed into the darkness.

All I could do was listen, prevented from helping Matteo directly and my song in somersaults to circumvent my limitations. "Take Father up on his offer. Unmake your declaration and ask him."

"Never."

"Then live with the consequences."

A star rose over my brother's head, kind of dull and dingy, and certainly not laudatory, but a star. Matteo dragged me back to Father's office, where he and Mamma and Ceres still waited, pacing and nervous, their consternation so thick, I near choked on it.

Matteo threw me forward. "Antonio's chart, sir, Claudio wants to see it."

If Matteo's command caught Father off guard, he didn't show it. He stopped his pacing and retook his seat, his song matter of fact. "Claudio's already seen Antonio's chart. I gave it to him."

Matteo dragged me back. "You've had it all this time?"

I didn't exactly answer. "Father told me to do what is proper."

"Proper." Horror took over his expression. "You burned it. Without consulting me."

He turned on Father. "Tell Claudio what it said."

"I can't. I never looked at it. I couldn't."

Charts piled on Father's desk. Matteo pawed through them, unrolling one, then the next. "But it's all here. In these charts. Our beginnings, our ends, the path we choose from one point to the other, all the possibilities."

He indicated one star, then another, using statements to get around his declaration that he'd never again ask Father. "I do not understand how you could not look. Do not understand why you have no curiosity as to what killed your son."

I didn't want to hear the conversation which followed. Didn't want to hear Matteo admit he didn't have Dante's and Ilario's charts, didn't want to witness the hollering and hand-waving, the frustrations and invectives.

A new star rose over Matteo's head, this one duller and dingier and even less laudatory looking than the previous. "Maybe I'm talking to the wrong person."

He swept all the charts to the floor and left. Again.

This time I skipped all the staring and went right after him. All the way to the festival fields. The sun sank below the horizon, the musicians began playing their tunes. The sentinel wisps began to announce him. "Behold Matteo, Panduri's Heir, the new, the unfamiliar, the. . . ."

Matteo furrowed through the dancers, straight for Salvatore, who had been first on the scene.

". . . the determined and direct. . . ."

Matteo yanked Salvatore from his square. "What happened to him? Why did he leave? How come he didn't take his fiddle? Why did you let him go?"

Loudly and obviously, and in front of everybody. And without the excuse of being drunk.

Things got awkward. The wisps rushed through the last of their announcement. ". . . the inquisitive, the overreactive, the apparently angry and annoyed."

The wisps clapped their hands to redirect our attention. "All should nod to him and get on with the party."

People started in on the nodding and bobbing. Matteo let go of Salvatore and went to the stables. He tossed a saddle on one of the horses, led it down the path and around the bend, all the way to the garden. The animal jigged left, then right, Matteo's emotion enough to make us all skittish.

I grabbed the bridle, took a moment to calm the beast. "Where are you going?"

Matteo laid a hand on each of the pixies, their caps fading and long-past due for replacement. "I have no idea. I don't even know why I took that horse. It's not mine."

Somewhere, from his cross hanging in a church someplace along the silhouette of that new horizon, Papist Jesus wept. I wanted to weep with him. "You have to find a better way to express yourself. You can't keep burning your bridges on the flames of self-recrimination."

"You're asking to hear my confession."

"I'm telling you to stop whining." I pulled a journal from beneath my cloak, leather bound and hefty. I took a few seconds to riffle through the parchment, of the highest quality and commissioned from Salvatore's father. I didn't know if my idea would help, but I couldn't keep doing things which didn't.

I handed the journal to Matteo. "Write it down. Everything. What you regret, what you don't, what you hope, what you don't, what you can't have, what you wish you could, and what you never knew you wanted. Get it all out, in pen and ink, then throw it on the fire."

He paged through. "I ask for confession, you tell me, 'Write a book and burn it.' You're supposed to be my cleric."

"I'm supposed to be your brother. What did you expect?"

Matteo kicked the stump, the stump Antonio left when he chopped down the tree, the tree Matteo grew on a promise, for a garden where we used to stand, one for all and all for one, the three of us together, our eyes to the horizon, and watch Dante and Ilario's constellation rise.

He slammed the journal to the ground. "I expected Antonio to live."

Twelve

*W*hy Matteo behaved as if I'd had a different expectation regarding Antonio's survival was a mystery I took a long and private year to ponder. From my room at the monastery, the simplest, the most meditative. The room with the clerestory windows.

I sent a sprite to sing him a song: *How is Mamma?*

He sent one to read me a riddle: *If you came to see her, you would know.*

My sprite returned a refrain: *I will see her soon.*

How soon?

Soon.

After winter?

I didn't answer.

A last sprite fluttered outside my window: "He asks, 'Do you promise?'"

Intentions are cheap. My repertoire overflowed. I'd see Matteo, find some way to guide him, help him, keep him focused on his course.

Do all the good acts my vocation required and a few it didn't. Just as soon as winter passed. And I sobered up.

As any good Gentle Guardian should.

Spring sprang early, greener than I'd ever seen, bursting with buds and chicks, lambs and kids, the air thick with the scent of peach blossoms. I walked the hills outside the monastery, my good intentions lost among the lushness. Week passed into hopeful week, every day livelier than the day before, but chicks remained in their nests, berries did not ripen, and the daffodils would not stop blooming. Dawn belonged to Luciana, and it arrived earlier every day as is scheduled, but the dew lingered, and the sun's angle did not change.

I didn't care. I was enjoying it all. Then one morning, music woke me from a restless sleep, resounding enough to send my bottle crashing and Topo scrambling across the floor moss. "Get up. Go home."

I tumbled from my cot, stinking of brandy and beer, the voice clear as if I'd spoken it myself. "Antonio?"

All that returned was a tune, soul-wrenching with memory.

Birdsong swelled, sudden and sweet. I glanced out the window. Grain waved in the fields, their heads growing heavy with seed. Flowers bloomed in a frenzy. Lambs, yesterday small and near helpless, pranced in the meadows, their coats thickening as I witnessed. The sun rose high, arcing across the sky as I'd never seen.

I washed my face, pulled on pants, tossed my cloak over my head.

Midsummer's finally approached, its pace frantic.

Something was wrong.

Matteo grabbed me the moment I arrived, ignoring Topo's hissing and holding me tight. "I'm glad you're here." His song was tense, his words soft and sincere. "Mamma's asking for you."

"What for?"

"I don't know. She's been keeping to herself. Father says she wants to think." Midsummer's sun raced to the horizon. Matteo watched. "I have to find Ceres, we have to go. The people will be waiting."

He was twitchy. Nervous. Running hands through his hair and talking in sprints. He donned his cap, pulled on his waistcoat, both deep blue, the buttons silver and sparkling. Fit for Panduri, fit for her Heir. "Tell Mamma I love her. We all do. I'll see her later."

Father stood guard outside Mamma's bower. He grasped my shoulders and held me at arm's length, gaze flicking left, then right, like he'd forgotten what I looked like, expression tender as I hadn't seen since I was a child. "We didn't want to upset Matteo, saw no need to distress Luciana."

"Sir?"

"Your mother wants you to hear her confession."

Confession.

Every breath I'd ever taken pulled away from me. My heart followed.

This eventuality comes to every cleric. Every cleric who is not an orphan. For me, this eventuality brought another complication. Of charts and compositions, scores and scrolls piled in my study, still not organized as Antonio had asked, still not arranged in any way that he trusted I would. And abject terror that Mamma's confession would prevent me from being able to present any of it as Antonio had planned.

I stalled for time, asked for details, demanded explanations, searching an excuse to slip away, reason to return in a few hours, unwilling to believe this pass had come, and berating myself for all my poor choices. "Why didn't you send for me sooner? How long has this been going on? Does Ceres know? Ursicio? Have you tried every medicine, every salve, checked her star chart, checked ours? Have you sought out every possibility, Inside and Outside, to keep her from leaving us?"

Father let me go on, answering as best he could, more patient than I'd ever known, more matter-of-fact than I'd ever expect. Plotting a memory I'd carry into the years to come, one Matteo would resent not having shared, and not understanding—this is because of who I am, because of what I do, because being Cleric and Confessor sucked worse than being Heir.

Outside or Inside.

So help me, Papist Jesus.

In the end, I had to stand at Mamma's door, undecided whether to go right in or knock first. "I can't."

Father gave me a nudge. "You can."

"No. I can't. I don't have my prayer beads."

The beads were for me, not Mamma. Tools. Something to hang onto when the world seems unsteady, something to fumble with when the right words won't come. I'd trained my whole life for this moment and all the moments like it. And I didn't have my prayer beads.

As Gentle Guardians went, my performance was shit.

Festival music wafted through the windows, bright with promise. Daylight failed. "Father?"

"Yes?"

"Your spring was beautiful. Thank you."

"Mamma wanted to see it, unhurried and full." He glanced out the window. Stars emerged, twinkling in deepest blue. "I have to go."

Panic grabbed me by the balls and squeezed. "Now?"

"Every year ends in winter whether we wish it or not. It's Midsummer. I have to dance."

I'd seen Father angry, Father calm, Father drunk and disorderly until forests fell at his feet. I'd seen him negotiate the *signori* until I feared his nose would lengthen like Pinocchio's with his necessary fibs. Never had I seen Father so resigned, so accepting, so resolutely certain a path had run its plotted course.

I went in. I heard Mamma's confession. A song I can't sing here. A song I can't sing anywhere. Can't notate to anybody, can't conduct for any chorus. I thanked her for her care, thanked her for raising me well, grateful for the burden she'd assumed, and ashamed of my resentment over the burdens I'd been compelled to carry. "Matteo told me you missed me. I didn't understand."

"Neither will he. Be kind to him. Always be kind." She squeezed my hand. "You must go. It's Midsummer."

And I had to dance.

First to find me on the festival fields was Luciana, luminous and lovely, ripening with another. She pointed. "Look at my husband, always resourceful."

Ursicio played a human Midsummer's pole, a toddler in his arms, another on his back. He and Luciana's olders ringed him with flowers from above. The middlings wove in between. I silently thanked Antonio for having made our sister this better arrangement.

Luciana threaded her arm through my elbow. "I haven't danced alone with another adult in so long, I'm not sure I remember how."

My panic subsided. "Come." I pulled her toward the crowd. "I'll dance with you."

We found Matteo and Ceres, then moved with them through the steps, our songs buoyant, our rhythm in sync.

What a relief. No lonely wives side-eyeing me, no curious maidens misconstruing my cloak. Just heel to toe and back again, the way we used to dance, all of us, for hours, before boundaries and birthrights, politics and polemics, before marriage and death and every soul-killing concern of the grownup world sent us spinning. Each in our place and certain the other would always be there to dance with us.

This was Midsummer. The core of who we were. As individuals. As family. As a people. And I wanted to enjoy it like this one last time.

Matteo stumbled. The music faltered. Across the field, dancers misstepped. Matteo groped for me, the knowledge writing across his face. Luciana cried, a kitten orphaned in the night. She whirled, eyes wild. "Father. I must find him."

I looked to the horizon, to where the night's darkest hour had already worn through, the sky lightening through my tears, bringing the dawn Luciana was helpless to delay.

Midsummer had passed.

—

The hours that followed flew by in surreal dissonance. Flowers draped from every doorpost. Fanfares played from every clearing. Frills and festoons embellished the pathways. Glamour spells gilded the lilies.

Matteo and I sat on the sill, watching and listening from a window in the Gathering Glade.

"Looks more like a celebration than a castoff." Matteo pointed to where willow wisps darted tree to tree, frosting the ripening fruit with pinpoints of light. "Did we make the wrong announcement?"

"The people show their love for Mamma, for Midsummer. They pay homage to Ceres and the coming Equinox."

He tossed me a candied violet. "We'll see how excited they are when Panduri's star finally heads into winter."

"You're being an ass."

"Mamma was dying, and you let me dance."

"Did you have a good time?"

"Glorious, amazing." Matteo made a masturbatory gesture ill-suited to the circumstances. "Ceres and I fucked like we haven't fucked before."

For a poet, Matteo could be crude. I checked behind doors and down halls to ensure no wives or children, servants or villagers were within earshot, then inspected the levels in the bottles and sniffed Matteo's breath. He was as sober as I was supposed to be. "Yet you're so glum."

"Because we were only fucking, not making love. Nothing resulted."

He meant a baby. "You can make love without conceiving children and you can conceive children other than just at Midsummer. Look at Luciana."

Matteo hopped off the sill. "Let us not discuss our sister's marital practices, nor highlight her bounty."

"Fine, then look at Ruggiero and his wife. Or you with the Careri."

Silence can ring. I'd never noticed.

Matteo recovered quickly. He swept an arm, addressing an imagined crowd. "Behold. Panduri's Heir and Legendary Past Protector is taking advice on sexual matters from a priest."

He checked the contents of my flask, foolishly left in view. "How's that abstinence vow coming?"

He examined the offerings piled on the reception table. Ditties and singsongs, baked goods and pottery, horseshoes and daisy wreaths, lady's slippers and so much more. Messages of condolence, large and small, paid in all manner of consideration available among the powers of Panduri. The sprites who'd delivered the offerings hopped off their branches, wings at the ready, waiting to complete their missions.

Matteo waved them off, then returned his attention to me. "I've always wondered about that. Ruggiero's child, I mean."

"Ruggiero wanted an heir. His wife may have thought to have one would please him, dispose him more kindly toward her."

"Hmmm." Matteo opened a note. Butterflies released to the upper reaches, flitting from one crystal dewdrop to the other. The sprite who went with the message flitted with them, announced the sender, and darted into the day. "Perhaps Ceres does not feel so well-disposed toward me."

"Perhaps Ceres thinks you are the one who is ill-disposed."

"Don't be ridiculous. I love fucking her. I love she enjoys it, too. And I love she's the mother of my child."

Again with the fucking. The only place Matteo cloaks sex with primroses is on paper. "Much as I'd love to continue this conversation, I have duties to attend. So do you. The people are gathering, and it's not fair to leave everything to Luciana and Ursicio. Where is Father?"

Not in his room, nor his study. Leaves scattered across Dante and Ilario's garden, forlorn and forgotten. The archives were dank and cold, the entrance sealed tight, and no indication Father had been to collect Mamma's chart. Luciana didn't know, neither did Ursicio. Not the house brownies, nor the groundskeepers, nor any *signore* or *signora* arriving to pay their respects.

Matteo whispered to me. "Find Salvatore. Have him find Father. Hurry. We can't hold the service forever, and we can't hold it without you."

Finding Salvatore took nothing, he was snacking in the kitchen. Finding Father? Not so much.

"The *duca* is overcome with grief. He will join us when the time is proper." We made the excuse over and over, then went through the offerings, stalling for time. The Gathering Glade came alive with song, with limericks, with yarns. Dragonflies spewed fire, fighting beetles drew their swords. Grasses waved, weaver ants made cloth, and lacewings draped delicate doilies under the teacups. Each offering's accompanying sprite announced the sender, performed her duty and headed out to join the party.

Then a Platter of Plenty crashed to the floor. The platter's sprite darted, back and forth, her anguish obvious. "This is from the harvesters, with happy remembrances of Duca's wife. I am disgraced. How can I let them know I'm disappointed in my duty?"

Niccoli was swift to the rescue. He picked up the platter, mended the breaks with a word, then coaxed the produce back into place. He tipped the platter's sprite with a sugared strawberry and sent her on her way, her commission complete.

And still Father did not appear.

Ignazio was quick to take advantage. "Our enemy sits opposite our border, exhorting the *folletti* to increase their din. Our brave protectors plug their ears. Perhaps it is time we opened our minds to one more capable of fixing that which is broken. Perhaps it is time we reconsidered the succession. Pass it to one more bountiful, more able to keep track of his *duca*, one whose star is already on the rise."

Niccoli placed the platter on the buffet. "Father, enough. A plate is an object. A settlement with our enemy requires a change of heart and mind."

He returned to his wife, his brood forming an orderly orbit around him, heirs and protectors and clerics aplenty. Niccoli kissed each on the cheek, seemingly happy with his place among them. But Ignazio's seed of doubt had been planted, left to germinate with Father's absence and growing wild among the crowd.

The murmurings began. "The *duca* is absent, heartsick and weak. He is not able to perform his duties."

Matteo looked to me, but I could not fix Father's absence. Could not realign all the cockeyed stars by which we'd lately steered our courses. I offered what I could. "Perhaps we should talk about this tomorrow. Or the day after."

Ignazio's gaze went stormy. Clouds accumulated and lightning struck in the distance. The air grew heavy, the humidity climbed. Men rolled up their shirtsleeves, women fluttered broadleaves to fan their faces. Conversation continued, the shadows lengthening under the coming tempest.

Salvatore returned, spoke in Matteo's ear. Matteo drew him close, as one might when accepting condolence. "Look for him some more. Do not return empty-handed."

He clapped Salvatore on the back and again sent him off, then pulled a handkerchief from his pocket and made a big show of wiping his eyes. He mopped at his forehead. "Niccoli, a cooling breeze if you could. The *duca's* placed himself in seclusion. We will continue the service without him and ask your indulgence for continued support and uplifting of his star."

Matteo stifled Luciana's protest with a shake of his head. He focused on one guest, then the other. "Please, no unhappy faces. Dry your tears. The wife of the *duca* was about life, she was about love. She was Midsummer, and she would like nothing better than if we danced."

He'd become Heir, and I got my first glimpse of the *duca* he would someday be. Cold and calculating and coldly calculating. Head to toe his father's son.

Every bone in my body grew icy.

The musicians took up their instruments, the dancers their marks. I readied myself to sing the laments and acknowledged another lesson—the necessity of ritual. The actions and attitudes and acceptances that mark the turning of our courses, peg us to our paths, assure us of our place among the spheres, and set our spirits toward our star's rising.

I recited the words, offered the prayers, performed the benedictions. I did all that was right and proper, pleasing to the Deep Lore and according to the monastery's teachings while the musicians played Antonio's compositions, my hope to settle my dead brother's relentless presence.

After I concluded, Matteo drew me aside. He wrapped his arms around me and held tight, much as he had when I'd arrived the day before, and spoke in a voice so low, it was obvious he meant that only I should hear. "I declare to you now, by every god you believe in, and those you do not, including the Papists' Jesus, no matter what the bastard orders you to do, if you burn Mamma's stars, I will cease to call you *brother*."

Thirteen

Salvatore returned Father from wherever he'd gone, far too intoxicated to be left on his own. Luciana, bless her, didn't care. She threw her arms around him. "Where were you, Poppa?"

Her voice was bright, her attitude open. Like a morning glory. Father kissed her brow, his attitude apologetic.

I helped Ursicio lead him down the oak alley, then departed, trusting my brother-in-law's resourcefulness would get Father into bed without putting too much stress on the shrinking violets. I stalked back through the alley and into the mansion's main clearing. I downed a cider, downed a brandy, downed a whiskey, intent on Matteo. "You had no right. No reason for continuing without Father, for forcing me to be part of your pettiness."

Matteo pointed to the children, to Luciana and Ceres, helping the fireflies light the lamps. "I did it for them. How about you?"

"Everything I do is for them, for you." I switched to almond liqueur, a specialty we distill at our monastery. "For Panduri."

"Yes, you're a saint. A paragon. Just like Salvatore. Servant to Panduri's star, a reflection we can all but hope to emulate."

I'm a cleric. I'm supposed to listen in compassion, offer council without judgment, hold myself neutral in all matters, look to the Deep Lore for guidance and beyond all, keep my temper. "You're a jerk."

Luciana covered her eldest's ears. "The children are listening."

She sidled up to me, took my hand and dropped something into my palm. A pearl of wisdom, warm and welcoming like Luciana, and backlit by my sister's gentle glow. "I love you, but you are wrong. Father cared for Mamma. He couldn't bear to cast her off. Matteo made things easier. Please. We are family. Embrace your brother. Forget your fights."

She laid a hand on my cheek, the way Mamma used to, then turned to her children and snapped her fingers. "Come, chickens. It is time we leave."

Her announcement struck me like a slap. "I'd hoped you'd stay here tonight."

Summer poppies nodded sadly in the corners, baby's breath whimpered by the windows. Luciana clutched her amulet. "I haven't the heart. Without Mamma, what is this place?"

Ceres drew Luciana close. "It's your home. It will always be your home."

"My home is here." She laid a hand on the bulge of new life growing within her, then picked up her youngest. "And here." She took Ursicio's hand. "We continue our course. After the twilight comes the dawn. I plan to do Mamma proud."

Matteo went with me to see them out, his son sleeping in his arms. "We were once like that. United. Now look at us, spiraling off in bits and chunks, forming our own constellations, creating our own risings and settings. I don't want my children fragmented. My son deserves better."

"Sounds like you've decided your son deserves siblings."

"I've decided recrimination chills even the warmest bed."

"So you've decided to fill out your roster, ensure Luciana's bounty has no reason to rival yours, and clog the lines of succession."

"Enough." Ceres stood behind us—and, of course, must have heard every word.

I tried to apologize. She put up a hand. "Stop, just stop. Stop hiding under that fine cloak, so sanctimonious and smug. Even when you're here, you're not, an oracle who sends counsel from some lofty pinnacle. Making judgments, making observations, and always from a safe distance. And don't let me forget my happy husband."

She poured herself a whiskey, lifted it to Matteo. "Yes, my husband may as well be with you. We scratch each other's itches, but love? Connection? Ha!"

She went to the window. "Tomorrow, farmers will tend their fields, mothers their children. Cloudworkers will sculpt, lightworkers will spin, watercrafters will flow in sparkles over the rocks. And all this will happen while Panduri's Cleric grumbles to his brother about the quality of his commitment and Panduri's Heir grumbles to his cleric about the quality of his marriage."

She turned to us and drained her glass. "Luciana does not worry me; she may yet be Panduri's hope. But dear Ignazio, Panduri's thoughtful negotiator, is able to talk the sky into torment, convince the clouds to cry, make what's bad seem good, and what's good unreliable. Beware Ignazio. He's the wolf, and soon he'll be at the door. How long would the Panduri we love, the Panduri we serve survive and thrive under Ignazio's self-absorbed and self-aggrandizing leadership?"

The monastery teaches us a closed mouth makes a happy drunk.

I was never much of a student. "Ah. You like stories. Just like Matteo. Good. Talk to your husband. Have him tell you our tale. Our family is adept at making adjustments and we know well the consequences of a bitter choice."

"You mean because Antonio died." Ceres sounded hurt, confused. She wasn't entirely innocent in the mess, but she'd never signed on for anything like the quagmire that was my family. No sane person would.

But I was a man possessed, unable to stop myself. Tired. So, so tired of doing what my stars said I should. So, of course, I didn't. "I mean the Deep Lore figures out what it needs, then ensures its outcomes. Everybody needs to stop acting like Matteo is a substitute. Matteo is exactly where he needs to be. Exactly where he's supposed to be. Exactly where he was meant to be."

Ceres put down her glass. She looked to Matteo. "What's Claudio talking about?"

"Nothing. Claudio speaks from the bottle, not his heart. He won't remember any of this once he sobers up."

Because that is the way of our people. Forget because the facts are too hurtful, replace because then we don't have to forgive. I headed for the door, having said more than I should, far more than was wise, and expecting a hangover to match in the morning. "Then I'll wish you both goodnight."

Matteo rang a bellflower. "Wait. I'll have one of the grooms ready a horse."

"What for?"

"You're not going back to the monastery?"

"I'm going to bed." I pointed past the wallflowers and down a hall where I used to sleep. "Unless Ceres has turned my room into a conservatory."

"Don't be ridiculous. Ceres hasn't turned anything into anything. This is your home, as much as Luciana's, and if Ceres wanted a conservatory, Father would grow one for her." Matteo picked up his son, took his wife's hand, and headed down the moss-covered hall which led to their apartments, his dismissal hanging like acid in the air.

Mist crept in, the fire damped. A mournful sound whistled through the huckleberries creeping along the rafters. The room felt strange and I a stranger in it, a shade disconnected. An asshole shade who'd been rude to my sister-in-law and hateful to my brother because I was no longer a part of what now happened here and Matteo no longer who I remembered.

He'd handled the *signori* well during Mamma's castoff, held off Ignazio on his own. I'd been spiritually absent, unwilling to give guidance because I felt underappreciated and overused. Matteo had gone on without me, navigating his stars by what signposts he'd found on his own.

Matteo hadn't planned to be Heir, but he was, and he was moving forward. He and Ceres's orbits were imperfect, awkward, but their brief bouts of honesty indicated their orbits were moving toward convergence.

Matteo had followed his star, the star I'd tossed into his path on a whim, a star that moved to a song over which I no longer had any say.

It was time for me to move on.

Move on where? To do what? I had my vocation. Charts to interpret, penitents to confess, Panduri's course to gently guard.

"They are better than nothing," Antonio had told me before my first time.

We were in a public house, the same we'd visited after Matteo's disastrous encounter with Ruggiero, the encounter that led to Matteo's more disastrous encounter with the woman of Careri. We were young, then, all that tumult still several Midsummers into the future. So young. And Antonio was so . . . definite. About everything. "I'm third son, I'm not supposed to want more."

"If Matteo and I ran away to Outside, you would be Heir."

The thought alone made me lose my knees. "Yes. I suppose. But I wouldn't want it. I'm not like you. Not born to it." I picked at my sleeve, feeling stupid. "When I'm not singing, I talk to the cat."

Antonio laughed at that. He pulled out his fiddle and played. A progression of chords rippling like water over rocks, then a series of subtle, slow notes which tugged at my gut. His music drew a deep emotion, a longing I struggled to capture, struggled to give voice. A call to boldness, to adventure, to be the best possible in things I had not tried, and to which I was not destined. I sang a counterpoint, shallow and saucy and unrestrained. A crowd gathered. Some hummed along. Then a girl, no, a woman, stepped forward.

Antonio never broke his tune. He bounced his bow across the strings, contorting so his elbow could push my ale a little closer. "Say hello to Pieta."

It didn't feel proper, didn't seem right. I told Antonio as much. To be a cleric comes with a vow of chastity, the first of the many I would break.

"You haven't yet taken the collar. You haven't shaved your head."

"It doesn't matter. I either am, or I am not."

"Then tonight you are not." Antonio put down his fiddle, got hold of my shoulders, and pushed me into Pieta's arms. "Never presume what you are supposed to be born for is who you are."

Rebellion is a lesson learned in regret, its remedies harsh, and too often, as Matteo learned those several years later, paid by others.

After Mamma's castoff, I wanted to know—if I'm not whom I'm supposed to be born to, was it possible to find out who I was? Matteo begrudged everything, and he was Heir. Father divulged nothing, and he was Duca. Antonio did what was best.

The Deep Lore allows for sabbaticals. Recommends them, in fact. Nothing pinned me to my post. I had secretaries, like Father. Assistants, like Matteo. I went off to find myself. First in bottles, then in whores, then in situations I dare not commit to record, pursued in secret in locations only I would know, for reasons which mattered only to me.

My cloak grew threadbare, my beard long. My penis rubbed raw in unexpected places.

I took a break. And a bath.

I cut my beard, cleaned my teeth, combed my hair, by then as long as the Papists' Jesus's. Or so Antonio once told me the Papists' Jesus looked like. "With wounds in his hands, in his feet, where they drove the nails. Blood dripping from his side, where they drove the sword."

Antonio had shown me his own hands, wiggled his own feet, pulled up his shirt and demonstrated a sword driven between the ribs. "The Papists sit in great stone buildings while the sun shines, so they can adore him in the dark. Adore him while he hangs from wooden planks arranged like this."

He crossed one forearm over the other and held them in front of his face. "Then they drink his blood."

"The Papists sound lovely."

Antonio made a grunting sound, halfway between horror and happiness. "They're beasts. Slow and lumbering and backward."

"Then don't go."

He shrugged, mumbled something about it being interesting. And Antonio's stories certainly made Outside sound interesting, in a wavy, warped kind of way. I became his vicarious companion in his secret vagabond life, took him at his word, believed him that nothing more than curiosity was involved. Because I was young. Because he was Antonio. Because I did not know then what I knew later.

My memories of that time with Antonio became a cage. So I became a hermit. A hermit who came into town to fuck, to drink, to eat good cheese, then disappeared before the consideration was due. Then I became a hermit who hollowed out a tree and slept within until my fingernails grew into the wood, like our ancestors in the time before their star's rising.

I did all the things I had not been charted and none to which I had. To the hurt, I provided no comfort, to the confused, no clarity, to the penitent, no absolution, to the recalcitrant, no reason to reconsider. My star had been plotted for the light, so I cast it into darkness, a phony, a fraud, one whom I did not recognize, in need of my own ministries, alone in the world.

Matteo sent a sprite: "Our courses wobble. Come home."

He sent another: "Please."

And then an onslaught: "How could you leave us?"

"Why did you go?"

"Did you think we wouldn't miss you?"

And, most poignant of all: "Tell us how we're supposed to go on."

The tree's bark, once comforting on my back, suddenly felt coarse, the cloud-filled sky, oppressive. My balls ached, my ass itched and when I reached to scratch at either, my back twinged.

I dreamed of fresh-risen cream and berries ripe from the vine, mattresses stuffed with dandelion fluff and sheets spun from star-light. The forest night, once mysterious and deep, filled with mon-sters, with strange cries in the night. Fire ants caught in the folds of my clothing, fungus in the folds of my crotch. Still I stayed, uncer-tain of my place in the constellation, my position in the dance, my purpose in caring at all.

A soul in winter either wakes or dies.

I crept out of my hollow, beard thick with burrs and my scalp crawling so badly I almost gave up my promise and shaved it again. I wrapped my hand around Antonio's amulet, never far from my heart. "I have no idea what I was born to, less who I am. I'm dying and I don't know what to do. Give me a sign, like the Papists ask of their Jesus."

It started to blizzard.

Which forced me to seek better shelter. And a blanket. Forced me to admit I needed to find my own way, seek my own path, discover my own song within the music.

Or so I told the milkmaid after spring finally came. "You see, I have no home. I've lost myself, my sense of worth."

Somebody burst into the barn and dragged me off her.

"Salvatore! How are you?" I indicated the milkmaid. "Meet Giulietta."

"Charmed." Salvatore took the bottle from my hand, threw my cloak over my head and pushed me out the door. "Let's go, Romeo. Midsummer approaches. You have to dance."

Fourteen

Salvatore dragged me over hill, across dale, all the way back to Dante and Ilario's garden. Matteo was taking an ax to the stump Antonio left when he chopped down their tree, his cuffs rolled to his elbows, his son and infant daughter nearby.

I dove for the baby, picked her up and away from the flying wood chips, then grabbed my nephew by his hand and pulled him back.

Salvatore didn't look concerned. "Don't worry, Matteo's got pretty good aim." He dropped a candy into my nephew's palm and left.

I cleared my throat.

"Claudio!" Matteo sounded uncommonly cheerful for a man wielding an ax. His chest heaved. Sweat poured under his armpits. "How nice you could come. We need your help, my children and I. This garden. Look at it. Unacceptable."

Every flower overgrew the next, every hedge had gone wild. The marble pixies were the saddest, near covered in moss, their little purple caps disintegrating with neglect. I'd decided the one closest to the fountain was Dante. I don't know why. Ilario liked the water best. "Do you ever think about them?"

Matteo dragged a sleeve across his forehead. "I think about them every Midsummer."

"I mean as individuals. As Dante. Or Ilario. They weren't interchangeable. Dante was taller, Ilario's hair was lighter. They looked like you."

Matteo nodded toward his son. "They looked like Cosimo."

True. And Matteo missed the hint. "Dante liked to build things. Ilario liked to take them apart."

"Puzzles." Matteo put down the ax. "They were two sides of the same coin. Both sides liked puzzles. Dante liked to put them together, Ilario liked to see how they worked."

Matteo dipped an empty carob pod into the stream and took a drink. He dipped again and offered it to his son, then tapped his temple. "Dante and Ilario were like your poppa. They liked to figure things out."

Matteo took his little girl from my arms and placed her among the leaves of a lady's cushion, well clear of the perimeter set by the wood chips. He pulled a trowel from his back pocket and placed it in his little boy's hands. He pointed toward the pixies. "Dig there a while, Cosimo. A hole about this big. Like we talked about." He squared up his fingers, demonstrating a rectangle half again as long as it was wide.

My nephew toddled off. Matteo again picked up the ax. He dropped its head to the soil and leaned on its handle. "Dante and Ilario were like Uncle Giacomo, always looking for the secret behind the obvious. They were way smarter than me. I'm always looking for the obvious behind the secret. Always looking for the reasons people do things. Like this last year, I decided to do as Ceres told me, decided to get out among the people, get to know Panduri. Antonio did it all the time. Walked among them like he belonged, so comfortable you'd never know he was Heir. That got me thinking."

Uh-oh. "Thinking about what?"

Matteo patted his pockets, first his pants, then his shirt. Like he was looking for something. "Got me thinking about the maestro, and his daughter. You remember her, she married the air spinner. They had a child, then the air spinner died. I got to thinking how odd it was the maestro came to Mamma's castoff, but not her. Mamma was always so kind to her. Then I remembered she hadn't been to Antonio's castoff either. He was her child's benefactor. I'd have expected to see her."

My tongue grew raspy, dry enough to cure fish. "Did you ask the maestro?"

"Yes. He told me that after the earthquake she'd gone Outside, took the child. I guess the quake scared her, and having lost her husband, she didn't see much hope she'd marry again, certainly not to anybody as well-regarded as an air spinner. The maestro told me he chose to stay Inside. 'To provide a link, in case either ever decides to return.'"

"You found that odd."

"I found it sweet, insightful. And puzzling. I mean, how had she crossed? All those *folletti*. I asked the maestro. He told me attitude is key."

Matteo dug through his vest, turning the pocket linings out clean. "How obvious is that? We don't cross because crossing is hard, it's dangerous. Salvatore ages a decade every time he goes, yet Giacomo went Outside all the time searching for Dante and Ilario. He crossed that valley like the *folletti* weren't even there. Maybe Giacomo didn't find crossing hard. I guess the Careri woman, the mother of my child didn't find it hard either. I can't tell you how it relieves me to find out her attitude got her across, not a set of wings."

I was cranky. My crotch itched. I wanted a bath and I couldn't figure out where the conversation was going. "So you decided to chop out the stump. A metaphorical vanquishing of your frustration over all you didn't know."

"I'm chopping out the stump because it's ugly. Because Antonio should have done it when he took down the tree. *Their* tree. Its fruit. Do you remember?"

Sweet and tempting, with a taste that left you reaching for more.

Matteo went to the pixies, to where his son was digging. He

reached over the little boy's head and retrieved his doublet, hanging over Dante's arm. He went through the doublet's pockets, felt along the seams and lining. "Dig for one thing and something else surfaces. And really it was quite amazing. Unexpected. All these years, so many questions, I found my answers planted at the base of that stump."

I should have left, should have turned around and toddled off, just like my nephew. But I was curious, too, just like Dante and Ilario. And Matteo was still holding the ax. "What answers?"

"This answer." He drew something from one of the doublet's pockets and threw it at me. "Catch."

Whatever it was I caught dead center because . . . instincts. A bit of iron, very like the one I wore around my neck, very like the one Matteo wore around his, that his children wore around theirs. The bit of metal worn by each of our citizens to connect us to our world and to each other.

The impressions conveyed by this one crept over my soul like hoarfrost over a pumpkin, despondency and despair, gloom and melancholy. I dropped it. "Giacomo's amulet."

Matteo scooped it up. "Guess I shouldn't have thrown it like that. Wasn't thinking. Giacomo's memories carry quite a kick."

"This is why you brought me home. To force me to hold our uncle's amulet, experience the horror of his passing."

"You weren't horrified. You were happy he was gone. He scared you, and you were happy we were shed of him. Nope, nope, don't protest. Antonio didn't like him, either. Now me, I always held out some affection, always thought Giacomo left us because he couldn't find our brothers. All this time I thought Antonio took down their tree so he wouldn't be reminded. The secret was Antonio took down that tree so he wouldn't forget." Matteo hefted the ax. "Or did you already know?"

Every truth was impossible, every lie worse. My mind did backflips, my heart flip-flops.

Matteo arced the ax back and up, bringing it down on what

remained of the stump in a shower of splinters. "Never mind. Once a cleric, always a cleric. I don't know who said what to you that binds your tongue, but finding that amulet makes me wonder if Antonio buried it there on purpose. Makes me wonder if more than laziness made him leave the stump. Makes me wonder if maybe he hoped one day I'd find it. Maybe Antonio meant to leave me a trail, an explanation for why he tried to run that Midsummer, for why he finally crossed. Like he never meant to go for always, only meant to finish what Giacomo hadn't. Meant to find Dante and Ilario, maybe go exploring with them, and with them, he planned to return."

He looked up. "Why else would he leave his fiddle?"

Matteo put down the ax and headed for Dante's Wall, retrieved a volume from its opposite side. Not a volume. A tome. Three inches thick and bound in leather. He held it up, spine out, and waved it inches from my nose. "So now, having figured all that out, I am finished. The pages are filled and I thank you for the suggestion."

He pointed to the pixies, to the dirt pile my nephew by then was fashioning into pies. "That's what all this digging is about. I intend to bury this confession here, along with my other frailties, for good or ill."

Drag me back, blather on about the maestro, then throw Giacomo's amulet at me and swing an ax at the stump. Yet something in the way Matteo dug under the roots gave me hope, gave me purpose. Matteo was done. He'd made his confession, and his grief was over. He'd come through, and Matteo thought the secrets were settled.

Maybe because it was Midsummer, maybe because I hadn't drunk anything since the day before, hadn't eaten since two days before that, but I got a little giddy. "Don't bury the confession, burn it. We can't do anything about the past, only the future."

Matteo paged through the journal. Ran a finger down one ink-laden parchment, then the next. "Ah. That's where you're wrong. You can do plenty with the past. Regret its events, address its mistakes, like the one you and I need to address now."

Dread, deep and dragging, cinched my balls in tight. "What mistake?"

"Your job. Father gave it to Tendi. Tendi is now head of your order. It is done."

The hopelessness, the despair, the sense I had no place to return to, no place where I belonged, no idea who I was, no inkling who I was supposed to be. It was all real, I just didn't understand why. "It must be undone. Tendi has neither the desire nor the temperament."

"He has Ignazio's backing, he doesn't need anything else."

"Except Father's approval."

"Yes, well, the absence of Panduri's Guardian is a gap even Father could not cover." Matteo snapped the journal shut. "He had no choice."

"He's Duca, of course he had a choice."

"He has the choices the *signori* give him. Ignazio suggested your disappearance was some plot of the Careri, to leave Panduri without guidance during this terrible time. He sent thunderheads and lightning strikes with demands for your return. Whipped the *folletti* into a fury. Their bells were unceasing, sent everybody into a tizzy." Matteo's voice dropped. "Some crossed. Salvatore could not retrieve them. We don't know where they are."

I learned yet another lesson—being third did not mean I escaped my responsibility. Being third only put my concerns last. "This has been a lovely talk, very illuminating. I'm going back to the woods."

I turned and walked off, but a single word, shimmering and stark, rooted me in my path.

"No."

I cursed my proximity, which made me susceptible to Matteo's power, cursed my inability to get free without my brother's say-so. "Let me go. I have no position, no responsibilities I must attend. You don't need me. You're pulled together and sure, your family growing and your star on the rise."

"You mean this?" He pulled off his cap, deep blue as twilight. "These?" He yanked buttons moon-washed in silver from his vest. "Nothing but a show for the *ducato*. A demonstration to the people that Panduri is whole and happy and its course proceeding as expected. Things are not fine. Clouds refuse to fluff under sunshine, seeds are slow to germinate, the hedgehogs are in open revolt, and the cream keeps going sour. Even the snapdragons are snarling."

"Snapdragons always snarl."

"You don't understand. Everything has changed since Mamma's passing. The *signori* stalk my path, presuming I hold some sway with Father. Ignazio dogs me daily, hoping I'll crack."

He looked to his children, the one sleeping, the other digging in the dirt, blessedly oblivious to the intimacies unspooling within inches of their innocence. "I sent Salvatore to find you because I need an assistant, an ally, somebody on whom I can depend. Father moves in a fog, more often in his cups than in his office. His power is on the wane, and I have no idea what I'm doing."

My cloak grew heavy, my collar tight. Matteo still had plenty to learn about power. "You drag me to a garden you no longer care for. Ask guidance I'm no longer authorized to give."

"You told me to write down a confession you never intended to read." Matteo took the trowel from his son and dug deep, flinging the earth to the heavens. A clod flew into the fountain, plopped through a pad of duckweeds, and set them quacking. His son clapped his hands and laughed, then hung from the fountain's lip and quacked with them. Matteo groped behind the pixies, to the place where he used to hide his bottles and retrieved the box in which he used to keep them, large and locked and, as I saw once he unlocked it, empty.

I confess, I was disappointed. "Why did you send me all those sprites?"

"Sprites?"

I repeated the messages. "'Why did you leave us? How could you go?'—"

"—'Tell us how we're supposed to go on.'" Matteo got pale and paler. He put up a hand. "Stop. Stop."

Matteo closed the box over the journal. He locked the box, placed it into the hole, then called his son over to help him cover it over. He tousled the boy's hair. "Go, count the honeybees and the bluebirds. Your uncle and I still have a little to say to each other."

The boy ran off. Matteo picked up the trowel and waggled it at me. "I didn't send those sprites to you. I just sent them. Told the sprites, 'Deliver these to my brother. He's broken my heart.' I meant Antonio, and I expected the sprites to return, to tell me they could find no recipient. None ever did. Now I know why."

Matteo looked to the sky, then to his feet. "When you left, I worried you'd gone Outside. I even set up a tent, camped a while at the edge, just in case. Because I presumed you'd done something stupid. It never occurred to me you'd done something deliberate. Well, I can be deliberate, too. And while you were off drinking, and dreaming, and fucking every hidey-hole willing to take you, I've been poking around a few of my own."

I was angry, confused, relieved in my dismissal, appalled in my sudden lack of direction. And still curious, always curious. The curiosity would never end, and so I asked. "What did you find?"

"That my brother's death is a mystery nobody thinks I have a right to know. I've had a year to think about it. A year alone, without your intractable and intransigent counsel. A year to figure things out, to work out the puzzle, and what I figured out is that Antonio was destined, he was charted, but at his end, Antonio was only a man, flawed as any, and I cannot spend the rest of my life resentful over what he did not tell me, angry about what you cannot. My children are growing, I have a *ducato* to tend. Giacomo was not Legendary, and if Ignazio has his way, Father will cease to be Renown. I either continue my course or Panduri will not continue hers."

He gave me the trowel and dropped the key into my palm, closing my fingers over it. "In case you decide to read it. It's a confession, but only for me to myself and does not bind you in any way. My offering to you, free of encumbrances, no conditions set forth. Because someday you may want to share it. Because someday, somebody may care."

A trowel, a key, and yet another burden. "You find me intractable."

"Like a mule stuck in a mud pit."

Fifteen

Fine for Matteo to ramble on about how he wanted to remember Antonio, to despair of the secrets he didn't know, decry the truths he'd uncovered. Fine for him to explain to me, least able of any to tell him *yea* or *nay* or *I don't want to hear about it.*

He was Heir. Powerful beyond measure. His wants of highest import, his needs higher still, his lacks ignored, his contrary acts excused because as Matteo rose, so did Panduri. And all its generations.

I spent most of that Midsummer staring at the twilight from the window of my boyhood room, a cantankerous Salvatore by my side. I held up my wrists. "You don't need the bonds. I won't run away."

Salvatore shifted his seat, his only indication he'd heard. I settled back onto the branches of the window seat, my gaze drawn by the cliff edges separating Panduri from everyplace else. Perhaps it was Midsummer. Perhaps it was the need to speak with somebody who would not betray my trust. I tried again, pointed to where mists obscured the other side. "How far did you go?"

Salvatore grunted. I thought that was all the answer I'd get, but he roused himself and came to gaze at the cliff edges with me. "I went

131

into their city. Their buildings are made of glass and supported by a metal like our irons, but cold and lifeless."

"Antonio said they call that *steel.*"

"Yes, silvery like the stardust we use to tip our arrows. I tested the metal. It was worthless against were-beasts."

"Our elementals would be fascinated." Noble gassers and rare-earthers, glass magicians and semiconductors.

Salvatore's face grew grim. "The maestro told Antonio he thought it best they not know. He said Outside is full of wonders, wonders we might mistake for magic and so feel at home, wonders that are often toxic, slowly fouling their water and their air. The maestro told us by the time we realized their magic was harmful to us, we might not be able to curb its effect."

The maestro tells us everything, and he knows when it's best not to tell something. "Someday, I'd like to go back. Not forever, or always. For a little. Now that I'm no longer a child. To see, to understand, to get some sense of what Antonio felt."

"His iron doesn't tell you?"

"I don't have the heart to listen." I settled back against the sill, feeling grumpy. "Matteo buries his journal and thinks himself absolved, but the rest of us have to go on, chained by loyalties and lore we aren't even sure how to interpret."

Salvatore turned his direct and honest gaze on me. "You could tell Matteo that much."

I shook my head. "Too easy. In my family, it's so much more intriguing to wander past each other, attempting to read a mood, a facial expression, a hook of a thumb."

"Your family is exhausting." The music grew louder. Salvatore leaned out the window. He twisted, I presumed to get a better view. "My sisters have joined the pipers."

He tilted an ear. "Listen, they're playing one of Antonio's compositions."

I wondered if Matteo had ordered it. Or maybe Father. "You should go. To cheer them on."

"Your brother ordered me to keep you safe."

I hopped off the sill. "Did he order you to keep me safe here, or only to keep me safe in your sight?"

"He ordered me to keep you safe."

I again held up my wrists. "Then release my bonds and keep me safe among Panduri. It's Midsummer. We're supposed to dance."

When I was a boy, Midsummer meant music, it meant treats, it meant playing long into the twilight, basking in starshine, waking on fields speckled in silver. I wanted to recapture that wonder, so spent my time with Luciana's children, with Matteo's, promised Salvatore I'd be there when he returned. We gathered moonbeams, attached them to ribbons, then ringed the dancers and tossed the beams into the skies above them.

A girl approached. No, a woman, hand outstretched. Her cheek was smooth, her eyes kind, her breasts . . . nice from what I could see of them, and her dress simple and pretty and bursting with buttercups. "Can we dance?"

I looked behind to see to whom she spoke.

She ducked around me. "I'm speaking to you."

Her song was flirtatious, friendly. Not intrigued by my cloak, because I wasn't wearing it. Nor interested in my wealth, because my wool pants and rough-spun shirt sung more of plowman than Duca's son.

I felt a push, just a touch, like somebody nudged me from behind, but nobody was there. Except the woman, and she wanted to dance, to get to know me, ignorant of my identity, unaware my vows made me unavailable.

I wanted to accept. Be like Matteo, or Antonio, or any of the many at the celebration. Dance for pleasure, or purpose, for fun, or my heart's desire. Because I was nobody, or somebody, like everybody else, like none other.

Because I was not Matteo nor Antonio, because I was not the

duca's son nor the Heir's brother, because I had not been born a cleric but made one. Because Panduri's needs came first, all others last, because I was no longer her Guardian, never her Protector, not all that Gentle, and certainly not Legendary.

I was Claudio, and I had no idea what I wanted to do next. Except dance. With this girl. No. Woman.

My one truth, and the only reason I could not.

I bowed to her. I shook my head. I stepped away. I went to practice targets.

Fifty-seven lost arrows later, Matteo joined me, bow in hand, quiver at his hip. "Salvatore's supposed to be keeping you safe."

"I'll remind him the next time I see him."

Matteo took his place by his targeting stake. "If you're trying to split Antonio's arrow, forget it. It's enchanted, cursed. I can't decide which."

I drew again. "Don't you have a wish you have to grant, a boon you have to bestow?" I sighted and let fly. The arrow went as far astray as the others. I pulled another from my quiver. "A procession you have to lead?"

"Already led it. It was very nice." Matteo tapped the hat, large enough to cook soup, then pulled it from his head. "This thing is hot. It makes my scalp sweat. Antonio never told me."

"Antonio never told anybody anything."

"He told you plenty."

I let my arrow fly. "Nothing useful."

Matteo dropped the hat at his feet. "We don't have to be like Antonio."

I threw my bow at his hat and went to find my arrows.

Matteo searched with me. "Antonio loved making music under the moonlight. You and I should give it a try. Not that we'll sound as good without him."

I kept on searching.

So did Matteo. "Or we could do something else. Antonio loved plenty under the moonlight. Wine, women, fishing."

"Antonio never fished."

"Are you sure? Seems I saw him once. Maybe twice. No matter. Certainly, the wine and the—"

"Woman."

Matteo stopped searching. "Excuse me?"

"He loved one woman under the moonlight. The wine, the cavalier music-making, the disregard for his role, your rights. Yes, in abundance. The woman, one. Only one. The talk of whores, of Midsummer fun. An act. From the start."

"The one he refused to speak of." Matteo crossed the space and got hold of my cowl. "Who was she? Why was she unsuitable?"

"I cannot tell you. I can never tell you." I pulled his fingers from the fabric, took the arrows Matteo had gathered, and shoved them into my quiver. "For the rest of my life, you're going to speak of Antonio and these questions will rise. Sometimes I'll be able to correct the misconceptions, most of the time I won't. Then you'll come at me from another direction, ask in a different arrangement. I probably still won't be able to say anything."

I backed away, stumbling over tussocks and clods, then pulled the quiver up over my head and tossed it into the woods. Tried to. It was pretty heavy. "You'll never stop. Because you don't think of me as Claudio, a man on his own. You think of me as Antonio's brother, Antonio's cleric, Antonio's confessor. You'll pick at one, then the other, with comments and accusations, observations and queries, until one day, there's nothing left of me."

"Listen, I was only—"

I put up a hand. "Stop. Maybe all you meant by any of this was to make a nice memory. It's no use. Even with all your powerful words. Antonio is dead. The music is gone, and without music, song is just screeching into the night."

So began my life of abstinence. Not by desire, by despair. Not from devotion, but dejection. Forbidden to leave, I was like the lonely wives, and like them sought solace in the only place left to me, beneath my monk's robe.

I went to see Father. To reclaim my position. Being an ascetic is easier from the top.

Father refused. "The *signori* would never allow it. In a year, maybe two, we can revisit the question, give them time to forget, remind them you're still the *duca's* third son. Until then, Tendi is agreeable and he's doing fine at the job." He stared at me a while.

I checked my cloak, my sandals, wiped at my mouth, wondering if a bit of breakfast were stuck there. "What is it?"

"Your hair."

Still waving and wild and long as Papist Jesus's. Perfect for a life of disgrace. I spent most of my days in the archives anyway.

Matteo came to see me. I sent him away. He claimed he needed chart interpretations. I told him to send them to Tendi. He railed from the other side of the door, declared I couldn't hide forever, couldn't pretend I wasn't there. I told him I could, because I already had, and the Papists' hell would freeze over before I'd let him get close enough to compel me to do differently.

I wanted to tell him more, so much more, about pride, and presumptions, and how just because he could do something didn't mean he should, but we were broken, Matteo and I. Those bits of myself I saw in him twisted my soul, squeezed me dry, sent my dungeon at being held a prisoner so high, I couldn't admit the truth—I missed my brother.

Midsummer approached, and I took to wandering the streets. Salvatore wandered with me, charged with my constant and consistent protection. A cleric with a bodyguard seemed ridiculous, so I left my cloak at the mansion, and we walked about pretending to be only friends. Topo always came along, draped around my neck like a muff. One day, I saw the woman in a clearing. The woman from Midsummer Past. The woman who'd asked me to dance.

Topo hopped off my neck and headed toward her. I waited, presuming he'd return. Then I decided to head home, presuming he'd follow.

I felt another push, not a touch, nor a tap, nor a nudge.

A shove. In the direction of the clearing and after Topo. The woman got to him first. "Your cat likes me."

I wasn't any good at simple talk. When a cleric's around, people either want to confess or keep their mouths shut, worried I'll find they need to confess. But this lovely, pleasant woman didn't know to do cither. I wasn't wearing my cloak. My hair was Papist Jesus. She thought I was like anybody else.

She looked to Salvatore. "Your friend doesn't speak."

"A cat caught his tongue and refuses to give it back."

Topo hopped out of her arms and onto my shoulder. She scratched him behind his ear. "This cat?"

Again, Salvatore answered. "No, his shameful cousin."

Her dress was yellow, her spirits high, her hair twined with buttercups. She carried a large green and yellow basket layered with lamb's wool and spooled silk. "Ah, well I have just the thing."

She shuffled through the spools, pulling a tangle from the collection. She placed it into my palm, her touch decisive. "I spun this yarn special, guaranteed to loosen the most tightly-stitched sensibilities, full of folderol and flights of fancy. I'll unravel it for you."

I hefted the tangled threads and finally found my tongue. "You're a yarn spinner."

"The best." She curtsied, then pulled out a spindle and gathered the thread. She began to spin her yarn right then. "If this cat is your familiar, then you might be a magician, and if this cat is a shapeshifter, he might be a parrot, and because he sits on your shoulder, that might make you a pirate."

"This cat is just a cat and we call him Topo."

She flicked the spindle under my nose. "Clever. You named a parrot for a mouse."

"*Shhh*. Topo thinks he's named for a lion."

We were doing fine, talking like couples talk. I wondered if I should invite her for cider. Or see if she'd like to go for a walk.

She tilted her head and scrunched her brow, like somebody was speaking in her ear, then dug back into her basket. "Wait. You don't need yarns, you need something made from yarn." She pulled out a skein, purple, and a couple of needles. She started to knit, the needles flashing and clicking. "This won't take two ticks."

I watched, fascinated, wondering what magic she might be producing. She was Panduri, as much as Matteo was, as Antonio had been. She was the gravity which held our constellation together. The reason any member of the nobility did what we did.

Or we were supposed to.

And she and Salvatore would get along just fine.

I handed the threads to him, bowed out of the story, and made my way to Dante and Ilario's garden. Ceres was there, basking in the last of spring, swollen with new life.

I hesitated on the edges, standing on the splinters that still remained from the stump, still shamed by my hateful comments to her after Mamma's castoff, embarrassed that two years later, I still hadn't apologized. "You look happy."

"Come." She waved me closer, took my hand and placed it on her belly. "Say hello to your nephew."

All the women I'd touched, in intimacy or friendship, never had I touched one in that way. The mound was smooth, too taut, the life within singing the faintest and most hopeful of songs. I pulled away, uncertain of the propriety of our encounter.

She resettled my palm, covered my hand with hers. "Wait."

Something jumped under my fingers, like a fish in a quiet pool.

Ceres chuckled. "That was a foot, I think."

My eyes filled. I loved Matteo's children, loved Luciana's, would have loved Antonio's, had he given me the opportunity, but Ceres's generous gesture granted me a glimpse into the wonder of it all.

How could a man not want this? How could the Deep Lore deprive him of this blessing? "Thank you."

She stood, her hand supporting her back and gazed at the pixies. "I've never lost a sister or a brother. My parents and grandparents are all alive. But for Antonio, I would not yet know what it is to forget, but sometimes I sit here and I see what joy there is to remember."

Ceres left me, her other children requiring her attention. I settled beside the pixies, picked at the tassels on the remains of their purple caps, not in the least certain why I'd come.

A scrap of parchment fluttered between Dante's little stone fingers. I plucked at it, but the parchment wouldn't release, melted to the marble by an ancient bit of taffy, no doubt left there by Matteo on Midsummer Past. I leaned in close and read the parchment where it lay.

In dreamlike guise our longings lie;
The lacings frail at times untie.

The hand was Matteo's, the ink faded, the bottom edge torn, the song rising from the sentiment poignant and sweet. I checked the other pixie, Ilario's. Another bit of parchment fluttered from his fingers, adhered to the stone by another bit of taffy.

Revealing loves decreed unspun,
Cast off in silence, one by one.

Parchment is parchment, one sheet much like the other, but not all parchment was made by Salvatore's father, nor bore his watermark. Matteo must have torn these from this journal. Perhaps on the day he buried it, perhaps before. He'd given me a key and a trowel. All I had to do was find them.

Topo dashed through, a wad of purple in his mouth. He dropped the wad at my feet, a couple of knit caps, and a note—*You forgot these.*

How had she known?

I replaced the yarn spinner's caps for the threadbare ones on the pixies, then walked down to the river and retrieved Antonio's fiddle, still hanging where Father had placed it in the willows, its polish dulled, its strings four Midsummers out of tune. I buffed the instrument as best I could, tuned it as best I knew, then played the fiddle under the moonlight and conjured memories of my brother, feeling lonelier and more remorseful than any being should have to feel.

After a while, I returned to the mansion. Not to dig out the key, nor to uncover the trowel, but to search out my razor. My Papist Jesus days were over. Born to them or not, our destinies are written in the stars, and though I'd never seen my chart, I had every reason to believe mine were beautiful.

On that last twilight before Midsummer, I closed my fingers around the razor's mother-of-pearl handle and committed myself anew, not as an untried boy, but a mature man, convinced in the act of binding, I could free myself, convinced by accepting my burdens, I'd one day be able to grant them release.

My brother had left me a trail written in parchment, straight from his heart, a trail he meant for me to find, a trail I meant to follow. Circumstances had sent us spiraling—those still with us, those who'd gone. The heavens had not placed me at Panduri's axis, but I could still do what I might to return us to our orbits, each in our places, forever one for the other, twinkling in a mantle of deepest blue.

Sixteen

The next morning, Father let me know the heavens had not placed me at *his* axis either.

"But—" My shaved head. My renewed vows. My good intentions.

"Glue feathers to your scalp if it makes you feel better, Claudio. Tendi stays where he is."

"You told me to wait a year."

"Wait another. Give your renewed commitment time to take hold." Father handed me a stack of scrolls. "Meanwhile, there's filing."

Charts piled on every table, gathered in every corner. Wandering ivy had crept over the nettle, and chain vines imprisoned the sparring ficus. "Where are your secretaries?"

"I let them go. They were always poking about my cabinets, moving work from one place to another, bothering me about my correspondence."

"That's their job."

"Now it's yours." He rummaged on his desk, rearranged papers and pens. "Have you seen Matteo?"

The ducal mansion is large and ever-changing, new rooms grown as needed. I'd been hiding deep among its roots. Father hadn't seen me in months. And he wanted to know about Matteo.

I headed for the door. "I'll find him."

Matteo found me. Ten steps outside Father's office. He grabbed my arm and whirled me around.

My scrolls went spinning. "I'm supposed to file those."

"Father's secretaries can do that."

"Father let them go."

"No, he didn't. He sent them to me." Matteo dragged me down the hall and pulled me into his study. "See?"

Every star plot in my brother's study was aligned in the same direction and sorted by declension. Matteo's verbs were color-coded, his verse arranged by form and meter, his every simile slotted into its spot. Even his adjectives hung in logical groupings, each by an individual thread. "Can I borrow a secretary for the archives?"

"Take them all. I'm going mad finding things for them to do." Matteo ran a hand over my head. "You cut your hair again."

"Lice."

Matteo hesitated. Maybe he thought I was serious. Then he smiled. He wiped his fingers on his pants, anyway. "You're still angry with me. I get it. Don't be. Midsummer is upon us and the midwives say Ceres may deliver before its end. I'm going to name this one Bartomeo. For Father. People always say he has good stars. How is he?"

A string of notes fiddled off my left ear. One of Antonio's tunes, but discordant. "When is the last time you saw him?"

"Last week, I think." He gazed out the window. "Maybe last month. No matter. I've been busy. Research. Have you any idea how long the Duca-who-was lived?'

"None."

"Me neither. I can't find his chart. Ours are there, all in their slots, still trapped behind a spell deeper than any blue. But before our generation, before The Great Upheaval?" He showed me empty palms and shook his head, then pulled a glass from a drawer, a bottle from another, pulled the cork and poured himself a drink. He waggled the bottle at me, eyebrow raised.

The fiddle music grew louder, my desire to clap my hands over my ears to shut it out overwhelming. I glanced at Matteo's bottle.

But…vow. Shaved head. Good intentions. I waved him off. "Those charts were probably burned, as they should be."

"Then there should be a space, a place where they once were, but there's nothing. No indication the Duca-who-was ever was. It's like our family sprang from the firmament, fully-formed." He drained his glass and slammed it to the table. "What's Ignazio got on Father?"

"No more than Father has on him." The revelation flew from my mouth. The rebound came as quickly, pain deep in my solar plexus, and a burning in my throat. Not physical, not really, but complete in recognition of my failure.

He'd been so congenial, focused on a different topic. I knocked his glass from his desk "You tricked me."

"You told me I couldn't ask about Antonio. You never said anything about Father."

I headed for the door.

Matteo beat me to it, arms spread jamb to jamb. "I used to think it was about Antonio, about Ruggiero. I thought Ignazio was motivated by revenge. Then it seemed it was only about power. Every day I must cast yet another agreement. Nothing momentous— drizzle for the new shoots or sun for the harvests. Yet Father's consideration drains faster than he can recoup. He's huffing to make the strawberries sweet enough, or the grain heads full and plump. I told Father to stop paying Ignazio, to let Nature take her course. Father told me if Nature took her course, Antonio would still be alive, there'd be no vendetta, and I'd be doing as I was charted without all the misplaced reproach. I'd ask Father what he means, but you know I can't because of that stupid declaration I made."

He flicked his hair out of his eyes. "I can't ask, but you could."

"Get out of my way."

"No." He looked up the hall, then down, his manner going from good-tempered to tortured in a twinkle. "I've been checking the casts, and something is coming, a reckoning of some sort. I can't tell what it is but feel like I should. I wake in the night with the sense I've forgotten something, or overlooked something, or misplaced it, or maybe never had it at all. Every evening I make my plans. Every morning I wake raring to do battle. Every night I have to admit, 'I may not take this hill today.'"

Hill. "You mean the charts."

He paced. Back and forth. "I mean Father. He tells me nothing, teaches me nothing, explains . . . nothing. I am Heir, and I am alone in my pursuit. He won't even eat with me unless Ceres and the children are with us."

"He asked if I'd seen you."

"Because he wants to know where I am. That's why he sent me the secretaries. To keep an eye out for me, let him know when I'm heading to see him. So Father has time."

"For what?"

"To hide whatever he's doing in that office. Go back there, poke around. He trusts you."

"If this is why you've been banging on the doors to the archives, you're going to be disappointed."

"I'm not asking you to do anything improper. Just asking you to have a look around. You know, knock a few scrolls off his desk, pick them up, hide them under your cloak."

"You want me to steal scrolls from Father's office."

"Only until you have time to file them properly." He took hold of my shoulders and drew me close. "Antonio's gone. I did not watch my words, and the Deep Lore took him away, cast me into his role. I have things I need to know, to understand, to calm this hurt, help me go on. You're my brother. There's nobody else I can ask."

I wanted to draw Matteo close as he drew me, wanted to tell him all I knew, explain all I could, but Matteo had walled himself off from any help that might do him good, craving only the help that might drive him to ruin. Nothing I offered would be of aid. "You could ask Father."

Matteo released me. He flopped into his chair. "We just had this conversation. Battles. Hills." He picked at a fingernail. "Declarations."

"All I'm saying is show Father some compassion and unmake your declaration. It's awful to be separated from a child, gut-wrenching."

Matteo stopped picking at his fingernail. He sorted through the piles, pulled out parchment, then pens, his intention to go back to work obvious. "I'm not a dolt. I understand Father misses Antonio."

"I'm talking about you, idiot. You've spent more time with Father than he's spent with all his other children combined, yet you act like you need dispensation to ask him a question."

Matteo leaned back in his chair. He tapped his pen against his teeth. "Says the man who's been hiding among the scrolls."

He put down his pen and got out of his chair. He went to a Venus claptrap nestled among the blanket ferns. He spoke to it, murmuring words both cajoling and commanding until it opened its jaws. He thanked the claptrap, pulled a chart from its depth and handed it to me. "Unroll it."

I did, laying it on his desk, my heart swelling to see to whom it belonged. Matteo's son. That of the Careri.

I traced one path, then the next, the stars lighting under my fingertips. All the possibilities. I looked up. "He's beautiful."

"Yes." Matteo's gaze flitted from one planet to the next. "Most days Ignazio comes and talks to Father. Those days I listen at the door. Their words are sometimes fast, sometimes slow, but never loud enough for me to hear. Just bits and pieces. About the vendetta. About parentage. About duty and honor and birthrights and boundaries. Father gets angry. Ignazio gets angrier."

He put a finger at the chart's point of origin, his child's conception. "They're talking about my son, I think. Perhaps Cosimo because we told everybody he belongs to Antonio, perhaps my child with the Careri, but I think Ignazio knows. About both. I think he's always known. That's why he didn't argue when Father put up Tendi to take the fall when the *signori* claimed the Careri was a spy. Ignazio knew the time would come when he could use that knowledge for his own gain. For blackmail."

Matteo raised his gaze to mine, his concern engulfing, soul-sucking, with tentacles so patent I could almost hear them slurp. "I need something I can use, insurance against the day Ignazio's bill comes due. You've been in those archives a year, pawing through the charts. Surely there's something you can tell me that won't upset the Deep Lore."

He was never going to stop. This would never end. I'd presumed Matteo's yearning was for Antonio, but it was for so much more. His children, their future, seeking answers I could not give to questions he didn't even know to ask.

I listened to the song rising from the chart. "I sense no danger. Nothing immediate."

Matteo's gaze grew wistful. "Whatever connection his mother and I made with his creation, I sense she's providing him love and nurture, sense whatever his living arrangement, it is satisfactory. But the Careri are not us, and they are less like us every day. Their star is slipping, my child's voice grows distant, and if Ignazio presents him any threat, his mother may not perceive it."

We always think we have time. For one more conversation, one more argument, one more chance to say, "It's all right." Or "I understand." Or "I love you." So very connected to each other, it never occurs to imagine the day that connection ends.

We'd lost Dante and Ilario. We'd adjusted our orbits, corrected our courses and continued, certain that time would be the last time, and since it had already happened, it could not happen again. Then we'd lost Antonio. "Someday this vendetta will end."

Matteo's head snapped up, expression keen. "When?"

"When the time is right."

"What else can you tell me?"

Not enough, not ever. Not much more than I already had. Matteo's answers did not reside in charts and plots. Not the answers he needed to hear. Of love and loyalty, caring and consideration. Of sacrifice and soul-searching, of putting aside our own small concerns for the sake of concerns which are larger.

Matteo was figuring things out but understood nothing. And the man who could explain was down the hall, not thirty steps away, his tongue untethered by the chain the Deep Lore commanded of me.

Thirty steps and all could be clear, yet Matteo, the man with all the words, could not find enough to ask.

"Fine, I'll poke around." I straightened my cowl. "You're coming with me."

It's not Midsummer unless everybody's fighting.

Matteo started out brilliant. Strong and stalwart and determined. "I am Heir, sir, by misfortune if not by design. If there is some truth by which Ignazio holds sway, I must know, must plan, must find some way to safeguard my child."

"Keep your face forward, your heart on what you have, not what you've lost. We continue our course, and that which is most important will follow."

"They do not follow. They chase. From a sound sleep, in the middle of a busy day, in moments of quiet contemplation. Unexpected, unbidden, rising from a well I fear will one day swamp my children. We must do as Antonio wanted, settle this vendetta, find a path to goodwill. Whatever this fight's source, we must find its finish. Until we do, my child is in danger."

We grow older, we grow softer, more robust in our illusions, more fragile in our truths. Our griefs become more bitter, our joys fuller and more rare. Like Dante's and Ilario's puzzles, each piece depends on the other, and when the lynchpin fails, expectations collapse.

Father and Matteo railed on, one after the other, rehashing every hurt, every slight, every bit of rebellion or bull-headed authoritarianism.

I looked at the door, sorry I'd thought this a good idea and lonesome for Mamma's gentle intervention.

Luciana arrived, her light sweeping away the shadows. "Stop it. All of you. Midsummer approaches and you're scaring the children."

Matteo looked out the window of Father's office, the largest, the most impressive, the window from which Father surveyed the entire *ducato*. The sun dipped to the horizon. Matteo left.

And Father kicked me out.

For what reasons did we war?

For ego, for missteps, for fear, for loathing. Of ourselves, not the other. Of what is, not what might be. And all the while, you think you'll have time, one more opportunity, to get it cleared.

Toward the end of Midsummer, I returned to Father's office, buoyed by the birth of Matteo's third, confident in my convictions and determined to convince Father. That it was time to end the vendetta, to face Ignazio, to explain to Matteo. We needed to plot a new course, do all those things which should have been done at first and must now be done at last.

I entered without knocking, pursued by a persistent rumbling, of earth shifting under my feet, into a space filled with stacks and sacks, mounds and molehills, and all of them arrayed near the fire.

And Father, feeding the flames, casting one document, then another, movements frenzied.

He reached for another parchment, a star chart, one I recognized. He took a moment, eyes widening in what I presumed to be surprise, then broke the seal and unrolled it, his gaze studious and steady. He ran a finger over one pathway, then another, all the possibilities, but the stars would not light under his fingertips.

Compassion, whole and helpless took hold of my heart and squeezed. I cleared my throat.

Father looked up and I had the impression he was glad to see me. "Lately I doubt my path, regret I was too rigid, too sure. A softer course might have saved Antonio, made Matteo feel more secure."

Claudio

He rattled the scroll. "Antonio's chart. I thought you'd placed this in the archives."

So did I. "Let me interpret it for you." With joy, with sorrow. With deep examination of how we'd arrived at this pass. "Perhaps after we can discuss how much we should tell Matteo."

Father nodded. To this day, I wish I'd waited my second statement until I got a response to my first. Because a nod is not permission if I do not know to which it refers. And I could not get clarity at that moment because the rumbling, present through the recent miseries, increased, near shaking me from my shoes. Then the chart dropped from Father's fingers, the gentle green glow of Father's amulet went dark and Father slumped over the pile in his lap.

The rumbling ceased. The ground grew still.

The nettle nearest Father began to brown, the wolf's bane to howl. Father's spirit rose over the ashes and the man who all had known as Bartomeo, Duca of Panduri, launched his spirit skyward and blew away on the breeze.

Taking Matteo's answers with him.

Antonio

Seventeen

The Midsummer I took my brothers exploring, Father brought us back. He made the long climb to the cliff edge, our irons his guide, then followed our trail down, all the way to a friendly farm. "The fighting is over, Antonio. Time to come home."

I didn't want to come home, none of us did. We'd eaten porridge from a bowl freshly-steaming on the farmer's stoop, fresh cream from the barn. We'd filled our pockets with apples, then faced the waves under a sun-filled sky that hid our presence, and listened to the salty tales of sea creatures.

"Please let us stay." We dug our toes deep into the sand, curious and hopeful. We showed Father the apples, small and succulent and bursting with life. "Please let us explore more."

Father made us empty our pockets, then clasped my shoulders, his music jagged and worried. "You must stop listening to your uncle's fancies. You are Heir. That is decided. Outside you are a wisp, a breath, a shade, the reason the farmer's children have nightmares."

"The maestro can see us. So can his daughter."

"His mother was born Inside. That's why he visits, why he's decided to stay."

Because Inside is better.

I still swiped an apple. Dante and Ilario swiped the rest.

Father joined me for his castoff. We stood helplessly by while my brothers and sister struggled to make sense of what had happened. Claudio dug through Father's cabinets, considering, rejecting, his movements frenzied. He talked to Matteo, cowering with his bottle in the doorway. "The people are gathering. Tell me what we should cast off with Father."

"His disappointment in me."

Luciana snagged Matteo's bottle and emptied it into the sparring ficus. "Ignazio's arrived. Go out there and handle him."

Matteo pulled a flask from his pocket. "Handle what?"

"His petition. He's brought Niccoli with him and plenty of consideration to convince the *signori* it's time Panduri chose a new Duca."

"Let him. None of this is mine anyway. It belongs to Antonio. It's always belonged to Antonio. I'm a beggar at the door, a thief in the shadows, sad and sorrowful and . . . and. . . ." Matteo's voice fell to a mumble. He rummaged through his pockets, checked a couple of shelves, like he was searching out an S-word to finish his sentence.

Luciana snapped her fingers and lit a flare. "Don't be ridiculous. The people don't care who is Duca, only that somebody is."

She knocked the flask from Matteo's hand, went to Claudio and flung back his cowl. "Stop all that rummaging. Counsel him."

Claudio tugged his cowl back up over his head. "Matteo, listen to Luciana."

"Shut up." Matteo retrieved the flask, crawling on all fours to find it. He took a pull, then slumped against the jamb, resting forehead to palm. "Holy crap, Antonio. Why'd you have to go off and die?"

I felt those words like a slap. My scar, jagged along my cheek, throbbed, not like it would had I been alive, but deeper, more impossible, with the low ache of a pain that can never be excised. At my side, Father sighed, the sound whistley and thin, a wind blowing in from a great distance. He touched my wounds, pale and see-through under my shirt, his finger lingering over the worst, the one closest to my heart. "I shouldn't have placed the *folletti*."

Father had placed them as a buffer—to catch Panduri's children should they cross. A last desperate effort. Because those apples we'd swiped were unexpected. They were unknown and unknowable in our world, fomenting a curiosity Panduri was unaccustomed to accommodate, and Dante and Ilario passed out all they had. Soon every child worked puzzles, every child posed questions, every child posited quandaries, plagued with the unquenchable thirst to know. "Can we go there? Can we see it? Can we touch it? Can we bring it back here?"

I embraced Father, embraced his dejection. I conjured every memory I'd ever had of how his shoulders felt under my arms, willed them to give his shadow substance. "The children would not stop. The Careri would not help. You had no way to know what would result."

The men built walls the children breached. The women cast spells the children ignored. Every dictum Giacomo issued, Matteo overspoke. Every lockweed Father planted, Dante and Ilario picked. Sorrowful songs swelled across our landscape, and Claudio crawled into corners, hands over his ears.

Ignazio, mellifluous and motivated, rewarded the *folletti* with fresh cream and sweets, soft rains and fair skies, earning considerable consideration each time he enticed the little imps to give a child back. But *folletti* are wild, unbeholden by our rules. In time, the seeds Father planted failed to constrict them, the stars Giacomo cast failed to control their course.

At the last, Father placed the Protectors, Panduri's last bulwark, our buffer to the buffer. Not to keep the Careri out, to keep the children in, and the *folletti*, like so many good intentions, became a power unto themselves, a history lost to our forgetfulness, replaced with another less likely to raise questions.

Of why we'd placed the *folletti* in the first place, of why my brothers and I tried to leave at all. Of an Upheaval Greater than the First, the earthquake which preceded it, the dissonance and discord and harsh words that followed. The many trills and flourishes it seemed better to quash, the qualms and misgivings it seemed prudent to cast off. The melody of that time was altered, with intention and by consent, then replayed until it rang true, and the details of what actually happened were replaced, by necessity, with an agreeable fiction. "We should have told Matteo."

Matteo hoisted himself off the floor. "Should have told me what?"

Claudio and Luciana looked at each other, their confusion evident in a blankness of thought following Matteo's question. Father looked surprised. "Can he hear us?"

"He still wears my amulet." Never far from his heart. "Claudio does, too."

And I perceive them, every thought, every emotion, sometimes even when I've blocked them out.

Matteo flicked at his ear. "That's Antonio's fiddle." His face brightened. "Maybe I can't be Duca. Maybe I'm going mad."

Luciana pulled a pen from Matteo's pocket. "You are not going mad. You are going to be Duca. Because you're going to make a declaration. Spell it out so all can see. Proclaim to the people, let all who witness know, you are Matteo, the Duca-who-now-is and your place will always be with Panduri. Do it now, do it with gusto, or cease to call me *sister*."

Matteo took the pen, Luciana's light dawning his features. "You have a lilt I've never noticed."

"And a left hook you can only imagine." Luciana balled her fist. She reclaimed the flask, and shook it inches from his nose.

To his credit, Matteo didn't flinch. Not much. He also didn't try to get back the flask. He turned to Claudio. "And you agree."

"A few hours of circumspect behavior from you is all we ask. Then you and I and Luciana can get as drunk as you want."

"Together."

Claudio crossed his heart. "Promise."

Ignazio's voice wafted in from the Gathering Glade, supercilious and strong. "A day of sorrow, of ending. Surely we cannot continue until the matter of the succession is settled."

Beside me, Father's shadow stiffened. "Do you think Niccoli perceives Ruggiero?"

I think Niccoli spends a lot of time seeking the same kind of answers Matteo sought.

Matteo drew himself up. He ventured further into Father's office, rifled through hedgerows and boxwoods, poked in cubbies and knotholes, until he found the right parchment, substantial and smooth, of the kind he favored for casting charts. He waved the pen at our brother and sister. "Out of here, both of you. Let me think."

Matteo dipped his nib to the inkwell, panic pooling in every pore. He struck his knuckles to his kneecap, one at a time and in succession left to right and back again, and I knew he was counting meter, deciding stresses. He played with the parchment, folding it this way, then that, caught up in the emotional whirlpool of the living.

In the Gathering Glade, persuasion took the center. Luciana's, then Ursicio's, Claudio's above all. Seeking calm, seeking support, seeking to keep our constellation together.

I played a tune, running fingers over an imaginary fret. I'd learned it sometimes helped.

It didn't. Matteo finished his folding and twirled the construct across the room like a maple seed caught in a gale. The ground rumbled.

I jostled Father's shade. "He's doubtful."

"He's drunk." Father floated by Matteo's elbow, laid an unformed hand on Matteo's shoulder. He whispered into Matteo's ear, his music a delicate crackle. "Think of green gardens growing. Think of your children playing among the blooms. Think of those times that were good, and find a way to think well of me."

Matteo sat straighter, looked skyward. "I do not hate you, Father. Neither do I love. Not now, maybe someday. Until then, I will set my emotion to poetry and commend you to the spheres. For Claudio's sake, for Luciana's. Then will I seal this room, along with our sorrows. Journey well."

He dug for another parchment, finer and smoother and stronger than the first, and wrote. Father and I leaned over his shoulder to see.

So did Giacomo. As always. My constant and ever-present reminder of my failings. He read: "*In hopeless circles, the past lies. The soul grieves deep in stalwart guise. Within the heart's slow, steady beat, is found the bitter and the sweet.*"

Giacomo dug an ephemeral elbow into Father's rib. "Very nice."

"Yours was nicer."

"He looked up to me. But that comment about sealing the office. Impossible." Giacomo smacked his forehead. "A *duca* must always occupy this office."

"A *duca* will." Father clapped him on the back. "No complaining. This is all your fault."

Because Giacomo started the fighting, about boundaries and birthrights, the roles we were born to, those we were not. He wailed and he hollered. Stars fell from the sky. Our planets grew shaky, our orbits warped.

Dante and Ilario tired of it. They decided to go exploring. "Not forever, nor always."

Just until the fighting ended, until our stars returned to their places. So Dante and Ilario spiraled their curiosity to the cosmos, lassoed the moon and set sail across the sky. The last we saw of them were as pinpricks on the horizon. We wished them fair winds and farewell, to explore where we didn't, to see what we hadn't, to experience what we couldn't. And all without mention they'd been with us at all, their existence stricken from memory, their star charts, then a garden, our only and very private proof Dante and Ilario ever had a place in Panduri.

Or so Matteo wrote out for Father's castoff, not for speaking or reading, but only for himself, because Father had asked him to remember what was good, though Matteo was unaware. And Dante and Ilario, though they'd left us, had been good.

Matteo threw down his pen, grabbed up the parchment, and ran for the door, a man who'd found his words, his purpose, his place. A man who'd become what he'd always sought. . . .

Giacomo lifted an eyebrow. "Legendary?"

"Enough." I took my place at Father's side. Finally. Finally. I had a protector who could buffer Uncle Giacomo. "We are family. For better or worse. Now we must be for Matteo. For Panduri."

I glanced from one to the other and hoped I projected resolve. "We'll work together."

A cheer rose in the glade. The people. Happy to see their Duca. Then Matteo, rising over all. "As our kind negotiator has already stated, this has been a trying time, a time of sorrow. Thank you, Ignazio, for your heartfelt concerns. Always Panduri's path lies at your center. Let us cast off those worries, secure that our course is clear."

I watched him from Father's window. The tallest, the most impressive, from which Father had surveyed the entire *ducato*. Matteo stood strong, arms outstretched, making calming movements with his hands. The clouds cleared, the sun strengthened. Matteo's turn had finally come.

I reached for Father, wishing to share this moment. Father held back, so did Giacomo, fingers to lips, heads tilted, concentration intent.

Matteo's voice again rose over the hubbub. "We are not at an end, we are at an edge, a crossing to a new beginning, a fresh course. Ursicio, beloved brother-in-law, Panduri thanks you for your service and restores you to the bosom of your family. Salvatore, son of the *ducato*'s parchment maker and known to all, shall succeed you as Legendary Protector. My gift to the *ducato*, and to its future, will be enough consideration for our Faithful Finder to retrieve his place among Panduri's noble lords."

The crowd again cheered. Giacomo made a series of clicking noises, like tumblers falling into place. "He's good at this."

"And Ignazio, your constant dedication to our cause, to keeping the *folletti* constrained, keeping Panduri's course clear, to you will go a special title which I now declare to be true, for you and your heirs forever, Panduri's Wise and Constant Counselor. May your skills forever smooth the path before us."

I turned to Father. "With Ignazio as Counselor, Tendi as her Gentle Guardian, what is Claudio to do now?"

"What he's been doing. Everything. As Matteo well knows, having a title is not required to perform the office."

Not every arrow aimed is true, nor every landing mortal. Father's gibe struck close enough. And it stung. "I meant no harm, no hurt." I was young. Desperate. "I had no idea what would result."

"That time is finished," Father's voice grew reedy, his spirit wraith-like. "Those memories belong in the past."

An awful certainty vibrated under my fingers, a diminished chord, acrid and bleak. "You can't leave. You don't know how it's been. There's only Giacomo and he fights all I do."

"I miss your mother."

I missed her, too, that willowy memory my heart never quite let be replaced by the mother Panduri's needs decreed. Given the choice, I'd be with her now, except . . . "If not for me, stay for Matteo. For Claudio."

Father sighed, dry as dead leaves. "What either lacks, the other will provide. My presence will only slow their progress."

Outsiders bury their secrets with their bodies. Insiders cast them off. I still carried mine; all I'd left were the questions. Sometimes, when Giacomo finally leaves me, sometimes, while the living sleep, I retreat to the shadows and ponder the starkness of my unintended crossroads, weigh what other paths we might have coursed, what other stars we might have followed.

Father tapped a spectral finger to my elbow. "You can come with me. Giacomo, too. Let us leave all to their fortunes and find our places among the spheres."

Giacomo laughed at the invitation.

And I showed Father where I'd hung my bow. "I made Matteo a

promise. Words and music, always together. Then I claimed Matteo's stars, and also claimed his purpose. I can't continue my course until I make things right."

I'd hoped Father would understand, hoped he'd champion my position. But his shade had already thinned, his need for absolution fading, his spirit near ready to ascend. He'd seen my brothers and sister unite in mutual support, seen Matteo make a successful crossing, seen him push back on Ignazio, take the mantle of Duca. Father had done his duty as best he was able, by us, by Panduri. He'd earned the right to do as he pleased.

Still, I tried. "Stay."

Father shook his head. "The living's need for the dead exceeds the dead's need for the living."

"What about the dead's need for the dead?"

But Father was already gone. Leaving me no trail to follow, no trace to hold onto.

And leaving me with Giacomo.

Eighteen

$\digamma$or what reasons did we war?

Claudio always explained it best. "Because people do stupid things, at stupid times, with stupid consequences."

"Yeah?" Matteo handed Claudio a journal, bigger and thicker and more impressive than the one Claudio had handed to him, the leather engraved with grace notes, the hinges plated in star shine. "Write it down. Every complaint, every grievance, every frustration your Deep Lore dictates you endure. Lock it in a box. Bury it by the pixies. Give the key to somebody who cares."

Some things don't change, although Matteo's work in the garden that first spring after Father's passing was commendable.

Still, Claudio grumbled. He tucked the journal into his cloak, then looked to the spot the stump's memory left bare. "It's ridiculous to send Salvatore all the way to Careri to find a tree."

"Not a tree, a fruit. For the seeds. From that Papist legend Antonio told us, the apples that grew in the Great Garden at the origins of the stars. Ceres wants to try and grow her own."

The blood drained from Claudio's face. "How do you know Careri has such a tree?"

"We had such a tree. Before Antonio chopped it down. Why wouldn't Careri?" Matteo flicked a finger under Claudio's nose. "Don't look so worried. Ceres isn't planning to bake pies with the produce. She thinks the knowledge the fruit conveys will grow us a window onto how Careri thinks, their needs. Aid us in our negotiations. I don't understand your consternation. You told me yourself, 'peace is its own reward.'"

"Since when do you listen to me?"

"Since I need an ally with the *signori*."

"Talk to Ignazio. He's your Counselor. Wise. Constant."

"And expensive." Matteo put a fine point on the prickly pears. "I'm not letting Ignazio anywhere near the Careri. Ursicio's resourceful, he can deal with them."

"You brought Ursicio back from the border."

"To keep an eye on Ignazio." Matteo grew thoughtful. "Look, there's nothing complex here. We'll talk to the Careri. We'll make nice. We'll convince them to help us clear those damned *folletti* from the valley. Then we'll go back to making pasta together."

"We never made pasta together."

"We'll start."

Claudio sunk deeper into his cloak. "This is stupid."

Matteo stopped his pruning. "Making peace with one's enemy is not stupid."

"You don't even know why we're fighting."

"Borders. Birthrights. Trade brands. Who the hell cares?"

"Maybe the Careri do."

"Maybe they don't." Matteo put down his pruning shears. "I'm ending this vendetta, with or without your support. The *folletti* are quiet for the moment, but the day will come when Careri will offer them something we can't, some treat from the Outside impossible for us to counter."

Matteo pulled a parchment and plenty of planets from a sack

resting against a croaking toadflax. He apologized to the flax for the disturbance, then laid the parchment on the ground, tossed the planets onto its surface, and followed with a generous sprinkling of stars.

He waved Claudio over to his work. "What do you see?"

Claudio traced, first one path, then the other, the stars singing under his fingertips in a way the Papists could never imagine with their Hanging Jesus and sepulchral teaching. "I see the possibility."

"More than a possibility. This vendetta has run its course." Matteo unrolled a second chart, then a third. "Look here. And here." He pointed to one declension, then another, all coursing toward synastry from what I could tell. "Been casting charts on this for weeks; all come up the same. And it's the damndest thing."

"What is?"

"I can't find this vendetta's start. It's like the entire conflict sprang from the ether. I see no reason we can't follow these casts and find its finish." He peeked under Claudio's cowl. "If you keep up with that face, it's going to freeze that way."

A single qualm, then a second, stuttered across Claudio's underpinnings, bouncing from one point of uncertainty to another. Support Matteo? Deflect him? He glanced to his feet, and I felt his trepidation that memory of the Upheavals might be enough to agitate the Deep Lore and again set the ground shifting.

Claudio pushed the charts aside. "The Careri are nothing like us, however they might appear. They've been apart too long. They do not remember the old laws."

"You'll remind them. The maestro can help. You should be thrilled. You're getting your old job back. This moment it is declared, Claudio again heads his order as Panduri's Gentle Guardian."

Claudio flung back his hood. "You're releasing Tendi from his vows."

"Releasing him? Are you mad? I need Tendi here to assist in negotiations." Matteo rolled the scrolls and stuffed them back into the sack. He arranged them and rearranged them but they wouldn't return to the neatly packed bundle they'd been. "Is he any good with filing?"

Claudio made a strangled sound like chokeweed hung up in his crotch.

I saw Matteo review his question and realize how it sounded. "Only when he's not negotiating. Tendi calms things, brings order from chaos. You should see my study. I'm half-buried and it's only getting worse. The secretaries are driving me to distraction, always with questions and appointments. They want me to move to Father's office. Tell me I'll have more room. And the *signori* are like goats, nibbling at my time."

He flicked one hand, then the other. "This one wants a moment, that one a minute. They think I should be in Father's office, too. The only time I get privacy is when I'm fucking my wife. Even then, I'm so frazzled I've no idea if I'm coming or going."

Claudio peered at him, his brows scrunched toward their middles, his eyes squinched at their corners. "Matteo, Father doesn't have an office anymore. Father's dead. That office is yours, meant for the *duca*. People want you to move there because that's where the *duca* is supposed to be."

Matteo scratched at his jaw. "Who says?"

"The Deep Lore."

"You mean . . . all the time?"

"Of course not. You have to sleep, to eat. Play with your children, go for walks. But when you're needed, you're supposed to be in that office, to be in Panduri, because Panduri without its *duca* is just another star shining in the night sky."

Matteo's gaze went distant. "Shit. I thought using it to store all of Father's crap would be enough. No wonder Antonio kept trying to hand me the job. Well screw him and damn the Deep Lore. I'll make a declaration that this Duca can do as he pleases."

"I don't think that declaration would hold. The Deep Lore is pretty deep."

"I'm a poet. I can be deep, too."

"You need to survey the *ducato*. That office has the best windows."

"Does it?" Matteo retrieved his pruning shears. "Do you remember

165

how much time Antonio took deciding where to grow this garden? The measurements, how carefully he placed each object, planted each plant, directed each sightline?"

I, who now experienced even the brightest sunshine under shadow, felt the shadow that crossed Claudio's soul, so chill I couldn't decide if it sprang from confusion or comprehension.

Matteo tapped Claudio's shoulder with the tip of his shears. "Ah, something Panduri's cleric may not know. Amazing. Perhaps that cowl prevents you from seeing past your nose."

He flicked his head toward the mansion, every limb line of its sprawling canopy clear in the slanted light of the waning day. "See, there's my room, yours, Antonio's. Luciana's bower. Mamma's." Matteo pointed his shears window to window, a conductor leading his orchestra through the score.

He stopped pointing and went to work on the insufferable bullheads, using the shears to coax the blooms back into place. "Remember when we all shared our space? Before we grew the wall-flowers because we thought we wanted to be alone."

Before Dante and Ilario left us, he meant. Before being with those still here became unbearable because of those who were missing.

Matteo tugged at his ear. "Giacomo told me what's missing is sometimes more important than what's there. He told me that was the secret to Dante's and Ilario's puzzles, to remember, that someday the information might be needed."

Claudio gazed at the mansion, at leaves greening with spring, and vines crawling along the trunks. Then I saw it, that wondrous way his face relaxes when he works something out. How his music rings true and the light of knowledge comes up in his eyes. "Father's windows are not there."

He dodged and weaved, angling from one vantage to another, backward and forward, corner to corner. "Father's windows aren't anywhere."

"Exactly. For all their tallness and impressiveness, there's one tiny portion of the *ducato* the windows in Father's office do not survey.

This garden. I've had plenty of time to think this through since Father left us. Plenty of time to ponder the reasons for why things are. There's plenty of wrongs need righting, plenty of stars on a tilt. I've been poking and prodding and charting and plotting, and guess what hasn't happened in all that time?"

The wary look in Claudio's eye returned. "What?"

"The ground hasn't rumbled, the rocks haven't moved. For better or ill, Panduri is in her proper place and I intend to make the most of it."

He sat back on his heels, surveyed the garden, an air of satisfaction settling on his shoulders. "If a man with no talent in gardening can turn his thumb green, then a *duca* with reason to know can learn the things he does not. About Careri, about the vendetta, about why we fight, why we don't. I am Duca, I am Panduri, and I declare now, that which is not bound by the Deep Lore is free for my taking, that which is not bound by your vows belongs to me. I want to know what happened to my brothers, want to know why my uncle despaired. I want you to find their charts. I want your help interpreting them."

He again returned to his pruning. "And I want to talk to Salvatore."

Matteo didn't see Salvatore just then. Salvatore was at the border. Matteo sent for Salvatore, but Claudio counseled with Ursicio and together they made damned sure Salvatore had good reason why he couldn't return. Matteo's urgency dulled under the myriad other items he had to attend.

Somewhere in that myriad, probably to prevent Matteo from heading to the archives and turning everybody's stars on their ears, Claudio dug out the charts no longer locked down by Father's spells, the Deep Lore, or discretion. The charts archived in Dante's and Ilario's slots. No other. Matteo's disappointment filled the well again gathering around him.

Giacomo's shade poked his head through the wall of Father's office. "Those charts won't fool him. Matteo already knows they're fake."

"Matteo doesn't remember."

"Someday he will."

Not that day. We watched Matteo unroll the charts on his desk, watched him trace the stars, one path then the other, all the possibilities.

I took a place close to my brother. The charts were good. And clear. I looked at Giacomo. "Whose are they?"

"A set of twins born the same day as Dante and Ilario, sons of a farmer whom Matteo has never met."

"A farmer." Parentage cannot be changed. "That was chancy."

"All I had to do was obscure their origins. Your father and I decided to take the risk. Matteo's spirit grew dark, his words sparse. You were all desperate to know how Dante and Ilario fared and we couldn't be sure of their fate. So . . . poof! As long as those twins live, so do Dante and Ilario."

Giacomo came all the way through the wall and looked at his boots, at the remembered candies and treats overspilling their tops. The better for throwing to the crowds. "I didn't mean for what happened to happen. Matteo surprised me that day in the garden. I thought you were all gone. I thought I was alone."

"So you perused their real charts."

"Matteo saw me." Giacomo looked at the pixies. "I loved them, you know. I loved their garden, too."

"You had a hell of a way of showing it."

"You fixed it, at least for that moment."

By cutting down the tree. "Then I ran and it all went bad, anyway."

"Your father tried to fix that, too, tried to replot what I'd done while you meandered among the Outsiders. But star casts were never his talent. Your father gave up, hid all our charts, then sought to distract Matteo by convincing him to retrieve you."

I hadn't "meandered" and I wasn't about to discuss my sojourns with Giacomo. "Until I saw him there with Matteo's son, I didn't think Father cared about the garden."

"Who convinced Matteo's tree to grow? Who kept things green

Antonio

during your interminable and childish absences?" Giacomo indicated the window of Matteo's study, and the garden clearly visible
beyond. "That was petty of you."

It is hard to get emotional in my current state. When the heart's
beat leaves the body, the pulse by which the spirit lives goes with
it. Gone are the ups and downs, the rights and wrongs. There is no
flutter to make a discovery, no despair to be proved wrong. Extremes
disappear without the blood rush of love or loss, rage or joy.

Giacomo is unpleasant, but he is not intolerable. To see Claudio
worry is uncomfortable, but not compelling. Matteo's swings, happiness to dejection, are of interest to watch, but the frustration they
engender is a thing of memory, one I have to conjure when I try to
understand. "I was not being petty."

Claudio stayed while Matteo studied the charts. Day turned to
night. Matteo stretched, his frustration flexing until I heard every
joint in his back crack. "These are not right. I worked backward from
the last point of which we can be certain, the day they left us. Their
origins are obscured."

Giacomo popped his head back through the wall, hope feathering
from his epaulets. "Show him." His words exited slithery and sly and
snuck their way right up Matteo's nose.

Matteo sneezed, then showed Claudio where he meant. "I need
to compare Dante's and Ilario's charts to others in the family—
Antonio's or Mamma's—to see where those planets converge."

I remember little about dread, but I saw it creep up Claudio's craw.
"I have no authority to offer any other chart to you. Not today, not
tomorrow. Whether I want to or not. Whether it would be better for
you to see it or not."

"Claudio, what can it matter?"

"Neither do I have the authority to explain why. We live our lives
by the Deep Lore, whether we accept it or not, and that is how it is,
be you Duca or no."

They railed at each other, into the night and into the next day.
Matteo coming at Claudio from one angle, then the next, and always

Claudio answering in that same, sullen way— "I cannot offer any other chart to you." —until the repetition rendered the phrase meaningless, and Matteo failed to grasp the clue hiding within.

I glanced at my wounds, traced the cuts and bruises left to fester, glowing in the harsh light of truth, with no way to make Matteo watch his words, no way to release Claudio from mine.

No way to warn them, if they persisted. No way to make sure they understood—fuck with the Deep Lore, the Deep Lore fucks back.

After all the hollering and hand waving was done, after Matteo got drunk and Claudio got drunker, both woke, hung over and grouchy, their fight forgotten in the greater concerns—the first overtures to the Careri, the increased fracases with the *folletti*, the charts still to be cast, grain to be ripened, weather to be mapped, and rainbows to be polished—the dailyness that made up the life of the *ducato*.

Claudio returned to his work and his worry, Matteo to his ever-present duty to keep Panduri on her course. Giacomo watched his opportunity drain away, then made daisy chains from the dregs and dragged them down the hall to Father's office.

Ceres followed him, Topo in her arms, stopping at Father's door. She could not pass through without opening them. She could not open them because Matteo had ordered them sealed.

"Leave him be," she said to the vine-twined wood. "We cast you off with the proper petitions and prayers. Be assured the memories we keep are enshrined in respect. Go in peace and let Matteo find his own way."

Matteo came to collect her. "Father is not here, Ceres."

"The Deep Lore says always a *duca* should occupy this room. The living *duca* won't, so the dead *duca* does."

"The dead *duca* doesn't. You hear a creaking in the trees."

On the other side of the door, Giacomo rattled his chains, his shadow stiffening until he became almost solid. Topo hissed, struggling in Ceres's grasp.

She let him go. "I do not hear a creaking. Look at this cat."

"Proof then that Father cannot possibly be haunting his office. Topo adored him. More than he adored Antonio." Matteo reached for Topo but the cat backed to a corner.

Matteo kissed Ceres on the cheek. "Topo is reacting to me."

Ceres returned with him down the hall. They left Topo to spit and slaver. Giacomo settled into a corner and stewed on his miscalculations.

I take my victories where I may and declare this round to me, but from the silent corners of my cold dark cage, I confess to disbelief. After all Matteo's demand for those charts. After all the talk of what is missing versus what is there. After all the possibilities. Matteo never looked to the one chart not forbidden to him by the Deep Lore or love. The one chart that would have provided Matteo the key to Dante's and Ilario's puzzles.

The one chart Claudio offered, as he always does at the ending of a life. The one chart Matteo refused, so Claudio could never offer again. One chart of several Giacomo was determined Matteo should see.

Matteo never looked at Father's.

Nineteen

The following Midsummer Giacomo came out of Father's office long enough to berate my brother's poor preparation for his task. "Did Bartomeo never explain the politics of forming friendships among the nobles?"

"Ignazio's no friend."

"All the better to keep him close. Matteo's talent is words, Ignazio's is twisting them. Matteo should be securing alliances, strengthening resolves, yet look at him among the *signori*, silent as a penitent, sitting while Ignazio stands. But for Claudio and that ragamuffin Salvatore, Matteo would never speak."

Salvatore's no ragamuffin. "He hasn't been around in months."

"Ah. Yes. Keeping him cloistered." Giacomo rocked back on his heels. "A waste of intrigue. All secrets eventually surface."

Not if you weight them with enough guilt. "Standing is difficult without the amulet. You know that." And sometimes Matteo's shin nagged at him.

"I wondered when Matteo would figure out that trick. I'm surprised Bartomeo never taught him."

I don't wonder. Removing the amulet is risky, reckless. A disconnection I'd mistaken for freedom, a drug I'd believed I could master. "Father strove to be truthful except when he couldn't."

Ignazio's voice rose above our contention. He rounded the circumstances, careful to avoid the most heated conversations, then ran a handkerchief across his forehead and turned to Matteo. "Midsummer approaches. Perhaps the *duca* could table this discussion until cooler heads prevail."

"The vendetta will end. What does it matter the season?"

"Negotiation ends nothing. It only creates new issues which must be addressed. The border is quiet, the valley is still. What do we gain from shaking the beehive?"

"You mean what do you lose."

Ignazio cocked his head. "Duca?"

Matteo stood, as I'd learned by now he hated. Not because he wasn't wearing his amulet, nor because the shadow of the snapped shin unsteadied him. Standing drew attention. Since taking on Father's role, Matteo craved solitude. Still, he stood and faced Ignazio.

Because he was Duca. "I've been through the charts, invoices new and old, the tally of consideration you've been granted for your dealings with the *folletti*. There are many ways you might serve Panduri, with your glib tongue and ability to skirt an issue." Matteo held up a pile of parchments, tied in string. "This way, I tell you now, will not continue."

Ignazio can convince any adversary he works in their interest, make any setback appear favorable. Hand him goose poop attached to thorny stems, he'll thank you and call it a bouquet. And all without tripping up his iron. His demands of Father had never been direct. Father's capitulations to Ignazio never subtle. "As you decree, Duca. We should proceed with negotiations as you deem fit."

The *signori* made murmurings of approval, gave nods of encouragement.

Giacomo groaned, the sound like branches blowing in a high

wind, creaky and ominous and over-the-top. "No good will come of this conversation. Still, our boy was magnificent."

He whisked a feathery kiss across Matteo's brow. And returned to Father's office.

Matteo dismissed the *signori*. He turned away and slipped his amulet back onto its chain. "Claudio, Ursicio. Your indulgence, if you please."

They waited while the room emptied, then until the hall cleared. Matteo leaned on a pile of filing. "Where is Tendi?"

Claudio closed the door. "Making sense of the current conundrum. Whatever Ignazio has billed for his most recent dealings with the *folletti* you should strike from the record. The little imps are in an uproar."

"No doubt Salvatore is assisting."

Ursicio upturned his palms. "It's a delicate situation."

"Make the situation less delicate. I ordered Salvatore home for the festivities."

"I do not see how that is possible, Duca. Midsummer approaches, and there are still so many matters Salvatore needs to settle."

I saw Matteo's resolve start to bend, the slightest calculation whether to impose his will or again allow himself to be handled. A vision of Father flashed in Matteo's mind's eye, an admonishment delivered on one of the Midsummers I'd refused to appear. "Nature does not hurry, yet all things are accomplished."

Unexpected. To me as well as Matteo. I don't think either of us ever thought of Father as a philosopher.

Matteo got brisk. "Your *duca* requires you help Salvatore settle all those many matters. Use your resources. Midsummer will wait."

Ursicio glanced to the window, to a sun hovering two fingers above the horizon. "The people—"

"—will wait also. The Heir is happy playing with his blocks, his father is here, eager to speak with Panduri's Protector. Take the time you need but bring Salvatore back from the border. Bring back Tendi, too." Matteo flicked his head toward the door. "Go."

Ursicio hesitated, a moment, then two, then he bowed and departed.

Matteo waited while our brother-in-law's footsteps faded down the moss-covered cobbles. He waggled a finger at Claudio. "Don't start. You tell me Salvatore cannot tell me more than he's already said. I get it. I'm calling Salvatore back because I miss him."

"Oh." Claudio's music took on a sympathetic lilt. "And Tendi? Don't tell me you miss him, too."

"I miss his filing. Being Duca is messy when the Heir is not old enough to be Heir." Matteo pulled a bottle from beneath the blooms of a *sub-rosa* bush and a couple of glasses from under its leaves.

He poured for both. "Tendi's not needed at the border. Nobody is. This vendetta is bullshit. It exists because we all go to the border and act like it does. Half of me believes the only reason Father pursued it was to let Ignazio earn consideration. Why, I cannot fathom. The other half of me doesn't care. I am Duca. When I say this vendetta is done, it is done."

"Then why delay Midsummer? Salvatore can join the dancing once he arrives."

"I'm not delaying anything. If people want to dance, they should dance. Once Mamma walked out there with Giacomo. He even wore the hat."

Claudio bit his lip. "With Antonio."

"With me. I don't know why. I was very little. Maybe Antonio was complaining. He never liked Midsummer. One time he told me, 'The people don't care. Throw a few flowers at somebody, proclaim, "Behold, the Heir." Poof! We have an Heir.'"

Matteo searched among his papers, lifting pens, moving inkwells. "Sometimes I wonder if our Deep Lore is no more than we make it. Look at the Careri, all this time paying it scant attention; still their stars orbit. Look at me, blathering on and not so much as a hiccup shivers my timbers. Or maybe the power is in the hat. Maybe that's why it's so big."

I hadn't heard Claudio laugh in a world of days. His music bounced off the canopy in a joyous euphony.

Matteo downed his drink and poured another. "I'm releasing Tendi from his vows."

Claudio blew his whiskey back into his glass. "You cannot release a man from his vows so he can file."

"Does the Deep Lore forbid it?"

"Not exactly."

"Then it's done. It's nice to be Duca." Matteo glanced from parchments to star casts, piled in molehills and mountains and every height in between. "I could move into Father's office, then I'd have more room. My wife would be pleased. She wants to turn this space into an aviary."

A tic formed at the edge of Claudio's eye. I felt him swallow.

Matteo flung himself into his chair. "But this isn't about how much room I have, or Ceres's redecorating. It's about letting Tendi choose his path. I'd pay him well to serve Panduri here, as my assistant, but if he'd prefer some other pursuit, so be it. What's important is wherever Tendi lands, it will be on his own two feet, earning his own consideration, deciding its disposition."

"Why do you think Tendi even wants those choices?"

"Everybody wants choices." Matteo sorted through a pile of scrolls. He picked up a pen.

Claudio reached a wistful finger to the bows hanging by the door. He mouthed the poem carved into Matteo's, then ran a finger over mine, humming the musical notes. "We never practice targets anymore. I mean together. Like we used to."

"Because that damned arrow of Antonio's is unsplittable." Matteo tapped the pen to his teeth. "You never play Antonio's fiddle."

"It caterwauls under my bow."

Matteo tossed his pen into a pile of pronouns. "I hate Midsummer's Eve."

A frisson of familiarity, of longing, a modicum of discontent, emotions I'd all but forgotten rose from a well I'd thought had run dry. Matteo believed Midsummer was about sex. Claudio about family and connecting. For me it was about escaping expectations, about avoiding being what people wanted to believe. I'd presumed Matteo wouldn't experience this part of it. The weight, the responsibility. Unable to celebrate, constantly watched, barred from the one thing every man desires, Inside or Outside, the freedom to determine his own course.

I don't feel much in my current state, but regret respects no boundaries.

Ceres charged through the doorway, Matteo's youngest in her arms, his second oldest hanging onto her skirt. "I just talked to Luciana. Are you crazy? This is your first Midsummer as Duca. You can't make everybody stand in that field, sweating, because you think Salvatore might tell you something about your dead brother you don't already know."

Matteo opened his mouth. I guess he thought he'd explain. Or something.

But Ceres splayed her index and middle finger and shook them inches from Matteo's nose. "Two hours. That's how long you have to decide where you want to live, the past or the present; then I take the Heir to the field and wear that damned hat myself."

She swept out, autumn leaves trailing from her skirts.

Matteo looked after her, his expression troubled. "I don't like when she talks that way in front of the children."

"Your youngest is barely on solid foods. He won't remember."

"He will when he least expects it." Matteo summoned a sprite. "Please tell Niccoli his *duca* requests cool breezes to placate the people."

He let the sprite select what she wanted from the bowl of treats he kept on his desk, then watched her dart into the stagnant sunset, her fingers sticky with taffy. "Imagine living a life so simple. Imagine being able to fly while living it. Listen to us, Claudio. Day in day out, Midsummer to Midsummer, niggling at each other over the Deep Lore. Maybe our answers lie elsewhere, maybe in the one place they've always been, with the one man we've always gone to, the one man who'd know, the one man who tells us everything."

He stood. "Come, let's go find the maestro."

Interesting how Matteo chose that moment to make that statement because in that moment, the maestro knew more than he ever had, but he'd never be able to tell Matteo. In that moment, the maestro became another piece of our past broken loose from the puzzle, stopping briefly before he spiraled into the spheres for a spectral embrace, a greeting, and for me, a goodbye.

Matteo did not sense him. Claudio did but put down the sudden racing of his heart to other worries. He made excuses for why Matteo should not visit the maestro just then but could certainly visit him later. Matteo made arguments why then was as good as later and Ceres had just granted him two unencumbered hours to go.

A different sprite arrived and the fight ended. Neither would visit the maestro. Not ever, for always. Nobody would. The maestro could never again be visited because the maestro was dead.

Matteo held off Midsummer so he and Claudio could cast off the maestro with fancies and filigrees and sunbeams to spare. He whispered to Claudio. "The maestro's daughter is not here. What should we do with his chart?"

"He has none. He was born outside. The maestro never had a place in Panduri."

That observation pinged Matteo like a sprung fiddle string. He rubbed his eye. "Of course he had a place, secure as yours or mine, a place where the Deep Lore has no dominion—our hearts."

"The Deep Lore says otherwise."

"The Deep Lore is an ass." Matteo walked off. He cast a chart for the maestro, plotting a life well-lived, a tale well-told. He asked Claudio to interpret it. "I want to know why the maestro came here. I want to know why he left what he knew to learn what he didn't."

"I don't need a chart to answer your question." Claudio threw open the shutters and waved Matteo to the scene beyond. "What do you see?"

Matteo looked. "The grain stalks are uneven and the cloud edges are ragged."

Antonio

Regret came up in Claudio's heart to see our extravagant and effusive brother reduced to administrative details. "The maestro saw a world more expansive than any he'd ever imagined. 'Outside is full of information,' he once told me. 'Housed in great libraries. Enormous tomes, sorted by topic, referenced by number, full of facts and figures and ripe for the picking, but useless because we lack the knowledge of how to make them serve our souls.'"

Matteo imagined all that knowledge splashed across parchments, imagined how he might make use of it for the betterment of Panduri. "I should bring the maestro's chart to his daughter, the moment this vendetta is settled. I should also bring her child's, the one Antonio cast. Maybe cast another chart for her."

I felt Claudio's heart pace up a notch, felt a trickle of sweat work its way under his collar. "I don't think the Outside could hold so many possibilities. Better the charts stay here, then both the maestro's daughter and her child will always have a place in Panduri."

Matteo's shoulders slumped. "Maybe she doesn't want a place here. Maybe she does not even know the maestro is gone. Perhaps she no longer feels the connection from Outside."

Matteo looked at the window, to where the sun still hovered two fingers over the horizon, as it had for days, despite his wife's threats. "Ceres wants another."

"That's why you're still delaying Midsummer. You do not share her desire."

"Don't be ridiculous. A child is a blessing. Every child." He returned to his desk, cast a cautious eye over the charts piled there. "Any child."

Giacomo swooped through the wall of Father's office, riffling Matteo's hair and scattering the star charts. He smacked my shoulder. "I told you. Didn't I tell you? One day this consideration would come due."

Always Giacomo makes more of everything than what it is, even in death, but a blossoming uneasiness tested my mettle and found it wanting.

Claudio noticed, must have felt the somber notes echoing from my misgivings. He gathered the scattered charts. His expression went solemn, the light in his eye, dark. He picked one from the flotsam, one I recognized from the day Matteo had shown it to Claudio. "You're not thinking about whether you're aligned with Ceres, not worried about whether you want another child. You're thinking about this child. That of the Careri."

Matteo swept the chart from Claudio's hand. "I'm thinking about my son. This cast, as you so eloquently explained to me, ensures his place in Panduri."

Giacomo threw back his head and bellowed.

Claudio paced, his agitation enough to churn butter. "This is why you're ending the vendetta. Not to make peace with your enemy. To connect with your child." He stopped pacing. "You want to go Outside."

"Only to Careri. Only to make sure Ignazio can't do him harm, can't wager Panduri's welfare for his well-being." Matteo bowed his head. "He's my son. I don't even know his name."

And we'd reached another edge. Had I Giacomo's ability to feel, I'd have bellowed too, dismayed the maestro had so swiftly sought his place among the spheres, distressed his daughter had not returned, jealous Matteo still felt his child's connection so keenly, and wishing, how I wished, Matteo would make an effort, any effort, to connect to me.

Matteo pushed past our brother. He grabbed my bow off its hook and headed out the door.

Claudio chased after him. "Wait. You can't go Outside. Flame. Fire. Destruction. Ash. You have to stay. Panduri needs you."

"For Papist Jesus' sake, Claudio. I'm not going Outside. I'm going to get Midsummer started. Then I'm going to practice targets."

Twenty

atteo eventually made Tendi his offer. Tendi chose to accept, much to Claudio's surprise.

Not to mine. I know what it means to pass in a role for which one is not intended.

Ignazio didn't like it. Outside the monastery's constraints, Tendi's talents expanded, calming every chaos before its amelioration was needed, straightening every path before Ignazio could twist it to his favor.

"You can't rearrange people like pieces of a puzzle," Ignazio complained to Matteo halfway through the following spring. "Does Tendi again become his family's heir? Does his brother become a protector, his marriage dissolved? He has seven children. Are they now to become bastards?"

Niccoli spoke up. "Father, no child is a bastard." Lately, he'd been hanging about. Panduri's counselor-in-training. Wise. Constant. All that.

"Indeed not." Matteo pulled out a marker and retrieved a dictionary from where he kept it by the syntaxes. "I am going to strike that word from our lexicon."

Ignazio took the marker away. "If you do, what will we call father-less children?"

Niccoli took the marker from Ignazio and returned it to Matteo. "Every child has a father. Somewhere. The other details would be for Tendi and his brother to work out."

"Fine." Ignazio shifted another pile. "The first detail Tendi should work out is attention to the proper filing of documents required for this negotiation. I can find no ley lines, no crop circles, not a single stone henge among these scrolls."

Matteo tossed the marker into a collection of semicolons. "Why do we need them?"

"The Careri have rejected our preliminary offers. They do not con-sider our trade goods lucrative."

"Star dust. Wind song. Brook babble. How can those not be con-sidered lucrative?"

Niccoli splayed his fingers before him. "Outside those are consid-ered unimportant."

Ignazio shook his head, his manner mournful, his music crafty, seeking something other than what he spoke. What he sought, I could not discern. "Our cousins have changed," he said. "The Careri no longer value consideration. They value tangibles. Objects. Things."

Matteo dropped into his chair. "I do not care how we come to this agreement, only that we do."

Ursicio, ever resourceful, piped up. "I know of a cave filled with pretty rocks that might serve, emeralds and opals and such. The gnomes sometimes pick-ax them out of the walls so the children can play with them."

"Anything, let's just get on with it. If the Careri like shiny objects, give them some of that substance the gardeners use to make stepping stones. The heavy metal that washes down the rainbows."

Claudio peeked his head from around a pile of bailiwicks. "Gold?"

"Yes. No iron, no moonbeams. Nothing that might draw them here, nothing that might light their way at night." Matteo drummed his knuckles on the desk. "Ignazio, tell me what we need to make those trades."

"Outsiders are very concerned with ownership. They want everything staked out and fenced off. It's very odd. We used to oblige them back when Insiders went Outside and Outsiders came here, used to make documents called *deeds*, others called *titles*. They're distinctive, large with substantive borders, and signatures at the end. Outsiders like to decorate them with many medallions, what they called *seals*, I suppose a way to close the matter. Theirs are melted wax—possessing no magic we could divine, but we used to affix ours with starshine, weighted with iron, a way to ensure those objects we gave them always had a place in Panduri."

Ignazio perused another shelf. "I don't think any of the documents we've found thus far can be repurposed. The Outsiders won't take them seriously."

"Why not?"

"Because our parchment is made from plant husks. They like to make their agreements on parchment derived from animal skin." He grew thoughtful. "They use the skin to make their leather, also. Instead of wood bark." ̄

The horror on Matteo's face would have made the Papists' devil cry. "How do they get the skin without harming the animal?"

"They can't, so they eat the animal."

All the sorting and searching stopped. The group grew solemn. Some looked at their shoes, others at their belts.

"Yes. Well. I told you they were odd." Ignazio shuffled through another cabinet. "I can't imagine anybody would leave dead animal skins lying about, and certainly I'm not finding any in here. They would require special filing."

His tone became cultured and cloying and brimming with good intent. "Perhaps among the files of the Duca-that-was?"

Every self-substantiating conviction giving structure to my evanescent existence went wobbly. Giacomo rose through the tree roots, blooming like fungus after a rainfall. "You shouldn't have taken my bet."

"Matteo can't go in there. He declared that office sealed." Covered over in blanket bushes, secured with tangle twine. "He'd need a powerful unmaking, and maybe a machete, to dissolve that declaration."

"His need for his child is the most powerful power there is." Giacomo spread his arms wide. "Would you like to go for double or nothing?"

I wanted to go for the days before those things I wanted Matteo to know had been eclipsed by those I did not. When the roles we'd presumed were those we assumed. When I was still alive, still hopeful, still in tune with my brothers. When we moved in symphony, each for the other, and had no reason to believe our orbits would ever cross our purposes. "Sure. I'll take that bet. Double or nothing."

Giacomo laid a finger on Claudio's shoulder and spoke into Claudio's ear. "Now is the time for Matteo to reopen Bartomeo's office."

I laid a finger on Claudio's other shoulder and whispered into his other ear. "Encourage Matteo to leave the past where it is."

Claudio all but pissed himself.

We could have saved the intrigue because Matteo went berserk, flinging invective and diatribe from the shelves. "That room is sealed and it will not be unsealed."

Claudio cleared Matteo's study. "The hour is late. Let us consider these matters tomorrow, or the next day. We have plenty of time before Midsummer. I will ask Tendi to lend his talents at the monastery. It is possible some of those documents are stored there."

Then he tried to calm down Matteo.

But Matteo was on a rampage. "Panduri's star will set before I let Ignazio set foot again in Father's office. The moon will outshine the sun before I grant him a glimpse at any of Father's star casts."

And so on.

Claudio went his way, back to the monastery to pick up a fresh set of platitudes and a stiff drink. I felt his certainty that Matteo wouldn't be poking around Father's office anytime soon.

Matteo raged until Claudio was well clear of the mansion, and he no longer had to keep hollering to cover the way his iron all but shouted any lies. He scooped the invectives and insults back into their bucket, donned a set of heavy gloves, reached into a barrel cactus, and withdrew, of all things, a machete. He hefted it, headed down the hall, and laid into Father's door with a mighty swing and a mightier declaration. "This extant and eternal seal is now extinct."

There are chord combinations resonant enough to plow a field. Matteo used his words in the same way. The twine binding the entrance snapped, the hemmingwood hedging the doorway collapsed, and the lockweeds unraveled. Father's door swung open, creaking on hinges in desperate need of oil. Matteo tossed the machete to the side and stepped past the jamb. For the first time in two Midsummers.

Giacomo stormed after, arriving with the force of a gale. He danced before Matteo, step-hop-hop, step-hop-hop, twirling on the third step-hop. He flung his arms wide and bayed, a fox on a scent.

Matteo stepped right through Giacomo's tumult, then he turned and spoke to the air. "I know you're here, Antonio. This office must always be occupied by a *duca*. That was your birthright, your charted destiny. Besides, Father's not the type to hang around. I also know you wish I'd leave well enough alone. Those seals I planted twined faster than I could ever manage."

Matteo walked right through Giacomo again and headed for the center window, the tallest, the most impressive, the one from which Father had once surveyed the entire *ducato*. He tore at the vines tangled there, but I'd grown them thick and fast in the two years since their seeding. Matteo retrieved the machete and swung it to the left, to the right.

The vines gave way. Matteo leaned out the sill and threw the machete into the twilight, then shook his fist at the rising moon. "Help me or hinder me, my life is mine to ordain, and so I declare, forever, for always, your shadow will no longer torment me. Father's secrets will no longer torture me. I am Duca, and so long as it pleases and serves Panduri, this room and all its mysteries are now beholden to me."

No high note is sustainable. The drama of Matteo's entrance quickly stuttered under the sheer volume of his task.

Invoices and agreements, trades and consideration exchanges. Marriage arrangements, mistress arrangements, heir nominations, protector assignments, and monk's tithes piled higher and deeper than seemed possible. Matteo sorted through stack after stack. "Did Father never throw anything away?"

Ceres rolled her measuring tape around her wrist. "Your desk won't fit in here. I'll find someplace else for it. You'll have to use your father's."

"Leave my desk where it is."

"It will get covered in bird droppings."

"Then hold off on the aviary."

Ceres came close and wrapped her arms around his waist. "I don't really need an aviary. I just wanted your study cleared. I thought we could move the children in there."

Matteo didn't seem to be paying attention. He held a star plot up to the light, holding it over Ceres's head to do so. "I can't figure out how Giacomo put these charts together. There's nothing straightforward in their casting. Every single one of them shifts with the circumstances, but there's no key, no notation to help decipher their angle of inclination."

Giacomo stopped poking in the grate. "Sometimes Matteo exhibits a lot less imagination than I'd hoped to engender."

Maybe Ceres thought so, too. "Why does it matter? Everybody those charts and casts concern is dead." She let go of Matteo.

Matteo put down the chart. "I heard what you said. Why do the children have to move?"

"They're plenty old to have a room to themselves. Midsummer approaches." She trailed a finger down his arm. "And, well . . . you know."

"I like keeping my children close."

"Close, yes. But they can't sleep with us forever. Someday, they'll get married, and their husbands and wives might object."

I expected Giacomo to laugh, say something crude about Matteo and Ceres's intimate details, most of which they pursued under bushes and behind hedges, but Giacomo grew serious. "She wants more."

I presumed children. Giacomo shook his head. "More of Matteo. More discussion, more walks, more sharing of what's important, one for the other."

Old pathways that were no longer possible for me to pursue, pathways I sure as hell didn't want to discuss with Giacomo. "You don't have to stay here. You got your wish, Matteo's taken over Father's office. Go get some fresh air. Midsummer approaches. You should see the figs."

I cupped my palms, the gesture suggestive. "Plump and juicy and more than you could handle."

"And miss the meteor showers when Claudio finds out what Matteo's up to? Absolutely not."

"Matteo's up to nothing. He's clearing away dried leaves. Watering the plantings. Fencing with the sparring ficus."

"Digging into fields your father meant to leave fallow."

My head began to spin. Word wars with Giacomo were ten times worse than word wars with Matteo had ever been. I needed a rest.

Giacomo would not be budged. Every cabinet Matteo entered might be the one Giacomo wanted, every cubbyhole cleared might yield the secrets Giacomo needed to be revealed. Hemmed in by birthrights and boundaries, the roles we were born to, those we were not, Matteo had my love, forever, for always. He had my trust. But like Giacomo's charts, what he lacked—and what Giacomo desperately wanted him to uncover—was the key.

Matteo seemed plenty ready to assist, so deep had grown the roots of his obsession. The drive that had Matteo inspecting every nook and combing every cranny Ignazio had so badly wanted to investigate.

Not regarding me. After his dramatic speech during the symbolic removal of the seal, Matteo didn't think about me at all. Matteo thought about his son, that of the Careri. Matteo sought the reason Ignazio appeared so determined to get into Father's office. He sought that singular, extremely damning item Matteo was certain Ignazio wanted to keep buried. The one thing Matteo worried he might someday need to use as ammunition to protect his child.

Word reached Ignazio. Perhaps a little birdie told him. A bombastic, histrionic, self-aggrandizing windbag of a birdie who flew to Ignazio in the night and whispered into his dreams. A birdie who told Ignazio the time had come to clear his course, settle his accounts, claim his rights. A birdie who didn't believe Ignazio had a course to clear, an account to settle, or a right to claim, but wanted to keep Matteo on edge. A birdie who wanted Matteo to keep digging.

Ignazio knocked, and Matteo refused to open the door, declaring through the crack in the jamb, "I'll find the deeds and titles myself." Then he dug into the documents with a renewed vigor.

I did my best to convince Claudio back to Matteo's side, visited him at his room at the monastery, the simplest, the most meditative, the room with the clerestory windows. I played long into the night, the measures crescendoing into cacophony, but Claudio slept the sleep of the exhausted. From the burdens he carried, the ones he refused to lay down. Leaving Matteo to search alone.

I retreated to my corner, dejected and defeated.

My crossing from life had been a surprise; to find Giacomo waiting, a shock; to uncover his intentions, a personal insult that made all my actions until my passing pointless. My initial salvos in this struggle were meant to settle Matteo, to move him along his course so I'd be free to find my place among the spheres and continue mine. I didn't understand Giacomo was entrenched for a siege.

The maestro used to tell me the most consistent characteristic of novelty is its rapid transition to commonplace. And so happened with Matteo and his mission in Father's office.

Daybreak to sunset passed, then sunset to dawn. Matteo sorted and piled, piled and sorted. His eyes grew grainy and his back achy. He found a deed or two and stopped to admire the medallions. A couple of titles surfaced. Matteo stopped to admire those medallions, too.

I took hope.

But Giacomo had been at this longer than I. He'd spent every moment since the Great Upheaval planning for this revelation and had devoted all his death to ensuring its execution. He'd haunted Father, hounded his every attempt to maintain the decided course. So when Matteo pulled yet another forgotten chest from the shelf and confronted yet another collection of casts and declared to the silence, "If what I seek is not among these fossils, I shall set it all to flame and go walking with my children," Giacomo let out a howl, deep and expansive and scary as shit.

A howl that echoed from one corner of Panduri to the other. A howl that gathered wind as it went. A howl that returned through Father's window, the one in the middle, most expansive, most impressive, from which Matteo could now survey the entire *ducato*.

Casts from the collection Matteo had just confronted skittered across the floor and hung up in the eaves. They blew across the hollyhocks, blocked every nook Matteo had inspected, wedged in every cranny he'd cleared.

I was jealous. I can play my music when the wind is right, but the transportation of objects is beyond my capability. Still, I thought Giacomo's ploy would backfire, thought Matteo would give up and torch it all. But I'd forgotten Matteo's deep need for organization, his delight to see every cast in its place, every chart in its cubby, the distress he suffered when stars did not align, and his desire, even amid the piles and mounds, to find a purpose in all the chaos.

Giacomo breezed past Matteo. He dropped a clump of casts at his feet. Matteo reached into the pile already scattering in Giacomo's wind, his move reflexive. He noted the seal was already broken, then looked to the notations on the scroll's edge, the signs and symbols that told him he held a birth chart, not a transactional one. He continued along the notation, as I'd learned he always did, his gaze sweeping to the end of the line, the owner's name.

Antonio, first son of Bartomeo.

Twenty-One

Two months before I chopped down Dante and Ilario's tree, Father told me those stars a man refuses to define will define him. I thought Father was talking about love because, at that time, love was all I thought about—or rather sex, fresh and fascinating, heady as flight and surely the womb from which all true music birthed.

Later, Father expounded. "Do not allow events or emotion to delineate what the Deep Lore has already engendered. Use your gifts wisely, Antonio, always mindful how attitude and actions might alter your course, and the courses of those dependent on your orbit."

Or to reduce the admonishment to an inscription succinct enough to fit on Matteo's bow: *Forsake not thy spirit, nor honor lost condone. Maintain well thy merit, by these things, thou art known.*

By then, Father had made it clear he'd been speaking of destiny, so I split Matteo's arrow, pinning his destiny to my will because by then I'd decided Father was an ass, the Deep Lore a lie, and love a precipice from which I'd never stop falling.

Death and disappointment have tempered me.

I no longer think Father is an ass.

Matteo laid out my stars on Father's desk, his music screechy and shrill. He traced one path, then another, scraped across wounds long scabbed over, his heart's cadence taking dips and twists worthy of an acrobat.

Giacomo whooped his victory. He stomped about Father's office, shaking the sparring ficus and setting the creeping nettle on edge. I retreated to a corner, unable to give the nettle comfort and certain Matteo would figure it out soon enough, certain my time on this plane would be done, certain I'd leave a failure.

But Matteo's spirit did not dawn with comprehension. He went to Father's window, the largest, the most impressive, and held the chart to the light, turning it this way, then that, his spirit confused.

"He doesn't understand." My turn to dance and stomp. Because Giacomo had cast my chart. "Matteo doesn't have the key."

Giacomo stopped stomping. He rummaged through file and shelf, tossing papers and parchments. Matteo's jaw dropped.

I imagined how this must look to my brother from his limited corporeal perspective and smacked my uncle across the shoulder. "Stop. You'll drive him mad. The key isn't here. I destroyed it the day I took down the tree, chopping it into as many pieces and burning it on the same bonfire."

Giacomo paused, the wheels in his brain click-clicking at an alarming pace. He launched out the door, sucking the air after him—

—and pushed Claudio through it.

Matteo turned on Claudio. I saw his thoughts move from the situation he did not understand, the self-propelled papers and parchments, to one he did. He rattled my chart. "You told me you burned this."

Claudio's thoughts followed a twisting and curvy trail: remonstrance he'd fallen for Matteo's melodrama, annoyance Matteo hadn't told him what he'd planned to do. Claudio had come back to the ducal mansion because he'd heard my voice, though he'd thought it a dream and couldn't conceive what it meant.

His gaze moved from pile to pile, regretting he hadn't had the courage to do this when first he'd found Father, knowing immediately what Matteo thought Claudio had burned and wishing he'd been born fourth son, maybe fifth, and some other, unnamed, unimagined sibling could be standing where he stood and facing Matteo's ire. "I didn't tell you I burned Antonio's chart. I told you Father told me to do what I thought proper, so I put it in the archives."

"Thus ensuring I'd never find it. You could lose your dick down there if it weren't attached. So how did it end up here?"

I saw the truth bubble behind Claudio's teeth, felt the pressure as it struggled to exit, that Claudio hadn't a clue how the chart had come to be in the office, only that it was there when Father died, and Claudio had left it. "What does it matter how the chart got here? It's here now."

"So are you." Matteo rolled up the chart and held it out. "Interpret this."

Claudio put his hands behind his back. "I can't."

"You are third son, Panduri's Gentle Guardian. It's your job to interpret charts."

Claudio went wobbly, his vows pulling him this way, then that, like Matteo's request for interpretation had reached out, grabbed Claudio's amulet and yanked it from its chain. His music pitched from possibility to possibility, high, then low, until he chose a refrain he could voice without offending the Deep Lore. "Not this chart. Not for you. Not ever."

Matteo gazed at the papers and parchments he'd witnessed flung from the shelves, at the casts scattered from the box. "The spirit, our heart, that which makes us who we are is like a wind, isn't it?"

Claudio calmed. His footing grew steady. "I've heard the Deep Lore describe it so."

Matteo went to stand by one of the piles. "Then it's Antonio. It's all Antonio. It's always been Antonio, because that chart is here, and you know it was there, and it's just like him to die and refuse to leave. Damned arrow is still stuck in that damned tree. My destiny will be bending to Antonio's will long after my memory has dispersed on the breezes."

Giacomo flicked a paper clip at me, which I found annoying more because he could when I couldn't than because he did.

Matteo and Claudio both looked to where the paper clip landed. Matteo picked it up. He showed Claudio. "See."

Claudio took a long and patient breath. "You think our dead brother is hanging about and tossing paper clips."

Matteo threw the clip at Claudio. "Look at this place. I'd never make a mess like this."

Claudio followed his gaze. Doubt picked at his mind. For Matteo, maybe for himself. I couldn't tell. "You didn't do this."

Matteo swept a hand over the scattered scrolls, at pages fluttering in the rafters, those caught on crannies. He nodded at the corner, the one I happened to occupy, but I think he only meant to point out a couple of parchments. "Antonio is here, I tell you. Whatever vow you made him, he means for you to break. Whatever limitations he put on you, he means for you to reconsider."

Giacomo shuffled off the upper shelves to stand beside me. "My consideration is on Matteo."

"Claudio knows his job."

"Double or nothing?"

Again with the double or nothing. "Fine."

What did it matter? In our flighty existence, double meant nothing, and nothing was all I had to lose.

Matteo again laid out my chart. He traced a random pathway, and I saw he had no idea if the star he followed ascended or descended, if the path continued or the course ended. Sadness gripped me, a welling at the hollow of my throat, an echo of the amulet I no longer carried, but which Matteo did.

His hand went to his breast, his music solemn, his confidence spent. "There must be more here. Plenty more. Maybe a chart the Deep Lore will allow you to interpret. Help me, Claudio, and we will find our answers together."

I wished I had a match. I wished I had the ability to strike one, toss it into the papers and set it all to flame.

Claudio gathered some of the documents. "Fine. I'll help you. After we get some air. Ceres tells me you've been caved up here for days. The children think this room has swallowed you whole."

"What would make them think that?"

"A yarn spinner told them."

"Does she wear a dress of buttercups?" Matteo dropped into his chair, his stance casual, his tone barbed.

I didn't think Claudio would answer. Didn't think he'd acknowledge the question at all, but longing caught at the back of his throat. Yearning tugged at his chest. "Salvatore told you."

"Didn't have to, I saw the two of you talking at Midsummer. You should have danced with her."

"She didn't know who I was."

"All the better. Sometimes I wish I could return to the time before Ceres knew who I was."

"No, you don't." Claudio tossed the documents back to the floor. "That would mean giving up your children, your life, that would mean going back to what you were, frustrated and miserable and certain all Antonio wanted was to keep you at his feet. You're trying to put me off kilter, trick me into saying what I shouldn't, reveal what I can't. I came today because you needed me. I don't know how I knew, nor why I listened, but I can't keep seeing to your happiness if you can't spare even a fraction of that care for mine."

"Fine. Leave the chart. It's very pretty, even if it's illegible. Perhaps Ceres can use it for wallpaper. I have this problem with every one of these charts which Giacomo cast. An entire generation. Does your Deep Lore absolve you of all the questions that will not be answered for fear of the answers performing your office might?"

Claudio was done being genial. His every muscle tensed and I felt the hair pick up on the back of his neck. "Do not blame me for that which Father or his Heir failed to provide."

Again, Matteo missed the clue hidden in the umbrage. "They

provided plenty. Father provided this mess. Antonio provided a bow, a fiddle, and a desk scattered with ancient consideration exchanges and a pile of truly appalling musical scores I hate worse than him because they're here and he isn't. I've got to do this all by myself, manage everything guided only by your veiled and uncertain counsel. Perhaps I should ask Ignazio. His skills may find me some way to negotiate these charts."

The air between my brothers pulsed. Claudio glanced at the box, the box Giacomo had toppled, the box from which Matteo had told Claudio my ghost had blown my chart. "Not all doors have only one key."

Matteo went alert. So did Giacomo, nose in the air, like Claudio's hood was red, and Giacomo was a wolf.

He lunged for the box. So did Matteo. I couldn't tell who did the most flinging, the living or the dead.

Claudio watched, his heart conflicted, then a song swelled in the distance. Bubbly, effervescent. Overflowing with joy.

A fresh breeze blew through the window, a different kind of wind, not dank and chill as what Giacomo blew, but warm and welcoming and smelling like spring.

Claudio grabbed our brother's arm. "Listen."

But Matteo was intent, responding to Giacomo's will.

Claudio dragged Matteo off the floor. "The people are calling for their Duca."

"No, they're not." Matteo flipped through one page, then the next. "It's not Midsummer yet."

Ursicio burst into the room. "You're supposed to be in the glade. The *signori* are gathering. Didn't you get my sprite?"

The sprite arrived just then, out of sorts and breathless. She didn't waste time with excuses for tardiness. "Tendi sends word, Duca. He got the *folletti* calmed down enough to send our offer and has received a positive reply. Ursicio adds a post-script which I'll quote to you now. 'Ignazio's a snake, but he made those colored rocks sound more valuable than honey bees.'"

The sprite helped herself to a candied marshmallow from among the treats on Father's desk and departed. Matteo went to the window. He turned to Ursicio. "That singing's for me."

Ursicio nodded. "Yes. The people are rejoicing. The Careri have accepted our offer. The vendetta is over."

Giacomo finally found what he sought among the flotsam in the box. He drifted the scores by Matteo's feet.

Not the scores Matteo had just referenced; the ones I'd left on my desk and then asked Claudio to arrange with all the other documents.

Oh no.

Giacomo drifted a different set of scores. Scores I'd sent Matteo from the border with a heartfelt request that he listen, but which Matteo had returned to me. Scores I'd talked Topo into dragging to Matteo's pillow, then convinced Topo to sleep beside, because in shock from having died, I still thought it best Matteo know the truth. Scores I'd now sink in a quagmire if I could do more than hulk ineffectually from the corners and bemoan my failures. *Those* scores.

Matteo didn't notice, treading over them on his way to the door. Which caused Giacomo to wail a misery nobody paid attention to, because they were too busy paying attention to something else.

The vendetta was over. The *signori* were gathering. The people wanted to hear their Duca speak.

Twenty-Two

The *duca* wanted to speak to everybody, the details regarding the cessation of hostilities with the Careri coming out in the breaths and heartbeats and pulses of a new dawn. Matteo left Father's office to hear them. He returned to his study and there questioned his advisors at length. "What of the *folletti*?"

"Gone." Ursicio burst closed fingers outward in a slow arc. "Without the strife, there is no reason for them to linger and the Careri will keep them well-supplied with treats in exchange for our trinkets. The Careri have offered to act as go-between for any deals we might want to make with Outside, therefore providing us the buffer the *folletti* once provided against contamination."

From the silhouette of a new horizon. From light-filled towers reaching to the heavens. From that place Matteo desperately wanted to believe Dante and Ilario had gone exploring.

Salvatore bowed. "Midsummer approaches. The draw of the Outside will be strong. Perhaps Duca should consider delaying our journey until after Midsummer departs."

"Nonsense. We have plenty of time before twilight. Or we could invite the Careri to celebrate with us."

"No, Duca." Tendi, Salvatore, and Ursicio spoke as one, their tone enough to bring every one of Matteo's exclamation points to attention.

Ursicio stepped forward. "What we mean is, perhaps we can discuss such an arrangement with the Careri once we become more accustomed to each other. As it is, we do not enter their gates. You will understand better when we get there."

Matteo went a little pale. He spoke a word to settle his punctuations and, I had the impression, his nerves, then glanced to Salvatore. "Keep an eye, Faithful Finder. We don't want to have to send you to retrieve anybody."

Giacomo got in close to Salvatore, inches from his nose. "He doesn't trust Matteo."

Neither did I. "What's he got planned?"

But the concerto had moved on and Giacomo was paying close attention to the next movement. Something to do with the colored rocks, the rubies and opals.

Niccoli explained. "The Careri plan to trade them for something called *electricity*. Lightning that travels along a metal filament. It is how Outsiders light their lamps."

Lanterns hung from the higher reaches of Matteo's study, powered by fireflies that flitted through the branches, free to pursue their own interests until nightfall. Matteo envisioned their gentle glow knotted in chains, lamp to lamp, lighting during a storm and bursting into flames. He shook himself. "Seems inefficient and dangerous."

He dug through the papers on his desk. "I found a document that dates from the time before the Great Upheaval. Plant husk, not animal skin. I could not bear to hear the spirits of the poor creatures scream. I had Claudio cast all I found to the winds with the proper laments."

He handed Ignazio a parchment, covered in medallions and ancient as dust. "This detailed the conveyance of five enchanted beans to an Outsider named Jack in exchange for his mother's milk cow. A shrewd bargain for Jack, and considering how Outsiders treat their animals, a lucky break for the cow. I've removed all words referencing both and replaced them with those which are proper for the conveyance of the gold."

Claudio leaned over Ignazio's shoulder to see. "They only want the gold, have no interest in the rainbows?"

Ignazio shook his head. "None."

"I don't understand. What do they use when they want to shine a little extra happiness on a newborn?"

"They use nothing. They don't cast birth charts anymore. They've replaced them with something called a *birth certificate*, more impressive and substantial than their deeds and titles, but lacking in destiny. Some Outsiders still cast stars, pay homage to the Deep Lore, but those practitioners are now rarified, grouped among a class known as *charlatans*."

"Charlatan." I felt the softness on Matteo's tongue. "Such a pretty word. A chatterer, one who utters silly talk. No doubt their greatest of storytellers. They must be revered." Hope flared in his soul, a wish for tales, for adventure. A wish to find out what had happened to Dante and Ilario, some notion the Careri charlatans might know.

Tendi sighed. "The Careri don't spin stories anymore. They recite histories."

My music grew plaintive. Claudio tilted an ear, like he'd picked up the refrain. "If Careri no longer pays heed to the Deep Lore, where do they seek guidance?"

Tendi put out his hands in a helpless gesture. "The Outsiders give a lot of credence to a concept called *modernity*, a faith called *science*. The Careri are much taken with those notions."

"Science." Again Matteo tasted the softness. "Another beautiful word. Like the sound a sorrowful warbler makes at the end of her song."

Consternation rose behind Claudio's inquiries, a well of misgivings moving in unquiet circles. "I do not think the *duca* should go."

All the sorting and arranging and pen scratching stopped.

Matteo clapped his hands. "Signori, to the kitchen if you will, for a meal before we depart. Everybody should pack snacks. We cannot risk eating anything the Careri might offer. Gentle Guardian, a moment please."

Unlike Giacomo, I'm no starcaster. In life, I was often unable to see past my nose. Death has taught me to recognize when a situation has become untenable. Such a situation developed while Matteo was waiting for the others to file out. I perceived it in the way he listened to their voices fade as they crossed the colonnade. How Matteo led Claudio to Father's office. The ominous cadence by which Claudio followed. The finality with which Matteo closed the door behind. "Explain yourself."

"The Careri beg for gold, not sunshine, ask for silver, not moonbeams. Blue skies don't interest them, but a hunk of lapis lazuli sets their hearts aflutter. We cannot risk Panduri to people who have forgotten what is truly valuable."

"You heard Ursicio. This is a goodwill trip, no more, and only as far as their *ducato*'s gate. So long as I don't enter Careri, I never leave Panduri."

"Then why go at all?"

"My presence assures Careri of our trust in the arrangement, the pleasantries to be exchanged a seal more impressive than any medallion. I will meet Careri's Duca face to face, then I will return." Matteo glanced to the window where the rising sun still touched a last connection to the horizon. "In plenty of time for Midsummer."

Claudio flopped into Father's chair. "All that way and you don't even see Careri."

"I will see something better, the end of this vendetta, the end of Ignazio fleecing our consideration, and the end of generations of second sons forced to hang about the border fucking sheep."

"Hang about with the Careri, we might be tempted to eat those sheep." Claudio picked up a pen and flicked it at Matteo. "I've been your brother a long time, so let us at least be honest. You want to go because you want to see your son, you want Salvatore to help you find him. That's why you all but fainted to learn nobody actually passes through their gates."

"I can find him myself. I need Salvatore to keep the others busy while I do so."

"I cannot allow it." Claudio got out of Father's chair and headed for the door.

Matteo beat him to it, blocking Claudio's path and trying to look like he wasn't blocking him. "I'm Duca."

"And I'm Gentle Guardian, beholden only to the Deep Lore, and surpass your authority in those matters which might affect it. However, in this, I'll speak to you as your brother. The risks are too great. Not for you, for your child."

"Nobody's risking anything. I just want to get a look at my son, assure myself he's all right. Nothing more." Matteo's manner was supplicant, his music sincere, and his iron silent. Because he'd crossed fingers behind his back, a trick I'd used plenty of times.

A trick that obviously fooled Claudio. He stopped trying to get past Matteo. "What will you do when you find him?"

Matteo drew Claudio close. "I'll leave him a trail."

Claudio clasped Matteo on the shoulders, held him at arm's length. "Impossible. Your son is only six Midsummers. Your effect on him could be catastrophic, Careri's effect on Panduri could be the same. Let Ursicio handle this negotiation. Send them our baubles, send them our gold, enjoy the silence of the *folletti*, then leave the Careri to their lives, leave us to ours."

Giacomo roused himself, moved a little closer. "Your brother is a kind soul, but sometimes dimwitted."

Claudio wasn't a father. He couldn't conceive of the agony at work on Matteo, the unrelenting gnawing that drove his actions.

Matteo moved to Father's desk and leaned against it. He put out his hand. "Give me your cloak. I want to show you something. Something important. About Antonio."

Curiosity crept in from Claudio's secret corners, overcoming the caution he typically took in his interactions with Matteo. The need to know what Matteo might have discovered, to know how his cloak might reveal it. Claudio shrugged the garment over his head. He handed it over, crossing Father's office to do so.

Matteo draped it over his arm. "Your cloak is heavy. Meant to hide a multitude of sins."

"And confidences."

"So it might be used for good or evil."

"As with the Deep Lore, always the intent of the cloak bends toward the good."

"All that hiding didn't help Antonio. He died."

I expected thunderclaps, expected lightning. I expected the ground to shift, forests to shudder, birds to fall from the sky.

Claudio didn't even blink. "You blame me for Antonio's death." His tone was casual, his heart in torment. Over the fiddle. And the question which rose more reliably than the sun—Why hadn't I brought it with me when I crossed?

Matteo wasn't thinking about my fiddle. "I blame your cloak. I blame the constant conflict the Deep Lore requires, choosing between what you know as a brother, what you know as a cleric. What you fear to divulge, what you fear to keep hidden. Yet, your silence is stupid. Antonio's death is a puzzle, but his reasons for crossing are clear. He didn't want to be Duca."

He shook the cloak. "I don't want to be Duca, either. Not today. Today, I just want to cross that valley, go to Careri, and meet my son."

Claudio stacked charts. He lined the edges up flush, and I saw him wishing he could stack his emotions as neatly. "You can't meet your son. You know that I'm right, and you know I can't let you."

Matteo didn't know any such thing, a certainty I felt fill his insides until there wasn't any room left. "Your cloak is mighty. Symbol of your office. Symbol of your power. Without it, you are like Luciana, or Salvatore, or any in Panduri. Without your cloak, your office does not exceed mine."

A vision of Claudio's cloakless, Papist Jesus days rose in both their mind's eye. Matteo's plan rose clear in mine.

Both my brothers beelined for the door. Matteo got there first, got it open and got out. Claudio threw himself after.

And Giacomo caught him. Grabbed Claudio out of midair, tight around the ankles and pulled him back.

Matteo pulled the door shut, then sealed Claudio in with a word. "Close."

Claudio scrambled up. He launched himself at the door. "You can't leave me here."

"You're already left. You'll find marshmallows in Father's drawers, and whiskey on the sideboard. If you need to piss, use his window, or the sparring ficus. If you get bored . . . I don't know, straighten the shelves."

"The *duca* must always be in Panduri. Must always occupy this office."

"A *duca* always *will* be in Panduri. A *duca* already *does* occupy this office. You, Claudio. Next in line should anything happen to me. So settle in. I'm invoking a silence on this doorway. What you further have to say, say now, because once I leave nobody will hear you, no matter how much you holler, until dawn next appears or I do."

Claudio rattled the handle, kicked at the jamb. "You only go to the gate. Salvatore will be keeping watch."

"Time moves differently Outside. I'll slip in quickly, get out faster. Be done with my business in the time it takes Ignazio to move from one paragraph of the negotiations to the next. Careri's orbit may be slipping, but it has not yet been captured by Outside." Memory of Matteo's Midsummer with the woman of Careri rose in Matteo's mind, her assertions of what rules still applied. "The Deep Lore may not be as binding, but the Deep Lore will still hold sway."

Claudio stopped kicking and rattling. "So will your words."

I felt bad for Claudio, hated to hear his calls. But I was little more than a concept, an idea, a collection of missed opportunities and poor choices chained by secrets I began to doubt mattered anymore. I didn't have the power to free my brother.

I didn't need to. Even if tradition named Claudio Duca in the event anything happened to Matteo. Even if Father and Giacomo had charted that possibility in Claudio's stars, the Deep Lore is a force no one should fuck with, and come dawn, whether Matteo appeared to lift his seal or not, the Deep Lore wouldn't force Claudio to stay.

But it would force Giacomo.

I think Matteo expected the crossing to be exciting and different. Certainly, he worried the valley would fill him with dread. But once the party's mounts made their descent, Matteo settled into a boredom near-numbing in its banality. Because the valley without the *folletti* was hot. The valley without the *folletti* was humid. Less colorful than it had been, half as wide as I remembered, filled with branches that did not sway on their own, leaves that needed wind to move, and paths that did not guide their way. The valley without the *folletti* was unremarkable, uninteresting, and full of midges. Because the valley without the *folletti* was just a valley.

I sat on Matteo's shoulder and took advantage of the occasional breezes. My music faded along with the birdsong, more dead than alive, like everything on the Outside.

"How do they stand it?" Matteo shifted his pack, the pack where he'd concealed Claudio's cloak, and took a drink from his bottle. Panduri water, clean and pure and invigorating in the stagnant landscape. "Even the air lacks nourishment."

"They call that component *oxygen*." Niccoli rubbed his chest. "The maestro once told us this thinning happens at the tops of tall peaks, but the phenomenon accentuates the further we ride from Panduri, though we lower our elevation."

Ignazio drew a little ahead. "Perhaps it is fortunate our Gentle Guardian chose not to join us. We did not consider the effects of such imbalance on the Deep Lore."

Salvatore let his mount fall back. "Take deep breaths. It helps."

—

The Careri's Duca was charming. He was even-tempered and polite. Older than Matteo, but not by much, shorter than Matteo by even less. His eyes were a little lighter, his locks a little straighter, but his every question was keen-edged as Matteo's. About the terms of the agreement, the particulars of the deliveries, the details of the *folletti's* new constraints. And how the *ducatos* might consider moving forward together.

Matteo admired Careri's tall stone wall, examined their gate. "Such a nice idea. No doubt borrowed from Outside. Secure. And so very private." His words struggled in the magic-poor atmosphere to outline a crack in the stone. Something discreet and temporary through which Matteo might slip.

Matteo could have saved his efforts. Careri's Duca smiled a smile disarming enough to win wars. "Might I invite you in? We still have hours before Midsummer and we've arranged a small reception, with music and song. Nothing fancy, just a token to welcome our brethren and show our delight to see our orbits again align."

Ursicio offered a polite refusal, Ignazio offered one politer still. Tendi demurred, Niccoli looked nervous, and Salvatore gave a frank shake of his head. All looked to Matteo.

"We'd be delighted," he said.

Twenty-Three

When we were young, the maestro had tried to tell us the true nature of the Outside on those twilights when Matteo spoke excitedly of all the wonders Dante and Ilario might explore. "Outsider places look interesting, but Outsider lives are boring. Filled with facts, not fun. Complaints, not delights. They remember their hurts, ignore their stars, and do not connect face to face, but through tiny plastic boxes clutched in their fists which require all their attention."

Matteo thought about that, laying a finger alongside his cheek. "What is plastic?"

Careri had no plastic that I saw. It had no televisions, nor laser pointers, nor those tall black cylinders that answer questions when you address them by name.

Salvatore was not fooled. First he made them leave their horses outside the gates, then he made them leave their snacks with the horses. "Heed the maestro's warnings. Take only memories, leave only footprints. Eat nothing, drink nothing, accept no gifts. Keep track of your baubles, give like for like, value for value, and keep your business short. Midsummer approaches and if we don't leave in time, we will be caught in the in-between."

He turned, looked in each of their faces. "Above all touch nothing made of iron. The metal will bind you here as it does in Panduri, and you would always carry a piece of this world with you."

He melted into the crowd gathered in the *piazza*.

The Careri Duca introduced Matteo and the others to one *signore*, then another. They were offered sauced plums and glazed peaches, fine wines and luscious cheeses. Matteo accepted one then the next, offering opals and rubies in return. His pockets emptied of baubles and became stuffed with the produce, the potted plants beside him grew drunk on his tippings into their roots. Still the offerings and the introductions came. Their men were handsome, their women beautiful, young, and vibrant. The air, which even in my quiet, slow-flowing state I'd thought dull upon entry, started to shimmer under their energy.

And the questions, the Careri's never-ending questions. About life in Panduri, our history with the *folletti*, how we celebrated Midsummer, what our processions were like. Did we still sing the old songs, dance the ancient dances, nourish ourselves on our stories, live in towns made of trees, and sleep unencumbered under the stars?

Ignazio answered, his responses long, his words careful to convey nothing of who we were or how we were or why, but the longer he talked, the more questions arrived. Friendly, curious, but with an edge of avarice all on the Outside seemed to hone, that need for more.

I'd long ago given up finding words to describe it.

The *duca* continued his introductions, going from least among the nobles to the first. Matteo noted the difference in dress, the lessening depth of their bows to him. I noticed a flicker of confusion the introductions should not go in the other direction. Finally the *duca* introduced him to a *signora*, beautiful in mistletoe, her gown fragile as snow flurries, her gaze reflective, like ice. "May I present my wife."

Matteo bowed, low and respectful.

She smiled at him. "A pleasure to finally meet you."

She offered a representation of a baby, crafted in linen, stuffed with plant husks, with hair of yarn and eyes made from buttons. The cloth baby wore an amulet like those of Panduri but carved of seashell. "We understand Panduri's Duca has children."

Matteo didn't understand the connection.

Tendi leaned close to Matteo. "They call that a doll. The maestro told me Outsiders consider them toys, pretend babies Outside children like to play with and feed and put to bed."

Matteo turned the doll over. "Looks like a puppet." Pinocchio popped into his mind. "But without the strings."

He held out a bauble to the *duca's* wife, his largest, his most impressive, a diamond sparkling with a thousand facets. "Perhaps as a complement to your dress."

The *duca's* wife seemed amused by the offer. She left the bauble hanging between them, unclaimed. "You have children," she repeated.

Other noble wives gathered around the party, other dolls appeared, other offerings made—to Niccoli, to Ursicio, even Ignazio—their presenters beautiful, their laughs musical, their manners yielding. The exchange bauble was always refused and always with the trailing comment. "We understand you have children."

An uncomfortable air settled about Matteo's shoulder, an itch he couldn't quite reach. The Careri Duca returned. He poured out wine, full and rich, the fragrance both foreign and familiar. "Perhaps we can come to further terms. The wires are already being laid for electricity, and our water now flows to our kitchens through pipes made of pee vee cee."

Matteo groped for a bauble. "Surely we can speak further, but we have plenty of fireflies and water already flows to our kitchens from streams the water nymphs are happy to redirect as needed." He pressed an emerald into the Careri *duca's* hand. "What is pee vee cee?"

"An Outsider material. I'm not sure of the exact composition, but I understand it's a type of plastic."

A memory of the maestro rose with the word. Matteo brought the wine to his lips, his intent to pretend to drink. He inhaled the wine's fragrance and memory of the Careri, who'd been first a woman, then a bird, took the maestro's place, along with a reminder of why Matteo had come.

The edges of the *piazza* filled with jugglers and clowns, acrobats somersaulting on tightropes, whirly-burlies playing hurdy-gurdies. All manner of crafters had set up their stalls. Weavers and papermakers, clayworkers and cobblers. Sugar lacers and glass sculptors and butterfly shapers. So like Panduri, yet their setting so different.

Matteo excused himself, desperate for air. He moved past the entertainers and into the alleys, twisting left, then right, his music growing anxious. His impressions faded, his emotions muted, like he'd wrapped them in fuzzy wool.

He found Salvatore leaning in a doorway tossing an apple.

"Thank what gods there be. You still have our snacks. I'm near faint from hunger." Matteo snagged the apple out of the air, mid-toss, and took a bite. The fruit was juicy and sweet and filled him with the will to learn all he could.

Salvatore knocked the apple from Matteo's grasp and pounded Matteo's back.

Matteo spat out the bite.

Salvatore grabbed his collar. "Keep your hands where I can see them and no crossing of your fingers behind your back. Tell me truly. Did you swallow any of that apple?"

Matteo put up his hands, fingers splayed, then pried Salvatore off his neck. He coughed. "Let me guess. You did not find that apple in my kitchen in Panduri."

"I found it on the buffet table, while the rest of you were ogling the ladies." Salvatore scooped the remainder of the apple off the street stones and pulled two others from his pocket. He showed Matteo. They were deep in color, their skin without blemish, and their fragrance . . . oh the fragrance rising in Matteo's nose. So sweet I near again felt alive.

Salvatore secured them under his cap. "These are Outsider apples, the ones Ceres keeps going on about. The apples from the knowledge-bestowing tree. The Careri must trade for them."

Delight fought with dizziness and sank Matteo to the stoop. He asked leave of a potted rose bush on his way down. "Excuse me."

Salvatore sat with him. "They don't speak to the plants here, have no awareness of their sentience. The Careri have lost the ability to feel them, the language to make them grow."

Matteo waved at the enclosures rising on all sides. "I haven't heard a bird sing, nor felt a fresh breeze since we passed under the archway. I thought it'd be simple—enter the *ducato*, pick up his trail, but there's not a glimmer, nor a shine, nothing to pull me toward him."

Salvatore didn't ask who, didn't ask what Matteo meant. "I've kept watch on this place. By order of Antonio, by order of the Duca-who-was. Your son is here."

Matteo's hackles rose, so high I half expected them to take his skin with them. Then the hackles settled. Matteo wanted information more than he wanted to be insulted that he didn't know the full extent of his Finder's duties. He stood. "Take me to him."

"I can't." Salvatore thumped a fist to the doorjamb. "The walls are too thick, the magic too thin for me to find him. Do not be worried. Your son is strong and steady, coddled and cared for, considered Careri's best hope for the future."

Surprise is an emotion I remember, but no longer understand. In my current state, new information is new information, consumed and collated and filed for future reference. But Salvatore's revelation jolted me. And so doubled its effect on Matteo. "Hope should be their most lucrative commodity. Everybody here is so young, so enthusiastic."

"So cordial, so friendly, with questions aplenty and answers few." Salvatore tapped under his eye. "Yet something is missing."

Matteo glanced about him, at houses rising stone to stone, streets paved in brick, silent, but for the hubbub rising from the *piazza*. He overlaid Panduri, the sights and smells and sounds to which he was accustomed. He imagined the people gathering for Midsummer. The young and the old, married and not. And Ceres standing with Luciana, their brood surrounding, looking into the distance and wondering when Matteo and Ursicio would return.

Alarm bells clamored and clanged in Matteo's mind. He pulled the cloth baby from his vest, examined the yarn hair, the buttoned eyes, his heart in a gallop.

Salvatore snatched it from him. "Did the Careri give you this? Who else got one?"

"Ursicio and Niccoli. Maybe Ignazio. For our children. I think they're toys."

Salvatore put his ear to the doll's chest, his face going pale. "These aren't toys, they're talismans. He thrust the cloth baby back at Matteo. "Listen."

I listened with him, at a *lub-dub* soft and steady enough to shatter illusion. Felt the rise and fall of a chest trying to draw breath.

Matteo let out a strangled cry. "Children. I see servants, and craft folk, noble people in good supply, but nowhere in Careri have I seen a child."

Above, the clouds cleared. The sun, which had seemed pegged to its place raced to its descent. The maestro's voice followed, clear in Matteo's ear. "Plastic is moldable, able to be compelled to any shape, serve almost any purpose. Its appearance is often cartoonish, and too often so authentic it is impossible to discern from what is real. Plastic rarely wears out, never decays, yet offers no nourishment, no delight to the senses. *The best I can say of plastic is plastic is useful.*"

Horror crawled over Matteo's equilibrium and took over his expression. He shoved the cloth baby back into his vest. "We have to leave."

He and Salvatore returned to the reception intent on gathering their group, but the *signori* swept Matteo back into the fray. He shook hands, exchanged pleasantries, greeted one *signora*, then another. Their responses were always interested, their welcomes always sincere.

The receiving line lengthened, the sun's height over the horizon grew short. The dread which had not visited Matteo in the valley found him. A sucking, hollowing sense of wrong that tunneled his vision, wobbled his knees, made Matteo think he lost a bit of himself with every introduction.

He got hold of Niccoli, greeting people to his side. "I feel more prisoner than guest."

Niccoli swept his gaze behind Matteo, left, then right, his music wary. "The negotiations are too easy. Their *signori* accept every offer my father makes."

He flicked his head toward Ignazio, speaking with a group near the buffet. Sweat beaded on Ignazio's forehead. He raised his glass to his lips, stopped, like he'd remembered the admonishments to abstain, then raised the glass to his lips anew, a buoy bobbing on a wave.

Of goodwill. Of friendship. And if they stayed much longer, they'd be swamped.

The bit of apple Matteo didn't realize he'd swallowed took hold, the juice he couldn't prevent from trickling down his throat took effect. Matteo's presumptions of his surroundings fell away. He saw Careri from a new angle, and I saw it with him.

The *signori* aged, the *signoras* grew warts. The craftspeople gnarled and the acrobats transformed to flies spiraling a strip of sugar paper being paraded around the square by a green-capped gnome. The offerings on the buffet tables grew sparse. The fruits became washed out and pale, the herbs lost their fragrance.

Matteo dug into his pack and withdrew what none knew he carried because a cleric's cloak hides plenty, and what the cloak best hides when it needs to, is itself. He hefted the cloak, lonely for Claudio's guidance, certain he'd missed something, or misplaced something, or forgotten something.

The something kicked at him. The cloth baby, giggling from beneath Matteo's vest.

For everything they'd accepted, foods and fancies, Matteo and his companions had given something in return. The ladies had given them cloth babies, children meant for pretend, then refused the baubles offered in thanks.

That did not mean Panduri's obligation had been met.

Matteo peeked at the cloth baby, at the yarn hair, and the button eyes, at the seashell hanging about its neck. Then I saw along with Matteo, the pearl hidden within the shell, the tiny pellet of iron. Tiny, but poison, enough to bind any of them to Careri should he touch it.

Matteo smacked Ursicio on the shoulder, drew the others in close. "If we do not leave, we shall become part of this place. Niccoli, corral your father. Tendi, find the horses. These women are not what they seem. They hope to mate with us. Those cloth babies they offered are payment for real ones. Use your handkerchief to avoid touching them directly and drop all you received behind a bush. Keep your speech pleasant, your movements casual. Give no indication of your disquiet but get yourselves past the gates. Salvatore will help you. Wait for me in the valley. And Ursicio—"

Matteo caught our brother-in-law by the arm. "If you can't find the horses, go on foot."

Then Matteo threw Claudio's cloak up and over his head, pushed past Salvatore, and disappeared down an alley.

Salvatore chased after. He was Panduri's Finder, and a cleric's cloak was no match for him, but I felt something shift in my brother, compelling enough to lend speed to his determination. Compelling enough to fan a flame in me I'd long thought dormant. For the spark of two spirits joined as one, the glimmer of a care beyond my small concerns. Shaking me from my complacency, dragging music from a soul I'd begun to fear I'd let stew too long in Giacomo's self-absorption.

Matteo's son. His melody as clean and clear as mine once was, the notes marking his path sparkling and true. A path that propelled Matteo around a corner and into a garden.

A garden where a tree grew. A tree bursting with apples. Not green like I'd swiped from the farmer's field all those years ago. Nor red like the apples in Panduri. These apples were yellow, fresh and bright as the rising sun. Under the tree, even fresher and brighter, sat Dante, or maybe Ilario, in purple cap and vest, working a puzzle.

The boy looked up. The connection sealed, a shot of the Outsiders' electricity reaching from one soul to the next. The boy got to his feet. "Hey! I know you."

"I know you, too." Matteo crouched beside him. He examined the puzzle, then pulled a bauble from his pocket and slotted it into a likely place.

He and the boy watched, breaths stopped. The structure held.

The little boy clapped his hands, then cartwheeled across the garden. He climbed into the tree, hand shading his eyes and looked to the horizon. He smiled at Matteo. "Do you like to go exploring?"

Twenty-Four

The boy wasn't Dante or Ilario, unless time had gone into reverse on the Outside. Still the wish flickered across Matteo's heart—that one of our little brothers had survived, that he'd been off exploring and had returned to the Careri garden, wanting to go home.

This boy's eyes were lighter, his hair straighter, his frame slighter, closer to Matteo's than either Dante's or Ilario's. Matteo's wish subsided in an instant. His heart filled with joy at having found his son. Still, there was a tug, a pull, a lingering thread that both circumstances might be possible.

There are no tears in my cold, heartless condition, but that does not mean I do not feel Matteo's.

The boy wasn't scared at all. He possessed enough of his mother's shape-shifting talent to make himself small enough to fit in Matteo's pocket, and enough of Matteo's talent to declare, "I will not be seen."

Salvatore arrived and tried to hustle Matteo on his way. Matteo shrugged him off, dug the cloth baby from under his vest and dropped it by the puzzle, a wire and plastic construct which appeared to have no solution. Matteo smoothed the talisman's yarn hair and touched a finger to the seashell wrapped iron hanging about its neck. "A cloth baby for my son. We are now evened. I will care for him with all my will and send you tidings when I can."

Before he left, Matteo reached to the tree's lowest branch and swiped an apple. Then he swiped two.

Matteo galloped into Midsummer twenty minutes into twilight, his pockets turned out, but for the one which contained his son. Unnoticed by Panduri because he still wore Claudio's cloak.

Bells rose from the valley, triumphant, robust, kind of screechy.

Matteo got off the horse. He kissed Ceres on the cheek. "The *folletti* are back. Better ask the musicians to play louder."

He doffed the cloak, donned the hat, and led the Heir onto the festival field. Then, as happens in instances when great hurt is avoided, he danced as he hadn't since he was young, slipping his Careri son from his pocket and sliding him in among the other children. "No more hiding. Find your place. And say hello to Cosimo. Wait." He pulled the child back. "What are you called?"

"Spero."

Hope.

Matteo tasted the syllables, serene and comforting on his tongue. He drew the child close. "That's a good name. Good and short and easy to remember."

Matteo woke early the morning after Midsummer. Ceres woke earlier. Matteo found her in the kitchen, stirring the porridge, their youngest at her breast, their third and fourth hanging off her skirts. She pointed her spoon toward the corner. "Who is that little boy? The one playing with Cosimo."

I watched a dozen answers work their way through Matteo's mind, a hundred urgings to express his pride, his joy. In all his planning, and in all his spontaneous action, telling Ceres had somehow escaped Matteo's attention. "Spero."

Ceres scooped her hand under the baby, swung her around, and switched her to the other breast with a practiced swoop. She didn't even have to put down the spoon. "The boy is your son, isn't he? The child of that other, that woman. The one who caused all the trouble. He's the reason you were so eager to go to Careri, so insistent it had to be you and not an emissary."

"She didn't cause the trouble. I was a willing participant." Matteo's music went awkward and artificial and far too bright. Like one of the Outsiders' plastic electrically-charged lamps. "How did you know?"

"I have eyes. That boy could be Cosimo's twin." She placed bowls on the table, placed the children around them, then pulled something from her apron pocket and showed Matteo. "I also had a bite of one of these."

The apples. The green ones Salvatore found on the Careri buffet, the yellows Matteo swiped from the Careri garden. "It packed quite a punch."

Her eyes got a little vague and she looked to the treetops. "I've been really curious about something called *calculus*."

She dropped the apples into a sack and handed the sack to Matteo. "Put these in your father's office, someplace the children can't get at them."

Matteo stuffed the sack into one of his boot tops, alongside his treats. "Are you angry?"

"About the apples or the boy?"

"Spero. I told you. He has a name."

"A beautiful name. And he has a mother who gave it to him." She looked corner to corner and, so help me, under the table. "Where is she?"

"I didn't bring her."

"You drag that boy all the way across the valley and you don't bring his mother." She aimed her wooden spoon at the door. "Take him back. Now. She must be frantic."

"I didn't drag him anywhere. He followed me."

"Matteo. Please. He's not a puppy."

The two of them went back and forth like that for a while. I turned to Giacomo. "How did it go with Claudio?"

"Awful. I thought at least he'd poke around the shelves, but all he did was write."

"Write."

Giacomo nodded. "In that big leather journal Matteo gave him. His confession, I think. Boring as shit. Then he prayed. I had no idea being Gentle Guardian was so dull. How did your father stand it?"

Those were good years, happy years. What little of them I remember. "It's not dull."

Ceres screeched. The children looked up from their porridge, eyes round. She lowered her voice. "Have you lost your mind?"

I hadn't a clue what I'd missed, but Matteo's emotions were coming to a boil. "He's my son."

Ceres's spoon went back to work. She pointed out Cosimo. "He's your son, also." She pointed out the next. "So is he. And she's your daughter."

She hefted the baby in her arms. "So is she. You risk Panduri because you cannot abide that you behaved foolishly in your youth. You take that child from his mother because you resent that she tricked you."

She drummed the spoon on the cooking pot. "The vendetta was over. The *folletti* were gone. You could have met with her. Talked. Maybe arranged to visit sometimes. But no. You had to choose the most impossible of courses."

"Not impossible." Matteo swept his arms from one end of the room to the other. "He's one little boy. This place is huge."

"Just like that." She snapped her fingers. "Just slot him in with the rest of the children, hope he forgets, hope nobody remembers how many children we have. You're Duca. You can't fart without somebody hosting a picnic to celebrate."

"Maybe I could leave him at Luciana's." Matteo rested his elbow on the table and his cheek on his palm. "She has so many, she may not notice."

"Your sister's no idiot. She knows how many children she's birthed."

"It's just for a little while." Matteo's voice rose to a desperate pitch. "Just until I can figure out what to do next."

Ceres put down the spoon. She adjusted the baby's sling and patted her hair into place. "Fine, Matteo, you figure things out. I'll take the boy to Luciana's for you."

Relief welled from that same stagnant pool a hopeless man draws comfort. Relief that Ceres seemed to understand. Relief that if they could just get through the next minutes and hours and days, somehow, someway, they'd get through the next years. Then Ceres finished her thought.

"And we'll all go with him." Ceres got the children out of their chairs. "Adventure time, everybody. Pack your nightshirts."

Matteo raced his family to the door. "Look, Ceres, I didn't plan this. I only meant to see him, find some way to keep a connection. But if you saw Careri, saw how it is, you'd understand why I couldn't just catch a glimpse and walk away. They're nothing like us, not anymore. Nothing's real. Nothing's true. Nothing is as it must have been before The Great Upheaval."

Ceres flowed the kids past Matteo like water past rock. "I'm sure you're exaggerating."

"I'm not. Ceres. Please. Listen to me." Matteo spoke low and urgent. He looked over his shoulder. "The Careri don't have magic anymore. All they have is illusion."

Ceres took off her apron and hung it by the hearth. "Then Luciana's shall be the perfect place for this child, for all the children, because Luciana's house is so filled with light and love there is no room for deception."

She swept out.

Giacomo scratched at his neck. "That went poorly."

I make music, not intrigue, and Giacomo's self-satisfied timbre pulled all my bass notes from wherever they'd been hiding. I grabbed him by his collar. Rather, I thought about grabbing him by his collar. In death, thought has to substitute for action. "Shut up. You planned this. You were hoping Matteo would take his child. Hoping he'd bring him back here."

"How else can Careri be saved? Our stars once orbited each other, but Careri's is collapsing. Under a single Duca, our stars will unite."

"They won't unite." I shook one fist, then the other, then banged them together in front of his face. "They'll collide. Panduri and Careri won't become one, we'll implode."

I cupped my hands crossways, one over the other like I were compacting a snowball, then grabbed at the place my amulet should have been, that small knot of spirit energy in the base of my throat I sometimes felt when my emotions did more than remain steady. "Because Outside can't become Inside."

"Are you sure? Have you tried?"

Something surfaced, a sensation I wasn't aware I could still feel, creepy and crawling and buzzing with flies. "This is what you wanted for Dante and Ilario. This is the reason Father let them set sail."

"Your father had no business interfering. Neither did you."

He meant how I pretended to want things peaceful, then riled the *folletti*, used my music to spook their spirits, kept them riled to keep Matteo home. "I was trying to fix the mess you made."

"Then you left him. Crossed. No explanation." Giacomo tapped his temple. "Matteo sometimes tells himself you were going to get his son. Deludes himself maybe you were planning to retrieve the baby for him yourself."

Always we want to believe the best, cushion our losses, color our memories. I didn't know if that's what I was thinking. I wanted to check on the child, make sure all was well, my further plans uncertain. "I'd assigned that task to Salvatore. Told him if the opportunity presented, he should. To never let the *duca* know I'd given that order."

That's why Salvatore had left Matteo and his party mingling by the buffet table. He'd sought the apple that fell from Matteo's tree, not the ones Ceres wanted.

Giacomo threw up his hands. "Then why are you all up my back-side about this?"

"Because I wanted that child for Matteo's love, not his ambition. Leave Matteo be, leave Spero be. The Careris' current *duca*, and Spero's Careri father both have to die before Spero can become Duca. Plenty can happen in the meantime."

Giacomo made a dismissive gesture. "Plenty can happen now. All Matteo needs are the right words and those two are out of the way."

He rubbed his palms together. "The vendetta is back in business. Careri's magic is waning. Matteo's star can finally rise."

All my cuts and bruises festered, especially the one closest to my heart. "Was I in Matteo's way?"

"Don't be ridiculous. You merely forgot your fiddle. In Panduri, we forget things all the time."

But we don't forget that which gives us life, gives us breath.

Those moments before my decision to take myself out of Matteo's equation suddenly blurred. I looked at the sky, so bright and blue, and longed to feel the sun's warmth on my face, to see my stars rise unencumbered.

By guilt. By regret. By the interminable levelness of living in the in-between. "You've been with Matteo since the beginning. Since you flung yourself from that tree. All our crossed signals, my mislaid plans. You botched them for us. I'll bet you talked the Careri woman into crossing our border. I'll bet you threw her into Matteo's path. I'll bet you even got hold of Ceres's iron and made it pull toward mine."

I concentrated all my newfound reasoning on him. "Right?"

Giacomo wasn't listening. He was on his way down the hall, fol-lowing Matteo to his study, a spirit on a mission.

Which I guessed when I got there had to do with all the call-ing and hallooing and knocking coming from behind the door to Father's office.

Giacomo laughed. "Oh yeah, I forgot to mention. Matteo forgot about Claudio. Your brother is still sealed in the *duca's* office."

And truly, angry hornets would have been calmer. "Where the hell is my cloak, you son of a sea dog?"

Matteo gave up on any apologies, intrigued by the idea of a sea dog. "Your cloak is on my bed, I think. No. On Cosimo's. He and Spero were using it to make a blanket fort."

"Who the hell is Spero?" Claudio was itchy and scratchy and needed a shave.

I wrinkled my nose along with Matteo. Claudio didn't smell so good, either. "Spero is my son."

Matteo caught Claudio up, more or less, on what had happened over Midsummer, and especially in the last hour, Ceres leaving and whatnot.

Claudio forgot about his cloak. He started poking around shelves, going through boxes and bins. "Why does the boy think he's here?"

"Spero, Spero, his name is Spero. And he thinks he's visiting his cousins. Which he is."

A sprite arrived from Careri with the unfortunate news that one of their children had gone missing. Also lamenting the *folletti's* resurgence. "Our *duca* worries the two events are connected and requests the urgent assistance of your protectors, and any finders, to aid in the boy's return."

Matteo made a big show of looking worried. His hand crept to his amulet and I felt him search the words that would keep his iron honest. "Panduri receives this news with great consternation. Assure your *duca* of Panduri's deep concern in this matter." He handed the Careri sprite a treat and sent her off.

He waited until she was only a pinpoint in the distance, then called in a second sprite, one of ours. Matteo instructed her to relay the message from the Careri *duca* and added, "The valley will be perilous. And noisy. Our brave protectors are to plug their ears and steer clear. Our Faithful Finder is to find something better to do with his time."

He saw to her payment, then turned to Claudio, now knee-deep in scrolls and tossing them into a large wooden box at a feverish pitch. "You're making a mess."

"I'm cleaning it up. Because I'm so damned sick of it all. Of pissing out windows, of shitting in the sparring ficus. Sick of sorting, and soul-searching, and considering all my poor choices."

He clamped the lid on the box and shoved the box forward. "Do your own damned filing. I'm getting my cloak, getting a beer, then going back to the monastery and getting a bath. And if the Deep Lore strikes me dead for my dreadful housekeeping during my time in the *duca's* office, I hope to Papist Jesus it does so before I have to hear one more damned confession."

He headed out the door. "There are still marshmallows in the desk drawers. I got sick of eating them, too."

Giacomo whooped and he hollered, he stomped and he brayed. "And that went perfectly."

I pointed to the box. "I take it Claudio didn't spend his time in here writing and praying."

"Not much. And now Matteo will put the pieces together. Maybe not today or tomorrow, but eventually."

He stopped stomping. "After all, Matteo is his father's son."

Well, so was I. And I was tired and sick as my brother, as in need of a beer.

Matteo looked at the door, uncertain what to do about Ceres, what to do about Spero, how long it would take Claudio to forgive him. He wasn't worrying about star casts and scrolls, boxes and bins, the roles we'd been born to, the ones we'd assumed.

He was worried he'd lose his family, trying to figure some plan to keep them all together. And Giacomo was here to keep Matteo on that anxious edge. As he'd always been. Ever since I'd cut down that damned tree.

Because Giacomo demanded everything. And I felt nothing. Because I'd let myself feel that way. Because I'd preferred the drudgery of despair to the joy our spirits are meant to dance.

No more. Not for me. Not for Matteo. I'd made him a promise. Words and Music, always together. From what I could see of the contents of the box, all Matteo needed was already there. First. And Foremost.

Antonio

I took a metaphorical bite of the apple, dug deep into my love for my brothers, then drew my imaginary bow across my imaginary fiddle and played as I'd never played before. A tune stalwart, yet sentimental, melodious, and meaningful.

Fanciful. Fulsome. Forceful enough to fling a few of my scores and a couple of scrolls at Matteo's feet in a great big honking phlegm-filled ball of truth—no matter how the stars eventually arrayed for Matteo, I'd had no right to obscure their paths.

The flinging turned out to be easy. As the maestro had told us, attitude is key.

Matteo neatened up the musical scores, his need for order overwhelming, then picked up one of the scrolls. He looked to the notations along its edge, as he always did, the signs and symbols that told him he held a birth chart, not a transactional one. His gaze swept to the end of the line, to the owner's name.

Claudio, second son of Bartomeo.

Confusion lumbered across Matteo's mind, his first presumption that the chart had been mislabeled. Then he checked the second chart.

A mental drumroll, then a cacophony of bells inwardly announced my brother's Underlying and Long-Past-Due-For-Finally-Telling-Him Premise.

Matteo, most bewildered, most caught-off-guard, most obviously in-the-dark of all.

Such neat, clean script, and written in Giacomo's distinctive hand:

Matteo, first son of the Duca.

The Duca

Twenty-Five

This tale begun in other ways,
Now searches for its end of days.

The Midsummer everything changed, I found Antonio standing before the waterfall which trickled down the far end of our room. He was dressed in my deep blue vest and cap and was surrounded by tailors. Ripping a seam here, letting down a hem there, moving buttons and buckles, adapting collars and cuffs.

I looked to Mamma, embellishing acorn caps for Dante and Ilario. "Why?"

"A mistake has been made."

No kidding. Antonio was bigger than me. How come nobody noticed? Why had they fitted those clothes to me at all?

I lounged in the corner and watched the tailors adjust him and pin him and tell him to stand still. Finally, they produced the head-gear and placed it over Antonio's cap.

"Hey! You're wearing . . . *p-p-p*-Uncle Giacomo's hat."

"Impossible." Antonio tapped a finger to one of the pleats. "This hat is meant for the Heir."

"How can it be only for the Heir if—" I again tripped over Giacomo's name, bruising a knee.

229

Mamma *tsk-tsk-tsk'd* me. "Remember what the maestro told you."

"A *g* is not a *p*. I want to make *je* like jelly, not a *pah* like pot." I'd been practicing, just like the maestro told me. Wanting to please Mamma, wanting to please *pah-pah* . . . I mean Uncle Giacomo, until my tongue knotted for the trying.

That didn't mean I was ready to give up the hat. "Tell him, Mamma. Tell him the hat can't be only for the Heir if Uncle . . . Giacomo wore it."

"Matteo, leave Antonio to his preparation." Mamma settled the caps on Dante and Ilario, then took their hands. "Let's find Claudio. It's time to make the patty cakes. What does it matter who wore the hat? Antonio wears it now. That's all we have to remember."

Because the parts we didn't have to remember were unpleasant. Those parts hurt. The hollering, the arguments, the threats, and the torment. Father bound Uncle Giacomo with tangleweed. Giacomo cracked the earth under their roots. They shouted and cursed, struggled and carried on, causing an Upheaval so Great we gave it a name and marked all our Midsummers from its cessation.

The ground stopped shaking. The weepers stopped wailing. The stars stopped falling from the sky. We let Antonio wear the hat, forgot he ever didn't, and continued our course. Until an Upheaval Greater than the First sent Dante and Ilario exploring and the rest of us sprawling, this time into a spiral from which we never recovered.

We groped along, doing our best, and neither Mamma, nor Father, nor Giacomo, nor any adult ever explained why any of it happened at all.

And neither did Claudio's magic box of documents, all dating from around that time and, unfortunately, cast by Giacomo. I'd heard of hieroglyphics. The maestro told us, covering page after page with simplified outlines of birds and trees, eyes and mouths, even stars and planets.

Antonio liked to trace those. "Why draw them? Why not cast real ones?"

The maestro tousled his hair. "Would you do the same with the birds and trees?"

"Or the eyeballs!" Claudio found that idea ridiculous, his laugh joyous enough to cheer even the grievous ginger snaps.

The maestro made other marks. "All writing is no more than what we make of it. Unintelligible until you have the key."

Or an interpreter. Or both. I sent Claudio a sprite. And our birth charts. "What the hell?"

He returned the sprite. And the charts. Postage due. "In seclusion."

Well, fuck Claudio. I didn't need him. I was Duca. First son of . . . the Duca.

The Duca-I-didn't-know-ever-was. Never saw documented in any file. Never heard mention made among the *signori*. Always whooping and hollering and howling at the moon.

Giacomo.

I wasn't stupid. I'd figured out that much from the notations on my and Claudio's birth scrolls.

I sent them to Claudio again, along with another sprite. "Seriously. What the hell?"

He returned them. And her. Again, postage due. "Seriously. In seclusion."

I needed a drink. I sent the sprite again. "But I can't read the charts."

"In seclusion."

"I don't have a key."

"In seclusion."

I'm confused and I'm hurt, I'm nervous, uncertain. I don't know what this means, why you chose now to try and tell me. What this might have to do with my sons, whether my knowing will challenge Panduri.

In. Seclusion.

Well . . . fuck Claudio again. "You're being a dick."

I waited a minute, then an hour, then half-a-day. His sprite finally returned. "I'm not being a dick. I just can't answer any questions."

"Sure you can. How high is the sky?"

"Endless."

"How many fish in the sea?"

"Enough."

"How far can you see on a clear day?"

"Forever."

"Why did Antonio leave?"

Silence. Even the crickets stopped chirping.

Without information, all that's left is assumption. Stories to cover the empty spaces between what we know and what we don't.

Assumption 1: Antonio left because he wanted me to be Duca. Because I was supposed to be. And he wasn't.

Assumption 2: Because Antonio knew the information that was in Claudio's boxes, knew what that information meant.

Well, fuck Antonio, too. Why didn't he just tell me?

And fuck Giacomo. How come he'd stopped being Duca? Why did he hand me over and make me be Father's son?

And fuck Father. Because. Just because.

And my goodness. Was Mamma even my mamma?

I unrolled scroll after scroll. I turned them this way, then that. I held them to the light, squinted and squinched and sounded things out, trying to squeeze any information from the jumble before me. I went on like that for a while. I even scraped at the paper, peeled it layer by layer. In case the chart I was trying to read was a decoy for the chart I actually could, as the maestro once told us smugglers on the Outside sometimes do to hide priceless works of art.

Day passed to twilight, then to night, then to day, then to twilight, then I lost count. I shoved the box, harder and further than Claudio had. I could assume all I wanted. I'd never solve the riddle of Antonio until I solved the underlying premise.

I sent Claudio another sprite. "Why did Giacomo and Father fight?"

All that returned was the gentle *shush, shush, shush* of surrender sloshing between my headbones.

For days.

Then a furor carried in from the valley, the *folletti's* screams rose to an unbearable pitch. I went to Father's window, the tallest and most impressive, saw what was coming, and ducked.

A sprite careened into the comforting cozyslippers, missing my head by a hairsbreadth. She was one of ours, of Panduri, and bearing a message from the Careri Duca. "Hello. We hope you are enjoying your summer. Our *ducato's* child is still missing . . . any word?"

Her voice was shaky, her ears blistering from the *folletti's* fever. I let her choose what marshmallows she wanted and thought how to word my answer so my iron would not betray me. "Tell our new friends we have no new word of their missing child. Then send notice to our brave protectors of our grave concern over the arrival of this message. They should take a high road, one well clear of the valley."

I handed her an extra sweet. "Except Salvatore. Tell Salvatore to put on his stocking cap. His *duca* orders him to take a long summer's nap."

Because fuck Salvatore, too. Because Antonio was first on the scene when Antonio died, but Salvatore was second. Father's finder, Antonio's constant and consistent shadow, the man who knew everything, told nothing, and always followed orders.

I was first. I was foremost. I was tired and crabby and hungry as hell. I'd had enough, and I was angry about all that had happened, angry I'd felt so guilty, angry I'd blamed myself at all.

For Antonio's death, for Father's distance, for Ruggiero's rage, for Mamma's fading away.

I sent Claudio another sprite. "How about if I burn the whole thing down?"

He returned another. "First—burn your confession."

The sprite handed me a key and a trowel. And a match.

Well, fuck Claudio a third time, and thank him for the idea. For the trowel, for the key, for license to be incensed and insulted, wounded and aggrieved. And to burn my goddamned journal.

I went to the garden and laid in with the trowel, flinging dirt, flinging curses, my house empty, my bed emptier, my heart raked raw. Till I got to the box, in the place where I'd planted it, dinged and dented and worn for the wear.

I unplanted the box and unlocked it.

And did not find my journal. I found two parchments, instead.

Made of plant husks, not animal skins, thank Papist Jesus. Distinctive, large, with substantive borders and plenty of signatures, sealed and medallioned and far more impressive than the one I'd found regarding Jack's shrewd exchange of his mother's milk cow for the magic beans. The seals on these parchments were affixed with star shine, weighted with iron, the intent of the maker obvious. To ensure these two parchments and whatever they detailed would always have a place in Panduri.

They were birth certificates. Birth certificates of the sort Ignazio had described, cast by Outsiders in place of charts. One for Dante. The other for Ilario. A name clearly marked on the line labeled "Father"—Giacomo.

Their place of birth—Careri.

The name in the line labeled "Mother" was a *signora* I'd met, introduced to me in the receiving line in Careri, dressed in icicles and snowflakes, eye keen, her smile cold. She'd given me a cloth baby. Told me how pleased she was to finally meet me.

The wife of the Careri Duca.

Impossible. She'd been young, she'd been vibrant, barely older than Ceres. And she must have understood Uncle Giacomo had children, too.

There's always that moment, crystalline and clear, that divides how things were with how things are, defines what one believed from what one now knows. That moment when all the running ends, the illusions fail, and facts must be faced.

This is what Claudio wanted to show me, what he'd wanted me to know, what he couldn't tell me. The reason none of us worked together, why we worked at odds.

Our underlying premise.

Who we are, what we were supposed to be, the roles we were born to, those we were not . . . was a lie.

On the Midsummer Dante and Ilario left us, Giacomo promised, "They're not going forever. Not going for always. They're going exploring and someday they'll return."

I threw myself after them. Then Father held me back. So I fought and I flailed and I refused to be calm. Because Antonio had taken us. Antonio had caused our sickness. I turned on my brother, scratched at his face, digging hard with my nails, drawing blood, and a scar which would always be with him.

And declared, "I wish you'd never been born."

Dante and Ilario's Wall still stood because when the one did not tear down what the other built, what they made together was invincible.

But what of Dante and Ilario?

I balled my fist and jammed it into the construct. In despair for all I'd known, all I hadn't, the mistakes made, and the opportunities missed. I pounded and pounded, gulped back voiceless cries, blinked back unshed tears. Until I no longer felt the impact of bone on stone. Until my flesh flayed from the muscle. Until all that remained was my rage, scorching, consuming, collapsing to ash.

Then I slid down the wall, my hand broken and bloody and cradled to my chest. Hopeless. Hollow. Grieving deep.

For the loved ones I'd lost. The ones who'd been stolen.

And the ones I'd never possessed.

Twenty-Six

*F*or what reasons did we war?
Because shit happens.

Three days after I deconstructed my agonies on Dante and Ilario's Wall, I wished *I'd* never been born. My fist swelled and my temper simmered.

Oh, and Antonio finally realized no matter who our fathers were, no matter how dead he was, I deserved the chance to talk to him in person. He found me working in the garden, took a look at my hand. "I see you've been figuring things out."

I wrung out the rag and kept on washing. All the blood and anguish, the assumptions, the anger. "It's only cuts and bruises. They'll heal."

"You have questions. Ask."

"Why did you place the garden here? Why didn't you want Father to see it?"

"The one has nothing to do with the other. The garden is here because Dante's Wall is here. Father couldn't see it, but not for me not trying. I spent days checking the sight lines, adjusting the angles. I couldn't find a way to make the garden visible from Father's window."

I pulled my flask from my hip pocket, uncorked it and drank. "Why did Dante and Ilario build the wall here?"

"Because their hearts were not in Panduri. That's why they went exploring."

I drank again, this time staring where the stump had been. "This wasn't just Dante and Ilario's tree. This was actually Dante and Ilario's tree. The seed you gave me to plant was from one of the apples they swiped."

"The fruit was so delicious and I didn't think them bad. I wanted to prove to Father the curiosity they engendered could be controlled with the proper guidance."

"So you made an offer to the Careri."

To be fair, Antonio looked sheepish. "I just suggested if they sent an apple from the tree in their garden, perhaps we'd each find a reason to work together, rather than fight."

"So they sent the woman, Spero's mother." I drank yet again. "That's how you knew she was Careri. Not because the maestro told you."

"She'd set her sights on another kind of apple."

"So we come full circle."

"Only me. I'm dead, part of your hopeless past. All I can do is go in circles. You, however, must move on." Antonio took the flask from me. He poured it out where I'd chopped out the stump, then exchanged it for a vial, tuneful and small, the vial he'd given me after my run-in with the trolls. "I found this in Father's office, lying beside your flotsam of frustrations. It should help with the fever."

I shook the vial by my ear, turned it this way, then that, fascinated by how the tones shifted. "I have a fever." Except for my temper, I didn't feel hot.

"Blazing. High enough to roast marshmallows. That should please the children."

Yes, the children were back. That's why I was washing the gore from Dante and Ilario's Wall.

"And Ceres."

Ceres, too.

"Luciana wants me to talk to you."

And Luciana had come to visit. She and her whole brood. I'd forgotten how many she had. They were planning a party here in the garden. I really needed to clean the mess I'd made, make it pristine, pretend everything that had happened . . . hadn't.

Antonio sat beside me. "You really need to return the boy."

"Spero." Perfect. Energetic. Curious. Forever asking questions, poking around in places the others didn't. He was everything that made the Deep Lore crazy. "The party is for him. To welcome him into the family."

"He's older than Cosimo."

"Only by a few months."

"The Deep Lore is clear. You'd have to name him Heir. Declare Cosimo Protector. Rearrange them like pieces of a puzzle."

I threw the cloth back into the bucket. "Our parents did."

"And it didn't work. Because the best puzzles have only one solution."

Antonio was so confident, so sanctimonious, so . . . smug. "Not our puzzle. We were settled, we were fine. But for *you* taking us Outside. What in *hell* were you thinking?"

"I was a boy, a few years older than Cosimo. I wasn't thinking. I was reacting."

To the fighting, the hollering, the sudden return of rancor. To details everybody decided I was too young to have to remember.

I turned my attention to Giacomo, standing beside Antonio. His skin was sallow, his cap was deepest blue. "What's your excuse, *Poppa*?"

The tips of his ears perked up. And I'll swear his complexion cleared. "It's so nice to hear you call me that. I'd forgotten how much I missed it."

"You don't deserve it. You gave me up. Caved to Father."

"For Panduri. At least that's what Bartomeo told me. And the *signori*. Blame them."

"I'll blame you. For everything I don't blame Father." I looked past him, past Dante and Ilario's Wall, past all the mixed messages and crossed signals. "Isn't he coming? The least you all owe me is full attendance."

"Bartomeo won't come. He did his best. So he got to leave."

"Best at what?"

"At doing what the *signori* told him to do." Giacomo hopped to the top of Dante and Ilario's Wall. He hopped in one giant step. Gianter than even a giant could have taken given the wall's height. A small giant.

"And you had to stay." I retrieved the rag. That wall wasn't going to wash itself. All those tiny bits of disappointment and rage ground into the crannies, all that chagrin clinging to the edges. Then there were those secret places, the complex spirals Dante and Ilario always delighted in including—the ideas not considered, the paths never taken. "Because you were Protector, you were Legendary."

"Because I was Duca and you won't move into the *duca's* office."

"Seriously. I move into the *duca's* office and poof! You can leave."

"So the Deep Lore claims. And the Deep Lore does not like being ignored. Believe me, I know."

Giacomo settled into his spot. He crossed his feet in front of him. "In the days of the Great Upheaval, I thought the *signori* wouldn't care what I'd done. When they did, I thought Ignazio would use that sugar-laced tongue of his to convince them it wasn't so bad. When he didn't, I thought your mother would stand by me. When she didn't, I figured anything I did after that wouldn't be important."

What he'd done. "You mean at the beginning. You mean conceiving Dante and Ilario."

"I mean bringing them back here. I mean letting them go. I mean dropping myself from that tree." Giacomo's face grew grainy, and his visage blurred. "My plan would have worked just as well if I'd left them in Careri."

"You conceived them on purpose." Somewhere between my hand-bashing and my first doses of Antonio's musical magic vial, I'd convinced myself Giacomo's making of Dante and Ilario was an accident, unintended. I'd been impressed by Giacomo's creation of the birth certificates, was already halfway to writing one for Spero, had already affixed a half dozen medallions.

Like father, like son and all that. "I don't understand."

"Let's just say, I too had a brother who didn't like the role into which he'd been cast."

He couldn't mean Father. Father had hated charting stars, had avoided taking the center until he could not avoid it.

Giacomo looked to the heavens. "Your sorry excuse of a Gentle Guardian has all your answers." He pointed. "Ask him yourself. Here he comes now."

I didn't ask who he meant, didn't take umbrage at the insult. I was feeling much the same about Claudio. "He's not coming. He's in—"

Claudio rounded the curve on the path, pace brisk. He walked right past me, his face in a jumble and Topo cradled in his cowl.

"—seclusion."

Claudio sat by the remains of the stump. Rubbed at the bridge of his nose. Ran a hand over his head.

"Hello?" I felt silly greeting him like a question. I was standing right there, but Claudio gave no indication he'd noticed me or my wash bucket. "Claudio?"

Antonio laid a hand on my shoulder, solid and steady and warm to the touch. Not what I'd expect from a spirit. "He can't see you. Can't hear you. Because you're with us."

His statement felt ominous, filled with that dizziness that comes with drunkenness, that unreality that surfaces when one is overtired. I flicked Antonio's palm from my shoulder, feeling petty, and puny, and too close to puking to care. I snapped my fingers in front of Claudio, then hop-step-stepped, hop-stepped. "Claudio. Hey! Claudio."

Topo hissed. He crawled out of the cowl and onto Claudio's shoulder, back arched, fur bushed. Claudio *sh-sh*-shushed at him, scratched him behind his ear, then pulled a journal from beneath his robe.

No. A tome. Bound in leather, half again as tall, twice as thick, and far more impressive than the journal Claudio had handed me.

Also tattered and worn. The leather stained, the parchment picked at, the hinges scratched.

Unexpected. I'd given Claudio that journal as a gibe, a way to shut up all his constant and incongruous counsel. It never occurred to me a cleric would ever have anything to confess.

Claudio opened the journal and laid it on his lap. He dug a pen out of his collar, then riffled through the parchment, ink-splotched and crammed with writing. An air of despair, of failure, forlorn and dreadful rose from the pages. There were moments of laughter, sometimes a snatch of song from notes I saw marked in the margins, but the overwhelming miasma was one of sorrow, of regret, of opportunities missed and chances not taken.

Claudio turned to the last page. He began to write.

Giacomo leaned over and read out loud. "'*We grow older, we grow softer, more robust in our illusions, more fragile in our truths.*'" He looked up. "And everybody says *you're* the poet."

Our conversation was too cavalier. We should be speaking in weightier tones, using better words, better sentence structure. Behaving with decorum. After all, at least two of us were dead.

I gave up on the washing and got off my knees, hand throbbing. Then I grabbed Antonio by the collar. "Why did you cut down the tree, sheepfucker?"

I tilted my head at Giacomo. "Because he hung himself from it? Listen to him talk. He wasn't worth the effort, certainly not worth the time I spent growing the damned thing. He didn't do what was best, he did what he wanted."

"Well, well, look what mule is calling the donkey stubborn." Giacomo got down off the wall. He got into my face, his blurry edges coming back into focus. "Do you love your wife, or was she forbidden fruit? Is that why she always smells of apples? You were Protector, prohibited to marry. Yet you did and set Antonio's course on a tilt."

"Antonio set his own damned course on a tilt. He had a woman, unsuitable and secret. Then he left her. Left us all."

Antonio pried at my fingers. "I didn't leave her. And I never fucked sheep."

I grabbed his collar all the harder. "Then who is she? Why didn't you tell me about her? Why couldn't I know?"

"You didn't come for me. You let Salvatore go instead."

"Because you wouldn't have listened, you pompous, self-serving ass. Returning you was my first duty as Protector, and I'd have found you, ordered you to come home, and you would have gone on. Because you shoved my words around like they were nothing. Shoved me around like I was less. I'd have failed and I'd have had to explain my failure to Father." I released him and swept an arm. "Behold Antonio, the insecure, the inconsiderate, the inconceivably unable to perceive how much I worshiped you."

Antonio had run as an experiment. To test my reaction. See if he could trust me. He was working his own puzzle and never gave me a chance to be part of the solution. I lowered my arm. "I fucking hate you."

I shook Antonio's magic vial by my ear, hoping it would take my mind off things, but the notes had grown discordant. "I don't like this hallucination. I want to wake up now."

"You're not asleep."

Claudio had once made mention of the Papists' purgatory. Had I arrived? Doomed to scrub at my sins from a never-ending wash bucket? "I'm dead. This is no hallucination, this is the way things are."

Giacomo flicked forefinger and thumb to the back of my skull. It stung. "You're very much alive, my boy. For now. But if Claudio doesn't stop pouring his heart on those pages and pour some water on the mess you made, that could change."

"What mess?" I presumed he meant the wall, but that was finally clean.

"The mess you made in the *duca's* office. By the hearth. You are passed out and senseless beside it."

"Don't be ridiculous. I'm right here. Feeling fine." I glanced at my hand, swollen and sore. "Mostly."

Giacomo shook his head. "Nope. Only your spirit. And only for a while. The rest of you has a lump the size of a *scungilli* behind your ear. You hit your head on the way down. Claudio has to find you, or. . . ." He pulled up a fist from his neck, strangling himself on an imaginary noose.

The imagining became intolerable. My hand, bruised and festering, grew shaky. I wanted to blur the image, the way Giacomo had blurred his visage. Wanted to replace what I'd seen with an agreeable fiction. "Somebody will find me. Everybody's home. Everybody's around."

"In your mind, because that's what you want. Ceres and the children are at Luciana's house. Racing turtles last we checked. You sent the secretaries and servants home hours ago. Claudio's your last hope. Thing is, Claudio's in no rush to see you. Claudio's here for his own reasons."

Claudio snapped the journal shut and threw down his pen. He produced a trowel and started digging, flinging dirt. He hit the box on the third fling, cleared the earth around it, removed it and shook it by his ear.

The box didn't make any sounds. It was empty.

His realization washed across the garden and pooled at my feet, nervous and gnawing. He knew I'd found the birth certificates.

Claudio whipped around. He sniffed at the air. He dropped the box, left his journal, and ran for the mansion.

Well, that was very exciting. Claudio would find me soon enough. He'd slap my cheek, dump cold water over my fever and all this would be done. I felt kind of stupid. Felt like I should have been kinder. I mean, Antonio was dead. What was he supposed to do about anything now? I hadn't seen him in years. And soon I'd no longer be able to see him.

I got hold of Antonio's hand and shook it before it faded. "Thank you for coming. You can go now."

"Go where?"

"To . . . you know. Where Claudio says. Among the spheres. Say hello to Father for me. Give Mamma a hug. And if my worst fears are true and Dante and Ilario are up there, too, tell them I'll keep all their stories safe."

Giacomo snorted. "If that's all it took, Antonio would have left at the first. Claudio's been offering prayers for forgiveness and release since the start."

I got uncomfortable, like some trickster had dumped thistles in my underwear. Like I'd mixed up the brides at a double Promise. Like something tacked Antonio here, kept Giacomo around. Some piece of the bigger puzzle, some— "What are you two doing here? Or am I making this all up?"

Antonio pulled out his fiddle from wherever it had been hiding. He tucked it under his chin. "Matteo, we don't have much time. You're not hallucinating, you're not making any of this up. We're really here. You're really sick. So the veil between us is thinned. So please, shut up and listen. Or you won't survive the coming storm."

"But Claudio's headed to the mansion. Soon everything will settle."

Antonio dragged his bow across the strings, a tune both foreign and familiar. A tune of return. "The Careri Duca is not going to play at being patient forever. He's coming, Matteo. Coming for the boy. And he's got a plan. You need a plan, too. A plan better than mine. A plan a whole lot better than Uncle Giacomo's."

Antonio laid into the refrain, eyes closed, the notes rising with their own light. His silver buttons gleamed and a swath of hair, iridescent in the tiny glimmers, escaped its binding to fall across his face.

Tuck of the chin. Set of the shoulder. Tremor of each finger for the *vibrato*.

Every detail carried importance I now understood, exquisiteness I wished I'd given more notice. Each a beginning, each an end, and each whispered.

Pay attention. Have a care.

Remember.

I grabbed Antonio's fiddle and smashed it to the ground, every one of the seventy sirens screeching in protest. The neck broke from the body, the strings popped and lashed across my cheeks. Blood, warm and coppery, trickled into my mouth, made its way under my collar. I lifted the remains of the fiddle to Antonio, my heart wrapped around my words, and desperate to remember his. "It only has cuts and bruises. Cuts and bruises only. They will heal."

Antonio caught me by the collar and dragged me across the garden. "Don't you leave me, Matteo." He smacked me across the face. "I mean it. Don't you dare die."

Dante and Ilario's garden faded, replaced by the corridor outside Father's office. I wasn't standing, but kneeling on the moss-covered stones, yawing and lurching and coughing so hard my chest near exploded.

I grabbed for Antonio. In that blink he became Claudio. So I grabbed for Giacomo. My hand passed right through him.

"Too late. I'm fading, too." Giacomo's voice got reedy and annoying. "Looks like Claudio got the pitcher plants into the act. Good. You'll probably live. But leave the wreckage for later. Because trouble is on the way. Big trouble. You don't want to be distracted."

Giacomo dissipated. His every feature disconnected from the next. And he was gone.

Twenty-Seven

Claudio knelt over the remains of Antonio's fiddle. "What the hell?" He picked up the instrument, fitted a tuning peg back into its hole, ran a finger over the scroll. "Seriously. What the hell?"

We were in the corridor outside Father's office. And yes. The fiddle looked bad. It looked really bad. Not quite so bad as what I thought I'd done to it in my hallucination, but still, pretty bad, the neck cracked, the body scratched, the strings sprung. "You were playing. Well, not you. I mean, Antonio. I mean, you were Antonio."

I held up my hand, as if that somehow explained anything, the throbbing so bad I half expected it to pulse with its own light. "When your head is not shaved you look a lot like him."

"Antonio."

"Yes. Yes. And trouble's coming. Giacomo told me. We're supposed to get a sprite."

"From . . . Giacomo?"

"Don't be ridiculous. Giacomo can't send sprites. He's dead."

"You're covered in soot." Claudio stood, fiddle still in hand. He pulled a handkerchief from beneath his cloak and wiped it over my face.

Only soot? I reached to where I thought the strings had lashed at my cheek, ready to trace a scar like Antonio's, except fresh and raw and dripping over my shirt. There was nothing. Just . . . soot. As Claudio had said.

I took the handkerchief from him, remembered where Giacomo had said I was actually supposed to be. And made a few assumptions. "I got too close to the grate."

"I'll say. Thank goodness I found you in time. Honestly, I thought you were dead and call me coward, I almost didn't come, but circumstances have so devolved." He looked at Father's door, closed tight, though when Claudio would have closed it, I couldn't imagine, what with all the dragging and slapping and pleading and whatnot.

He pulled at his collar. "I had no business leaving those boxes there, without guidance, without explanation. It never occurred to me you'd take such drastic action, but what's done is done, and we'll need to figure something else out, but first let's get you cleaned up and I'll send for a folkwife to have a look at that hand, and then we could—"

What Claudio thought we could do remains a mystery because his blather made my ears ache. "Shut up. I have something to show you."

I headed for my study without curiosity over what Claudio meant by drastic action, by devolved circumstances, or why he'd now decided to return. I headed for my study, propelled by a different goal than propelled Claudio, a different need than that which drove him. I headed for my study, dug out the charts he'd given me two Midsummers past. Charts I now understood were meant to mollify me, make me stop asking questions. Charts which had seemed wrong.

Claudio followed me and I waved the charts in his face. "You told me these belonged to Dante and Ilario. They don't, you . . . you—"

I couldn't call Claudio a bastard, I'd stricken that word from my lexicon. "They don't, you . . . cleric. These charts are fakes. You knew it, but you gave them to me anyway, gave your Duca false materials. I should . . . I should—"

What I thought I should do also remains a mystery, because

Luciana burst through the door, open and honest and sunny as midday. "What's that smell? Are you roasting marshmallows? Matteo, why are you still here? Word is spreading. The *signori* are gathering, the people are waiting for you to speak."

Papist Jesus. How long had I tarried in that garden with my dead brother and uncle? "There's no reason for the people to be waiting. Unless it's Midsummer again already."

"Are you drunk? We just had Midsummer." Luciana came close and smelled my breath. "What happened to your clothes? Why are you all wet?"

I patted my pockets. Drunk sounded like a wonderful idea, then remembered Antonio had traded his magic musical vial for my flask. And my clothes . . . covered in soot, my collar undone, one sleeve rolled to my elbow, the other shirt cuff opened and bedraggled and flapping about my fingers. "I think the water was from Claudio. You see I had a fever, and—"

"Never mind." Luciana got hold of my arm. She dragged me to the door. "Claudio can help you clean up. A quick bath. And a shave. The people won't wait. There's such a ruckus."

"What ruckus?"

Claudio got hold of my other arm, pulled me away from the door and pushed me toward the window. "Ignazio. Can't you hear him? He received a sprite. He's been going on about electricity. And something called pee wee pipes. Are they an instrument?"

"Pee vee cee. And no, they carry water. You wouldn't know what Ignazio's been saying. You've been in seclusion."

"I removed myself from the world. I didn't remove my ears from my head. Listen."

Ignazio orated in the Gathering Glade. He swept one arm, then the other, engaging and persuasive. "The Careri are clear in their desire to rejoin our orbit. They have much to offer, wonders from the Outside. Games we can play on tiny boxes, and a way to receive news without having to tell each other."

"Do the Careri now read minds?" I didn't see who asked that

question, but the voice sounded simple, plain, and suspicious. Probably a gnome. They don't engage and hate being persuaded.

"No. The Careri have devices, powered by electricity. Electricity comes from the sun, from water, from wind and oil, coal and gas. For cooling, and warmth, light and convenience. The ways of the Outsider are strange, but we should not eschew that which might improve our circumstances, nor ease our lives."

"What ease can the Outsider provide?" Ursicio. Ever resourceful. Always pleasant. Like rutabagas when they're stewed properly. "We already have warmth from the sun, water for drinking, wind to cool, oil to fry, coal for our cookfires. And who among us doesn't have plenty of gas after a nice bowl of beans?"

Laughter swelled, rolling in like a wave.

"Very funny, Loyal Ursicio. And all excellent points." Blessed Tendi. Patient and calm and bland as potatoes. "Ignazio, our Wise and Constant Counselor also tells us lovely stories. We so appreciate his tales."

Tendi's voice amplified in a way that let me know he meant I should hear, and I should get ready. "I see the *signori* are gathering. Please, Panduri, return to your homes and your work, your families and your diversions. There is no rush. No need for decisions now. We can discuss this matter tomorrow. Perhaps the day after. Or maybe after the harvest."

Murmurings of assent followed, then drifted into the distance.

Luciana began to pace. "Has Ignazio gone mad? Did he take something from the Careri? Has he offered something in return? Ursicio told me you all turned out your pockets before you left. This is bad. This is really bad. You are Duca. You must counter this influence, this sudden curiosity. I'll help Ursicio settle the *signori*. Meanwhile, I think—"

What Luciana thought at that moment also likewise remains a mystery because a screech arrowed through our conversation, like the sound of a thousand damp fingers squeaking across clean crystal. I clapped my hands over my ears and vaulted for the window. Storm clouds gathered in the distance, past the border. Over the valley a cacophony chorused, the volume ratcheting past ridiculous.

And a pinpoint, barreling in and trumpeting an alarm.

"Antonio warned me about a storm." I pointed. "Here comes the sprite Giacomo told me would be arriving."

"Giacomo?" Luciana stopped pacing.

Claudio drew Luciana aside and spoke to her in a tone too low for me to hear over all the *folletti's* racket, though I could imagine. About a fever and a lump on my head, how I'd claimed Antonio had been playing his fiddle, Giacomo was in the garden. . . .

The sprite streaked through the window, then cartwheeled across the floor moss to slow her speed. She dropped a cloth baby at my feet. The same cloth baby I'd left in exchange for my son. "The Careri *duca* sends this message. 'Return the child, or suffer the repercussions.'"

She pointed out of the window, toward the borderland where a new cloud bloomed over the valley, dark and dystopian and spreading with a speed no weather does. "The *folletti* are rising. I barely got through with my wings."

Claudio was quick to offer the bowl of candied violets I kept on my desk. "Why are the *folletti* rising?"

The sprite tapped her nose. "Can't you smell?"

All I smelled was the roasting marshmallows, sticky over my lips like I'd buried my face in them.

I guess Claudio smelled more because he clutched my shoulder. "Those aren't clouds. That's smoke."

Sprites are discreet, loyal, expected to keep what tidbits they overhear outside of their commission to themselves. But this sprite was one of ours. Her place was in Panduri. "Tell me more."

The sprite darted back, then forth, then back again, her amulet whispering of indecision, of conflicted loyalties. Finally, she lighted on my right shoulder, shuttered her hand to the side of her mouth to hide her lips, and leaned into my ear. "I think Careri plans to burn out the *folletti* and cross, Duca. Either that or he plans to drive the *folletti* before him. He has people from Outside to help. He calls them *mercenaries* and they are armed with something called *guns*."

The sprite made motions like she were aiming for a target. "Like bows but without arrows. Loud noises provide their power. I saw one of the mercenaries use it to stop a bear in its tracks. Scared the poor animal so badly he dropped where he stood and fell asleep."

The sprite stopped targeting. "The effects are profound. The bear was still sleeping when I left."

Luciana gasped. Her hand flew to her mouth.

My hand flew to my head, to the bump behind my ear which was every bit as large as dead Uncle Giacomo had said and now throbbed worse than my hand, because of all the screeching. I needed to do something, respond in some way. Fire, *folletti*. Gun-armed, prolonged sleep-inducing Outsiders. "I have to hide Spero."

The sprite twisted on her spin. "Is that the answer I should attempt to relay?"

Every vertebra in my spine got hold of the one beneath it and stiffened. "No. No."

Somebody finally used my son's proper name and it had to be me and it had to be in front of the sprite. Discreet or not, a sprite doesn't need to know more than she should.

Flattery might distract her. Sprites are as susceptible to sweet talk as they are to sweets.

I tapped Claudio on the shoulder. "This sprite has done Panduri a great service and has been very patient with me. Surely, Gentle Guardian, when you have a moment, it would be proper to sing a praise in her honor."

Claudio bowed, and, I'll swear, the sprite blushed.

I turned to her. "Can you carry another message? Or should I call one of your sisters."

"Don't be ridiculous." The sprite was smoke-shocked, gun-surprised, and breathless, but sprites have pride. They never refuse a commission.

"Thank you. Send to our water nymphs their Duca's wish that

they direct their waters into the valley to quench the fire. Send to our good protectors that they marshal the pitcher plants to pour out their bounty until the waters arrive. Also to be certain our sparring ficuses are in fighting trim."

"Of course. Any special directions for Salvatore?"

"Yes." I thought of Salvatore's stalwart and steady service, his assiduous attention to his duties. "Tell our Faithful Finder to find a better solution and implement it."

The sprite curtsied and took flight.

I took a seat. I was tired. And hungry. I reached into my boot tops, came away with an apple and took a bite.

The fruit was delectable and delightful and bursting with possibilities. What I thought I knew about the *folletti* shifted. I saw the *folletti* from a new angle, their behavior from a different perspective. They were distressed and dismayed, not angry. Vexed, not vicious, their frustration fomenting past tolerable.

Like a sprite behaves when she cannot complete her message.

I'd never thought of the *folletti* that way, as creatures with purpose, able to be frayed by their deficiencies. They were meant to buffer our contacts with the Careri, keep all in their proper places. And now something, or somebody, was frustrating their mission.

The apple's juice trickled down my throat revealing when last I'd tasted one.

In Careri, the apple Salvatore nabbed from the buffet table. An apple that made Ceres curious about calculus. An apple she'd placed in a sack and I'd stuffed in my boot tops, then forgot about. Apples she'd feared might be dangerous.

Right?

Maybe not.

I swayed, drunk on the apple's knowledge. Time expanded, a quarter hour happening in a few seconds during which I had plenty of time to examine another conundrum from a new angle.

All of Claudio's damned documents. Maybe Claudio threw those files in the box because *I* frustrated *him*.

The *folletti* broke into a new song, not so loud, but discordant and disturbing, like those scores I'd found in Antonio's study jumbled among a pile of ancient star casts and scrolls. Scores Claudio must have filed in Father's office at some point. Scores Claudio had ultimately tossed into the box.

Though the scores were not, at that moment, before me, I saw them in my mind's eye, listened to them with my mind's ear, the notes flowing in sparkles over their parchment like sun-danced water over rocks. I grabbed paper and pen and started writing, adding words, notations, flourishes and trills, then sat back and looked at what I'd written, at the miracle unfolding before me.

Boom.

Claudio didn't notice, he was still thinking at normal speed. And he was still looking out the window after the sprite. He shook his head. "The Careri Duca burns the *folletti*, you drown them. Perhaps we should take a step back, perhaps we should—"

But what else we should do also likewise and yet again remains a mystery because frankly . . . I didn't have time.

Twenty-Eight

Father's office was a chaos. Papers and parchments scattered into the corners, the creeping nettle cowered by his desk, and his sparring ficus looked ready to cry.

Claudio followed me in. "Well, that was rude."

"Luciana will be fine."

"I meant rude to me. Luciana's dandy. Gone to help Ursicio keep the *signori* settled."

"She's always so practical." Ash slurried in water puddled in front of the hearth. Gunk dripped from the grate. I poked at the goo. "Marshmallow. You left them in Father's drawer. I was hungry."

Claudio picked a bloom from the bottlebrush Father always grew by the door. He swept the sticky slime to the side. "You near incinerated yourself."

Not a fever. A fire. I plucked the bottlebrush from Claudio's fingers. "Leave that. Ignazio's getting ready to claim the *ducato*. I'll bet he's already on his way. I have to stop him. Help me search."

Claudio opened drawers. He closed them. He rattled boxes and baskets. "What am I looking for?"

"Those documents you left for me. The ones in the box. The ones I couldn't read because I didn't have the key. All those casts and scrolls and musical scores." I combed through nooks, nosed through crannies, looked under parchments and paperweights and piles of files. "Especially the musical scores. The compositions I found on Antonio's desk after he died. The ones that were all mixed up with the star charts."

I peeked under the creeping nettle. "Remember?"

"Oh." Claudio stopped searching. "About those papers."

"I know. You're sorry and all that. Don't be. I get it. I had to unearth Dante's and Ilario's birth certificates and figure it out on my own and you know why?"

"Because I'm a cleric and I'm not allowed to tell you."

Claudio. Always so literal. "No. Because I wouldn't listen to those scores while Antonio was still with us. Then I wouldn't listen to them again when Topo dragged them to my room and left them on my pillow. Because I was stubborn. I was hurt. I was angry and anxious and I don't like anybody telling me what to do."

I got down on my knees and checked under the desk. "Because without Antonio's music my words meant nothing."

"Matteo. Stop. Those scores you found on Antonio's desk aren't what you think. They're not—"

"—melodic. I know." I got off my knees. "They're disagreeable, unbalanced, discordant as shit. Like Antonio left out half the notes. That got me thinking about what you told me about solutions and puzzles."

"That doors sometimes have more than one key."

I waggled a finger at him. One that wasn't broken. "That's what Antonio left me in those scores. A second key to those star casts you left in the box. Because I'll bet he destroyed Giacomo's key when he torched Dante and Ilario's tree."

"Yes. And we should talk about all that, except listen—"

"No. You listen. His music, my words. Together they unlock the whole thing. All those documents and scrolls, all their secrets. Maybe

Antonio didn't want me to know those secrets once, but he wanted me to know them later or he wouldn't have sent those scores to me. You must have agreed or you wouldn't have left everything lying on his desk for me to find. Wouldn't have tossed them in the box."

I checked the hedges, pulled baskets from the shelves, snooped behind the whispering windwhistle. "Because you couldn't tell me, because Antonio told you, and you can't tell anything anybody tells you in confession."

A paper clip flipped between us. I picked it up. I waved it at Claudio. "See? So help me find the box, little brother. Or cousin. Or whatever you are. Then help me shove all its secrets up Ignazio's ass."

I tapped my toe, my mind halfway to assembling the words I needed to fend off Ignazio's. "We'll get him the hell off our backs, the rest of today's mess settled, then you and I will get drunk."

"If you want to get drunk we should get started now. The box is here. You left it behind the hearth." Claudio dragged it out, then he rooted to his spot, going still and serene, an oak bracing for a storm. "It's empty."

I dropped the paperclip, crossed the room, picked up the box, and patted my good hand around the interior, half-expecting to release a false bottom. "Where did all the papers go?"

Claudio pointed to the grate. To soggy ash and soot and, yes, burnt marshmallow.

"I burned them." Fire, not fever. Because I was angry, because I was raging, because my hand was infected and I was out of my mind.

Because I couldn't burn my journal. Because I couldn't find my journal. Because it wasn't buried in the garden. Because Claudio had taken it, left Dante's and Ilario's birth certificates in exchange. Because nothing was how I'd assumed, nothing was how it should be, and nothing was going the way I'd hoped.

Then I caught my foot in the creeping nettle, my shin gave way, and I cracked my head on the grate.

I let the box crash to the floor moss, then sank to the roots of the sparring ficus and dropped my head into my hands, even the throbbing one. "We are so fucked."

"Don't be ridiculous. They're just a bunch of papers. Everything you need to handle Ignazio is here and here." Claudio tapped his head, then his heart. "Because you're Duca. You have the office, the lineage. You even have the hat."

The floor rumbled. For the first time in a very long time.

Claudio jumped, his eyes wide and surprised and full of apprehension. "What was that?"

"The Deep Lore. I broke it. Or rather I burned it. Along with the hat."

"You burned the hat?"

I crawled to the hearth, dug through the ashes, and pulled the remains of a pleat from the back of the grate. "To a crisp. And everything else. That is, everything within reach. Including our charts."

"No, you can't mean that." Claudio's scooped through the goo and the gunk. "Without charts we're . . . chartless, gusting on a chaotic wind."

Without a purpose, a path, And without a place in Panduri. "Don't tell Ignazio."

"No wonder everything is going so cockeyed. I thought it was about your boy. It's about our charts. Everything is always about our damned charts." Claudio rinsed his hands under the water lilies, then rummaged on Father's desk. "Gather your planets and stardust. Get out your parchment and scrolls. Cast us new ones."

"I can't. Without a chart, I'm not Duca. I don't have the authority to cast them, or to instruct anybody else to cast them, or even to sit in this office and complain about it."

The rumbling grew deeper, cracking the earth beneath the floor moss. The shelves toppled. The wolfsbane lifted its blooms to the sky and howled. The framing on Father's window, the largest, the most impressive, the one from which I'd started surveying the entire *ducato—that* framing—cracked.

Claudio grabbed the front of my shirt and hauled me up. "Ignazio cannot know you are not Duca. He cannot know I now can't be Duca either. As Wise and Constant Counselor, he'd be next in line, and we cannot let that happen."

His voice was too shrill, his breathing too fast, his color too high. But Claudio was steady, brave as I've ever seen him. And determined. "If Ignazio is Duca, this office is his. These records are his. Dante and Ilario's garden, their constructs. Panduri. Everything. Is *his*."

I thought of Father. Thought of his secretive *sub rosas*, his low-pitched *sotto voces*. What Father knew he'd kept to himself. What Father didn't, he never disclosed. Even to me. Because he was Duca.

And so was I. "Go to my study. Bring me Dante's and Ilario's charts, the fake ones. Also, Spero's birth certificate. They're on my desk."

I sent him for other documents, anything star-sprinkled and medallioned, well-worn and creased enough to look like it dated from the proper period. Claudio moved back and forth and forth and back. The knowledgeable apple raised the destroyed records before my mind's eye. I interpreted them using the key the apple had helped me fashion from Antonio's scores. I erased and rewrote, rewrote and erased, then I looked out of Father's window.

My window. The *duca's* window. The window with the cracked frame from which I could still survey the entire *ducato*. "Shit. Here comes Ignazio. Let me do the talking."

Then I took off my amulet. Because I was going to be telling a lot of falsehoods. I handed it to Claudio. "Hold this for me."

"Are you crazy? You'll die."

"No worries. I'll talk quick." I brandished the birth certificates, rattled the scrolls and the casts. "I've got a plan."

A terrible plan. Based on bravado and bullshit. Backed by random charts, newfound knowledge, and my unique talent, the power of my words, and their ability to make what is bigger, more, what is not, less, and what is true, whether convenient or not, real.

Up against the biggest liar Panduri had ever charted.

And his son. Papist Jesus's Gentle sidekick. Signore Meek and Mild. Carrying a satchel.

Yes, I had a stinking and terrible and brazenly impossible plan.

Antonio would have been so proud.

Niccoli's talent is making the broken whole and he honed right in on Antonio's fiddle, lying in a crumpled heap atop Father's desk. "How sad. Seventy sirens worked seventy Midsummers to make that fiddle."

And all it took was one of Antonio's magic-infused vials of music to send it crashing. "That was an accident."

Niccoli looked at my hand.

I held it up. "This was an accident, too."

The fissure widening in the floor moss, the toppled shelves, the cracked window frame, the tallest, the most impressive, and . . . all the rest.

I shook my head. "Accident. Accident. Accident."

The ash and the slurry and the goo still dripping from the grate. "Is that an accident, too?"

"No. Marshmallows."

"Ah." Niccoli's features lighted. "I love those."

"Enough." Ignazio's attitude sliced through all the syrup. "It is time we settle this matter. You've stolen a child, one of the Careri. It is time you send him back."

"Spero came for a visit and will be returned when the time is right. I am his father, he is my son, and it's time he knew the rest of the family."

I held up Spero's birth certificate, patterned on those Giacomo had crafted for Dante and Ilario. I pointed to the seals and the medallions and to where I'd forged the Careri Duca's signature, taking care my fingers covered any indications the parchment had originally detailed an agreement between an Insider piper and an Outsider village regarding the removal of rats. "Spero is here with permission from his *duca*. This situation is nothing like when Giacomo retrieved Dante and Ilario."

Something glinted in Ignazio's eye, maybe surprise, maybe suspicion. "You knew Giacomo was once Duca."

"Always."

"And the *signori* installed Bartomeo to replace him."

"From the moment I was grown."

"Because Giacomo tried to use Dante and Ilario to claim Careri."

Dante. Ilario. Claim Careri. A *ducato* once part of our orbit, and upon whose orbit Panduri's star used to rise.

That information was new.

Every muscle in my amulet-less body went nerveless. Every assumption I'd ever made fell flat.

No wonder Father and Giacomo fought. "I found that out later."

Ignazio reached across the void and grabbed Claudio by his cowl. "Did you know all this, too?"

Niccoli pried Ignazio off. "Father. Let go. He can't say anything. The Deep Lore won't let him. Our visit isn't about Spero's need to visit his family, but about how he might be used to harm Panduri. How Panduri might be used to harm him."

"You mean how your father can profit from it all." Claudio adjusted his cowl. He straightened his collar. "How you can help him."

"I mean how we can settle a situation already sending our stars into a tilt." Niccoli leaned into Claudio, his tone honest and constrained. "Counsel your brother to put on his amulet before he falls down. Advise him to speak the truth. The solution will follow."

Put on my amulet. Tell the truth. Not while my cunning was supercharged on the Forbidden Apple. Not while I had scrolls and charts and hogwash to spare. Yet I sensed a sincerity I'd never credited to Niccoli, goodwill I'd presumed was a show.

Clear and certain and—despite my lack of connection because I wasn't wearing my amulet—strong. "Our sins always surface, as Giacomo learned to his sad and sorry detriment. So have your father's. He's made an arrangement with the Careri Duca. He wants Panduri in exchange for a child. A child who is son to me, Panduri's current *duca*. A child who is also in line for Careri's *ducato*."

I sorted through the starcasts until I found the chart Claudio had shown me the Midsummer he retrieved me from between the legs of Spero's mother. The chart which showed the generations of her *ducato*, the placement of her husband, and where Spero's star would someday fall.

Next, I showed Niccoli Spero's birth chart. Traced his star to its origin—me.

Last, I pulled Niccoli toward the window, pointed out the smoke, the tumult gathering over the valley. "Those *folletti* do not rise to get away from the fire. They rise to protest your father in this exchange, because as these star casts show, though Spero may be Careri's Heir, Careri's Heir also has a place in Panduri."

Niccoli leaned against the casement. "I know."

I placed my good hand on the piles of documents, ones with plenty of medallions of the kind Outsiders like, and dismissed Niccoli's agreement with the bad one. "Tell your father not to bother deny-ing. I've got the—" I stood straighter. "Wait. What do you mean, you know?"

Niccoli looked like he didn't quite know what to do with that question. "I mean I know. Ignazio's been my father a long time."

Longer than mine had been mine. "Then tell him I've got the proof right here, proof I intend to present to the *signori*. Proof of his double-dealings, complete with star seals and signatures."

Ignazio came closer, expression benign. "What proof? I see parch-ment and paper and a few bits of marshmallow. And I didn't sign any of it."

"No, but Giacomo did." I unrolled one Giacomo had, a list of instructions for the cloud sculptors from what I'd been able to interpret.

I held the list in front of my face long enough for Ignazio to see the signature, partly for the drama, mostly to hide the twitch starting at the corner of my eye. "The Careri are infertile, their generations have grown sparse. Their star is descending and threatens to send ours into a spiral. Giacomo was no paragon, no lover of rules. He was like you, Ignazio, born under a contrary star, but he was also Panduri's *duca*, first and foremost. You convinced him to take action, one that likewise encouraged his ambition, one you assured Giacomo would maintain our orbit and save a dying *ducato*."

"And what action did I convince Panduri's *duca* to take?" Ignazio's demeanor was casual, his tone politely interested, as if we spoke of matters of little consequence and not of his concern.

"You convinced Giacomo to conceive Dante and Ilario, perhaps even arranged the liaison with the wife of Careri's *duca*. It was a foolish and foolhardy plan, but Giacomo was no fool. He cast the plan here, in these documents, tested the possibilities in the stars. And your role in their casting."

Ignazio settled into the chair opposite the desk. "Only a fool makes a record of his secrets. And, as you said, Giacomo was no fool."

"Except Giacomo had a brother who did not like the role he was charted. A brother who'd presumed he'd become Duca once Giacomo's plan went awry. A brother the *signori* passed over because he, too, had been born under a contrary star."

I leaned on Father's desk. I had to, the ground was still shaking and without the amulet, my difficult shin was beginning to buckle. "Giacomo was like many of us, drawn to forbidden fruit. As you were, *Uncle* Ignazio, Panduri's Protector before Giacomo, and, I'm certain, nowhere near as legendary."

"Bartomeo was a priest. He liked to read. He liked to garden. He was shit at casting stars. Couldn't protect a willow wisp from a sugar rush. He should have refused the position."

My gaze darted, windows to shelves. To the walls Father had grown directly from the soil, the furniture Father had fashioned directly from the tree branches. Ignazio is a manipulator. He's a scoundrel and a schemer, scurrilous and too often just plain mean. I was sick of it.

I'll bet so was Father. "Father took the position to protect all he loved. Panduri. His children."

And yes, even me, his nephew.

My shin finally gave up and I collapsed into Father's chair. I'd been a fool. Made my assumptions, presumed the worst.

Claudio's right. I'm a jerk.

Ignazio swooped in, grabbing a stack of scrolls from my pile. He looked at the first. "This is fake. You've erased the original words and copied others."

He sorted through. "And what are these? Star charts for ducks, puppies, kittens. Are these chronicles of dastardly deeds and scandalous confessions, or listings of inhabitants for a children's petting farm?"

The race was done. I'd lost. I asked Claudio for my amulet, waited while he affixed it to my chain, then breathed deep the glory of connection. Outside had been interesting, intriguing and illuminating and plenty of fun. But Outside was torn from the gravity which held Inside together, and I decided then and there, Inside was better. "We had the proof. The documents, the signatures, the castings, and more."

Claudio and I stared soulfully at the grate, at the ash piles and marshmallow goo. Because despite our many failings, we are honest men.

Ignazio laughed. Coming from him the effect was kind of creepy. "Let me guess. It was an accident."

I nodded. "That doesn't mean there aren't copies. I will find them."

"You can't find them if you aren't Duca. My power is negotiation, I'll persuade the *signori*."

"My power is enhanced by truth. They will listen to me."

Ignazio put out his hands, the gesture conciliatory, his manner slippery as oiled fish, his expression . . . a little queasy. My guess from the way the ground kept shifting under our feet. "Matteo. Stop. There is a simpler solution. Let us negotiate. I'll pass over my claim. The *signori* can name Niccoli as Duca. Surely, the Deep Lore seeks such a solution. What else can all this earth-shaking mean?"

How far do apples fall from trees? "And who would be orchestrating that performance?"

Niccoli stepped between us. "I'd orchestrate my own. But I don't plan to take the stage. I've lost a brother to these frustrations, this need for more, the despair at feeling slighted. I've lost a sister-in-law and a nephew to its fruit."

He lowered his head. "No more. The poison of this tree will not be allowed to root in my generations. My wife, my children deserve better. I am done."

He lifted his satchel up and over his head and placed it on the creeping nettle. He squatted beside it, opened it and started removing scrolls. He handed me one.

I read the notations as I always did, the symbols that let me know I held a birth chart, then swept along to read the chart's owner: Matteo, First Son of the Duca.

Niccoli nudged the satchel. "You don't have to search for copies. I have them here."

Twenty-Nine

*N*iccoli had copies. He had star casts and scrolls, birth charts and consideration tallies. Niccoli had everything a man born to gentle guardianship should have. And he had it all in triplicate.

Thank you, Papist Jesus.

Niccoli handed me Claudio's birth chart. "These are only your recasts. Bartomeo burned your originals while he was still Gentle Guardian. He did so with all the proper laments and ceremonies and as was pleasing to the Deep Lore."

I reveled in the charts, in their existence, in the confirmation that I still had a place in Panduri. "Then they named Bartomeo to be Duca and Giacomo recharted our stars."

Niccoli nodded. "Yes, but plenty cannot be changed. Origins. Parentage. Facts my father used in these copies to drain consideration from Bartomeo. When Bartomeo died, my father presumed he'd one day be able to use the truth of your births against you, against Claudio."

Niccoli pulled one gossamer-tied bundle after another from the satchel. He rattled one at Ignazio, stewing by the sparring ficus. "You presumed a lot, Father. My obedience. My allegiance. My willingness to avenge what happened to my brother. But you forgot what was most important. You forgot my heart and my home is forever, for always with Panduri."

Niccoli handed me the scrolls. "Take them, with my blessings, but have a care. Grief is a journey that never ends. Don't let it choose your destination."

I unrolled my chart first, then Giacomo's, then Mamma's. I showed them to Claudio. "She belonged to me."

"She belonged to all of us. Mamma was meant for the Heir. Like Ceres."

"So she went with Father. Packed me up, packed up the hat, and rearranged us. And your mother?"

"Dead at my birth, I'm told." A flicker, the tiniest fleeting feather of regret fluttered from Claudio's core. "Antonio told me she sang sweeter than any songbird. He told me my talent comes from her."

"And Antonio's talent?"

Claudio put out his hands. "I have no idea."

The charts made no sense. "Antonio was bigger, but not much older. They could have left us in our places. Saved all the trouble. They even made me declare Cosimo to be Antonio's. Yet by any arrangement, Cosimo was the child of the Heir."

Claudio again grew silent.

Ignazio stopped his stewing. "Because aside from your looks, your tendency to overreact, and your facility with words, you were like Giacomo in one other way. Go ahead, Niccoli. Show him."

Niccoli traced my pathways, all the possibilities. They lighted under his fingertips.

I spotted the problem. "There. At my star's origin."

A defect no recharting could fix, no reimagining could alter. "I was likewise born under a contrary star."

Ignazio leaned back, his expression self-satisfied and final. "Thus, the reason for the *signori*'s constant concern and need to gather."

Sadness puddled at a spot over my heart, threatening to swamp me. "The *signori* gathered because they weren't certain the rearrangement would work. That's why Father and Antonio tied me to Midsummer, why Antonio was so desperate to keep me away from the border. Because the *signori* had changed the *duca*, not the Deep Lore, and the *signori* had no idea if any of it would take hold."

Claudio lowered his head. "You were Heir even when you weren't. Always at Midsummer's approach, the unknown factor, the underlying premise. Without you, the twilight might never have come."

Niccoli rerolled my scroll. "So now we are returned to our reason for being here and the reason for the current instance of the *signori* gathering. Your son. Spero. The *signori* know about him, know about everything. They have from the start. Most of the time they choose not to remember. Now they must."

I gathered the charts and the scrolls and dumped them beside Niccoli. "These are ridiculous. An illusion. We are who we are because of the choices we make, not because of stars tossed on a parchment."

"Yet you stand in the *duca's* office. Though your stars were recharted, though you eventually burnt them. Though you were rearranged and recast and trained to a role to which you were not born. You are Duca. All bow to Matteo, first son of Giacomo, despite the twisting of his planets. And as Matteo rises, so shall Panduri."

But under a contrary star. I looked out of the window—the tallest and most impressive—at smoke billowing in the distance, blowing left, then right. The *folletti* were rising, their consternation now coalesced into a general and annoying hum.

Over a boy I loved, one I began to realize I couldn't keep. Unlike Giacomo. "I'll always be a danger. So long as I'm Duca or any of my line, Spero might be Careri's excuse to make the same claim Giacomo hoped to with Dante and Ilario. Even if Careri never tries to claim Panduri, always there is the same danger from me. That I would do as my father and claim Careri as mine via Spero."

And what of Spero? What price would he pay? Had all the messing with the Deep Lore put an unwitting target on his back? Like Antonio, would he one day die and nobody understand how?

I grabbed my head. The effects of the Outsider apple were wearing off and a man could go crazy trying to work out all those possibilities. "I can't be Duca. It doesn't matter if I'm charted, or recharted, what the Deep Lore decides, or if the Papists' Jesus gets off his crucifix, crosses our valley, and declares me so. I can't be Duca, or Panduri is always at risk. From me, from Careri, from the day my Heir, my Cosimo, makes the same stupid Midsummer mistakes his father and grandfather did. I can't be Duca."

The words rose, each in shimmering perfection, lighting a path I'd never considered.

"Matteo." Claudio touched my shoulder. "Don't."

But the ground stopped shaking. It settled into profound silence. I put up a hand to stop my brother, taking joy in a freedom an hour earlier I'd have declared impossible, certain, absolutely certain, that in freeing myself, I also freed Panduri. "I can't be Duca."

I looked at Claudio. "You do it."

I've seen Claudio content, Claudio despondent. I've seen him rhapsodic and rapturous and angelic in bliss. I've seen him negotiate the intricacies of the Deep Lore until I feared his heart would fail from all the soul-squeezing turnings. Never had I seen my brother so horrified, so panic-stricken, so painfully stunned.

Oops. "Sorry. I don't know what I was thinking. Never mind."

Ignazio stopped moping. "Perhaps Niccoli will reconsider."

"Perhaps I won't." Niccoli lifted Antonio's fiddle. He laid a hand over the broken places, a finger along the frets. The neck uncracked, the strings tightened around the pins, the dents in the body smoothed. Niccoli presented me the instrument, whole as the day it had been made. "Here, it may be out of tune."

Somehow, I doubted that.

He dug back into his satchel. "Alas, my ability to make the broken whole does not apply to people, else my brother would still be alive, and Matteo's hand would be healed, but perhaps the ability applies to situations. Perhaps to puzzles. The only way I know to find out is to provide the key."

Niccoli pulled out a last scroll. He unrolled it on Father's desk, then waved me over to see.

We grow older, we grow harder, more entrenched in our dogma, more despairing of our dreams.

Antonio tried to tell me right after I snapped my leg. He told me we needed to find a creative way to end this vendetta or it would end us all. Then, for reasons unknown, he got on a horse and crossed out of this life, leaving me headaches and heartache and a course I was unexpectedly and grudgingly expected to follow.

We'd been rearranged, my brothers and I. My uncle and my father had cast our constellations this way, then that, looking for the best combination, their presumption Panduri's puzzle, and therefore ours, had only one solution.

They were wrong. Like Dante's Wall, the best solutions sometimes don't fit the puzzle. And no matter how many ways Father and Giacomo plotted our charts their puzzle would never resolve. Because they were still missing a piece. An unexplored permutation, an overlooked pathway outside Panduri's typical possibilities but well within all my generation held in common.

Giacomo's unconsidered child. The child I didn't know about until I looked at her chart, sunshiny and hopeful and always on the rise.

I turned to my brother, my cleric, my friend. I turned to him because in all matters regarding the Deep Lore he is my unwavering star. "Can a girl be Duca?"

As it turned out a girl—no, a woman—could. Or at least nothing in the Deep Lore said she couldn't.

"Nobody's ever thought to ask," Claudio told me later while we all sat together working out the ways and the wherefores and the whens.

I gathered the remaining pieces of our puzzle. Niccoli and Claudio, Tendi and Ursicio, Luciana above all, and yes, even Ignazio. I had to. He was and forever more for this and all his generations, Panduri's Wise and Constant Counselor.

Because intrigue is exhausting and the moment I had a chance and while I was still Duca, I meant to strike the practice from our lexicon.

Salvatore sent a sprite. "Panduri's Faithful Finder wishes to convey to the *duca* he has found the most obvious and better solution to our border problem and sends these words which I will now quote. 'I have offered enough sweets to carry the *folletti* into the next Midsummer and in so doing have made the *folletti* our friends, rather than our foe. They declare loyalty to Panduri's Duca and await his further actions to ensure our newfound peace. It seems the *folletti* do not like being cut off from Inside any more than we would. I guess somebody should have thought to ask.'"

Salvatore. Master of simple solutions. I sent the sprite off with new instructions. "Ignazio wishes you to convey to Careri his apologies for an arrangement poorly made. He requests the immediate cessation of all misunderstandings and assures an amicable and agreeable accord beneficial to both our *ducato*s will be swiftly made."

Ignazio wasn't ready to give up the fight. "You send a sprite offering friendship to the Careri, Salvatore sends one offering the same to the *folletti*." He snapped his fingers. "All the ill-will disappears."

He stopped snapping. "Ridiculous."

"Come." I waved the group to the window. "Look over the valley, look at all that smoke. Yet the sun is setting and no glow lights the twilight. Smoke, but no fire. The *folletti* are supposedly rising, yet none cross our border."

I laid out another chart, yet another cast of the vendetta, one I'd made before Ignazio and Niccoli arrived, while I did all the erasing and rewriting, and Claudio was trundling parchments back and forth. I showed the others. "When I visited Careri, I presumed they had no magic, only illusion. Now I think their magic *is* illusion."

I pointed out a star, powerful, yet pale, hidden by the light of a dozen others. "I think illusion is their *duca's* special talent, as fraught with pitfalls as any of ours, and as exhausting as intrigue. So I think the Careri Duca will welcome our tidings. I expect the moment our sprite arrives, the Careri Duca's Outsider mercenaries with their sleep-inducing guns will evaporate into the ether, as will the smoke and hopefully any ill-feelings."

Niccoli didn't seem convinced. "If their talent is illusion, any agreement Careri makes will be just as ephemeral."

"Which is why your father will not be involved. We need straight talk and simple transactions. We need qualities which are not easily twisted. The Careri divine what a person wants and turn his talents to their service. I'd declared freedom to pursue a life of my own and unwittingly helped create Spero. Ignazio wanted power, so Careri turned him, then Ignazio turned Giacomo.

Ignazio was halfway to protest, but I stopped him with a word. Negotiation is likewise exhausting and I needed a nap. "For this reason, Salvatore is immune, the only among us able to cross without detriment. His heart is only for Panduri and he has no curiosity. He cannot be swayed by the temptations of another world.

An uncomfortable thought rumbled between my ears. "The Careri are too clever, too practiced in the art of deception. We cannot fight them. Perhaps it is best for our orbits to diverge."

Luciana made a sound like a distant wind. Not a sob, more like an outrushing of air from her lungs. "You would no longer be able to see your son. And he is bright and beautiful. Don't make that decision yet. Only make the decisions you must. And speak to Ceres. She's grown fond of him as I. A solution will present when you aren't puzzling through it."

Claudio gave me the most to think about. "Whatever their illusions, from your description, from Salvatore's, it sounds like your boy's garden, the tree growing there were real. You've always believed his mother's love for him is likewise real. However you might feel about her, how she tricked you, that love and your son might be the only true things in Careri. And therefore, their only hope."

271

Thirty

Someday when all at last comes clear
and the secrets all been told,
I'll rest me well with books and beer
And hand back all their souls.

No new plan is easily implemented. Unbecoming Duca proved far harder and more cumbersome than becoming Duca.

The *folletti* still found plenty of fault, despite the infusion of sweets and the removal of Careri's influence. Their bells tolled particularly clamorous over their quota of marshmallows.

I left those negotiations to Tendi and Ursicio, confident in their resourceful ability to calm chaos. Then I offered Salvatore respite from all the sheep in recognition of his faithful and unrelenting service to Panduri. I sent him a sprite with the news that he was released from his position and was now free to take on his duties as his family's heir.

He was quick in his response.

So I sent for him. "What do you mean you want to remain Protector? You are first in your family. You are foremost. You must marry. Make new heirs. Go to work husbanding your family's hard-won and recently-restored consideration."

"I like being Panduri's Protector. I like being her Faithful Finder. I like living at the border in a tent all my own. I have sixteen brothers, half as many sisters. One of them can be heir. I'm happy to play second fiddle to any of them."

"A girl can't be heir."

"Are you certain? Have you asked? Because last time I checked, the Deep Lore was looking kind of flexible."

And there was the matter of getting clarity with the *ducato* across the valley.

Niccoli proved invaluable. "I don't think the Careri were being duplicitous when they sent Spero's mother to Midsummer. I think they were honoring a contract made among our fathers. That we would provide them a child. A child who could carry their *ducato* into the next generation."

"What were we to receive in return?"

"What they have been trying to provide us. The wonders of Outside." Niccoli flicked his hand, like he were waving a magic wand. "Electricity! Water pipes! And something new they are very excited about called *cold fusion*."

"Cold fusion. Sounds like what happens when snowflakes mate. Is cold fusion or any of Outside's other wonders necessary in Panduri?"

"Only if it is necessary for Panduri to change."

"Do you think Panduri should?"

Niccoli cranked his neck this way, then that, the way a man does when undecided. "I think Outside is closer than we think, their curiosities legion, their possibilities endless. I think Panduri needs to decide where her star lies."

I had something else to think about, one other detail to define before I gave up my rule. "How is your father?"

"Enjoying his grandchildren. I do not think my ability extends to people, but I think my children may be able to heal the hardest soul."

—

There was the matter of who would live where.

Ceres wasn't happy. "But I just finished with the aviary."

"We're exchanging for Luciana's house. It's huge. You can have three aviaries."

"Don't be ridiculous. What would anybody do with three aviaries?"

I'm not sure what anybody does with one. "We won't be exchanging until Midsummer. That's months away. Claudio and I promised Luciana we'd grow some new rooms here before I give up being Duca, else half of her brood will be sleeping in the branches."

And, of course, there was the matter of the star charts. Because in Panduri everything always comes back to star charts, and for all my sister's decisive, compassionate, and capable qualities, Luciana couldn't cast one.

I worked with her on the finer points. So did Claudio.

She was intransigent. "I don't understand what all this nudging is about."

Ursicio poured her another cup of tea. "Darling, you raise an orb every morning, bright enough to light the day. These are just a bunch of stars and planets."

"It's not just the nudging, it's all the arranging. Why must we be so constrictive? They're only infants. Can't we give them a little room to breathe?" She tossed the stars and planets back into the bucket and pushed the bucket toward me. "No, this won't work. I'm not set up for stars and the night. I'm the dawn. I like to get to bed early."

My talent is powerful, it's strong. It's more apt to get me in trouble than out of it, but one bit of my talent I'd been trying to cultivate was the ability to discern the larger meaning behind somebody's words. I put a finger under Luciana's chin and lifted it. "What is this about?"

"I'm afraid I'll screw this up."

"You won't. You'll do your best." I shoved the bucket back at her. "Please let's get on with this. I can't not be Duca until you cast stars making me something else. And Claudio also needs to be recast."

Claudio stopped ordering the meteors by weight and size. "I don't."

"You do. Because right now, while I'm still Duca, I declare you free to pursue your own life."

"I'm a cleric."

"Not all Promises are public. Father had a family before Mamma and I and Luciana came along. You can, too."

Claudio looked like he was thinking about that one. "I'd have to give up my position as Panduri's Gentle Guardian, give up my place when the *signori* gather, give up my room at the monastery, the one with the clerestory windows."

"I'll bet a hundred buttercups and a green-and-yellow basket filled with spinning yarns you'd find something better as replacement."

Luciana dug back into the bucket, sorting out comet trails and quasars. "Enough with all the familial bonding. It's late and I'm tired. Dawn comes early." She scooped up a handful of stardust. "Matteo, you first. What do you want to be?"

To say the room fell silent would understate the sudden vacuum into which all sound scrambled. In all my years, in all that had happened, nobody had ever asked me what I wanted to be.

In all of Panduri, I don't think anybody had ever asked anybody.

Luciana rattled my stars. She held them over the parchment. "Matteo?"

I looked skyward, at a twilight deepening to night and thought of all I'd already done, all I hadn't, all I'd wished I could change, all I didn't, the times I'd tried my hardest, and the times I'd been my worst. I decided there's really only one goal, one path any of us can master, even when we think we've done our best. "I want to be . . . better."

Luciana released the stars to the parchment. Then she and I and Claudio, and even Ursicio, bent our heads together to see where they landed.

And that brought me to Tendi. The ever-present question mark on the accounting of my past. I was still uncertain regarding Tendi. Still unsure of any further action regarding his future. "When you were made to take the blame for my liaison with the Careri, when you were ordered to the monastery, were you unhappy?"

"No, Duca."

"Why not?"

"I had no wish to marry. No wish to produce heirs. Women are beautiful and caring and of great value to our society, but I have no wish to join with one. I prefer men. The monastery has plenty. The Duca-who-was's kindness and wisdom saved my father and me a contention with the Deep Lore and gave me a chance at a path I could only have hoped for." Tendi returned to his filing. "Besides, I liked the work. "

Nobody liked the work. Some were better at it than others, but nobody actually…liked it. "You gave up your vows. You took my offer of freedom with alacrity."

"Because I had found one with whom I had wanted to spend my life. He's a protector whom I would otherwise be unable to see. So for your father's foresight, I am forever grateful."

A protector. One who was always first on the scene, whose service had been faithful enough to restore his place among the *signori*, yet had chosen to remain as Panduri's Faithful Finder, and allowed a younger sibling to take the title as his family's heir.

Or maybe not. Did it matter? Father had told me nobody would protest but also declined to tell me more. Because it wasn't any of my business.

I took that lesson to heart.

Claudio clung to the monastery in the days following Luciana's recasting of our stars. I finally tracked him down. He was in his room, the simplest, the most meditative, the room with the clerestory windows. Still his, until he decided otherwise.

I handed him his journal. "I didn't mean to presume about the yarn spinner. It's not my business what you do, who you fuck, or whether your hair grows Papist Jesus to your knees. All I meant was if you want to bury that cloak along with your confession and hand your crown of thorns back to Tendi, go ahead. Or don't. It's your life, and it's not fair you use mine to keep yourself tied in knots."

Claudio flipped through the journal. He wiped dirt from some of the pages. "I've been looking all over for this. Where did you find it?"

"I saw you drop it in the garden on the day you found me in Father's office. You were scribbling furiously. Giacomo even read a little of it out loud for us."

Claudio's gaze darted, chair to desk, cabinet to corner. "Giacomo."

"I told you I was in the garden, told you I was with Antonio and Giacomo, both of them as alive as dead people can be." I pulled my amulet out from under my collar so Claudio could see it, put up my hands, fingers splayed, so there'd be no question whether I was crossing any. "Call me liar if you must, hallucinatory if you're feeling generous, but right now we have other business to finish. I brought you your journal, which I read cover to cover. You owe me something of equal exchange."

I put out a hand. "Dante's and Ilario's charts, the real ones. I want them."

Claudio didn't even look surprised. He pulled them from under his bed like he'd been waiting for the asking, along with a couple of bottles. What secrets were left for him to keep? I knew them all. Claudio was truly free.

He handed the charts to me. "Antonio had these with him when he left. They returned with his things. You were so disturbed over his amulet, his wounds, that he hadn't taken his fiddle, you never thought to ask what else he might have carried. I don't know why he had them. I can only surmise. Maybe he hoped to find them."

"Dante and Ilario are dead."

Claudio's face washed over in the oddest expression. From confusion to consternation to comprehension. Like a wave far out to sea had finally come to shore. "Why do you think they're dead?"

In all the years I'd asked for those charts, all the years the three of us stood in the garden and tracked Dante's and Ilario's progress, death had never been mentioned.

Now it had. "I saw it happen. Not in front of me. On their charts. I was in the garden with Uncle Giacomo and hiding behind their tree. So I could watch him." Trace their paths. All the possibilities. "Then the charts just . . . winked out."

I meant to recount the facts, run through them like a list. And that's how I started. "Giacomo didn't howl, he didn't holler. He closed up like a moonflower at sunrise, curled into a ball. He made this awful high-pitched keening sound. Strangled and strained, wheezy and wet. Like a concertina that runs out of air."

Then I started pacing. "Nobody was there. Nobody could help. Mamma and Luciana were in the fields cutting lavender. You were at the monastery. Father had gone on a drunk. Antonio . . . I don't know where Antonio was."

I dropped to my knees. "I don't know where Giacomo got the rope, but he wasn't fancy about any of it. He was crazed and complex, larger than I'd ever known him, more legendary than I could cope. I tried to stop him, but I couldn't get close. His words were strong and certain, and if I'm not careful they sometimes return on the wind."

Claudio dropped his journal, then dropped beside me. He drew me to him, his breath warm on my ear. "What words?"

"'Let me go.'" I wrapped my fingers around Claudio's wrist, clasped him tight. "And he went."

I held to Claudio for what felt like forever, thinking I'd hold to him like that for always. But real life isn't like that, other things have to be done, so I finally fell forward, allowed the emotion to drain between the floor stones. "That's why Antonio cut down the tree. To give me something else to remember. Of him swinging the ax, instead of Giacomo swinging from the rope. Something as traumatic and disturbing and for which I could blame him. Give me another anger I could hold, and grant me the grace to rewrite Giacomo's passing the way that I wanted, to replace what had happened with an agreeable fiction."

So odd. I didn't cry. I didn't scream. I don't think I was even breathing hard. It was over. It was done, my grief cold, my memories intact and awful and all I had left. "Dante and Ilario didn't belong, so they worked their puzzles. I added to their constructs because I didn't belong either. I didn't want to be at the border so I could get in on all the sheep-fucking. I wanted to be at the border because I didn't know where else to go."

That's what would happen to Spero. He already sensed it, already worked his puzzles, more and more since he'd arrived. Someday he'd go exploring, unless I found a way to make him belong.

Claudio pulled the cork on one of his bottles. "I don't think they're dead."

I popped my head up. "Dante and Ilario?"

"Time moves differently Outside. Sometimes washes forward, sometimes back. You remember that tale of the Outsider who played *bocci* with the *folletti*? He thought he was gone for a few hours, but when he returned to his world, twenty Midsummers had passed."

Rip Van Winkle. One of our many cautionary tales against dabbling too much in the Outside. "What about him?"

"Those charts may have winked out because Dante and Ilario had moved beyond our world's ability to perceive them. I think Antonio hoped to follow, hoped to find them, hoped to find some peace for himself that a good life were possible out there."

Claudio lifted the bottle to his lips. "You believe what you want, but I think Dante and Ilario felt most at home exploring. They passed out those apples to the other children because they wanted to share that curiosity. Then they left and saw many places, learned many things. I think they lived to be old men. I think they each had a dozen children and then each had a dozen dozen grandchildren and I think on every Midsummer they looked to the stars and asked each other the same as we—'Where are Matteo and Claudio and Antonio now?'"

He stood. "I'm hungry. How about you?"

"That's it? I still don't know what happened to Antonio."

"He died."

"I don't know how, or why."

"Will knowing make him less dead?"

It wouldn't. And it wouldn't make me any less unhappy about any of it. Knowing wouldn't do anything for me at all. I'd never thought about that. "Death stinks."

"Death is. It happens to us all. Grief's the stinky part." Claudio dove under his bed again. He retrieved a leather-bound packet, cobwebby and dusty and worn about the edges, like it had been opened and closed and opened again, over and over.

He handed it to me. "Antonio's scores. The ones he sent from the border and you returned to him, the ones Topo dragged to your bed pillow. I never put these in the box and you've never heard them. They're worse than the others. I tried to sing them, and poor Topo disappeared for days. So here they are, they're yours and they involve matters unrelated to all the rest of it. Oh, and here."

He dug under his collar and pulled out his amulet. No, two amulets. He removed one from the chain and handed it to me. "This was Antonio's. His original, not the one I handed you when his body returned. At the first, I had no time to fix this, make it more palatable. At the last, I wasn't certain I even should. So I gave you a duplicate, one he'd asked me to make, one he never used, one I was able to fill with a few acceptable emotions until I figured out what better I could do. I'm a shit for not telling you, worse for keeping it hidden. Do what you want with all of it. I'm never talking about this again."

He headed for the door.

"Wait. Where are you going?"

"To get a snack. From now on, I move forward."

And so he did. And so did I. But first I had to listen to the scores. As discordant as Claudio promised. Then I had to add the bits of song Claudio had noted in the margins. Worse than I could have imagined. Then I had to add my words to work out the key.

What resulted was a whole damned opera. Start to finish.

Requiring many bottles to drink it all in because the *libretto* was so tragic and frustrating.

Antonio's iron was worse. I see why clerics adjust them. It's too much. It's all just too damned much.

Life is impossible. Death is more impossible. We do the best we can, continue from where we are, they from where they've gone. Until the day our paths again cross. That's how it's always been, how it will always be.

I miss Antonio. His absence sometimes feels more like a funnel, and if I'm not careful, if I don't hold tight to those I still have, I might go into a spiral from which I cannot recover. So I keep my face forward, my memories happy, and my heart open. And should he send another paper clip or fiddle refrain or snatch of song my way, I'm happy to hear his stories.

I returned to Claudio after I sobered up. Not to talk about it because he'd already told me he wouldn't. I went to Claudio because he's my brother. "I need you to set up a meeting."

Then I went to speak to Ceres.

Thirty-One

Forsake not thy spirit;
Neither honor lost condone;
Maintain well thy merit;
By these things, thou art known.

For what reasons did we war? Because we did not talk.
Instead, we exchanged insults and called it banter. Tore at each other and called it debate. Blathered and called it conversation. We presumed and assumed, kept our hurts close, our happiness at arm's length, obscured our feelings, cloaked our fears, and hung our most heartfelt concerns out to dry. We let our lives move past us, unaware a moment's music might be our last, a song might never again rise, a voice might never again be heard.

Because we forgot that quality that makes living Inside so much better than Outside, that which makes us invincible, immortal, never-ending. We forgot our ability to connect.

Ceres was straightforward, her estimation true as on the morning she first met Spero. "His mother must be frantic, out of her mind with worry. What decisions you make now will decide whether Spero finds his peace or lives in anguish."

"He has to go back."

"Of course he does." Ceres gave me a hug. "That doesn't mean he can't return."

Spero's mother wasn't so accommodating. "You had no right."

She waved her hands, sometimes pacing. "He is my light and my life, my reason for rising, the last thing I think about before sleep."

We spoke outside the walls of her *ducato,* in that balanced place between our orbits. A few tasks remained before I gave up my rule. That meant I was still Duca, my place still and forever in Panduri, and I could not leave. I wouldn't have wanted to if I could. I had Ceres, I had my children.

And I had Spero. "I had every right. I'm his father."

"He doesn't know that. He has a father here, a good one. That's who Spero knows."

"Will you ever tell him?"

She let that question hang unanswered.

Cheers rose over the walls. Happiness from Careri to have their Heir restored.

"Celebrations are planned." More hand waving. "Ceremonies. Careri will dance this Midsummer as it hasn't in memory." More pacing. "Don't you understand? Spero does not belong only to me, only to us. He belongs to Careri, the hope upon which our star will again rise."

She handed me a bundle, soft and squishy. Another cloth baby, dressed in a familiar red vest and cap and wearing ridiculously out-sized boots. Mine. "I made this doll from the clothes you were wear-ing on the Midsummer we created Spero."

My uniform. The clothes that had disappeared, the ones Claudio couldn't find.

She smoothed the yarn of the cloth baby's hair, then touched the cloth baby's amulet. Iron, not seashell. "What hold I ever had over you is terminated. What deceptions I made are regretted."

Not every wobbling course can be steadied. Still, I tried. I removed the boots from the cloth baby and handed them back. "Keep these. You can't see the possibility now, but someday Spero will want to walk his way across. Not forever, nor always. For a visit. I hope you will not fight him when he does."

And so I left. I had Spero's birth certificate, his star chart, and so long as the orbits of Careri and Panduri endured, I'd have hope.

The clearing was empty, the stalls closed, the trees quiet. The people had already headed for the festival fields. Time waits for no man, even in Panduri, carrying each to his destination whether he wills it or not. Midsummer finally approached and with it my last hours as Duca. I walked the grass-covered clearing, uncertain of the spot. When last I'd walked this particular corner of this particular glade, I'd walked with the Heir. Today I walked alone.

Because youth is foolish. Youth is impatient. Youth is impetuous and self-serving, sure of its rightness, unconvinced of its wrongs and youth does not understand: in the end, all vendettas fade, all hurts soften, all convictions are tested, and confessions heard. Antonio and I could have arrived in harmony, our places arranged as we liked, one for the other, and each for himself, had we been willing to compose our song together.

But youth also thinks it can figure everything out on its own. Leaving me memories, a fiddle, and a single burning refrain. "Why?"

Oh, and a package of truly horrible scores. Scores that finally yielded an answer, or at least a possibility, in the tale of a love unknown, a dream unrealized, a hope let go. The tale of a life which, for Antonio, became increasingly unwieldy and despairingly intolerable.

I'd been too wrapped up in my own travails to wonder why Antonio headed to this place, this neighborhood, on the night he left the Midsummer procession, the night he told me I shouldn't be

Protector, that I should wear the hat. Had I a thought in my head for anybody other than myself, I might have looked for him there on the Midsummer we couldn't find him, the Midsummer Giacomo hung himself, and the Midsummer Dante and Ilario set sail.

Because this place is where Antonio went when he needed to know something. This place is where Antonio came when he wanted to figure things out. This place is where Antonio sought comfort when the pressures of who he was, and especially who he was not, over-whelmed him. Where Antonio found a home, a life he could never pursue, a happiness he could never fully own, not so long as he was Heir.

Because she was Outside, and he was Inside. This place where the maestro had lived, and where Antonio's heart had resided. With the maestro's daughter.

Those we care about most are always a little fuzzy. Their hearts are too fragile, their emotions too raw, their souls too bright to perceive at close range. All we see are the parts, a blur of action, a flash of anger, a burst of laughter. Sometimes distance is required to bring those we love into focus, their hurts and their pain, their joys and their triumphs, that which drives them, that which they fear, that which would make them whole. Sometimes understanding comes only with their leaving.

Sometimes understanding never comes at all. That does not mean we should avoid the journey.

I lifted the fiddle and hoped mine here had not been in vain. "I need to send a commission."

She appeared in a twinkle, a little older, her wings a little worn for the wear, not quite so exuberant, nor so eager as the night Antonio and I had walked here together.

Just like me. I handed her the fiddle. "You said one day Panduri's Heir would need something sent and you would know exactly where it should go. I am no longer Panduri's Heir. I am only Duca for a few more hours. Are you still willing to accept this commission?"

Her expression gave the answer. Still . . . it's polite to ask. She took the fiddle and held it to her ear. "This commission does not say where it is bound."

I nodded at her, deep and respectful. "My brother left me a trail, compliments of Midsummer, his destination unknown. I will be forever grateful if you would ask the commission again, hear the answer with all your heart, then follow that trail to his joy."

As far as I know, the sprite never returned. Wherever the sprite went, I hope she's exploring. And wherever the fiddle went, I hope Antonio knows it's all right. I hope he knows I understand. I hope he knows I love him.

The transfer of my rule to Luciana went off with a ceremony and a procession and much throwing of flowers. With pipers and acrobats, light spinners and song. With a brand new hat, bigger, and heavier, bearing twice the braids and four times the pleats of the former. Luciana carried off the wearing like she'd been born to it. The people cheered.

Panduri did not care their Duca was now a woman, only that somebody was. They did not care who occupied the *duca's* office, only that somebody did. They did not care where Panduri's star rose, only how high. We marked our milestones as we always did, plotted our progress as we always had. We each found our places, our points in Panduri's constellation. And we danced.

The following Midsummer after Luciana became Duca was more exciting. We gathered in Dante and Ilario's garden to witness the planting of a new tree, one that would be widespread and strong and bursting with possibilities. One birthed from the apple I'd swiped from the tree in Spero's garden in Careri. A tree bearing the fruits of wisdom, from which Spero could always return. A tree where we could always find him.

"Use your words," Ceres whispered in my ear. "It's only bark and branches."

Claudio asked me to wait. He reached behind Dante's Wall and presented me a sapling. "I grew this from the root of the stump you removed, that day I found you wielding the ax."

The stump Antonio had left. A reminder. And also a promise. I touched a branch. "Very nice. And with all that ax-wielding, highly metaphorical."

"I don't think you have to help this one along. Curiosity typically outstrips itself, and without wisdom can be disastrous. But wisdom without curiosity grows stale. Let's grow both trees together, as they did in the First Garden. Then let us see what develops." He patted his pockets. "Shoot. I forgot a trowel."

Ursicio, ever resourceful, produced some. He showed them to the children. "It's time to dig. Let us plant with our best intentions. Who wants to help?"

Everybody, as it turned out. There was digging and delving and much flinging of dirt. There was discussion, then argument, planning, then tugging—this way, no that way, over there, over here—regarding the tree's final position.

We adults watched, our glasses full, our hearts fuller. We dodged mud clods, broke up melees, offered guidance our offspring ignored. They clamored for the anticipated fruit. "Someday we will taste one, someday we will touch one, someday we will bring one back home."

Eventually, the next generation got the seed and the sapling planted, a little bedraggled for all the trauma. Luciana poured out a pitcher plant into the earth surrounding its roots, then muttered to me and Claudio. "It will be a miracle if it survives."

I was willing to lay my bets. Like us, that sapling had been shocked, been broken, ill-used, and misrepresented. I crouched beside it and pressed my ear to the bark, listened for its heart. Of life, of love, of a yearning to heal. "This tree will be fine. So will we."

I glanced to the sky. "Come. It's time."

I faced the horizon, a brace of quivers crisscrossing my chest, a brace of bows resting by the purple-capped pixies. I watched with my family while my brothers' constellation emerged in deepest blue.

My middle daughter sat on my shoulders. She pointed to the horizon. "Where are Dante and Ilario and Antonio now?"

Claudio tilted his head toward his wife, her hair braided in buttercups, her body ripe with new life. "I know just the person to tell us."

My sister-in-law pulled a green and yellow basket toward her. She set it on her stomach and started choosing yarns, pulling one thread, then another, until the collection looked like a hopeless tangle. She took a breath and began to spin. "On a long ago Midsummer very much like this one, a quintet of brothers set off exploring. . . ."

She recounted the tale, the parts we'd chosen to remember, the happy times, the quiet times, the times we'd thought everything a great adventure. She spun the tale until she couldn't. Until she got suddenly quiet, her expression pinched and painful. Until the most unbecoming series of sounds escaped her lips, strained and strangled and peppered with swear words.

The end of the story would have to wait, because life won't.

The women gathered around my sister-in-law and spirited her away. Ursicio's and Luciana's olders filed all our youngers to the kitchen for honeyed lemonade. Ursicio and I piloted Claudio under the arch leading to the targeting field.

Claudio drew back. "I should be with her."

Ursicio pushed him forward. "There is nothing you can do or say that won't get you into trouble. Let the ladies handle it."

He lifted a quiver up and off my shoulder and settled it on his own. "You first, Matteo. I'm out of practice."

I shook my head and handed him my bow. "Go for one of the closer targets. Be careful. I've no idea where Topo's got to."

I don't know why I was feeling so authoritative and sure. I hadn't practiced targets since the maestro died.

Ursicio tested the draw, nocked an arrow, sighted on one of the hay-stuffed canvas sacks at the opposite end of the field. He squinted at the weapon's belly. "'*Forsake not thy spirit. . . .*' Did you mean this poem for me?"

Um . . . no. "The Duca-that-was-before-me had an odd way of offering guidance."

Claudio made a little hiccup, halfway between a laugh and that sound that happens when the food goes down the wrong way. "Father didn't commission that bow."

But, the poem, the admonishment. And stuff. "Who did?"

"Giacomo. He commissioned them all."

No wonder Antonio didn't keep his. I thought he left it because he was mad at Father.

Well . . . fuck. And fine. Let Giacomo's singular and futile attempt at fatherhood fail with spectacular legendarity. I'd had a better man to guide me, obtuse as his methods may have been. I'd had an even better man to teach me how to love. "Keep the bow, Ursicio. I'll use Antonio's."

Because I had all the words I'd ever want or need, memories aplenty. What I'd lack forever, for always, was my brother's music.

Sometimes that's just how the stars fall.

Ursicio's shot wasn't bad. He stepped away from his targeting stake and waved me forward. "Your turn."

I hefted Antonio's bow, sighted my target.

Claudio smacked his forehead. "Oh no, you're going for Antonio's arrow. You're drunk, you didn't bring near enough ammunition."

"Shut up." I flicked my head at Claudio's targeting stake. "Wait there. I intend to make this shot. You're going to be quiet while I do so."

I again drew and sighted.

Then I tilted, this way than that, Dante and Ilario's wind in my sails and the injury from my magic musical vial Midsummer returned to haunt my hand. I lowered the bow. "I can't. My grip's too weak."

Claudio came close, reached alongside my arm, wrapped his fist around mine. "We'll do it together."

We drew as one. Still I couldn't let go. Claudio relaxed his stance. "What's wrong?"

"Once I do this, that's it, it's done."

"Nothing's ever done. It just goes on to become something else. Keep your eye open, your heart alive, and maybe you'll see that something else in the last place you imagine."

I know Antonio wasn't there, know I felt no more than the weight of my wine, the weirdness of hearing Claudio sing the same words Antonio had set to music on the night he first offered me the hat. Still, I couldn't shake the impression Antonio stood beside me, instead of Claudio. Couldn't shake the feeling Antonio helped me with the draw. Couldn't convince myself the pain in my hand was the reason I heard Antonio's voice clear in my ear at the moment I let fly. "I haven't left you. Not really. You'll see me at your end."

That's how I finally split Antonio's arrow. Or maybe Antonio split his own arrow.

I cut off the congratulations Ursicio and Claudio started effusing. Really, who gives a damn? It's only an arrow, and all my cuts and bruises had long since ceased to fester. "Claudio, I've been meaning to ask you about something not composed in Antonio's scores. Regarding the child of the maestro's daughter. The child she birthed while married to our air spinner."

Claudio didn't answer. Cloak or no cloak I suppose there's still plenty he can't divulge. And maybe it wasn't any of my business. I had the child's chart, the child of the maestro's daughter. Someday, when the time was right, I'd take a look at it and see.

A cry went up from the ducal mansion. Cries of "It's a girl!" Then, "And a boy!"

And Claudio, in bright shirt and deep green britches, his hair returned to Papist Jesus. Laughing. And crying. His joy so true he could have been Antonio. An older, wiser Antonio, worn along the edges.

I clapped my brother on the back, our past finally in its place, our faces finally forward, then I handed him Antonio's bow and gave all our stars permission to rise. "Your turn."

Epilogue

I thought my tale with Antonio finished the Midsummer I finally split his arrow. Hours later, many hours later, long after Claudio met his twins, and I met my niece and nephew, hours after everybody had slept and danced and slept some more. Hours and hours later, but still an hour or two before dawn, I returned to the garden, sober as winter, and buried this journal. I unearthed the box where I'd placed my first journal all those Midsummers previous and found Claudio had returned my confession and reburied it with his own.

This journal joined them. The box was buried yet again. I found my way to the kitchen and had breakfast.

I never did look at the chart of the child of the maestro's daughter. I thought about it, Midsummer to Midsummer, but there was always another star that needed casting, or another child that needed tending. The chart could wait, life does not.

That's what I told myself. A more honest part of me feared the paths wouldn't light for me. Or that Antonio had cast it without a key. Or that I'd unroll the chart, have no problem reading it and likewise no sense of connection, of familiarity, no excuse to believe that

291

someplace I'd find a trace to hold onto. So I left the chart, secure the child of the maestro's daughter would always have a place in Panduri.

Then, one morning, many Midsummers after and just a few hours before she was to wear the hat, Luciana announced she wasn't going to, she planned to pass that honor to her oldest daughter. "Seems ridiculous I have to die before she gets her chance. Doesn't it make better sense that I'm still around to guide her if she gets stuck?"

We asked Claudio. He told Luciana she could do what she wants. Then he handed me Topo and made me tuck the cat into my vest. He ignored all the spitting and slavering and flicked his head toward the door. "Let's go walking."

Yes. Topo is still with us, on his ninth life and fading fast. He still hates me. Maybe a little less. But not by much.

Midsummers are different under Luciana. Most of the celebrations occur in the daylight hours before all the dancing.

Fine with me. These days, I also like to get to bed early.

It was an excellent Midsummer. Glorious. The acrobats twirling higher than I'd ever seen and the musicians excelling. "Listen," I said to Claudio. "One of Antonio's compositions."

"Is it?" Claudio's voice fell off, his tone disinterested.

"Luciana must have ordered it."

"Maybe."

I listened a while longer. "The fiddle player is good. Really good."

"If you say so." He wandered to the border of the festival field, close to the trail leading to the cliff edge.

The sun dipped toward the horizon. We started the long climb up, taking it slowly. My shin often gives me trouble these days.

Claudio and I had plenty of company. Lately, our young people have turned this climb into a tradition. To see the silhouette of a new horizon—light-filled towers and pinnacles soaring to the heavens. And sometimes to leave to go exploring. Never for long, never for always, never too often.

Topo hopped out of my vest and scampered up the climb. I waited, presuming he'd return. I felt a push.

And not from Claudio. In the direction of where Topo had scampered. I looked, and saw the cat, riding the shoulder of Claudio's oldest son. "Antonio," I called.

He headed toward us, scanning the crowd, his hair long and wild as Papist Jesus, just like Claudio's when he was young. His gaze met mine and moved on.

I shaded my eyes and called again. "Antonio." Then smacked Claudio's shoulder with the back of my hand. "What's wrong with him?"

"Perhaps he doesn't recognize you."

I tried a third time. This time waving. "Antonio."

My nephew finally realized I was talking to him. He nodded and smiled, then tucked a fiddle under his chin and played a happy little refrain.

Antonio's fiddle. And Antonio's refrain. And Claudio's oldest has no talent with music.

He came down the slope, threw an arm across his midsection and bowed. "You know my name." He scratched Topo behind his ear. "Is this your cat? He likes me."

His hair was too light, his eyes too dark to be Claudio's son, but he looked so much like Claudio, he could have been Antonio.

There was an earthquake, a great upheaval. But only in my heart.

Claudio caught hold of me. "Say hello," he murmured. "Be pleasant. Say something nice."

The young man waited. "Signore?"

Topo hopped off his shoulder and onto mine. For once, the cat was kind, purring and mewing and acting like we were the best of friends. "Your fiddle."

The young man held it out to me. "Exquisite, isn't it? My great-grandmother said my great-grandfather claimed seventy sirens worked seventy Midsummers making this fiddle. In Careri, I'm told that story is true. All I know is I was once offered a million euros for it."

Claudio touched the neck of the instrument. "It's beautiful. Is a million euros a lot?"

"A million of anything is a lot." The young man laughed. He again tucked the fiddle under his chin and played another happy refrain. "What would be the use? All I'd end up with is a million euros. I'd have to give up the music."

He played a little longer. Tuck of the chin. Set of the shoulder. Tremor of each finger for the *vibrato*.

Every detail carried an importance I hoped those who loved him understood, an exquisiteness I hope they did not fail to notice. Each a beginning, each an end, and each whispered.

Pay attention. Have a care.

The sun touched the horizon, and the light began to fail. The music cut off. The young man shoved a swath of hair off his forehead and looped it behind an ear. He bowed again. "I have to go. My mother told me not to drink anything or eat anything and not to stay past twilight. She kept telling me. *Inside is not like Outside.*"

To gaze upon him, whole and healthy and joyful. . . . "We have quite a reputation. But we understand and hope you will return. Be assured, you and yours always have a place in Panduri."

"Thank you. Perhaps next Midsummer. I'll bring my cousins, Dante and Ilario. They are named for my great-great-granduncles, the most adventurous and curious of explorers, renowned and legendary. Always first on the scene, and last to leave in a scuffle." He retreated up the climb, then turned and raised the fiddle. "Or so their story goes."

I started after him. Claudio held me back. So I kept an eye on his path until the sun set and the twilight deepened. Claudio pointed out a new star rising on the horizon. One I had not charted, a star I had not cast. A star I think I recognized.

I left the cliff edge with my brother, bid him goodnight, then found my trowel, returned to the garden, and unearthed my journal—to add a grace note, a postscript, a last verse to the song. Largely true, mostly fable, perhaps to pass into history.

Claudio once assured me a man cannot outrun his stars. He's never explained what happens when the man's stars outrun him. At the last, all extinguish. That does not mean their light does not continue.

Past you, past me, past all who remember, to rise in further skies, set on further shores. Further suns to further suns. Further moons to further moons. In this life, and beyond.

The Midsummer's Eve I ran away, my brother Antonio returned me. The Midsummer's he left, a piece of my heart went along. We do not own our lives; we borrow them for a while. At some point, all run their course. At some point, everybody crosses.

But if we are patient, if our eye is open and our spirits willing, twinkles cross back. Bright spots and blessings, gifts without strings, free and unencumbered and with the power to comfort, to heal.

A heart. Or a hope.

Forever, for always.

And to that I hold.

Notes

On a hilltop in Italy a few kilometers from Careri, in a comune in the Aspromonte region of Calabria, can be found the remains of Panduri, a once-thriving, and somewhat forward-thinking town for its time which had partnered with a local monastery to test modern farming methods.

Panduri possibly dated from pre-Roman times and is named for Pandora, the first human woman created by the Greek gods, upon whom they bestowed many gifts. Pandora's legend claims she opened a magic jar, releasing all manner of chaos and evil into the world. Pandora despaired until she heard a tiny voice speaking to her from the jar, and she realized Hope still remained. Pandora closed the jar, saving Hope for a better day.

Alas, the Italian town of Panduri was destroyed in the sixteenth century by a devastating earthquake which left only a third of the village's population alive. Her dead were never buried. Local legend claims someplace beneath the town's remains is a fissure leading to a cave possessed of a certain magnetism, the effects and details I have been unable, as of yet, to ascertain. Only locals know the cave's location—and it is said only they may withstand the cave's special properties.

Legends and rumors, the stuff stories are made of.

The townspeople who survived the earthquake packed up and moved to the nearby hilltop of Careri, where every year a ceremony is held to remember the town that was, celebrate the town that is, acknowledge her legends, and pray for the souls of those lost to Mother Nature and time.

Contrary to its depiction in *Deepest Blue*, the Comune of Careri is a thriving municipality located in a region where many a curious traveler has gone exploring.

With his reference to 'standing on the shoulders of giants' in Chapter Four, Antonio pays homage to the Outsider Isaac Newton, a man who knew about apples and how they fall from trees.

Claudio learned that peace is its own reward from Antonio, who recounted to him a story about the Outsider activist, Mahatma Gandhi, revered proponent of nonviolent civil disobedience to achieve positive societal change. Claudio passed that wisdom on to Matteo, who quoted the sentiment back to Claudio in Chapter Eighteen.

The quote in Chapter Nineteen regarding accomplishments and how Nature does not hurry was borrowed by Bartomeo, Duca of Panduri, from the Outsider philosopher, Lao Tzu.

Book Club Questions

1. Antonio and Matteo innately refuse to follow their charted paths, while others follow without question, such as Tendi and Salvatore, also Claudio. Which attitude is more detrimental to the individual, which is more detrimental to Panduri as a whole? If one of the characters had changed their approach, how might Panduri have thrived or suffered as a result?

2. Matteo wonders if the Deep Lore is what they make of it. Indeed, it does seem the Deep Lore molds itself to changing circumstances—but does that mean the Deep Lore changes, or only Matteo's understanding of it?

3. Was Bartomeo a good father? Was Giacomo a poor one? Were Matteo's estimations of either true or fair? Would Antonio have agreed or disagreed? How about Claudio? *Deepest Blue* is a story of perceptions, less of events. How does one's perception of reality affect the reality?

4. Matteo's desire to be at the border and Antonio's refusal to let Matteo take on his charted role are the driving conflict throughout Matteo's confession. Despite the *duca's* orders, and the single time he constrains Matteo with the stranglevine, there appears to be nothing holding Matteo in town. Likewise, Antonio suffers no apparent consequences because he stays at the border. How come Matteo doesn't stay at the border? After he is injured, why does he not return as soon as he is able?

5. Claudio is not born to his role. Is he as lacking in his performance as Panduri's Gentle Guardian as he claims, or has the recharting of his stars nudged him along a path that he ends up negotiating successfully? Or is Claudio successful, despite what his stars show?

6. In *Deepest Blue*, intentions often carry similar weight as action. Is the same true Outside, in our world?

7. Does Panduri's magic source from its physical existence, or from its people?

8. The experience of intense grief rewires our response to stimuli, especially stimuli directly attached to the grief. Matteo's grief is tied to Panduri and its distinction from Outside. How does Matteo's grief guide his course? How might his course have proceeded but for the grief experience?

9. Nowhere does *Deepest Blue* spell out how Antonio came by his knowledge of his and his brothers' collective past. What presumptions might be made about Antonio's story from those tidbits Matteo reveals?

10. Is Inside better?

Resources

$\mathcal{G}$rief is a journey that never ends. There are people and organizations who can help. Reach out.

MISS Foundation
A Community of Compassion and Hope for Grieving Families
www.missfoundation.org

The Compassionate Friends
Supporting Family After a Child Dies
www.compassionatefriends.org

The Dougy Center
The National Center for Grieving Children and Families
www.dougy.org

NCTSN
The National Child Traumatic Stress Network
Recognizing and Responding to Childhood Traumatic Grief
www.nctsn.org/trauma-types/traumatic-grief/kids-teens

Child Grief Support Directory
https://www.live-evermore.org/child-grief-support-directory

Acknowledgments

Writing a story takes time. Writing a good story takes encouragement. To those who lent a word along the way, I am grateful.

Sharon and Kelly, KC and Melissa, and the denizens of Perley Station. To Rails for the Resources and a special thanks to Lisa Miller for her always pivotal Story Structure Safaris.

Last, and best, thank you to my firsts, my foremosts, my forevers, my always, my reasons for rising: my husband, my children. Always close to my heart.

About the Author

*M*indy Tarquini grew up convinced there are other worlds just one giant step to the left of where she's standing. Author of the critically acclaimed and award-winning *Hindsight* (SparkPress 2016) and *The Infinite Now* (SparkPress 2017), Ms. Tarquini's writing has appeared in *Writer's Digest*, *BookPage*, *Hypable*, and other venues. An associate editor on the *Lascaux Review* and a member of the Perley Station Writers Colony, Ms. Tarquini is a second generation Italian American who believes words have power. She plies hers to the best of her ability from an enchanted tower a giant step left in the great Southwest.

Mindy loves the internet. Check out her website at www.MindyTarquini.com. Stop by her Facebook page at www.facebook.com/MindyTarquiniAuthor. Catch her on Twitter. Or Instagram. Follow her on Pinterest. Yes, there's even a little-used Tumblr. Say hello.

SELECTED TITLES FROM SPARKPRESS

SparkPress is an independent boutique publisher delivering high-quality, entertaining, and engaging content that enhances readers' lives, with a special focus on female-driven work.
Visit us at www.gosparkpress.com

Ocean's Fire, Stacey Tucker, $16.95, 978-1-943006-28-1
Once the Greeks forced their male gods upon the world, the belief in the power of women was severed. For centuries it has been thought that the wisdom of the high priestesses perished at the hand of the patriarchs— but now the ancient Book of Sophia has surfaced. Its pages contain the truths hidden by history, and the sacred knowledge for the coming age. And it is looking for Skylar Southmartin.

The Infinite Now, Mindy Tarquini, $16.95, 978-1-943006-34-2
In flu-ravaged 1918 Philadelphia, the newly-orphaned daughter of the local fortune teller panics and casts her entire neighborhood into a bubble of stagnant time in order to save the life of the mysterious shoe-maker who has taken her in. As the complications of the time bubble multiply, this forward-thinking young woman must find the courage to face an uncertain future, so she can find a way to break the spell.

Hindsight, Mindy Tarquini, $16.95, 978-1943006014
A thirty-three-year-old Chaucer professor who remembers all her past lives is desperate to change her future—because if she doesn't, she will never live the life of her dreams.

Above the Star, Alexis Chute, $16.95, 978-1-943006-56-4
Above the Star is an epic fantasy adventure experienced through the eyes of three unlikely heroes transported to a new world: senior citizen Archie; his daughter-in-law, Tessa; and his fourteen-year-old granddaughter, Ella. In this otherworldly realm, all interests are at war, all love is unrequited, and everyone is left to unravel the truth of who they really are.

But Not Forever, Jan Von Schleh, $16.95, 978-1-943006-58-8
When identical fifteen-year-old girls are mysteriously switched in time, they discover the love that's been missing in their lives. Torn, both want to go home, but neither wants to give up what they now have.

About SparkPress

SparkPress is an independent, hybrid imprint focused on merging the best of the traditional publishing model with new and innovative strategies. We deliver high-quality, entertaining, and engaging content that enhances readers' lives. We are proud to bring to market a list of *New York Times* best-selling, award-winning, and debut authors who represent a wide array of genres, as well as our established, industry-wide reputation for creative, results-driven success in working with authors. SparkPress, a BookSparks imprint, is a division of SparkPoint Studio LLC.

Learn more at GoSparkPress.com